SPECIAL MESSAGE TO READERS

This book is published under the auspices of

THE ULVERSCROFT FOUNDATION

(registered charity No. 264873 UK)

Established in 1972 to provide funds for research, diagnosis and treatment of eye diseases. Examples of contributions made are: —

A Children's Assessment Unit at Moorfield's Hospital, London.

•

Twin operating theatres at the Western Ophthalmic Hospital, London.

•

A Chair of Ophthalmology at the Royal Australian College of Ophthalmologists.

•

The Ulverscroft Children's Eye Unit at the Great Ormond Street Hospital For Sick Children, London.

You can help further the work of the Foundation by making a donation or leaving a legacy. Every contribution, no matter how small, is received with gratitude. Please write for details to:

THE ULVERSCROFT FOUNDATION,
The Green, Bradgate Road, Anstey,
Leicester LE7 7FU, England.
Telephone: (0116) 236 4325

In Australia write to:

THE ULVERSCROFT FOUNDATION,
c/o The Royal Australian and New Zealand
College of Ophthalmologists,
94-98 Chalmers Street, Surry Hills,
N.S.W. 2010, Australia

FORTRESS OF SPEARS

The Romans have vanquished the rebel alliance, leaving Calgus, Lord of the Northern Tribes, a prisoner of the chieftains he once led. But there's no rest. The new Roman leader's plan is to capture Dinpaladyr, the Selgovae fortress of spears, and return it to a trusted ally. In a select group of the infantry going north with the Petriana cavalry, Marcus Aquila burns for revenge on an enemy army that killed his best friend. They take the fort before the rebel army arrives. However, whilst disguised as Centurion Corvus of the 2nd Tungrians, he's only days ahead of two of the emperor's agents sent from Rome to kill him. And they are pitiless assassins. They know his real name, and too much about his friends.

Books by Anthony Riches
Published by The House of Ulverscroft:

WOUNDS OF HONOUR
ARROWS OF FURY

ANTHONY RICHES

FORTRESS OF SPEARS

EMPIRE: VOLUME THREE

Complete and Unabridged

CHARNWOOD
Leicester

First published in Great Britain in 2011 by
Hodder & Stoughton
An Hachette UK Company, London

First Charnwood Edition
published 2012
by arrangement with
Hodder & Stoughton Ltd.
An Hachette Livre UK Company, London

British Library CIP Data

Riches, Anthony.
Fortress of spears.
1. Aquila, Marcus Valerius (Fictitious character)- - Fiction. 2. Great Britain- -History- -Rome period, 55 B.C.– 449 A.D.- -Fiction. 3. Historical fiction. 4. Large type books.
I. Title
823.9′2–dc23

ISBN 978–1–4448–1234–3

Published by
F. A. Thorpe (Publishing)
Anstey, Leicestershire

Set by Words & Graphics Ltd.
Anstey, Leicestershire
Printed and bound in Great Britain by
T. J. International Ltd., Padstow, Cornwall

This book is printed on acid-free paper

For John, Katie and Nick

Acknowledgements

In the generation of any book there are always pivotal individuals, people without whose input the work involved would be made harder, less pleasant, even downright difficult. *Fortress of Spears*, although it's been enjoyable (and somewhat different, having been written in the main in a walk-in closet in South Carolina), has been no exception to that rule.

Inevitably the biggest accolade must go to my wife Helen for putting up with all that tedious stuff that I expect many writers put their families through — the 'it's not good enough' worries, the staring into space thinking about cars and cameras rather than writing, the 'I just had an idea for the book' as you crawl into bed at 2.30 in the morning, still fizzing with creativity and unmistakably wide awake, and finally the unutterable smugness of that completed-manuscript moment. All that would be bad enough, but it's even worse when the writer in question has to compress all that angst into one week a month at home.

For their patience in never once asking where the hell the manuscript was, Robin Wade (agent) and Carolyn Caughey (editor) deserve major credit. Perhaps I can crank out *The Leopard Sword* on a timelier basis. Francine Toon stood in for Carolyn with aplomb whenever Carolyn was absent, and managed my various whinges without batting an eyelid. And while I have only a hazy idea of what they actually do in support of the books, I know that Hodder's sales and marketing teams have to be doing a great job given the results they've achieved over the last two years. Ladies and gentlemen, whatever it is you're doing, thanks very much and please don't stop!

At this point I must also make a point of thanking Ian Paten, most excellent of copy editors, for his invaluable work in not only making sense of my inconsistencies, but helping me to avoid more than one embarrassing mistake.

As usual, I've exposed the script to a small and trusted group of friends in search of critical feedback, and so to Robin Carter, Paul Browne, David Mooney, John Prigent and Russell Whitfield, thank you, gentlemen, for your comments and typo spotting. I also exposed my concern about a lack of story development to my friend and business partner Graham Lockhart a few months back, only to receive the following advice in his broad Glesga accent: 'Just do what you always do. Invent some more characters and let them sort the story out for you!' Sound advice. I did, and they did, and so the lesson was relearned. Thanks, Jockzilla!

Writing *Fortress* also provided another text-book example of how the ancient-warfare community always pitches in to help when asked. Members of the highly rated Roman Army Talk website www.romanarmytalk.com

never failed to come up with answers to the most arcane of questions and provided a first-rate source of information (and sometimes entertainment!). Kevan White's excellent website www.roman-britain.org continued to be a compendious source on all things to do with the frontier area in which this story is set. And while I wasn't able to take up John Conyard's generous offer to try out the Roman style of riding owing to a protracted family illness that chewed up all my spare time for six months, meeting John and the Comitatus guys at Maryport was a great moment for me. John's fund of information contributed at least one little snippet of *Fortress* that I think he'll recognise.

Finally, on the 'learning more about being a Roman soldier' front, the year was also remarkable for the charity walk along Hadrian's Wall in full armour (and I do mean 'full' armour), sixty pounds of the stuff with all the weapons and shield. Adrian Wink at Armamentaria kitted me out in the full kit, David Mooney tried to get me fit before the event — and succeeded in getting me soaked to the skin and hugely blistered on more than one occasion — and Julian Dear walked the whole way behind me, variously encouraging, browbeating and taking the mickey out of me as appropriate. Carolyn drove a very long way to be there at the end of the walk, which was nice, and Robin, rufty-tufty type that he is, dragged me along the route in true infanteering style. Chaps, I couldn't have done it without you, and not only would I have missed the chance to experience just what the average Roman soldier was put through on a daily basis, but Help for Heroes would have lost a nice chunk of cash. Well done to all. I'll certainly never write another passage about Tungrians on the march without reflecting on just how hard it was to drag all that iron around. Speaking of HfH, it's not too late to donate. The wall-walk page is still open and you can find it via my website www.anthonyriches.com. As I write, the armed forces have been hacked by the Treasury once again, doubtless putting an even smaller number of men and women under even more pressure, which makes this the best place to start charitable giving for me. And off the soapbox . . .

Lastly, to everyone else that's helped me this time round but not been mentioned, to use that old cliché, it's not you, it's me. Those people that work alongside me will tell you how poor my memory can be, so if I've forgotten you then here's a blanket apology. Where the history is right it's because I've had some great help, and where it's not it's all my own work.

Thank you.

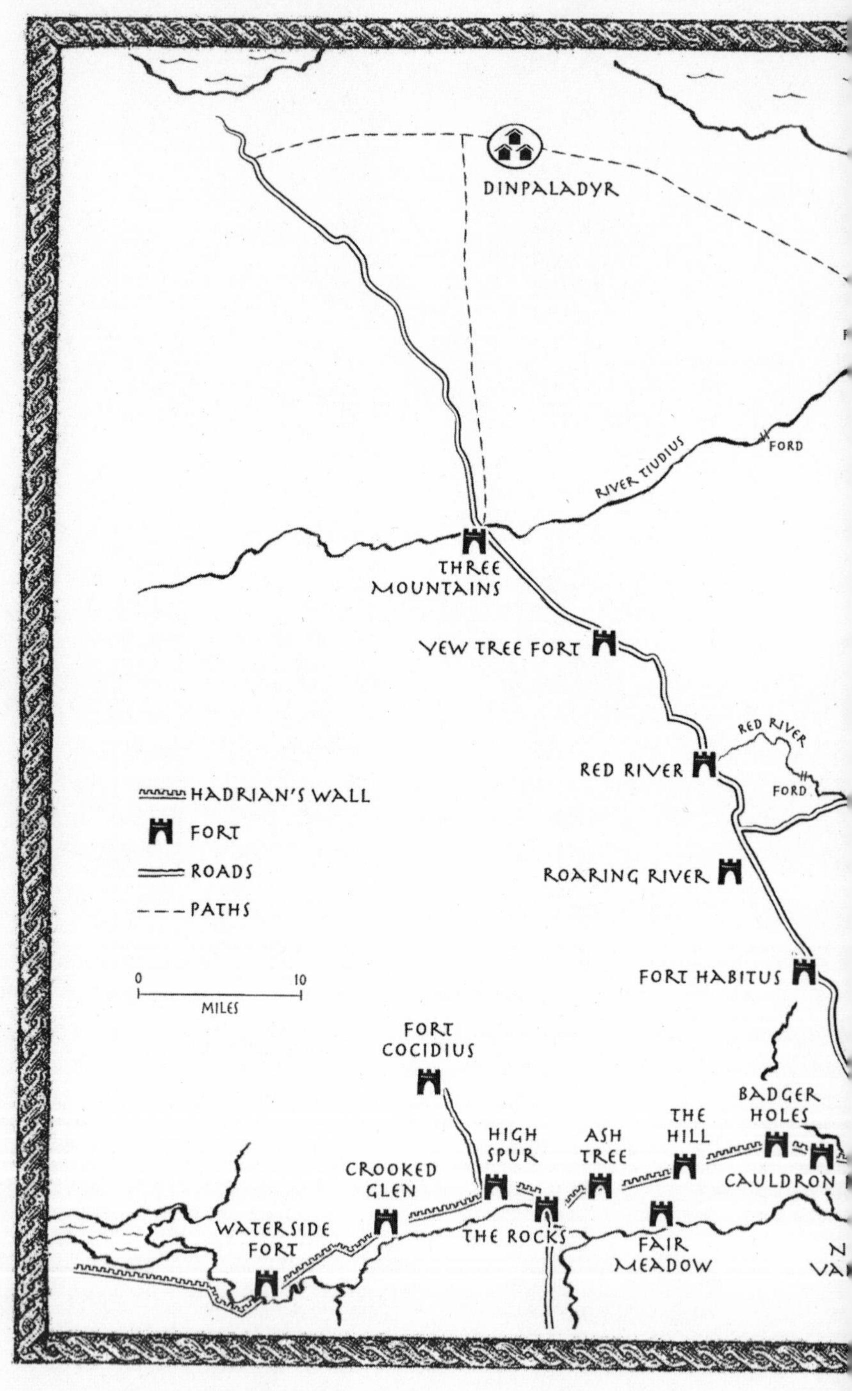
DINPALADYR
RIVER TIUDIUS
FORD
THREE MOUNTAINS
YEW TREE FORT
RED RIVER
FORD
RED RIVER
ROARING RIVER
FORT HABITUS
HADRIAN'S WALL
FORT
ROADS
PATHS
0
10
MILES
FORT COCIDIUS
BADGER HOLES
THE HILL
ASH TREE
HIGH SPUR
CROOKED GLEN
CAULDRON
WATERSIDE FORT
THE ROCKS
FAIR MEADOW

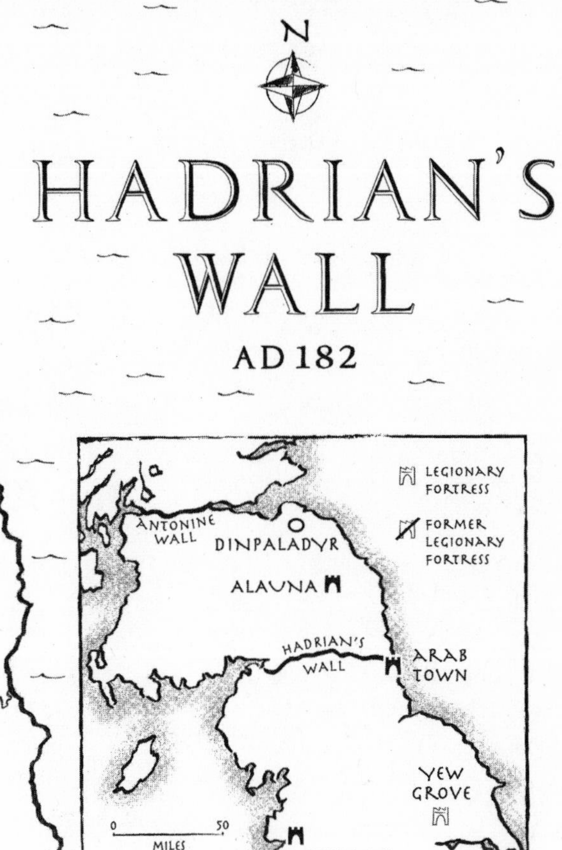
N
HADRIAN'S WALL
AD 182
LEGIONARY FORTRESS
FORMER LEGIONARY FORTRESS
ANTONINE WALL
DINPALADYR
ALAUNA
HADRIAN'S WALL
ARAB TOWN
YEW GROVE
0 50
MILES
VETERANS' HILL
DARK POOL
FORTRESS DEVA
ALAUNA

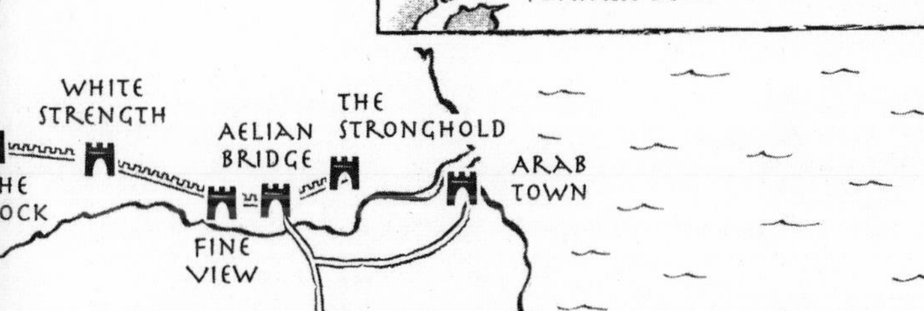
WHITE STRENGTH
AELIAN BRIDGE
THE STRONGHOLD
ARAB TOWN
FINE VIEW

Prologue

Rome, August, AD 182

The first of the young senator's bodyguards died slowly, choking to death on the cobbles with his sword only half drawn from its scabbard. He stared up at his killer with bulging eyes while the assassin turned away from him and drew his gladius, facing the younger of the two men with a grim smile. He had stepped out of a side alley in a street whose sudden quiet should have been enough of a warning to an experienced man, punching a half-fist into the veteran soldier's throat before the bodyguard had the time to realise that he was under attack. The senator and his remaining protector fell back a few paces, both men staring in amazement at their companion as he writhed and kicked in the throes of his death spasm.

Another man stepped from the alley's shadows in the killer's wake, and leaned against the wall of a shop in the late afternoon's warmth, his face set in an expression of boredom. Where the bodyguard's murderer was heavyset, with arms that rippled with hard muscle, the man that accompanied him was tall and thin. His voice, when he spoke, was agreeable, and almost soothing in the softness of its tone.

'Greeting, Tiberius Sulpicius Quirinius. Forgive me, but I can't help thinking that you've made something of a blunder in your choice of protection today. Hiring retired soldiers is all very well, but they do tend to know more about throwing spears at barbarians than the dangers of the streets, as your man here is so noisily demonstrating. And the savings to be had from hiring a boy to do a man's work are so often outweighed by the resulting costs. Wouldn't you agree, Senator Quirinius, given that you chose to chance a district as rough as the Subura with only these two innocents for protection?'

The prostrate bodyguard shuddered in one last desperate effort to breathe through his ruptured throat, and then sagged back to lie still on the stones. Quirinius drew himself up, staring at the taller of the two men with an air of confidence that he was a long way from feeling.

'What in Hades do you think you're doing? Who are you, to challenge an unarmed senator of Rome in the open street?'

The thin man smiled widely, spreading his hands in greeting.

'Who am I, Senator? I'm Tiberius Varius Excingus, and *I'm* one of the Emperor's corn officers. This is my colleague, Quintus Sestius Rapax. He's a praetorian officer, believe it or not, but he's never lost the taste for killing even after his richly deserved promotion to centurion. As to what we're doing? Well, you might be a senator, but you're clearly still wet behind the ears, or you might have been a little more careful in the last few hours.'

The praetorian's eyes were alive with calculation as he stepped in to face the remaining bodyguard. He nodded to the boy, barely fifteen from the look of it, then pointed back with his sword at the uniformed men who were guarding the far end of the street from prying eyes, his voice harsh from years of bellowing orders across parade grounds.

'You're staying to fight, then, eh, boy? You can still save yourself, if you run now. My men will let you leave, if you drop the sword and walk away.' He waited, watching the conflicting emotions play out on the boy's face. 'No?' The bodyguard shook his head, wide eyed and clearly terrified, but either unwilling or simply unable to turn and run, and the praetorian laughed softly. 'Just as well. They'd probably have killed you, if only for fun — or just because you've seen my face. And you, Senator, will you not be joining the fight? You've got no weapon, I suppose. Only a fool would have walked into a trap like this without a blade of some nature, but I suppose it's a little too late for you to reflect on *that* . . . '

He stamped forward, smashing aside the boy's raised sword with his own and putting a bunched fist into his face, hard enough to break his nose, then thrust the blade up into his defenceless victim's chest before he could recover from the blow, dumping him on his back in a fast-spreading puddle of blood. The senator looked about him, seeking a means of escape, but the shops that lined the street were closed, and the killer's walk towards him was more saunter than stalk. The taller of the two men spoke again, strolling across the street's cobbles until he was close enough for the senator to see the thin scar that lined the left side of his face.

'The bad news, Senator, is that you're not the only person you've doomed with your loose talk, and I'm afraid that the damage can't be limited to these two poor individuals. I'm told you have a young wife and an infant son, and so, regrettably, our next call will have to be on the pair of them. You have sisters too, I believe? Believe me, Senator, when the throne decides to remove a threat it does so in a particularly thorough way, to ensure that nobody stays alive who might later seek their revenge.'

Quirinius spread his hands, his voice wavering in desperation.

'Couldn't I . . . '

'Pay us off? You don't have enough money, Senator. Call on our better nature? I'm really not sure whether I've got one, but I can assure you that my colleague Rapax here most certainly does not. He enjoys these little diversions far too much to have any underlying decency. No, Senator, the time to be having second thoughts about all this was *before* you walked into Praetorian Prefect Perennis's office and told him your story regarding the death of his son, and exactly who it was that killed him. You blurted out that the fugitive Marcus Valerius Aquila was the murderer, and is hiding with an auxiliary cohort of Tungrians in northern Britannia under the name of Marcus Tribulus Corvus far too easily, I'm afraid.'

Rapax stepped closer to the young noble, smiling easily into the other man's eyes, then looked down at the stream of urine puddling around his feet. He shook his head, his voice a hoarse growl tinged with the barest hint of irritation. 'Take a moment to compose yourself, boy. A man should go to meet his gods with dignity.'

The senator stared helplessly back at the assassin's stone-hard face, his knees shivering with the imminence of his death. The praetorian raised his sword and expertly stabbed the point into the conjunction of shoulder and neck, watching dispassionately as Quirinius slumped slowly to the cobbles. The life faded from his eyes, blood gushing down his toga and staining the white linen crimson as it poured from the artery Rapax had opened. Excingus shook his head sadly.

'It's amazing how many people one man can condemn to death with just a few loose words. I hope you've plenty of energy left in you, colleague, for I fear we have a long evening ahead of us.'

1

Britannia, September, AD *182*

The barbarian scouts shivered in the cold pre-dawn air, staring out into the forest's black emptiness and waiting for the dawn that would release them from their task of watching the silent trees for any sign of a Roman attack. The youngest of them yawned loudly, stretching his arms out in front of him to dispel the stiffness that was afflicting all three of them before whispering to the small group's leader.

'There's nothing out there, nothing for miles. The Romans are camped out on the plain behind a wall of earth, not crawling round the forest like wild pigs. It's time we were back inside the camp . . .'

The oldest of the three nodded almost unseen in the darkness, keen to be warming his feet and hands at the fire rather than crouching in the shadow of a fallen tree and waiting in the cold for nothing to happen. He shook his head stubbornly, raising a finger in admonishment to both men.

'We've been trusted to watch this side of the camp, to sound the warning if we hear as much as a badger stirring the leaves, and that's what we'll do, until the sun's over the horizon and eyes are stronger than ears. If either of you don't like that, you can fuck off back into the camp and discuss it with . . . '

He started at a sudden sound, thinking for a moment that someone was wielding an axe at the palisade a hundred paces to their rear before he realised that the younger of the two men facing him had been punched sideways to the ground with something protruding from his ear. The stink of blood was suddenly heavy in the air. The older warrior slumped away from the log a split second later with an agonised, bubbling grunt. His eyes rolled upwards as the arrow buried deep in his chest took his life. Their leader ripped the hunting horn from his belt, grabbing a deep breath and putting it to his lips, only to shudder with the bone-crunching impact of an arrow into his own ribs. The horn fell from his nerveless fingers to the fallen leaves with a soft thud, and he stared stupidly for a moment at the short length of its feathered wooden shaft jutting from his chest, feeling his blood spraying from the terrible wound chopped deep into his body by its iron-tipped head. His vision narrowing, he sank slowly to his knees, caught for a moment between life and death as a noiseless figure ghosted across the forest floor towards him.

Without any sound that the dying barbarian could make out, the shadowy figure was abruptly beside him, a tall, lean man dressed in a grey cloak and with a Roman gladius gleaming palely in his right hand, his face painted with stripes of dark mud beneath a cross-crested helmet to match the forest's dappled moonlit floor. He grabbed at the tottering warrior's hair to steady him and lifted his sword to strike, angling the blade for the killing thrust. He looked into the dying man's eyes for a moment, then ran the gladius's razor-sharp blade through the helpless tribesman's throat and eased him down to lie glassy eyed in the leaves. Putting a hand inside the tunic beneath his mail armour, he touched a pendant hanging around his neck and muttered a quiet prayer.

'Unconquered almighty Mithras grant you safe passage to your god.'

He dropped into the fallen tree's shelter, staring intently at the palisade for any sign that the scouts' deaths had not gone unnoticed by the warband camped behind its protective wall. His brown eyes were pools of darkness in the night as he stared fiercely into the gloom, his fingers white with their grip on the sword's hilt. After a long moment of complete silence, other than for the rustle of leaves in the night's gentle breeze, he turned and whistled softly. A dozen men rose from the cover of the undergrowth fifty paces from the camp's palisade and crossed the space between the forest edge and the fallen tree with swift caution, weaving noiselessly around the stumps of trees felled to build the camp's wall. They dropped into the fallen tree's cover and were instantly still, each one of them aware that any unexpected sound might waken the barbarians sleeping beyond the palisade. Half of the small group were, at first glance, declared enemies of the other half dozen, their shaggy hair and long swords in stark contrast to the soldiers' close-cropped heads and short infantry blades. After a moment one of the barbarians bent close to the cloaked swordsman, speaking softly into his ear.

'I told you this was the place, Two Knives. They wouldn't have put men to watch the forest here without a quick route to safety back through their wall.'

The Roman nodded, whispering his reply.

'And since Qadir put the watchers down silently, we still have the advantage of surprise.' Behind the barbarian one of the soldiers, his helmet crested front to back to denote his status as a chosen man and the centurion's deputy, nodded recognition of his officer's quiet compliment. He finished slinging his bow across his muscular shoulders, and pulled his gladius from its sheath while the centurion pointed to the wooden wall looming over the stump-studded clearing. 'And the palisade breach is to the left of the hidden doorway?'

The barbarian nodded confidently.

'Yes, as we discussed. A twenty pace section of the wall from the hidden opening is ready to fall if the retaining bars are removed. And now, with your permission . . . ?'

He drew a long hunting knife from his belt and reversed its grip so that the silver line of its blade was concealed behind his arm. The Roman officer nodded decisively.

'Quickly and quietly now, Martos. There'll be plenty of noise soon enough.'

'Don't worry, Centurion Corvus, for the chance to twist my knife in Calgus's guts I would go silent for the rest of my days.'

The barbarian turned to his men, as the

shaggy-haired warriors clustered around him.

'There were three of them, one young, one old and one about my age. You, and you, you're the closest we have to them. With me, and *quietly*. Any man that makes a noise will have me to reckon with.'

The three men slipped away, quickly merging with the looming bulk of the timber palisade that had been thrown up around the barbarian camp.

⋆ ⋆ ⋆

Calgus, king of the Selgovae people and self-styled 'Lord of the Northern Tribes', knew the argument, if it could be deemed worthy of the name, was getting away from him too quickly for there to be any chance of his regaining control of the situation. For a fleeting moment he considered taking his sword to the Venicone chieftain who was so blatantly defying him in his own camp, but the half-dozen hard-faced killers arrayed behind the man, and the heavy war hammer carried over his shoulder, killed the thought before it had time to muster any conviction. He might have been standing inside his own tent, in the middle of thousands of his own people, but these flint-eyed maniacs would tear through his bodyguard and kill him before any of his men were sufficiently awake to react. Drust shook his head vehemently, flicking his hand in a violently dismissive gesture.

'This war of yours is doomed to fail, Calgus, doomed by your own hand, and the Venicone tribe will not stand alongside you while the invaders grind us all into these hills.' He flicked the hand again, the gesture inches from Calgus's face. 'Our part in this war is done. We will fall back to our own lands, and wait for the Romans to decide whether we're worth the trouble of pursuit.'

He turned to walk away, and Calgus reached out to take his arm.

'I had thought the Venicone under King Drust had . . . '

The Venicone leader spun back at the touch of Calgus's hand on the sleeve of his rough woollen tunic, his braided red hair whipping about his face with the speed of his reaction. His men froze as he lifted a hand to still their instant response, their eyes burning with the urge to fight, and he leaned in close to his former ally, speaking softly despite his anger.

'You thought there was more to us, perhaps? You wonder that I can walk away from a war not yet finished? There was a time not long distant when I would have agreed with you. I considered you a comrade, Calgus, a man I could stand alongside in the fight to evict the Romans from our soil, but hear me now when I warn you one last time. The next time you lay a finger on me, I will let these animals behind me loose on your bodyguard just to see who comes off best, and you and I will discover which of us is doomed to die at the other's hand. You thought me stupid, eh, Calgus? You thought I would never hear the rumours of your betrayal of our Votadini brothers after they had triumphed in battle for you, and that you did this because their king disputed your plans one time too many? Perhaps even simply because you could? My men were a cunt-hair from victory in their fight with the Romans at the ford, with more than a thousand heads for the taking, until Martos of the Votadini, a man deliberately betrayed and left for the Romans to slaughter by *you*, led his warriors into battle against mine at the crucial moment, and turned our victory into bloody defeat in a hundred heartbeats! Apparently even the Romans know better than you how to treat an ally, and while I'll have no truck with them, neither will I risk your friendship for an hour longer. You have poisoned our own people against us, you fool, and you will pay for that mistake with your own blood, and that of your tribe!'

Sneering disdainfully, he turned away and ducked through the tent's doorway, leaving Calgus staring after him. A soft voice spoke from behind him, although there was iron in the words.

'You must stop him, my lord. If he takes his men north we will not have enough strength to defend this place against two legions should the Romans attack.'

Calgus spun back to face the speaker, glaring with frustration into his seamed face before nodding at the old man resignedly. His adviser was a man of unerring instincts, even if some of his advice had resulted in more difficulty than had at first seemed apparent.

'And what do you propose, Aed? That I should beg our comrade to stay? I'll not make a fool of myself to no purpose.'

The old man smiled gently, spreading his hands out.

'No, my lord, I fully agree. Your authority must be maintained at all costs. I was simply about to suggest that you might have something to offer Drust in return for his continued support.'

Calgus frowned.

'What can I possibly offer the Venicone that would persuade them to stay and fight?'

'Something, my lord, which, since you have possessed it for less than a month, you will never truly miss. Something which you can always take back later, once the Brigantes south of the Wall are freed from under the Roman boot and swell your army to an irresistible size.'

Calgus nodded slowly as the realisation of Aed's meaning took effect.

'Yes . . .'

He hurried from the tent in the wake of the Venicone chieftain.

* * *

There was a long moment of silence before one of Martos's men reappeared from the gloom, gesturing the remainder of the raiding party forward. Marcus led his men across the ground between the fallen tree and the wooden wall in a crouching run, finding the gap in the palisade just as Martos had described it to the legions' senior officers the previous day. The two ends of the wooden wall were overlapped, making the thin gap between them almost invisible.

'Give me ten front-rankers and I could defend that little gap against a fucking legion . . . '

Marcus looked over his shoulder to find one of his men standing close behind him; the stark white line that marked his face from the point of his right eyebrow to his jawbone was still visible beneath the mud daubed across his features. While the soldier was hardly one of his more stealthy men, he had point blank refused to allow his centurion to accompany Martos's warriors to the enemy walls without his being one of the soldiers alongside him. Marcus pulled off his helmet, handing it to the other man.

'Here, Scarface, make yourself useful and take this. I'm going in to find Martos. Get your ropes in place, and be ready to guide the cohort in if I sound the call.'

The soldier shook his head with resigned disgust.

'If you're going into that nest of blue-noses with them . . . ' He tipped his helmeted head to indicate the Votadini tribesman. ' . . . then you'd best be looking like one of them.'

He fished a small bundle out from beneath his mail, handing it to Marcus, who opened it to find a mass of hair spilling out into his hands. He stared down at the object with fascinated disgust.

'This is . . . '

'It's clean, I washed the skin in the river only a few days ago. Put it on.'

Marcus's skin crawled as he pulled another man's scalp over his head, allowing the long black hair to settle over his shoulders. Scarface squinted at him in the darkness.

'Your own mother wouldn't recognise you. Try to bring it back, there's a soldier in the Sixth Century offered me ten denarii for it.'

Squeezing between the gap in the palisade with his gladius drawn, Marcus found the barbarians busy dragging the last of the guards into the four-foot-deep ditch that ran around the camp behind the palisade. Martos turned to him with a grin, shaking his head at the sight of a Roman officer with another man's hair draped across his head.

'It suits you. Perhaps you should have been born north of the frontier.'

Marcus slid his gladius back into its scabbard and covered the sword's gold-and-silver eagle's-head pommel with his cloak.

'The palisade is as you expected?'

The barbarian nodded.

'Yes. I told you there were pre-prepared exits on all four sides of the camp, and I remembered the location of this one perfectly. Twenty paces of the wall with the logs chopped almost clean away at their bases, the whole section braced into one solid section and then locked in place with wooden beams to stop it falling over if some idiot leans against it. We've taken down the bracing beams that hold the whole thing to the wall on either side, so all your men have to do is give their ropes a solid pull and the whole section will fall and make a nice handy ramp into the camp. And now, if you're ready, for Calgus.'

Marcus nodded, looking about him at the sleeping barbarian camp. In the pre-dawn gloom the tribe's tents receded into the darkness, the occasional fire kept burning to provide a quick source of flame.

'There will be men awake, even at this time.'

Martos nodded.

'Yes, it's certain. They know that the legions are camped on the plain close by, and that they may attack at any time, perhaps even today. Some men will sleep like dogs; others will lie awake for fear of the morning. But we will walk with confidence to Calgus's tent, and the men that are awake will see what they expect to see, their own people going about their leader's orders. Come.'

The half-dozen barbarians gathered around the Roman officer, following Martos's lead as he strode confidently into the heart of the slumbering enemy camp. They walked for a minute or so, angling to the left and climbing the slope away from the safety of the palisade, until Martos raised a hand to halt them. He looked around him and then ducked into the cover of a large tent, gathering his men to him with a gesture and whispering so quietly as to be almost inaudible.

'This is Calgus's tent. There will be guards at the entrance, so once we're inside I want silence until we have everyone inside either dead or gagged. And Calgus is *mine*.'

He looked around the group to ensure that he was perfectly understood, then dug the point of his knife's blade into the tent's side and drew it swiftly downwards, opening a long slit in the rough canvas wall. Marcus stepped in through the hole first with his gladius drawn, finding the tent's spacious interior dimly lit by a pair of oil lamps. The sole occupant, a stooped figure, stood with his back to him, and he bounded forward with two quick paces to wrap his arm around the man's mouth and jaw, muffling any cry for help with the fabric of his cloak and the armour that clad his sleeve beneath the rough wool.

'Guard the door, and keep that slit held tight.'

The two warriors moved quickly at Martos's whispered command, temporarily securing the tent against chance discovery, and their chieftain stalked around the captive until he came into the old man's field of view. Marcus felt him shrink away from the Votadini prince's harsh stare, and tightened his grip against any attempt to raise the alarm, but felt only capitulation in the way the old man held tightly against him pressed back in a futile effort to escape the nightmare unfolding in front of him. Martos lifted his knife to the old man's face, tapping a sunken cheek with the point.

'Aed. Not what I'd hoped for, but a fair start. I came seeking your master, but instead I have the sour, shrunken old fuck that drips his poison into Calgus's mind. Doubtless it was your idea that my warband be abandoned in the path of the Roman cavalry after the fight for White Strength, led into their path to be chopped to pieces, in revenge for the massacre of their cohort. And why? To get me out of the way, so that Calgus would be free to murder my uncle and take control of our kingdom.' He put the knife's point under the old man's chin, digging the sharp iron up into the sagging flesh until a thin runnel of blood ran down Aed's neck and into the folds of his robe. 'And now, thanks to you, I am a prince without his people. My family are either dead, or suffering so badly that I could wish them dead. So let's not bother with any of the usual denials, because if you don't answer me quick and straight I'll slice you open and pull your guts out for you to carry around for a while. *Calgus.* Where is he?'

* * *

Drust laughed in Calgus's face for a second time, his eyes bright with amusement.

'You offer me the Votadini's land, Calgus? You might as well offer me the moon, for all the cost to you, and for all the chance that I might be able to keep the ground you offer, even if I were minded to accept. If I wanted the Votadini's land I would have taken it long since, you fool.' He turned back to his men, pointing to the northern face of the camp's protective palisade. 'We need to be away from here before full dawn. You, take a message up the hill. The fence is to be opened, and our people ready to run north.' Turning back to face Calgus, he put both hands on his hips.

'The Votadini are nothing more than the Romans' lapdogs, Calgus. Their royal women drip with jewellery made in the south, and their men wear swords with keener edges than would be the case if they were locally forged. If we occupy the Dinpaladyr we'll have less than a month before a legion marches up, batters down the 'fortress of the spears' walls with their catapults and puts us all to the sword. The Romans like their trade with the Votadini, and through them with the rest of you fools, and they won't be abandoning that easy money without a fight. So no, Calgus, you took the Votadini's land and now *you* can defend it, or else run and hide when they kick down your gate and come looking for their revenge on you. I can run now, away to the safety of my own land behind their old north wall, and they will leave me well alone if they know what's good for them. They might even pay me tribute to keep me behind my walls and out of the fight. But you, Calgus, you have ruined their forts and slaughtered their soldiers. You could run to the ends of the world and they would still never stop hunting you. So if I were you I'd . . . '

His eyes suddenly narrowed at the sound of shouting from over Calgus's shoulder. Another voice joined the first, and a sudden scream of agony rent the air. Drust turned and roared at the men gathered about him.

'Get that fucking fence open! It's time to leave!'

* * *

The first Selgovae warrior through the tent door died silently, his throat torn open by a hunting knife wielded by the Votadini he'd knocked aside in his haste to enter the tent. He staggered three paces into the tent's half-light, with his lifeblood pumping down his chest and his bowels noisily emptying into his rough woollen trousers before he pitched full length to the pale turf.

'Lord Calgus! There are Romans in the . . .'

The second man was still only halfway through the flap door shouting wildly that the alarm was raised, when the first warrior's killer backhanded the short blade into his belly and ripped it out through his side, spilling the slippery rope of his guts and wrenching a grunted scream of pain from his contorted mouth as he fell to his knees. Martos shrugged into the old man's white face.

'Time to leave. Release him, Marcus.'

Aed barely had time to register the sudden cool air on his face as the Roman stepped back, lifting his arm away and pushing him on to Martos's knife before a sudden burning pain ripped into his body. Looking down in horror, he saw the weapon's blade protruding from his belly in Martos's expert hand, staggering in sudden shock as the Votadini prince pulled the weapon down into his lower abdomen before twisting it savagely and pulling it free, wiping the bloody iron on his robe. A rush of warm blood gushed from the wound, filling the air with its metallic stink, underlaid by the smell of excrement, and the old man dropped to his knees and bent double with the excruciating agony of his wound.

'Die hard, Aed. Hard, and *slowly*.'

He gestured to the hole in the tent's rear, stooping to pick up a small wooden box that rested at the foot of Calgus's bedroll and lifting the lid to peer inside, then angled the casket to show Marcus the contents.

'I should have known. Nothing but paper. I suppose Calgus's private letters might be of some value, if only to give your tribune something to read once the fighting's over . . . '

He tossed the chest to one of his men, and the small group stepped out into the dawn's pale light through the rent in the tent's back wall, Marcus quickly taking stock of their situation in the sure knowledge that if the presence of a Roman officer in the enemy's camp became known they would be beset from all sides in seconds. All about them warriors were crawling from their tents and reaching for their weapons, not yet aware of the interlopers in their midst, but only seconds from making that discovery.

'There's no time for slow and quiet now! Follow me!'

He drew his gladius and set off at a dead run down the path between the tents, sprinting towards the palisade where his men were waiting, Martos and his warriors close on his heels. The crude wig that had masked the Roman's features fell away and revealed his short cropped black hair, and a tribesman blinking away sleep in his path gaped in amazement, throwing his head back to shout a warning as Marcus's gladius ripped open his throat before one of Martos's warriors shoulder-charged him into the side of another tent without breaking stride. A chorus of shouts was following them now, alerting the men in front of them even if the cause of the uproar was still unclear. Bleary-eyed tribesmen turned to crane their necks, instinctively reaching for weapons as they sought the source of the commotion.

Martos drew level with the centurion, straining every sinew in his magnificent physique as he pounded along beside the man who had been his enemy only days before. A straggling group of Selgovae warriors was gathering across their path, hefting their weapons in readiness for a fight as the intruders charged towards them.

Marcus tossed the gladius into his left hand and drew his spatha on the run, flashing the long blade out and bellowing a rising scream of defiance as he ploughed into their midst, flicking aside a spear-thrust with the long cavalry sword and ducking under a swinging blade before upending the sword's owner with his leg hacked off at the knee, spinning away to his left in a double flicker of razor-edged iron. Martos matched the ferocity of his attack, hacking his way into the Selgovae with a fury that scattered the warriors, his men crowding in around him to protect their prince at any cost. A tribesman hacked down two handed at Marcus with a heavy sword, the blade sliding down his angled spatha as Marcus pivoted around his right arm, reversing his left-handed grip on the gladius's eagle-head pommel and backhanding the short blade through the swordsman's ribs before spinning again, tearing the blade free and cutting low, felling another warrior, both his hamstrings severed by the spatha's harsh bite. Two more warriors ran in to the fight, and Marcus turned to confront them, starting as a spear hissed past his head and punched the closer of the pair back with his eyes rolling back to show only the whites. The other man swung his sword up to attack, only to stagger as an arrow flicked through the throng of Votadini and embedded itself in his throat. A strong grip on the neck of his mail armour pulled the young centurion away from the fight, the four surviving barbarians and Marcus's own men forming a thin line against the gathering mass of enraged Selgovae warriors. Qadir and his two fellow Hamians were nocking and loosing arrows with a speed and accuracy that were, for the moment, felling as many tribesmen as were joining the uncertain warriors facing off the outnumbered Romans. Scarface grinned apologetically as his officer spun to face him, backing off a step at the look on Marcus's face.

'No time for that, Centurion, the fence is coming down . . . '

With a creaking, screaming tear of rending wood, the twenty-foot-wide section of the palisade that Martos had identified to him on their way in fell away from the rest of the wall. As the dust of its falling settled, Marcus saw the men who had dragged it down drop their ropes and take up their weapons, forming an unbroken line of shields in seconds. A lean centurion limped out in front of them, pointing with his sword and bellowing an order in a voice that carried far across the barbarian camp.

'*Tungrians, advance!*'

* * *

Calgus stared across the camp with mounting consternation, hearing the bray of trumpets that he knew must presage an attack by the legions. With a sudden flicker of fire in the purple dawn sky, half a dozen blazing fire pots arced high over the camp's southern wall, landing in gouts of flame as they shattered to release their burning liquid contents and set instant flame to both men and tents. Behind him Drust smiled knowingly, unsurprised at this turn in events.

'The Romans are inside your walls, Calgus. Your game is *finished*.'

He nodded to the largest of his bodyguards, tapping the back of his head. The man took two steps forward before punching Calgus behind the ear with as much force as he could muster, his massive fist hammering the unwitting tribal leader to the ground twitching and barely conscious.

'Nicely done, Maon, now tie his arms and legs, and gag him. He may prove a useful bargaining counter to have behind our walls should the Romans come knocking.' He turned away from the scene of chaos. 'Let's be away now, before the legions close the gap in the northern fence and pin us against their shields.'

The warriors around him turned at his command and climbed the gentle slope towards the camp's northern fence, its line of tree trunks now marred by a gap to match that ripped open by the Romans down the slope to the east. Drust looked about him and found the scurrying figure of his body servant, running for the king's tent, clearly intent on salvaging the most precious of his master's possessions. He smiled quietly to himself at the man's evident urgency.

'Very wise, little man. I'd have the skin off your balls were it any other way.'

He turned away, confident that his servant would be out of the camp with the warband's rearguard, and ran for the gap in the palisade, intent on making sure that no attempt to close the gap in the fence could be made before his men were all through it and into the safety of the forest. Behind him in the king's tent, and unseen by the hundreds of men streaming past up the camp's slope, the slave dropped to his knees and started to frantically cram his master's most treasured possessions into a goat-skin bag. He was reaching for the most important item of all when a ballista bolt, fired blindly over the camp's palisade by the legion artillery supporting the attack, punched through the tent's canvas wall and spent its lethal power in his body, spearing through his heart and covering the far wall with a spray of crimson arterial blood. His eyesight dimming, the dying servant reached out a hand to grasp the shining gold ring, then froze into immobility, his last conscious memory the agonising iron cold of the missile which had transfixed him.

* * *

Marcus and his men stepped clear of the Tungrian advance, and the cohort's leading century strode past them and into the enemy's stronghold, soldiers running hard for both ends of the century's line to lengthen the shield wall against a barbarian counter-attack as quickly as possible. The cohort's 2nd Century followed them in and veered to the left, their centurion shooting Marcus a quick grin as he ran past bellowing orders at his men, the 3rd Century breaking to their right. As the cohort's line grew in strength their spears flickered out to kill those tribesmen who had failed to retreat in the face of their remorseless advance. More centuries poured through the palisade breach and fanned out on both sides to further strengthen their foothold in the enemy camp, and Marcus saluted the cohort's first spear, clasping hands with him as the other man jumped from the palisade's wooden slope to the ground.

'I don't think I've ever been quite so pleased to see your face, sir!'

His superior officer smiled grimly, motioning for them to step aside as another century stamped up the fallen palisade's wooden ramp and hurried off into the fight. Marcus's friend and brother officer Rufius winked at him as he pointed up the slope with his vine stick, shouting the command for the 6th Century to form line in a bellow made hoarse by the twenty-five years of legion service he had completed before joining the Tungrians. First Spear Frontinius's chin jutted between the cheek pieces of his helmet as he stared out into the barbarian camp, watching as the sea of barbarian tents took fire from the flame pots being hurled over the palisade by the legions' artillery, the blaze's flickering light illuminating the enemy warriors as they crowded forward to join battle with their attackers.

'A job well done, Centurion Corvus! Now we finish these blue-faced bastards once and for good. Your boys will be along in a moment. Take them to the left, push up the hill and link up with the left flank of the century that went up in front of you. In the meanwhile our axemen will make this gap in the fence big enough that even the Sixth Legion's road menders will feel safe to join us. Ah, here's your century now . . . '

He pointed back into the empty space between forest and palisade, and Marcus followed his outstretched arm to find his 9th Century marching into view, their one-eyed watch officer striding alongside them with Qadir's brass-knobbed chosen man's pole in his hand while Morban, Marcus's veteran standard-bearer, was at their head. Marcus saluted the first spear, then trotted out to meet his men, returning the watch officer's salute and barking his orders to the men around him as Qadir retrieved his pole and dropped back to his usual place at the century's rear.

'Well done, Cyclops! To your places, gentlemen, we're turning left and advancing up the inner wall until we make contact with the century to our right, then we take our place to their left and keep advancing alongside them!'

He trotted over to the head of the century, returning the standard-bearer's salute and shouting over the crash of hobnails and the jingle of equipment as they mounted the fallen palisade's wooden ramp.

'Morban, take them left! Up the hill!'

The standard-bearer shot him a quick nod, then bellowed over his shoulder at the lanky trumpeter marching behind him.

'*Blow!*'

The trumpet's harsh note snapped the century's heads up, and Morban canted the standard to the left. Marcus stepped out in front of the marching century, turning to face the troops and raising his gladius high and pointing to their left.

'*Follow me!*'

He jumped down from the wooden ramp, watching the marching soldiers as Morban led them over the one-foot drop and up the slope to their left. Satisfied that they had made the turn successfully, he turned, gulped a lungful of air and ran hard up the slope, past the leading ranks of the century's column and on up the hill. He ignored the fact that Cyclops had broken ranks to run alongside him as he searched through the billowing smoke for the century that had preceded them, knowing that nothing he could say would reduce the man's protective instincts towards his officer. Toiling through the reek drifting slowly across the chaotic battlefield, he suddenly ran into clear air and stopped, aghast at the scene unfolding in front of him. The century that had advanced up the hill only moments before him was being overrun by hundreds of barbarian warriors, the soldiers fighting a desperate but doomed defensive action as their enraged enemy hammered against their faltering shield wall, one man after another going down into the trampled mud to be finished off with swords and spears by the rampaging horde. As he watched, the other century's centurion, anonymous in the drifting smoke, stepped into the front line with a bellow of defiance and started fighting for his century's survival. Without his even being aware of it, a growl of anger rippled in his throat as he watched his brother officer fighting for his life, and he put a hand on the hilt of his spatha.

'*No!*'

Marcus turned, to find his watch officer's one good eye fierce with determination.

'No use in your throwing yourself away. Take the lads in there and pull those poor bastards out of the fire, those that's left.'

He nodded slowly, turning away from the scene of his comrades' massacre. When he spoke, his voice was harsh with fresh purpose.

'Get back to your men, Cyclops.'

He ran back down the slope through the smoke, his mind working quickly, almost falling over Morban in the murk.

'Twenty paces more and then put them into line to the right, facing up the hill. No horns!'

The standard-bearer nodded at him and stamped away up the hill, while Marcus pulled a soldier out of the marching ranks and barked a command in the man's ear.

'Run back down the hill to the first spear. Tell him there's a century being torn to pieces up here and we need urgent reinforcement now! *Go!*'

He pushed the soldier hard, sending him away

down the slope, then turned back to the marching column. Morban, barely visible through the smoke, had the standard held horizontally over his head with its metal hand pointing to his right.

'Scarface! Make sure they make the turn!'

The veteran soldier snapped a salute and ran to march at Morban's shoulder, ready to stand firm once the standard-bearer made the right-angled turn to put the 9th in line facing the enemy, rather than risk encountering them in the vulnerable column of march. The line abruptly turned right, the soldiers following their standard without much of a clue as to what was happening. And just as well, Marcus mused, given what they would be facing in less than a minute. He stepped in alongside his deputy, pointing past the marching soldiers and up the smoke-wreathed slope.

'Qadir, there are hundreds of barbarians less than a hundred paces that way, and they've already torn up one century. When we march out of this damned smoke they'll throw themselves on to us like dogs on raw meat, so give me your pole and get your bow ready, you and your mates. Anyone that looks like they might be important, anyone with a lot of gold or that's shouting the odds a bit too loudly, put them down.'

The big Hamian handed over his six-foot brass-knobbed pole, unslinging the bow from across his shoulders and barking a command in Aramaic to the dozen or so other Hamians marching in the 9th Century's ranks. Marcus shot a glance back down the century's line, waiting a few seconds to allow the last of the marching soldiers to make the turn, then drew breath to bellow his orders.

'Ninth Century, halt!'

The column stamped to a halt, troops coughing and spluttering as they breathed in the thickening smoke from the rapidly spreading fires.

'To the left . . . face! Form lines of battle!'

He waited while the soldiers straightened their lines, the front-rankers raising their shields and hefting their spears, the rear-rankers crowding close to the men in front of them, ready to grip their belts and hold them steady once the fighting started.

'Ninth Century . . . '

Marcus's voice rang out over the short double line, the din of battle from their right muffled by the smoke and the distant roar of blazing canvas.

'When we march forward, we will soon come upon the remains of one of our sister centuries. They were surprised in the line of march, and never stood any chance of resisting the barbarians. You, however, are ready to fight, armed and armoured, drilled and trained to perfection. Any one of you is worth a dozen of those blue-nosed bastards. So we will go forward, we will find the men that killed our brothers and we will kill as many of them as possible before our reinforcement arrives. At the walk, *advance!*'

The century started forward as one man, and while Marcus had Qadir's pole ready to push between the shoulders of any man hanging back, he quickly realised that he wasn't going to need it. Ten, twenty paces they advanced, without any sign of an end to the dirty grey smoke what was making eyes water and lungs strain for breath, and then, in the blink of an eye, they were back out in the crisp dawn air with the scene of the other century's massacre laid out before them.

The slope was littered with corpses clad in the same equipment his men were wearing, their mail armour a dull iron grey against the barbarian camp's trampled mud. A few of the fallen soldiers were still moving, their wounds severe enough to leave them helpless but not enough to have killed them immediately. Half a dozen barbarians were moving among them, their swords black with the blood they had spilled, and, as Marcus watched, the nearest of them raised his blade in readiness to dispatch another of the wounded. Qadir snapped his bow up, and, with a sonorous note from the bowstring, put an arrow into his neck, dropping him choking and kicking to the ground beside his intended victim.

A couple of the barbarians closest to the dying warrior looked up at the sudden commotion, gaping in surprise at the 9th Century's unexpected appearance from out of the smoke even as the other Hamians shot them down with a swift precision that rivalled Qadir's. Forcing himself to ignore the dead and dying Tungrians scattered across the ground before him, Marcus pushed through the century's battle line and looked around him for some sign of the barbarians who had massacred his fellow soldiers only minutes before. The smoke eddied with the gentle morning breeze again, affording him a momentary glimpse of the fight taking place down the slope to their right. The Tungrian line was now fully embattled, struggling to hold back easily three times their own strength of enemy warriors who were throwing themselves at the shield wall with the desperate fury of men who knew that if they failed to break through the soldiers they were as good as dead. Before the curtain of smoke closed again he realised, with a sickening jolt, exactly what it was that the barbarians had impaled on their spearheads and were waving up and down in front of the Tungrian soldiers. He turned back to his men with his eyes blazing and the muscles around his jaw rippling as he fought to hold his temper.

'Ninth Century, right wheel!'

He held his breath for a long moment while the century swung ponderously through their quarter-turn to face down the slope. The Hamians were all at sea with the manoeuvre, still new to the disciplines of infantry fighting after choosing to join the century less than a week before, but the men around each of them gently pulled and pushed them through the line's reorientation, with more than one kind word or pat on the shoulder for men who had been derided as nothing more than a burden on the cohort only days before. Marcus smiled to himself despite his anger, acknowledging their justified change of status. The battle at the Red River's ford had seen to that in one desperate, bloody afternoon of seemingly doomed resistance to the Venicone tribe's assault.

Within a minute the line was aligned with the direction in which a swelling roar of battle was reaching them through the smoke, the soldiers looking anxiously down their ranks at him as he pulled both swords from their places on his belt, his face grim with purpose. Morban, now no longer the pivot for their swing to the right, scuttled down the line's rear to his place immediately behind their attack, the trumpeter running behind him. Marcus raised his voice again, steeling himself for the attack.

'Ninth Century, your enemy are down there, hidden in the smoke.' A few of the soldiers, he realised, were translating his words for those men around them with insufficient Latin to keep up with his angry words. 'When I give the command we will march down this slope until we have them in sight. They will be close, Ninth Century, close enough for you to smell the shit that will stream down their legs when they see us come out of nowhere at their backs.' A few men laughed, the delight of imminent combat evident in their wide eyes and flared nostrils. The rest of them were for the most part stone faced, working hard to hold their nerve with battle only seconds away. Marcus nodded to the trumpeter, who blew the advance strong and clear.

'Ninth Century, advance!'

As the two lines of soldiers stepped off down the hill, Scarface thrust one of his spears at the man behind him.

'You, pass this forward to me when I've put

the first one through some fucker's back, and make sure you're ready with it as soon as I've thrown this one, or there'll be a short and very interesting discussion once we've sorted these long-haired cunts out.' The men around him smiled despite themselves, as amused as they always were by his blend of bombast and single-minded purpose. Without taking his eyes off the ground in front of him, the veteran soldier hawked noisily and spat into the grass. 'The rest of you, stop your grinning and get your fucking spears ready to throw!'

Thirty paces down the slope, the century got their first glimpse of the enemy through a momentary gap in the smoke. The mass of tribesmen were pressing harder on the Tungrian line than before, clearly wearing the embattled soldiers down by the sheer weight of their numbers, and the cohort's grip on its foothold inside the barbarian camp had visibly reduced in size since Marcus's last quick look. Another ten paces saw the century within a spear's-throw of the raging tribesmen, and yet still undetected. Marcus lifted his sword and then dropped the blade. Whatever the trumpeter might have been feeling, his lungs seemed unaffected, a loud note from his horn pealing out over the battlefield and snatching the attention of the enemy warriors. The 9th Century's front rank roared their defiance, shaking their spears at the surprised barbarians, and Marcus raised his sword again.

'Spears . . . '

The men in the front rank leaned backwards, their left arms reaching forward for balance as they pulled their spears back until the iron heads were level with their helmets. Scarface turned his face and kissed the cold iron, feeling the blade's ragged edge on his lower lip, then locked his gaze on a warrior twenty paces distant in the barbarian warband's rear.

'*Throw!*'

The front rank took a collective two steps forward, exhaling noisily as they hurled their weapons into the enemy warriors.

'Spears . . . *throw!*'

Reaching back to take their second spears from the men behind them, the soldiers hurled themselves forward again, and launched a second volley into the barbarian rear. Dozens of the enemy were now out of the fight, some toppled to the ground, others on their knees or held upright by the crush of their numbers.

'*Form line!*'

The century was back in line within seconds, staring down at their enemy as a wave of confusion spread through the barbarians.

'*Swords!*'

The front rank unsheathed their short swords, a sudden pale gleam in the dawn light. Marcus pointed his sword at the enemy warriors, raising his voice to a roar.

'*Attack!*'

Scarface pointed his sword at the barbarian he'd decided to kill first, screaming his challenge.

'*Come on, you fuckers!*'

He bounded down the hill, the men to either side of him howling their own battle cries as they made their own charges, punching his shield into the barbarian's face and stabbing his gladius into his guts before the other man had the chance to recover from the blow. Driven by their recent experience of battle with the tribes, and knowing what would inevitably come next, the front rank pulled their shields together to form a defensive wall, while the rear-rankers stepped in close and caught hold of their belts, steadying them against the assault to come. With a roar of anger the barbarian warband slammed back against their defence, hammering at their shields and helmeted heads with swords and spears as they recovered from their shock and threw themselves at the new threat.

* * *

Tribune Licinius spurred his horse forward up the line of the 20th Legion's column to meet the scout riders racing towards him from the barbarian camp's northern face. His cavalry wing was strung out over the hundreds of paces behind him, still making their way through the forest that surrounded the camp, along a tortuous hunter's path that had been scouted as an approach route in the days that had followed the near-disaster at the Red River. Sending half a legion down the path first had been a necessary measure, given the need for the heavy infantry to break into the camp and defeat the warband before the cavalry could follow up and chase down any survivors, but their lack of urgency in the approach march had tested his patience beyond its limits. The lead rider reined in his sweating horse alongside the tribune's magnificent grey, his voice urgent as he saluted his superior and launched into a description of what was happening at the head of the column.

'The northern palisade has been breached from the inside, Tribune, and there's a warband running north in tribal strength. We saw their rearguard heading off into the forest, at least a thousand men strong, and they looked like Venicones.'

Licinius nodded, thinking quickly.

'Those tattooed buggers must have decided to quit Calgus's war even before the attack on the camp became evident to them. What about the legion?'

The decurion shook his head dismissively.

'Too slow and too late, I'd say, Tribune. The leading cohorts are just wasting time forming up on the open ground between forest and palisade, with no sign that they intend getting stuck in any time soon.'

Licinius's temper boiled over.

'*With me!*'

He spurred the grey down the line of troops followed by his bodyguard, seeking out the group of men that represented the point of the 20th Legion's spear.

'Tribune Laenas, might I ask exactly what the fuck you think you're doing?'

The legion's second-in-command, a tribune whose tunic bore the broad purple stripe of the Roman senatorial class, and a man unused to having his judgement questioned, turned away from a frustrated-looking group of the cohorts' senior centurions with a look of incredulity, opening his mouth to snarl a response that died in his throat when he saw who was doing the questioning.

'Ah, Tribune Licinius, we're, ah just making sure that we've got everything in place before . . . '

Licinius rode over his half-hearted explanation with a patrician disregard for manners, leaning in close and speaking in quiet but fierce tones.

'What it looks like, Tribune Laenas, is that you're dithering in the face of a fight. These gentlemen around you know that the time to strike was while the barbarians were still escaping into the forest. Since even my old ears can clearly make out the sound of battle from inside that palisade, I suggest that you get your cohorts through the gap those blue-nosed blighters have torn in the fence and get them into action. If, that is, you don't want to be dismissed and censured for lack of commitment by the governor. And let me make this very clear; if your soldiers aren't out of my way very quickly I will simply ride my cavalry through and if need be *over* them. There's a Venicone warband making their escape while we sit here wasting time, and I intend making sure that as few as possible of them get away, *if* you'll get your men out of my path.'

He sat back in his saddle with one eyebrow raised. Laenas swallowed unhappily, then turned back to face his officers.

'Ah, gentlemen, we will advance into the

enemy camp and join battle immediately.'

The legion's most senior centurion nodded briskly, his smile speaking volumes for his pleasure at the cavalryman's intervention.

'At the double march, Tribune?'

Laenas swallowed and nodded.

'Indeed. At the double march, First Spear Canutius.'

* * *

'It's a good thing we've got the advantage of the slope!'

Qadir nodded in response to Marcus's shouted comment. The century were starting to tire, the front rank becoming more interested in keeping their feet and fending off the barbarian spears than taking their iron to the enemy, who in their turn had burned through their first rage and were attacking with less vigour than moments before. A horn sounded across the smoke-wreathed camp from the northern palisade, and the front rank of a legion cohort swept into view through a gap in the camp's northern fence. Marcus shot the oncoming legionnaires a dark glance.

'About bloody time too.'

Qadir shook his shoulder, pointing across the Tungrian line.

'Look!'

Fresh troops were pouring into the space behind the Tungrian cohort, moving quickly to bolster their sagging line.

'It's the Second Cohort. First Spear Neuto

was never going to leave us in the sh — '

Marcus stopped in mid-sentence, his eyes suddenly caught by an object being waved around over the heads of the barbarians a dozen paces from the century's line. Qadir caught his stare and looked to see what had taken his attention. It was a man's head, still wearing the cross-crested helmet that denoted his centurion's rank, evidently hacked from his body and impaled on the point of a spear as a crude trophy with which the Romans could be taunted. As Qadir watched, Marcus's face went white with anger, and his eyes narrowed in calculation. He turned to the Hamian, reaching down and picking up a fallen shield, his voice stony as he turned to face the howling mob railing at the century's shields.

'Shoot to my right, and keep shooting.'

Guessing what was about to happen, Qadir reached out a hand to restrain his friend, but Marcus was too quick for him, pushing through the astonished rear-rankers and stepping into the front rank alongside Scarface. Stopping a sword-blow with his shield, he stepped forward and stabbed his gladius into the tribesman's throat as the enemy warrior fought to free his blade from the painted wooden surface, turning back to stare with a blank-eyed intensity at the wide-eyed soldiers.

'Guard my left.'

He turned back and stepped into the seething mass of warriors, hacking down a man to his right and blocking another sword-blow from his left with the shield, shouting a terse order over his shoulder.

'*Qadir! Shoot to my right!*'

The Hamian shook himself free from the amazement of seeing his centurion actually throw himself into the mass of his enemies and bellowed a command in his own language.

'*Hamians, to me!*'

Nocking an arrow and loosing it with one fluid motion, he sent the iron-tipped head through the throat of a warrior poised to bury his axe into Marcus's helmet. Ramming his gladius deep into another barbarian's chest and feeling the blade's reluctance to come free of the wound's tight grip, the young centurion released the weapon's ornate handle without a second thought, kicking the dying warrior back into the men behind him. Grabbing the axe from the tribesman tottering backwards with Qadir's arrow buried in his throat, he levelled his shield and hurled it horizontally into the press of the enemy, flattening another of the men facing him with a ruptured throat, then raised the axe two handed and gathered himself to attack again. Another Hamian reached Qadir's side at the same second, ripping his bow from its place across his back and reaching for an arrow with the same unconscious grace with which the chosen man exercised his craft. With only a split second's time spent finding a point of aim, he sent the missile into the fray around his centurion with an almost thoughtless speed that nevertheless sent another of the men facing Marcus staggering back into the men behind him in a spray of his own blood. At the same instant

Scarface shook off his own momentary panic, hurling a furious command at the front-rankers to his left as he waded forward into the barbarians.

'*With me, you bastards!*'

Slamming down his shield to block off a spear-thrust aimed at his legs, he thrust his sword's blade into the barbarian's throat and twisted the hilt, opening the warrior's neck wide in a shower of hot blood that flicked across the half-dozen men who had advanced into the barbarian mass alongside him. Glancing up, he was momentarily open mouthed at the sight of his officer hurling his shield into the warband's mass and grasping an axe two handed before throwing himself at the warriors gathering around him with an incoherent scream, clearly lost to his rage. The speed and savagery of his onslaught cleared a path into the heart of the warband as warriors fell away from him with their bodies rent by the weapon's heavy blade, those as yet untouched by the unexpected attack backing away from the berserk Roman. Qadir and his fellow archers were ten strong now, and their arrows were killing the warriors to Marcus's right faster than they could be replaced by the men behind them, the barbarians' eyes flickering from their unhinged enemy, his armour dripping with the blood of the dying men scattered around him, to the archers dealing out impersonal death to them from behind the Roman line.

Scarface and his fellow soldiers now formed the other side of their centurion's tenuous link to his century, their shields forming a diagonal wall from the century's line to Scarface at its farthest extension. A man fell forward into the seething mass of barbarians facing them, his throat skewered by a barbed spear thrust over the rim of his shield and then pulled back to haul him bodily out of the shield wall, and Qadir pushed a rear-ranker forward to take his place before lifting his bow to shoot again. The soldiers were holding out well enough, stabbing into the mass of their enemies and parrying the inevitable counter-attacks in a way that the veteran soldier knew could only last so long before they succumbed to the overwhelming strength gathering against them. He dragged in a deep breath, meaning to entreat Marcus to retreat from his exposed position, but before he could do so the axe snagged between a dying man's ribs and stuck fast. A warrior in the mass facing him stabbed at Marcus's face, the blade slicing a long cut in his cheek as he swayed backwards to evade the attack, releasing his grasp on the axe's handle as he bent to scoop up a dying warrior's sword from the ground beside him. Stamping forward, he hacked the sword's blade at his attacker's legs, dropping the man to his knees with the muscles of both thighs opened to the bone. Drawing his spatha, the Roman roared his blood-soaked defiance at the barbarians now visibly shrinking away from him. A single man stepped forward to meet him in the space that had opened around the Roman, one hand grasping a massive battleaxe, the other a spear on which the centurion's head was impaled, and as

Scarface realised whose the head was his eyes narrowed in pain.

'Oh, dear fuck . . . '

Marcus jumped forward to meet the newcomer's attack, a fresh flight of arrows punching into the men to his right as he stopped the barbarian champion's axe with crossed swords, halting the blade inches from his head before slamming his helmet's brow guard forward in a vicious head-butt which sent the enemy warrior staggering backwards, blood streaming from his shattered nose. He followed up with lightning speed, his spatha hacking off the reeling barbarian's right arm at the wrist before the other man ever realised what was happening to him. Thrusting forward with the barbarian weapon, he ran the warrior clean through, leaving the blade sheathed in his opponent's chest and tearing the spear from his grip. While the barbarians around him watched in amazed silence, he pulled the severed head from the bloody blade, tossed the weapon aside and tucked the grisly trophy under his left arm. Stepping back a pace, he growled a quiet order to Scarface.

'Fall back. *Slowly*.'

The tribesmen watched in silence as the Romans retreated to their line one pace at a time, never once looking back from their enemies, while the Hamians waited with arrows nocked and ready to fly. Regaining the relative safety of the Tungrian line, Marcus blew out a long shaky breath, tears running through the blood painted across his face between his cheek guards as he stared down into the pain-contorted face that stared back up at him. He lifted his head to watch numbly as the 20th Legion's leading cohort smashed into the barbarian rear less than a hundred paces from the Tungrians' place on the slope.

'I'll see you buried properly, Tiberius Rufius, and then I'll take as many of my men as will follow me, track down that bastard Calgus and make sure he dies in agony for you.' He turned back to Morban, who was standing at his shoulder, aghast at the death of the man who was both Marcus's saviour and his closest friend, his voice hoarse with sudden grief. 'Standard-bearer, at the slow march, retreat back up the slope. Now they've finally got here we'd best give the bloody legion some room to work.'

2

King Drust looked about him as the Venicone warband climbed the bare hillside high above the doomed barbarian camp, scanning the empty ground to either side before glancing back over his shoulder, panting with the effort of the climb up the wooded slope below. The forest's upper limit was five hundred paces behind the rearmost of the Venicone warriors, whose initial headlong charge from the embattled camp had quickly been reduced to a long loping stride as they had weaved their way through the densely packed trees. His warriors were marching in a long, straggling column as they climbed the mountain's unforgiving slope, moving in family groups of spearmen and archers whose breath steamed around them in the cold morning air. He spat on to the hillside's thin turf and grunted a comment at the leader of his personal bodyguard jogging along beside him.

'Perhaps we got away clean, but I doubt it. Those Roman bastards don't give up that easily.'

The other man grimaced at the pain gnawing at his chest, as the effort of the long climb started to tell upon him.

'Aye, and we're leaving a trail that a blind man could follow.'

The king nodded, looking back at the treeline again.

'Their soldiers will never catch us, not over

this ground and carrying that much weight in weapons and armour. It's their horsemen that worry me.'

'Worry you, Drust? I thought you and your tribesmen feared no man?'

The king looked up, to find that Calgus, still being carried over the massive shoulder of the man who had beaten him into unconsciousness, had regained his wits. His voice was weak with the after-effects of being stunned, but the acerbic note was unmistakable. He reached out and tapped Calgus's head with his knuckle, causing the rebellion's former leader to wince in pain.

'Calgus! You still live, then? I thought Maon might have hit you too hard, but I see your skull is every bit as thick as I imagined.'

Calgus smiled wanly.

'Insult me as you will, Drust, I can see that I am due a long period at your mercy before you sell me to the Romans. If they let you escape, that is . . . '

Drust laughed in his face, hefting his hammer with a grim smile.

'Oh, they'll do their very best to stop us, Calgus, and they might kill a few of us, but all they'll really manage to do is pick off a few weaklings and provide us with fresh . . . '

A horn sounded back down the slope, and Drust turned back to stare down at the trees. A single horseman had fought clear of the forest's thick growth, and was sounding the signal to alert his comrades of the Venicone warband's presence high on the hill to their north. Drust laughed at Calgus's expression, caught between hope and fear.

'It's a tough choice, eh, Calgus? To be carried off into slavery by me, or to be rescued by the Romans, whose strongest desire is to put you on a cross and watch the crows pull your eyes out while you're still breathing. Cut his bonds and put him down, Maon, I'll have your sword-arm free for more important work. Calgus can either keep up this gentle pace we're setting, or he can fall behind and find out what the Romans have in store for him.' He raised his voice to a bellow. 'My brother warriors, very soon now the Roman horsemen will be snapping at our heels, eager to take our heads for the bounty they will earn for each man they kill! We must keep moving, no matter how many times they attack! If they can stop us here, they will bring their soldiers up the hill to surround us and slaughter us from behind their shields! Keep moving, and use your spears to make them keep their distance. Archers, pick your targets well, and wait until you cannot miss before you shoot! We must keep moving, cross this miserable bump of a hill and make for our own land! The horsemen will give it up soon enough. And remember, brothers, tonight we dine on horse flesh!'

Calgus, initially unsteady on his feet after being unceremoniously tipped on to them by the massively built Maon, gritted his teeth and fell in alongside Drust, a cynical smile playing across his face despite the pain throbbing in his head and the weakness in his knees.

'*'Tonight we dine on horse flesh?'* And I

thought I was the expert at keeping the facts from my people!'

The Venicone king looked back at the forest's edge again, where another half-dozen horsemen had emerged from the trees and were trotting their mounts easily up the bare slope behind the warband.

'Enjoy your good humour while it lasts, Calgus, I'm away to find my body slave and relieve him of a heavy burden. Those bastards are going to keep us in sight until enough of them have gathered to start picking off the stragglers with their spears, and shooting arrows into us from our flanks. And you, Calgus, have no shield.'

* * *

'Look at him, strutting around like he had anything to do with the fighting.'

Soldier Manius poured a small measure of water on to his cupped palm, rubbing it vigorously on to his face to dislodge as much of the dried blood as possible, then poured another measure on to his sweat-crusted hair, grimacing at the dirt that came away on his hand. He shot another glance at the 20th Legion's first spear as the senior officer walked past the Tungrians, bellowing a command at his men, and nudged the man standing next to him.

'All big and brave when it's all done bar the shouting, but nowhere to be seen when the iron's flying, from what I've heard. A legionary from their First Cohort was telling me that . . . '

A roared command from their centurion, a twenty-year veteran with a battered face by the name of Otho, silenced him.

'Stand to, Seventh Century! Stop your moaning and get in line! There's work to be done and we're the men to do it!'

The voices of the cohort's other centurions were ringing out along the length of the defensive position that the Tungrians had fought grimly to defend in the dawn's pale light, urging their men back on to their feet.

'Good old Knuckles, now there's an officer who'll stand in line when the time comes. And you wouldn't want to trade blows with . . . '

'Anyone with his mouth still open, shut it *now*, or I'll come and shut it for you!'

Manius nodded to his mate with a knowing look, but kept his mouth closed. Otho glanced along the line of his men for a long moment, satisfying himself that he had their full attention before speaking again.

'That's better. We have new orders, Seventh Century. We are to search whatever parts of this camp the legions haven't already burned to the ground for anything that might be of value to the empire. There will still be a few of the blue-faced bastards hiding and waiting for dark to fall, so don't use the door of any tent unless you want your head taken off. Cut a flap in the side of the tent with your sword, have a good look through it, and if it's empty step inside to see what you can find. If you can see anyone inside the tent do *not* go in after him, but call on him to surrender. If you have to, surround the tent and use your spears to drive him out. And don't kill any of the bastards unless you absolutely have to, they're worth a lot of money to the empire. Tribune Scaurus will catch shit from above if we don't bring a few of them out alive, and we all know that shit rolls downhill! Inside the tent you may find weapons and personal effects abandoned in the battle. Do not *try* to hang on to any such item, not if you don't want me in your face. Any man found attempting to hide any booty will probably be flogged in front of the cohort, but he'll already have a set of lumps courtesy of this . . . ' He held up his right fist, the knuckles criss-crossed with the scars of fights long forgotten. 'Right, get to it! Seventh Century, *advance!*'

The centuries advanced slowly up the hill, skirting round the smouldering remains of tents which had caught fire during the battle and concentrating on those which had survived, enjoying the late morning's gentle sunshine as they searched the camp at as leisurely pace as their officers would allow. After an hour of slow climbing with nothing more than the occasional discovery and capture of a hiding barbarian to show for their efforts, the cohort entered the section of the camp which had been used by the Venicones.

Approaching the next in an apparently unending succession of tents to be searched, Manius's tent party went about their task in exactly the same way they had approached every other search that morning. Hacking an upside-down 'V' out of the tent's wall with his razor-edged dagger, the senior soldier looked cautiously through the opening he'd made, calling a warning back to his comrades.

'Body! Looks like he's dead . . . ' Dropping his shield, he stepped in through the hole with the dagger held ready to fight, looking round the tent's interior for any lurking enemy. 'Clear! This one's definitely dead, he's got a ballista bolt through his spine. Might be something here, though . . . ' Putting a boot on the crouching corpse's shoulder, he pushed the dead barbarian away from a small wooden chest. 'What have we got here? All the usual barbarian rubbish, I suppose . . . spoon, knife, cloak brooches . . . ' He slipped the jewellery into his purse, then frowned as he caught sight of something gleaming brightly in the sprawled barbarian's hand, reaching down to pry it loose from the dead man's cold fingers with his pulse quickening.

'So what's this, then, I wonder, all bright and shiny . . . ' He turned back to the rent in the tent's wall and called softly to the soldier standing on the other side. 'Look at this!' He held up the torc for the other man to see, hefting the weight of it. 'Weighs as much as my dagger! We should call for Knuckles . . . '

The look on his face belied the words, and his comrade took one look and nodded agreement with the unspoken sentiment.

'What, and have that old bastard walk away with enough money to put every man in the tent party on the street set up for life? That's ours, mate. We fought for it, and we're keeping it. Stuff that thing into your armour, under your shield-arm. That's our retirement fund you've got there.'

* * *

'We'll not stop them tonight.'

By late afternoon the Venicones were a dozen miles to the northwest of the barbarian camp's smoking ruin and still marching, while the Petriana's cavalrymen rode to either side and behind them. Battered shields and bloodied spears told their own stories, but for every half-dozen barbarian bodies spreadeagled on the hillsides in the warband's trampled wake, their backs arched in death by the impact of the cavalrymen's spears, the Petriana had paid the painful price of a dead rider. Tribune Licinius sat on his horse on a slope to one side of their path and watched the tribesmen trotting wearily across the hill's thin turf in the sun's slowly ebbing light, nodding his head at the decurions ranged alongside him decisively.

'They'll make another few miles before night falls, and camp in the open tonight. There's nothing to give them any shelter that they could reach before dusk. We'll have to fall back to the legions, get a night's sleep and some food into men and beasts, then get these lazy buggers back out here to renew hostilities tomorrow morning. After a day like today we'll all benefit from a few hours without having to stare at those bloody savages and their spoils.'

His men had watched in horror that morning,

as those riders foolhardy enough to risk a charge at the warband's flanks had been mobbed by the Venicones, seeing their fellow soldiers dragged from their horses and killed with a savagery that made their last moments a screaming bloody nightmare. Any man that had ridden to the aid of a comrade in such circumstances had achieved no more than to sign his own death warrant, and the horsemen had been forced to watch the swift and horrible demise of their comrades without any means of either rescue or revenge. Worse still for men trained to put the welfare of their mounts before their own, more than one riderless horse had been pulled into the warband and swiftly butchered for the meat to be had from its steaming corpse. While the cavalrymen had shouted enraged curses and oaths of revenge at the fleeing barbarians, their initial hot-blooded attempts to disrupt the tribesmen's flight had quickly reduced in intensity as the likely fate of any man that rode too close to their enemy sank in. For the most part they had ridden in sullen silence alongside their enemy, casting dark glances at men carrying trophies of weapons and armour torn from their dead comrades, or laden with heavy chunks of bloody meat.

'Should we leave scouts to keep watch on them, Tribune?'

Licinius shook his head at the question.

'I see no need. They're leaving a trail in the grass that we'll pick up easily enough in the morning. No, we'll not risk another man in pursuing these bloody-handed bastards, and tomorrow we'll have the rations to stay with them for a few days, and a few other tricks to make them sorry they've taken their knives to our horses. Come on, gentlemen, let's drag our men away from their dreams of revenge and take them home for the night.'

* * *

'So then he just says 'Guard my left' and jumps into the blue-noses like a madman. Grabs an axe and paints himself from head to foot with blood. There was guts and shit everywhere . . . '

Spotting Centurion Julius approaching over Cyclops's shoulder, the soldier known to his mates as Scarface snapped to attention, saluting the 5th Century's officer as he stopped to stand in front of the half-dozen men grouped a few paces from the door of their officer's tent. Looking about the group, the heavy-built centurion hooked a thumb over his shoulder, his black-bearded face creasing into its habitual sneer of disdain.

'You rear-rank heroes have got better things to be doing than encouraging this idler to spin his tales. Go and do them. *Now*.'

The soldiers took their cue, dispersing back to their respective centuries without a backward glance at the watch officer, who, making to leave in his own turn, found himself detained by a pointed finger and a hard stare.

'Not you, Cyclops. Nor you, Scarface. You two and I need words.'

The one-eyed watch officer nodded meekly,

recalling his previous encounters with Julius in the days before Marcus had taken an interest in him, and commanded him to drag himself free from his downward spiral of infringement against authority and ever harsher punishment.

'Where's your centurion, Watch Officer?'

Augustus pointed at the tent behind him.

'Not come out since we got back to camp, sir. He's . . . '

'And your optio?'

Scarface spoke up.

'With the wounded, Centurion. He sent me to collect some water.'

The centurion leaned in closer, hard eyes boring into Scarface's, and took a firm grip of the soldier's tunic.

'Best be on your way, then, hadn't you, soldier? But before you go, a word of advice. If I catch you boasting about what Centurion Corvus did today again I'll have you round the back of the command tent for a short and painful lesson in the lost art of keeping your bloody mouth *shut*. You're supposed to have a reputation for watching over him like a mother hen, and yet here you are, mouthing off to anyone that'll listen about what a great warrior he is. Perhaps you ought to be the one who's called '*Latrine*' behind his back; you're more deserving of the name than me from what I can see. Now get out of my sight.'

Scarface hurried away, red faced and chastened, but the burly centurion had already forgotten him as he turned back to the watch officer.

'It's true, then? He's shut himself in there and won't come out?'

Cyclops nodded silently, his misery so evident that even Julius, who under normal circumstances would have wasted no time telling the watch officer to pull himself together and get on with doing his job, was almost lost for words himself. He patted the other man on the shoulder and gestured to the line of tents behind him.

'Best if you make sure your men have got their gear sorted out, and then get them rolled up in their cloaks and asleep. The rumours are flying that we're back on the march in the morning, looking for more barbarians' heads.'

Cyclops nodded again, saluting the burly centurion and turning away to do his bidding while Julius stood and stared at the tent's closed entrance flap for a long moment before stepping through it. Inside he found Marcus sitting in near-darkness, his armour still crusted with the dried blood of the men he had killed fighting his way to retrieve his friend's head.

'Come on, lad, there's no time for this nonsense. You're a centurion, you've got men bleeding out there and you've left your optio to pick up the pieces. You need to . . . '

'He's dead, Julius. The best friend I had in the world . . . '

Julius followed his exhausted, vacant stare and started with shock. Tiberius Rufius's severed head was propped against the tent wall, his dead eyes staring glassily back at Marcus.

'Jupiter's fucking cock and balls! I don't

. . . you just can't . . . '

Words failing him, the big centurion shook his head in disbelief and reached down for the dead man's head.

'Leave. Him. *Alone*.'

The barely restrained animal ferocity in the Roman's voice froze Julius in mid-stoop. He turned to look at his friend, finding himself eye to eye with a face he barely recognised as the man he had watched pull himself from the edge of oblivion to command a century of Tungrians alongside him. Marcus spoke again, through gritted teeth, his face stonily implacable.

'You leave him *alone*, Julius. I haven't finished making my peace with him yet, not by a long march.'

The fight went out of him like a snuffed candle, as if he had nothing more to give.

'Just leave me alone with him. I need more time to say goodbye to him.'

Julius straightened, shrugging helplessly.

'This is wrong, Marcus. You just *can't* do this . . . '

The young centurion had slumped back against the tent wall, his entire focus on his dead friend's head. Julius shook his head in helpless exasperation and ducked out through the flap.

'*You!*'

The passing soldier froze at the bellowed command, snapping to attention and staring at him warily.

'I want a lamp and some oil to light your centurion's tent. Fetch them here, now!'

* * *

Tribune Scaurus walked into his tent as the sun was dipping to touch the western horizon, dropping his helmet and sword belt on to the rough wooden table and nodding wearily to his two senior centurions. After the rout and destruction of the Selgovae tribe's warriors, trapped in their camp and battered into ruin by two legions, and with their fleeing survivors hunted down by the auxiliary cohorts that accompanied the main force, he had been summoned to a senior officers' conference with the governor and his legion commanders that had lasted most of the evening. He turned back to the tent's door, muttering a quiet command to his lone bodyguard. The massively built German nodded, closing the tent's flap and turning to stand guard over his master's privacy.

'Arminius will make sure we're not disturbed. This information is for you and you alone, at least for the time being.'

Taking a cup of wine from First Spear Frontinius's outstretched hand, Scaurus raised it to the two men and tipped it back, swallowing the contents in a single gulp.

'Thank you, Sextus. Mithras unconquered, I needed that. It baffles me how a man as abstemious as Ulpius Marcellus ever reached the rank of governor. He certainly isn't one for handing round the drinks, not even after a successful battle. So, gentlemen, how are our men?'

Frontinius rubbed his shaved head before

answering, his features shadowed with fatigue.

'Our section of the camp is built and secure, Tribune, and the men of both cohorts are bedded down with double guards, in case any stray barbarian gets the idea to come looking for revenge in the dark.'

His colleague Neuto, the 2nd Cohort's senior centurion, nodded agreement.

'The First Cohort got the worst of the fighting this morning, so we agreed to let the Second take guard duty for the night.'

Scaurus accepted the decision without surprise. Since his promotion to command of both Tungrian cohorts after the untimely death of the 2nd's prefect, and with a promotion from prefect to tribune to reflect his increased responsibility and status, he had found the two former comrades worked so well together that his decision-making capabilities were rarely called into play.

'Any more dead?'

Frontinius ignored the wax tablet open in his hand, his tired face grim as he recounted the damage done to his cohort in the dawn battle to break into the barbarian camp.

'Yes, another two men dead from their wounds, so the first cohort has now lost a hundred and thirty-seven men today, eighty-seven of them dead and another dozen or so likely to die before dawn. The bandage carriers reckon that about twenty of the wounded will fight again given time, but the rest are finished as soldiers. Most of the surviving centuries are still at more or less effective fighting strength, though, since the majority of the dead were from the Sixth.'

The tribune nodded.

'Yes. The governor sends his respects and sympathy, as did Legatus Equitius on behalf of the Sixth Legion. He collared me afterwards, sent you his regards and told me that if there's anything he can do, short of giving us men to make up our losses, we have only to ask. Is there anything we could ask him for?'

The 6th Legion's commanding officer had been Frontinius's prefect until a few months earlier in the year, and their relationship had been a strong one. The first spear shook his head.

'Other than taking Centurion *Corvus* off our hands, given that once again he's the talk of the bloody camp and likely to bring inquisitive senior officers down on us like flies on freshly laid shit? No, Tribune, I don't think there's anything the legatus can do for us.'

Scaurus was silent for a moment.

'And how is the centurion?'

Frontinius shook his head.

'Julius found him sitting in his tent with poor Rufius's head and refusing to come out. Says he's had enough of leading his friends to their deaths, what with Antenoch a few days ago and now the best friend he had left in the world. Dubnus could probably have dragged him out of it quickly enough, but he's fifty miles away with a spear wound in his guts, which only leaves Julius, and he's about as sensitive with these things as I am. Added to which he tells me that the man very nearly went for him when he tried to reunite Rufius's head with the rest of him.'

Scaurus nodded.

'And there's not one of us that would relish being on the wrong end of that. Best you leave him to me then. First Spear Neuto, how's the Second Cohort?'

'No more deaths, Tribune, but then we only took a handful of serious wounds apart from the fifteen men who were killed this morning. Sextus and I have agreed that the Second will take the lead in our next battle, if there's a lead to be taken. And if there's a battle to be fought, given that we've just torn the Selgovae's fighting strength limb from limb.'

Scaurus rubbed a hand over his narrow face, his grey eyes ringed by the fatigue of the previous week's ceaseless activity.

'Whether there'll be any more fighting this year I couldn't say, but I can assure you both that this campaign isn't over. Not for us, at least.'

Frontinius frowned.

'For us . . . ? What about the rest of the army?'

'The rest of the army, Sextus Frontinius, has other fish to fry.'

The prefect unrolled the map he kept in his field chest, laid it across his table and weighted the corners with his helmet and weapons. He pointed to a spot on the map north of the wall that spanned the province to separate civilisation from the northern tribes, and a good distance to the east of the road that ran northwards from the wall, bisecting the tribal lands beyond the frontier.

'That's us. Battle won, and the Selgovae well and truly put back in their place.'

He tapped the map to the west of the road, indicating the Selgovae's tribal lands.

'They'll have to be kept in their place, of course, but a single cohort could probably manage that, given that we've killed most of their fighting strength today. The Cugerni and Vangiones cohorts ought to be more than enough force to keep their heads down. You know how that works . . . '

Both of the senior centurions nodded with grim faces, and Neuto's voice was harsh as he spoke.

'Oh yes, Tribune, we know how that works. Go in hard and do whatever it takes to make sure the stupid blue-nosed bastards are clear that they lost. Burn their villages at any sign of resistance, confiscate anything they're not clever enough to hide, and give them a winter they won't forget for a while. There'll be a skirmish or two, but they're out of the fight after today. And us?'

'We drew the more interesting job, I'd say.' The tribune pointed to the land to the east of the North Road. 'We're ordered to head north and east, and liberate the Votadini from whoever it was that Calgus sent north to rule them, once he'd killed King Brennus. Since we don't know how many warriors Calgus sent north with their new 'king', we're to advance at full strength and in full battle order, and we've been given six squadrons of horsemen from the Petriana wing to scout for us. The governor thinks that Calgus may have run for the safety of the Votadini capital, given that we've not found his body on the battlefield, which makes him very keen to liberate it from the last of his men and see what we find.'

First Spear Frontinius frowned again, raising a bemused eyebrow at his superior, his voice acerbic with disapproval.

'Two cohorts? Sixteen hundred men, even if we were at full strength? We ought to be twice the number, and with a bloody sight more than two hundred horsemen. Not only do we not know how many warriors might be waiting for us, but there's still the small question of the Venicones. The last I heard on the subject was that some weak-chinned fool in a stripy tunic dithered outside the barbarian camp for long enough that the entire Venicone warband was able to make a sharp exit through the north fence.'

Scaurus nodded sharply, his eyes signalling disapproval of the language his subordinate was using to describe a senior officer, if not the offended sentiment behind them.

'I know, First Spear, and I won't bore you with the excitement that little error of judgement has inspired among the great and the good, except to tell you that we've had a cohort detached from the Twentieth Legion under the command of the 'weak-chinned fool' in question attached to us. Apparently it was either that, or go home in disgrace for letting the Venicones escape from under his nose, so he's chosen to work under me for a few weeks as punishment.'

'And the Venicones?'

'Last seen running hard to the north, after a day spent exchanging iron and insults with the Petriana. Honours even, apparently, according to the first message riders back from the fight, with several hundred of their warriors killed by the cavalry as they fell out of the line of march with exhaustion, but fifty or so of Tribune Licinius's men torn limb from limb as a result of getting carried away and riding too close to the enemy with the excitement of it all.'

Neuto stared at the map for a moment before speaking, his voice rich with irony.

'So while the legions get to sit back and count barbarian heads, we go north with three cohorts, one commanded by some custard-livered aristo, and a couple of hundred horsemen, not only charged with taking the Dinpaladyr but potentially having to fend off the entire Venicone warband as well.'

Scaurus nodded, his smile tight.

'Almost, First Spear. But the legions won't be getting any time to polish up their armour. The one thing I haven't mentioned yet is going to keep them very busy until the snow comes.'

Both of the senior centurions' eyes narrowed. Neuto breathed the question in a hushed tone, his face set in the expectation of bad news.

'The Brigantes?'

Scaurus nodded.

'Yes, First Spear, the Brigantes. Calgus has the full-scale revolt he was desperate for, only just too late for it to do him any good. And we, gentlemen, will just have to manage with what we're given.'

* * *

'Curse this fucking rebellion. Another couple of days would have seen us on the Wall with the Aquila boy in our grasp. Instead of which we're sat here like spare pricks, waiting for the bloody army to get off their arses and clear these impudent Brits away, only these useless provincial bastards are too scared of a few uppity blue-painted farmers to get out into the countryside and do what needs to be done. The bloody Guard would go through this lot like a hot knife through butter . . . '

Centurions Rapax and Excingus were standing on the walls of the Waterfall Town fort, forty miles to the north of the legionary fortress at Elm Grove, staring out at the dusk's purple landscape in frustration. The praetorian was complaining bitterly to his colleague, slapping his palm down on the wall's stone parapet to emphasise his disgust with the soldiers manning the fort below them.

'All the way to the edge of the bloody empire in less than a month, changing horses three times a day until my arse feels like it's made of leather, and now we're sat here looking at the hills and wondering how the fuck we're going to get any farther north. A few of the locals get uppity and these cowards all run home to mummy, and wait for someone else to sort it out for them.'

Excingus laughed wryly, shaking his head in mock dismay.

'Yes, colleague, I have little doubt that your

fellow guardsmen would cleave a bloody path through these rebels, were they here. Which nevertheless leaves us with the same question. Do we wait for the legions to finish their business in the frontier zone and turn south to clear out these bandits, or do we make our own way north immediately, in pursuance of Prefect Perennis's orders? I think you can guess my preference, but I must defer to you in all such military matters.'

Rapax gave him a dirty look, tapping the hilt of his sword thoughtfully.

'Your preference and mine are one and the same, brother, to get north and find the Aquila brat before he takes flight again. It could be rough, though. Two centurions and a few guardsmen won't offer much resistance to a decent-sized warband, should we happen across one, even if the soldiers in question are praetorians. And I, unlike *you*, have fought against barbarians, in the last emperor's wars against the Quadi and Marcomanni. I've heard the screams of men staked out for flaying and disembowelling, men taken in battle or from the camp in the night, and never seen again except for their ruined corpses on the tribes' sacrificial altars. We can ride north tomorrow morning and hope to make our way through to the Wall without seeing another living soul, trusting that the advantage of surprise will be on our side . . . ' He grinned darkly at the corn officer. ' . . . since only a bunch of madmen would attempt such a thing. I'm sure my guardsmen will think I've kissed my marbles goodbye, but they'll do what I tell them readily enough. So the question isn't really a military matter, since militarily the idea of riding north from here without enough men to sweep away the tribesmen in our path is quite likely to prove suicidal.'

He raised an eyebrow at his colleague, inviting him to comment. The corn officer stared out into the darkening and silent hills to the north for a long moment before speaking.

'Agreed. Riding north tomorrow does seem to carry somewhat more risk than waiting here for the army to march south and restore order. If it were that simple the decision would already be made as far as I'm concerned, but I'm afraid it isn't. If we sit here for the best part of another month, what are the odds that the news of a praetorian and a corn officer coming north will reach the army in the north well in advance of our arrival? Pretty good, I'd say, given what we know of the average soldier's love of gossip. And if that news reaches either the Aquila boy or the men sheltering him from justice, I'll wager my balls to a denarius that he'll be away to another hiding place before we ever reach the Wall, much less find this Tungrian cohort he's supposed to be hiding with.'

He paused, smiling at his colleague's sour expression.

'Yes, and therein lies the problem with inaction, eh, Quintus? If we go home empty handed, having paused here for the legions to regain control and make it safe for us to proceed, I wouldn't expect all that happy a welcome when we get there. So no, the problem isn't military, it's more about balancing the uncertain risk of being killed or captured by the rebels against the absolute certainty of what will happen to us both if we go back without the prize. I say we go north tomorrow, and use your undoubted skills to avoid the barbarians and get us through to the Wall in one piece.'

Rapax grimaced, nodding his head reluctantly.

'In that case you'd better go and see the centurion of the guard, and get us some better directions than 'out of the north gate and don't stop riding until you see the Wall', and I'll go and break the good news to my lads. They're going to love this . . . '

* * *

'You there! Who's that sneaking round the camp after dark?'

Soldier Manius very nearly lost control of his bowels as he recognised the voice challenging him from the shadows of a pair of tents, the familiar sound of a gladius being pulled from its scabbard freezing him where he stood.

'It's me, Centurion, Manius!'

Otho stepped forward from the shadows, his familiar, ruined face creased into a frown.

'What in Hades are you doing out here? I was just about to put my bloody iron through you.'

Manius caught a whiff of wine on the centurion's breath and breathed a little more easily.

'I couldn't sleep, Centurion, so I came out

here to avoid waking my mates up, and to get some air . . . '

To his surprise the officer nodded sagely, puffing a snort of recognition from his flattened nose.

'Can't sleep? Nor can I. Too many good men dead . . . too many men . . . '

He staggered, and Manius put out a hand to steady him, pulling it back hastily as the drunken officer started at the gesture.

'Get your fucking hands off me! Get back to your tent and go to sleep!'

'Yes, sir!'

Saluting, the wary soldier turned away and walked back towards his tent, then slid into the cover of the shadows and watched while Otho weaved unsteadily away to his own bed, blowing out a long, slow breath of relief. Somewhere close by a man whimpered in his sleep, reliving some horror or other from the dawn's desperate fighting. Waiting until Otho was safely out of sight, Manius resumed his progress through the camp, using the rows of canvas tents for cover. His armour exchanged for a clean tunic and his cloak, with only his dagger for protection, he worked his way from the 1st Tungrian Cohort's section of the camp, through the 2nd Cohort's tents and on into the area reserved for the Petriana's cavalrymen. Skirting round the tethered horses, well aware that any one of them could kick him unconscious if he were unwise enough to present them with an unexpected presence in their midst, he made his way slowly and stealthily into the heart of the cavalry wing's lines, until he came upon the tent he was seeking. Several times the size of those around it, bigger even than that in which the wing's tribune worked and slept, it contained every stores item required to keep the wing in the field for an extended period. Loosening his dagger in the sheath hidden under his cloak, he stepped through the tent's flap to find its single occupant hunched over a scroll at his desk, his lips moving silently as he totted up the day's consumption of his precious equipment. Without looking up from his task, he spoke in an irritated tone, shaking his head slightly.

'And what might you be needing? A new sword? A couple of spears? Perhaps you lost your boots in the fighting today, eh? I swear I've not met a bigger bunch of robbers than . . . '

His voice tailed off as he glanced up to find the infantryman waiting silently before him, one hand sliding beneath the table's surface to reach for the handle of a club he kept there to discourage anyone with the idea that his equipment might be available without the necessary permissions and formal records. The soldier held up his empty hands in reassurance, reaching into his tunic despite the now openly wielded club and fishing out a piece of jewellery of quite abnormal proportions. The yellow light from the storeman's lamps shone from its ornate surface in a manner guaranteed to beguile a man whose entire life had been devoted to the pursuit of gold, and the club clattered unheeded to the floor as the supply officer advanced round his desk and stared dumbfounded at the heavy torc gripped in the unknown soldier's hand. Rediscovering his voice, he spoke again, his tone softer than before, as if he knew that this was a prize to be pursued with delicate care.

'Quite . . . amazing . . . ' He coughed, clearing his throat before continuing, adopting a more businesslike tone as the torc's initial impact on him began to subside. 'And so, soldier . . . ?'

Manius shook his head, his face tense.

'I'm not that stupid. If we're going to do business I need to be sure that my piece of the bargain will be between the two of us. If anyone outside of my tent party discovers I'm carrying the sort of coin this will earn they'll have it off me quicker than you could rob a new recruit of half a year's pay for his gear. And this little beauty is our retirement, me and my mates.'

The supply officer kept a straight face, nodding his understanding.

'There are thieves all around, my friend, and so I completely understand your need to remain nameless. Might I ask how you came by this . . . interesting . . . spoil of battle? It was my understanding that such a precious ornament would most likely decorate the neck of a tribal chief, and yet no such head is reported as having been taken today. How can I be sure that this is what it seems?'

The Tungrian snorted, smiling with little humour in his face.

'Oh, it's real, I can guarantee you that. We were first into the barbarian camp, once the fence came down, and when the blue-noses finally broke and ran it was my cohort that swept up the hillside, ripping through their tents and capturing those men that were trying to hide from us in them, taking them to be slaves. I found a barbarian hunched over this with the missile from a bolt thrower stuck clean through him. He was probably supposed to be looking after it when the artillery boys got lucky, but it was me and my mates that struck the gold they uncovered. So now then, what will you offer me for this pretty little trinket?'

The supply officer held out a hand for the torc, smiling at the reluctance with which the nameless soldier handed across the heavy ornament. Examining it closely under the light of one of his lamps, he nodded his head in appreciation.

'Quite lovely. Beautifully engraved, clearly authentic and once a suitable provenance has been dreamed up with a little more romance than some poor bugger getting an accidental bolt in the back, it'll be worth a small fortune from the right collector. I can't offer you any more than five hundred for it, though . . . ' He handed the torc back to the open-mouthed soldier, shrugging at the other man's obvious outrage. 'What were you expecting? Ten thousand denarii and a night alone with the prettiest horse in the cohort . . . ?' He sighed wearily, as if explaining the mechanics of fencing stolen tribal jewellery were a routine topic of conversation, and Manius narrowed his eyes at the storeman's well-practised act without the ability to gainsay his words. 'Look, whatever your name is, this stuff doesn't just sell itself. I'll sell it to a man in the south of the province, for a profit of course. He'll move it to Rome, to a businessman he knows, for a profit. He in turn will know the right dealer in such precious and risky items, a man who knows where the discreet and wealthy customers are found for this sort of rather specialised merchandise. And he in turn will take a profit.'

Realising that the Tungrian still didn't understand, he shook his head with a gentle smile.

'What you're doing right now is illegal. You should have handed this in to your centurion when you found it, and he should then have passed it up to your first spear, and so on. By now this little trinket should be on the governor's desk, with him feeling rather smug about being able to send it to the Emperor with his compliments. Instead of which you're sneaking around the camp and trying to find a buyer for it, and inviting me to join you in your crime. The dealer in Rome will have his wind stopped for good if he's caught trading this, since in reality he's robbing the throne of a nice heavy bag of gold. Oh yes, we all do it, but getting caught with this little beauty would be a death sentence to anyone in the chain I've described, and they're all going to want a nice big slice of it to take the risk. That's why fifty thousand paid to the dealer in Rome becomes twenty-five thousand paid to the man that takes it to him, which becomes ten thousand to my man in the south, which becomes five thousand to me — if I'm lucky. And I've got the worst risk of all, since I have to find the money to pay you here on the edge of the world, and I have to get the item in question across a country that just won't stop rebelling to my man in the south. That'll cost me at least a thousand, and probably more.' He sighed, shaking his head and raising both hands in the universal gesture of surrender. 'All right, and against all my commercial instincts, I'll give you a thousand. How many of you are there left alive in your tent party?'

'Five.'

'Well, there you go, then, that's a nice clean two hundred apiece, two years' wages and none of the usual deductions. A man can do a lot with that much coin. What do you say?'

The soldier's face darkened, but he knew he was left with little alternative.

'Go on, then. Give me the cash and I'll be away.'

The other man shook his head quickly.

'No can do, I'm afraid. I've only got a few hundred on me, and I'll have to borrow the rest from an associate. Leave the piece with me and I'll make sure the balance gets to you . . . '

The Tungrian shook his head disbelievingly.

'Right, that'll be easy with you not knowing my name.' He stuffed the torc back into his tunic, turning for the tent's flap. 'I'll come back to you tomorrow night, so you have the money ready and we'll have a deal. Any delay and the price doubles, to compensate me for *my* risk in holding it for you.'

He ducked out of the tent and into the night, starting his cautious passage through the camp to his own cohort's lines. The supply officer, once he was sure that the soldier was really gone, smiled broadly to himself as he reached for his cloak.

⋆ ⋆ ⋆

With the senior centurions away to their cohorts, eager to start their preparations for the next day's march north, Scaurus stretched his weary frame and opened the tent's door to find Arminius waiting for him.

'Go and get some rest, my friend. We're marching north tomorrow, and I'll need you fresh for the fight. Now, which way to the First Cohort's lines?'

The massively built German crossed his scarred arms and fixed the tribune with a level stare.

'You want me to go and rest? Look at the state of *you*.'

Scaurus raised an eyebrow, and took a breath, preparing to speak, but closed his mouth as the German bent slightly to speak quietly into his face.

'You will recall the day you took me prisoner? The day Thunaraz looked down from the clouds and threw his lightning bolts to gift you victory at the moment of your defeat, and condemn my people to defeat and slavery, curse him. I told you then, and I tell you again now, that I will fight for you, I will die for you, and I will worship your god Mithras alongside you, but I will never spare you my opinion. And it is my opinion that you do need sleep, and that you do not need to take any part in preparing your men for war tonight.'

The tribune's reply was quiet, but equally firm.

'There's one particular man that needs my help, Arminius.'

The German shook his head.

'No. You represent authority, and Centurion Corvus will surely never bow to authority while he has his best friend's head staring at him. Leave the boy to me, and get your head down. If I fail to reawaken his interest in life, then you can take your turn at persuading him later. Although if what I plan fails, Mithras alone knows what will be required to bring him back to life.'

Scaurus nodded wearily, patting the big man's shoulder with something approaching affection, then turned and closed the tent's door flap. Arminius stared at the canvas in silence for a long moment, then turned and walked swiftly for the 1st Cohort's section of the camp. As he approached the first of the cohort's sentry points, two men stepped forward with raised spears, the weapons' points glinting in the torchlight.

'Halt! What's the watchword?'

The German laughed, advancing until the spearheads were almost touching the mail shirt that covered his massive chest.

'Watchword? How the fuck would I know the watchword, you stupid bastards, I've been keeping guard outside the tribune's tent for the last hour, without the time to play your little soldier games. Now shift your arses out of my way or I'll put those spears where they'll never see the light of day again.'

The soldiers looked at each other uncertainly, but were saved from their dithering by the appearance of Julius walking briskly towards them.

'Let him through. He's too stupid to remember the watchword even if he'd bothered to find out what it was.'

Arminius stepped past the soldiers, clasping hands with their officer.

'Julius, it's good to see that you came through today's madness unscratched.'

The big centurion turned his right arm over to reveal a long shallow slice into the flesh of his forearm.

'Not quite unmarked. This will make a nice addition to my scar collection, even if I have a way to go before I can match yours. The warrior that did it is currently considering his lot from the roof of my tent, or at least his head is. Cheeky blue-nosed bastard. And to what do we owe the honour of your visit so late in the day?'

The German grimaced.

'There is a young officer who has taken to his tent, I believe, and refuses to consider leaving it for fear of causing the deaths of more of his friends?'

The smile vanished from Julius's face.

'Yes. His century is sitting shivering in their tents with their chins wobbling, and when I went to reason with him he nearly took my head off. We've got until dawn to get him back on his feet, or else he'll have to be left behind when we march . . . '

Arminius nodded.

'Leave him to me.'

Julius watched the German head off down the line of tents with tired eyes, then turned back to the sentries with a dismissive sneer.

'And the next man that turns up here without the watchword and shouting the odds, remember the golden rule. If in doubt, spears first and questions later. You call yourselves soldiers . . . ?'

Arminius found the man he was looking for without too many problems. Where the Tungrians had their tents laid out in straight lines, their Votadini allies' shelters were gathered around their leader's tent in a tight circle. He stopped at the perimeter of the huddle of tents and shouted across them, his voice a commanding bark.

'Martos!'

After a moment's pause a warrior that Arminius recognised as one of the prince's bodyguard strolled out to meet him, eyeing the German flatly and keeping his hands close to a pair of fighting knives tucked in his belt.

'Why do you call upon a prince of the Votadini and a free man as if you were his master, rather than addressing him with the respect that your slavery to the Romans demands?'

The German chuckled darkly, putting his hands on his hips with supreme self-confidence.

'Free men? You and your prince submitted to Roman rule just as completely as I, once you were betrayed by Calgus and defeated by these soldiers camped around you. And you are not the man I wish to speak with. Tell your master I need his help with Centurion Corvus.'

The Votadini warrior stared hard at him for a long moment, then turned on his heel and walked back into the cluster of tents. After a moment Martos stepped out of his tent and beckoned the German to join him. He took a lungful of the cold night air and stared up at the blazing stars in the coal-black sky above them, waiting for Arminius to negotiate his way through the tents. When the German stood before him he continued to stare upwards, speaking without looking at the other man.

'My kinsman tells me that you wish to speak with me. He told me that I had only to say the word and he would gut you like a rabbit, and I told him that taking his knives to you would be a very good way to die before his time. He is frustrated, like all of my men, not to have been turned loose to hunt down Calgus once his warriors were beaten, although I suppose that we will get over the disappointment. Especially as we expect he has run to the last of his men who currently hold our capital. So, you have my attention. What can I do for you that will not wait for daylight?'

His gaze came to rest on Arminius, who inclined his head respectfully.

'Prince Martos, our friend Centurion Corvus has taken to his tent and will not come out. Instead he sits hunched over the head of his colleague Rufius, terrified of leading any more of his comrades to bloody death. I think we've seen this before, you and I, and I think we both understand what will happen if he cannot be persuaded to change his mind.'

Martos nodded.

'He is a fugitive from their justice. Without the shelter provided by the Tungrians, he will soon be discovered. And when that happens, riders will be sent to this cohort to arrest the tribune and first spear, and take them to explain how they came to be providing our friend with a hiding place in which to escape from the Emperor's justice. They would join him in a slow and painful death, were he to be uncovered for who he really is. But why should this concern me? I like the man, but if he insists on cutting his own throat then little I can do or say will prevent him from doing so, and as for Frontinius and Scaurus, well, one Roman officer is much like any other, I would imagine.'

Arminius spoke quickly, his voice kept low to avoid their being overheard.

'We march tomorrow, to free your tribal capital from whatever hold Calgus still has over your people. My master is sympathetic to your people's plight, whereas the man that will probably replace him if Corvus is discovered is a Roman aristocrat, and cares no more for the likes of you and me than for any other 'barbarian'. Worse than that, he is a man of little courage from what we saw today. I fear for your people's safety if he becomes the commander of the force on which your tribe's survival rests.'

Martos eyed the German for a moment.

'You present me with little choice, then? Either we get the centurion back on his feet, or we risk losing the officer most likely to want my people free without the spilling of any more of their blood.' He sighed. 'Again I find myself drawn into matters for which I care little, when all I want is to be set loose to hunt down Calgus. Come on, then, German, let's put some strength back in this Roman's backbone.'

They walked quickly to the 9th Century's tents, Martos waving away the bodyguards who ran to join him as he strode away.

'Any man that can best me and this ugly German bastard deserves our heads.'

The 9th's tents were pitched in an orderly manner, and the soldiers were already tucked away and asleep, exhausted by the exertions of the day, but half a dozen men were standing around their centurion's tent with worried faces. Seeing the two barbarians approaching, Qadir and Cyclops sent the rest away to join their tent parties and greeted the two with respectful nods. Both men knew that Martos's intervention in the battle of the Red River had saved the cohort from being overrun, and Arminius was universally recognised as a man not to be crossed.

'He's still in there, eh, Cyclops?'

The watch officer nodded, indicating the tent's door flap with a wave of his hand.

'Young gentleman won't come out, won't eat or take a drink either. Just sits there staring at Centurion Rufius's head . . . '

Martos put a hand on his shoulder, gently easing him to one side.

'Leave him to us.'

The two men stepped into the tent, finding it

lit by a single guttering lamp whose fuel was nearly exhausted. Martos looked at Arminius, who nodded silently and backed out of the door, calling for more oil. Marcus was sitting on his bedroll, the severed head of his friend facing him across the dimly lit space, propped against the oiled leather of the tent's wall. The tent reeked of blood and sweat, and Marcus's armour and flesh were still caked with gore, the untreated cut on his cheek a line of crusted blood.

'I see your friend Rufius is dead. A pity, he was a steady hand in a fight from what little I knew of him. In my tribe, when a warrior brother falls in battle, we take a drink and celebrate his life. We commend his spirit to the gods, and pray that our exit from this life will be as noble as his. I have heard that he died with half a dozen dead men littering the ground around him. And I have also heard that you, Centurion Corvus, hacked apart a dozen men to take his head back from our mutual enemies. You Romans clearly have your own ways of marking such a glorious death, and such a feat of revenge, but this does not seem fitting . . . '

Arminius stepped back into the tent with another lamp, then busied himself pouring oil into the first one while Martos looked on, weighing up the exhausted and demoralised man slumped on the ground in front of him. He squatted in front of Marcus, looking into the younger man's red-rimmed eyes.

'So, Centurion, you have a choice. Come with us now, leave the past behind you and look forward to tomorrow. Come with us now, and we will drink to your friend's feats of this and other days. We will send him to his gods with our thanks for the time he gave us. Or you can stay here and wallow in your misery, and tomorrow we will be forced to march away and leave you with the legions, where you will eventually be discovered to be a fugitive from justice.'

He eyed the downcast Roman with a calculating eye before continuing.

'Rufius saved your life, before you found your new home with these people, right? When your father was executed by the Emperor, and your family slaughtered, it was Rufius who helped you to escape from the men hunting you?'

Marcus nodded, smiling wanly at the memory as he answered.

'He wasn't the greatest of warriors, but he was every inch a soldier. He stood alongside me twice with his sword drawn when he hardly knew me. He brought me to the cohort, persuaded me to change my name from Valerius Aquila to Tribulus Corvus . . . ' He shook his head with the memory of that cold spring morning earlier in the year.

'So you owed him your life twice over. Is that why you jumped into the warband today? You should have been killed in an instant, but between your men's efforts and the favour of Mithras, you killed a dozen men or more and walked out alive with what was left of your friend. Your name is on the lips of every man in camp, thanks to that moment of madness, and the story grows with every telling, as does the number of people who hear about an insane young Roman fighting with an auxiliary cohort. We march north tomorrow, and if you don't lead your men out of camp tomorrow morning, it will only be a matter of days before someone puts the pieces of your story together and you find yourself in irons, waiting for the carpenters to finish building not only your cross, but those on which everyone who has protected you will die in agony alongside you.'

Marcus stood up, stretching the stiffness out of his joints.

'So if I don't pull myself together I risk dragging everyone else into my private Hades? And what if I do march north? How long will it be before I see another of my friends hacked to pieces in front of me?'

He stared aggressively at the two men, challenging either of them to reply. Martos spoke into the charged silence, his voice harsh with emotion.

'How long? Who knows? We're warriors, my friend Marcus. We all live with death. None of us enjoys losing a friend, but none of us has much choice in the matter. Your father had you trained to fight, he made sure you knew how to throw your iron around. He gave you the skills you need to kill anyone that puts himself in your way. More than that, he gifted you the intelligence and aggression to survive, and perhaps even to take revenge for his murder when enough time has passed. But you won't make a life here without facing death the way you have today, and you will face it again and again. Your friends will die, Marcus, it's a fact of life. I've lost friends and kinsmen, and so has Arminius. You have two choices, Centurion, you can either learn to deal with it, or you give up now and spare those close to you by taking your own life.'

Arminius stepped in close to the exhausted centurion, gently tapping his bloody chain mail with a sad smile.

'And whichever you choose, you must make that choice quickly now. If you're not with us when we march tomorrow morning, you'll represent a death sentence to the man I've sworn to protect with my own life. And I cannot allow that to happen.'

Marcus closed his eyes and stood silently for a moment, swaying slightly on his feet with exhaustion, then opened his eyes and regarded them without any hint of emotion.

'Very well. You are both good men, and I trust your judgement. I will seek to deal with my loss, and not betray those left alive for the sake of those already dead.'

Martos put a gentle hand on his shoulder, guiding him towards the tent door.

'Good. Life is for the living, Two Knives, and the more death you see, the more you will come to appreciate that truth. Let's get you out of that mail and washed, and then the three of us can take Rufius's head down to the fire that's been set to deny the crows our dead, and reunite him with his brothers-in-arms. After that, I'd say that we'll all need a drink, and a chance to remember the man at his best before we leave him here for good.'

* * *

Stores Officer Octavius found his intended partner in the torc's purchase absent when he made his way to the man's section of the Petriana's camp. Enquiries as to the whereabouts of Decurion Cyrus were met with the combination of indifference and near outright hostility to which he had become accustomed in his service as a stores officer. The most helpful comment he got was from a man whose sword he had replaced with moderately good grace less than an hour before, prompting a temporary truce in the usual state of open warfare between the cavalry wing's fighting men and the storeman they were rightly convinced was making a small fortune from supplying their needs.

'He's out at the turf wall supervising the guards. One of the decurions stopped an arrow this afternoon, so Cyrus has gone over to make sure Double-Pay Silus is up to doing his job for now. I can take you over to see him if it's urgent . . . ?'

His look of appraisal was enough to put Octavius on his guard in an instant. The stores officer and Decurion Cyrus were well known throughout the wing as men with a shared objective, wealth and all of the privileges it could buy them. Cyrus was reputed, despite his relatively lowly position as a squadron commander, to be wealthy well beyond the expectations of any of his peers, or indeed the wing's senior officers. It was muttered that he had chanced across a large cache of barbarian gold in the previous few months, and had contrived to keep the majority of it for himself with a few well-placed bribes. As for keeping that portion that he had managed to retain to himself, his fearsome reputation for swift violence in the face of any perceived slight or wrong had guaranteed that nobody who had even the scantest idea as to what was kept in his campaign chest harboured any thought of theft. Octavius, detested though he was by the Petriana's men, carried no such threat, and any man that suspected the presence of easy gain in his doings would have little to put him off the idea of taking a knife to either the store's tent canvas wall or, should the necessity arise, its occupant.

'Nothing that won't wait. I'll catch up with him later.'

The storeman turned away with a quiet curse, but his mood quickly lightened with the realisation that the army was unlikely to be moving from their camp alongside the ruins of the barbarian stronghold for a day or two. There were sacrifices of thanks to be made to various gods, equipment to be recovered from the dead, wounded to be carried away for treatment and the corpses of the fallen to be gathered and burned. He was sure that the governor would be unlikely to throw battle-weary soldiers on to the road without a compelling need for such a course of action. He would have plenty of time to speak with his business partner once his night's business was complete.

* * *

Posting Arminius to keep guard on the command tent delayed the arrival of the latest piece of bad news at soldier level in the Tungrian cohorts by no more than an hour, and by the time of the morning meal every man in the Tungrian section of the camp was fully aware of both the facts as they were known and the inevitable speculation wrapped around them.

'Every fort on the wall burned out, I've heard, women and children raped and murdered and the greybeards pegged out for the crows.'

Morban shook his head angrily at the trumpeter's excited statement, reaching across their small tent and gripping the younger man by the tunic with an angry glint in his eyes. Short of stature and bandy legged, the standard-bearer was nevertheless solid with muscle, and a dangerous man when roused.

'Then you'll do well to keep your mouth shut and what you've heard to yourself. It's just a story to you, eh? Well, to some of your mates it's their women you're talking about being fucked stupid by those dirty blue-nose bastards. Some of them have kids too. So get your bloody horn and get ready for morning parade.'

He stamped out of the tent, his breath misting in the early morning chill, almost tripping over the child sitting outside, seemingly oblivious to the cold. The boy was intent on the knife he held in one hand, and was dragging the edge of its blade across a sharpening stone. He glanced up at his grandfather before returning his gaze to the weapon's edge.

'I thought I could hear you and that bloody stone, Lupus.' Morban squatted down next to his grandson, holding out a hand for the knife. The boy surrendered it reluctantly, and stared fixedly at it while his grandfather examined the edge, snatching his thumb away with a curse as the blade drew a thin line of blood. 'Cocidius, but that's sharp! Six more months of your constant sharpening and you'll have nothing left, lad.' He handed the weapon back, watching as Lupus slid it into the sheath on his belt. 'Look, Lupus, you don't need to sharpen a knife every day. This isn't normal . . . ' His voice faltered, foundering on the certainty that nothing he said was going to make any impact on the boy, who was staring at the ground in misery.

'Antenoch told me to make sure I always had a sharp edge on my knife.'

Morban nodded, blinking away the tears that were threatening to run down his cheeks. The boy, despite not having reached the age of thirteen years, had used the knife to hamstring a barbarian warrior at the battle of the Red River Ford, taking revenge for the murder of his friend Antenoch. He put a hand under the boy's chin, lifting his face until they were looking into each other's eyes.

'I know. It's not easy for me either. Antenoch was my friend, as well as looking after you when I couldn't. I . . . '

The boy started to cry, and Morban gathered him into his arms and hugged him tightly, feeling the child's body shake as he sobbed out his misery, and his feeling of helplessness intensified. After a few minutes the sobbing eased, and the standard-bearer was able to gently remove the boy's arms from around his neck and hold him out at arms' length.

'Come on now, lad, we've got a parade to get organised. I don't even know if Centurion Corvus will be join — '

As if on cue Marcus stepped out of his tent, pitched alongside that used by the standard-bearer and trumpeter, and looked about him. His eyes were red with fatigue, and his armour was still covered in dried blood, which was flaking away as the rings rubbed against each other with his movements, but his face had a determined set despite the exhaustion that shadowed his features. Morban took one quick glance and turned to bellow down the line of tents.

'*Qadir!* Two Knives is up and about! And you, lad, go and get your cleaning gear, he's going to need a bloody good brushing before he goes on parade!'

* * *

Storeman Octavius caught up with Decurion Cyrus shortly after breakfast, strolling through a surprisingly busy morning to find his would-be partner supervising a flurry of activity. Having enjoyed a few hours of sleep, he was aghast to see that the squadron's tents were being struck and loaded on to the wing's baggage animals, while individual troopers were fussing over their mounts and checking equipment with the solemn faces of men going back into the fight.

'What's happening? How can we be on the move so soon, and with the battlefield still littered with gear?'

Cyrus grinned down at him mirthlessly, shaking his head in dark amusement.

'Always the last to know, eh, Octavius? The whole camp's on the move, man, both legions going south to put a Brigantian rebellion back in its place, and we're going north to see if we can bottle up the Venicones and prevent them from escaping back to their lands north of the abandoned wall. Most of us, that is. Some poor bastards have been detailed to ride to the north-east with the auxiliaries and take back some fortress that Calgus still holds.'

The stores officer's eyes widened in near-panic, and he gripped the decurion's arm without being aware of the action.

'But I've got a deal for us . . . '

Cyrus reached out with his other hand and plucked the storeman's grip from his sleeve, speaking in a quiet but fierce tone.

'Not *now*. Can't you see the interest you're causing?'

Two or three men were already watching the pair with thinly disguised curiosity, and the decurion turned away to check the fastenings on his saddle, speaking quietly over his shoulder.

'What's so urgent that it can't wait a few days?'

'I've got a soldier from one of the Tungrian

cohorts offering me a bloody great big gold barbarian torc, and he says it belonged to a tribal chief. It'll sell in Rome for a hundred thousand, minimum, and I've got him on the hook for a thousand. We can probably make at least twenty thousand on the deal, if you can just lend me five hundred to make up the purchase price . . . '

Cyrus turned back to him, taking his spear and showing him its iron head as if to discuss some feature of its manufacture.

'Firstly, my friend, there's no way I'm going to put my hand into my purse with this collection of thieves and idlers watching. And secondly, both Tungrian cohorts are away off to the north-east with that aristo Felix and six squadrons, something about cleaning out a nest of blue-noses up north, so that torc's about to march out of the camp. It seems that your deal's walking out on you.'

3

Centurion Dubnus shifted uncomfortably on the examination table, feeling the doctor's cool hands gently probing around the fresh scar that would be his permanent reminder of the battle at the Red River. The spear wound had been inflicted by a barbarian who had run full pelt into his century's line and punched his weapon's iron head through the big man's armour, burying it deep in his side to put him out of the fight, and into the hands of the Noisy Valley fortress's medical staff.

'I can't feel anything to indicate any infection, Centurion, and your wound seems to have healed nicely enough. You're a lucky man. You can get back on your feet for a few hours a day, nothing strenuous, mind you, and no clever ideas about sneaking back to your cohort either. I know you're desperate to get back into the fight, but you won't be fit to get back into armour for at least a month. Do you understand what I'm saying *this* time?'

Dubnus returned her questioning stare with a rueful smile. He had been caught at his room's window a few days previously, watching the legionaries practising with their weapons when he was supposed to be confined to bed.

'I understand, Doctor. I'll sit in my chair and listen to the idiots comparing the size of their scars.'

She nodded firmly.

'Good. And no trying to make your way down the corridor unobserved either. You need at least another week of inactivity before we can be sure that your wound is really healed.'

He nodded, sitting up with the help of the doctor's orderly Julius, a quiet and good-natured man rarely without a smile on his face.

'Is there any news from the legions?'

Julius answered after a moment's silence, shooting a troubled glance at his mistress.

'Yes, Centurion, a message rider arrived last evening. I would have woken you when I heard the message he was carrying, but you looked so . . . '

'And?'

The orderly smiled at the questioning tone, but the doctor turned back to him and wagged a finger.

'Calm yourself, Centurion. There's nothing either of us can do, whatever the news might be. As it happens, the news is good, or so it seems. The rebellion is broken, their camp stormed and destroyed, and those barbarians who escaped are scattered, and running for their lives. And no, there's no detail as to which units took what part in the fight.'

Dubnus pulled his tunic back on gingerly, feeling the fresh scar tissue flexing with his movements.

'Doctor . . . '

She shook her head.

'After all that's happened in the last few

months I think you should call me Felicia, Centurion.'

'Very well, Felicia. Whatever fighting he might have seen, Marcus will have come through it in one piece. He's faster with two swords than I am with one, his century are determined not to let 'their young gentleman' come to any harm, and he's got Tiberius Rufius to keep him from making an idiot of himself. He'll be back here soon enough.'

Her eyes moist, Felicia reached out for the big soldier's hand.

'I know. And if anything were to have happened to him, I could cope with it. It's just the not knowing . . .'

Dubnus gave her a wry smile.

'I know. Believe me, cooped up in here, I know exactly what you mean. And now I must give you this.'

He picked up a small cloth-wrapped package and handed it to her, catching Julius's eye and tipping his head at the door. The orderly took the hint and made his excuses while the doctor unwrapped the cloth, revealing a small knife in a soft leather sheath.

'What . . . ?'

'It's for your protection. I asked the soldier that you discharged yesterday to bring it in for me. I want you to promise that you'll wear it until Marcus can come for you. You need to be able to protect yourself if the need arises. You know where a man is vulnerable to a small blade just as well as I do, and that one's long enough to open a throat if need be. It will strap around your leg above the knee, and be hidden under your stola. Promise me that you'll wear it.'

She drew the knife from its sheath, examining the razor-sharp six-inch blade with a critical eye well used to gauging the sharpness of her surgical tools.

'Dubnus, I took an oath to protect human life, not to take it.'

The big centurion shook his head, but his reply was gentle.

'These are difficult times, and you're too precious to my friend for me to see you without some way of defending yourself. What if the Brigantes break into this fort?' He took a deep breath in through his nose, then exhaled and raised a questioning eyebrow. 'And besides, it's not just about *you* any more, is it?'

⋆ ⋆ ⋆

The Tungrian cohorts marched two abreast down the well-beaten track that ran from the barbarian camp to the edge of the forest, and which would bring them out on to the flatter land of the Red River's flood plain. The gently waving branches above their heads cast sun-dappled patterns across their ranks until they marched out on to the rolling plain, leaving behind the forest in which Calgus had planned to ambush and destroy the legions, before the presence of his Venicone allies had been detected by a chance encounter with one of Marcus's soldiers. Emerging from the trees on to the plain's gently undulating ground, the centuries drew up in parade formation and waited for the other components of Tribune Scaurus's command to make their appearance. Marching at the head of his 9th Century, and still wrapped in the grief of Rufius's sudden and violent death, Marcus was nevertheless aware of a collective melancholy sitting heavily on his men, a feeling he was himself quite powerless to resist. When the cohort's column halted he stood his men at ease and strolled out in front of them, staring hollow eyed up and down the Tungrian cohort's line and noting with a sudden pang the absence of Rufius's 6th Century, and the stocky figure of his friend out in front of them. After a few minutes a column of legionaries began to emerge from the trees, their centurions drawing them up in front of the Tungrian line and standing them to attention until the cohort's full strength was arrayed across the plain. First Spear Frontinius spoke without taking his eyes off the legion detachment's flag, the representation of the leaping boar that the 20th had made its badge over a century before.

'We *are* honoured. The Twentieth's legatus has given you their First Cohort to play with. He must have a soft spot for you, Tribune.'

Scaurus nodded, watching as the cohort's five centurions walked the lengths of their double-strength centuries, checking their men's line and equipment with an attention to detail that would have done honour to preparation for a triumphal parade through Rome. He answered his deputy's question in a matter-of-fact tone, not taking his eyes off the legion cohort's fluttering detachment banner.

'Indeed. I believe that Postumius Avitus Macrinus had a good relationship with my sponsor, before he left Rome to serve in Britannia. Ah, here comes their tribune. I'd suggest, First Spear, that you leave the talking to me. No matter what the man says. This man is the son of a most distinguished family, and I'm not sure that he's going to find this very easy.'

They stood in silence as the detachment's tribune walked across the gap between the two cohorts, his first spear walking at his shoulder and one pace behind. He halted in front of Scaurus and nodded brusquely, while his senior centurion snapped to attention and stared blankly over Scaurus's head. A man of about twenty-five, Tribune Laenas was of above-average height, with black hair and a broad face which, unsurprisingly under the circumstances, was set in a look of deep dissatisfaction.

'Marcus Popillius Laenas, tribune, Twentieth Legion Valiant and Victorious, reporting for duty as ordered.'

Scaurus stood in silence, holding the younger man's gaze and waiting patiently. After a long moment's wait Laenas raised an eyebrow.

'Ah, is there something wrong, colleague?'

'A small matter of military courtesy, Popillius Laenas. I fear that it is usual for the officers of a detachment to salute its commander.'

Laenas raised both eyebrows with surprise. Scaurus nodded in confirmation, willing his face not to reveal the amusement he was feeling at the look on the other man's face.

'I am your commanding officer, Popillius Laenas, and when I gather my officers I expect them all to salute me, including you. When I give a command, I expect the appropriate respect and a speedy response, with a salute. In short, Tribune, I expect you to behave in a way that recognises our relative ranks while your cohort forms part of my command.'

The young aristocrat stared at him in amazement.

'You're seriously expecting me to salute you? But I'm . . . '

Scaurus nodded, raising a hand to forestall the other man.

'Yes, I know, you're a broad-stripe tribune and you've only ever saluted your legatus who, like you, is of the senatorial class. And I, as we are both only too well aware, am an equestrian. The broad stripe on your tunic far outweighs the narrow stripe on mine, and in any other situation I would be the one deferring to superior rank. If I meet you in the street in Rome some day, then I will be the man showing respect for his social better, and I will do so promptly and with all due deference to your rank. Today, however, Tribune Laenas, you will have to adjust to the idea of saluting me, and you will have to make that adjustment quickly. Unlike some senior officers of my class, I do not intend to ignore the correct disciplines of this military life which we have chosen.'

Laenas looked at him for so long that First

Spear Frontinius was convinced he had decided to be deliberately insolent, and was tensed for the explosion that he knew such a reaction would elicit from Scaurus, but, to his relief, the young tribune simply raised one hand to his forehead, a look of bemusement on his face.

'You'll have to forgive me, Tribune, I'm not used to taking orders from anyone below the rank of the legion's legatus. I'll do my best to remember in future.'

Scaurus nodded impassively.

'Thank you, Tribune Laenas. I'm sure we'll both soon get used to the idea, strange though it may be. And this is your first spear, I presume?'

'Yes, Tribune, Senior Centurion Canutius.

Canutius saluted crisply.

'Tribune, the first cohort of Twentieth Valiant and Victorious is ready for detached duty. We have seven hundred and forty-three men fit for . . .'

He stopped speaking as Scaurus raised a hand and pointed at something over Laenas's shoulder.

'My apologies, First Spear, but I think our detachment from the Petriana has arrived.'

The horsemen of the Petriana wing were indeed making their appearance, each rider leading his horse down through the trees and into the morning sunlight. More than a few of the cavalrymen were leading a second horse, and as the squadrons began to form up facing end on to the infantry cohorts, Marcus realised that there were thirty or so empty saddles among the two-hundred-odd horsemen of his cavalry squadrons.

Frontinius leaned close to his tribune's ear, speaking quietly to avoid being overheard.

'That's strange, I thought we were being loaned six squadrons? I can only see five. That, and a lot of riderless horses.'

Scaurus nodded thoughtfully.

'You're right. Let's see what Tribune Licinius has to say on the subject.'

The Petriana's commander was the last man out of the forest, and he strode briskly across to Scaurus with a businesslike air, a vaguely familiar decurion walking behind him and leading a magnificent spirited black stallion which jerked at the reins every few seconds, its evident desire to be away across the rolling ground at a gallop manifest in every movement. His own grey horse was waiting for him at the forest's edge, along with his personal bodyguard. Scaurus snapped to attention, followed by the three first spears and, a second later, Popillius Laenas. Licinius smiled lopsidedly, shaking his head gently.

'There's no need for you to be saluting me, Tribune, we're of an equal rank now and you'll only go embarrassing me in front of the governor or, worse still, a legatus.' He looked around at the three first spears and Laenas, favouring them with a wintry smile. 'Morning, gentlemen. Please do stand at ease while I take your tribune off for a quick chat.'

He took Scaurus by the arm and led him a few paces away from the group of his officers, stopping to talk once there was no chance of their being overheard.

'I haven't got long, so we'll have to make this quick. The rest of my command is champing at the bit to go north and get stuck back into those Venicone bastards. You've probably already worked out that I'm stretching my orders just a little, and giving you five full squadrons and one more consisting of horses whose riders were killed yesterday. We had a bit of a time of it, I'm afraid, so I'm assuming that you can spare me from giving you another thirty men by putting some of your own in their saddles. I'm putting my men under the command of Decurion Felix, a young man who's not just an excellent officer, but also very well connected, *if* you take my meaning. Unlike some sons of influence, however, he insisted on starting his service as a cavalry squadron commander, despite the fact that his father could have pulled a few strings and seen him start off as a legion tribune like that fool Laenas. Apparently he wanted to see the life of a soldier from the ground up, a position which I find myself forced to respect given the capabilities of a *certain* legion tribune not far from here.' He raised an eyebrow at the look on Scaurus's face. 'And yes, I can see you trying to work out where you've seen him before. He's the man you rescued from the Votadini during the disaster at White Strength.'

Scaurus nodded.

'Oh yes, now I remember him. He had a barbarian hunting arrow stuck in his armpit less than a fortnight ago, as I recall. Are you really sure he's fit for duty?'

Licinius nodded briskly.

'Centurion Corvus's wife-to-be seems to have worked miracles, got the bloody thing out without causing any more damage than it had already inflicted on him, and I'm told he'll make a full recovery soon enough. Just give him time for the wound to fully heal and you will find him to be not only an efficient officer, but a good fighting man to boot. I can't take him back into the fight yet, though, and I can't spare you anyone that's fully fit, so you're both going to have to make the most of it. Oh, and watch out for his horse, he's a magnificent animal but he's also an evil-tempered bugger. And now I must get back to my men, before they decide to ride north for revenge without me. I wouldn't put it past them either, not with the mood they were in last night. The best of luck with your mission to liberate the poor old Votadini!'

He clapped Scaurus on the shoulder and turned away, mounting his horse and riding back up the path with his bodyguard in close attendance. The tribune turned back to his own men, taking the measure of the decurion standing slightly apart from them.

'We've met before, I think, Decurion Felix?'

The other man nodded, raising his right arm gingerly in a careful salute.

'Indeed we have, Tribune. I was lucky enough to be saved from the barbarians by that large German gentleman standing behind you and one of your centurions. They found me as good as dead, with an arrow sticking out of my armpit and poor old Hades here not much better off.'

Scaurus nodded.

'You're the man that rode through the barbarian warband during the battle for White Strength and lived to tell the tale. You must have balls the size of goose eggs.'

The decurion tilted his head to acknowledge the compliment.

'Amulius Cornelius Felix, Tribune.'

'And I'm Gaius Rutilius Scaurus, tribune commanding First and Second Tungrian Cohorts, and temporarily appointed to lead this detachment. How long is it since you were wounded, Decurion?'

Felix frowned in concentration for a moment.

'Fifteen days, Tribune.'

'Just over two weeks? Are you sure that you're fit enough for field duty?'

The cavalryman smiled slightly.

'Not really, but given another week I'll be perfectly fine. In the meantime I'm more than capable of riding and issuing these layabouts with orders, and we have another four decurions who can do the running around until I can lift a sword again.'

'Tribune Licinius commends you as a competent officer, and tells me that you'll be worth the wait. He also tells me to keep an eye open for your horse?'

Felix smiled easily, pulling his mount's head down until it was alongside his own, stroking the animal's long face affectionately.

'What, dear old Hades here? He's what I suppose might be called a lively character, if he were a man. The first time I set eyes on him he was busy kicking lumps off another poor horse through a gap in the fence between them, and I knew straight away he'd be perfect for me. Just don't get too close to his hindquarters, because like any good soldier he doesn't like anybody or anything behind him that he can't see. And he kicks like a bolt thrower.'

'The tribune also explained why I can see so many empty saddles in your ranks, Decurion. He suggests that I find thirty riders from my three infantry cohorts, and group them into a sixth squadron. I think I may have an officer with the appropriate skills to lead them, but he'll need a good double-pay to help him knock them into shape. Do you have anyone in mind?'

Felix smiled easily, nodding slightly.

'A man with the tact and diplomacy required for turning infantrymen into cavalrymen? Oh yes, Tribune, I've got just the man for the job.'

* * *

'Fuck *me*, you lot have got to be pulling my bowstring!'

Decurion Felix's double-pay man stalked down the line of volunteers with a pained expression, shaking his head unhappily. Tribune Scaurus's announcement of a requirement for men with riding skills had prompted twenty or so men from each of the Tungrian cohorts to step out of the ranks of their centuries, ignoring the insults and abuse their fellow soldiers had rained upon them, and a similar number of legionaries had volunteered from the 1st Cohort. Marcus had stayed put with his century until Tribune Scaurus had taken him to one side, and bluntly ordered him to volunteer.

'For one thing, those men are going to need an officer, and you're probably the only man on the field other than me with anything like proper cavalry training. And for another, just in case I need to remind you, your heroics of yesterday have once again swollen your reputation in the army to the point where the wrong people are going to be asking questions. You'll be better off out of sight scouting out in front of the main force for a while, I'd say. You can take my man Arminius with you, it'll be amusing to see him on a horse again, and perhaps he'll be of some use to you.'

Nodding his understanding with an impassive expression, Marcus had saluted and walked out to join the group of men nervously waiting to see what being a cavalryman was going to mean to them. Double-Pay man Silus gave him an astonished glance before turning back to face the volunteers, recomposing his face into the expression of disgust he'd been wearing before noticing the centurion's unexpected presence.

'Cavalrymen? Most of you lot — yourself obviously excepted, Centurion — wouldn't have been judged fit to shovel shit out of the stables when I joined up. You're not bloody cavalrymen, you're just a shower of footslogging mules, and that's all you're good for. Come on, there must be some of you that want to fuck off now, and spare me the bother of telling you to bugger off once it becomes clear that you're all bloody useless? No . . . ?' He sighed and shook his head with exasperation. 'Are you sure about this, Decurion?'

Felix nodded tersely.

'Yes, Double-Pay, and preferably before the three cohorts standing watching us die of boredom.'

Evidently exasperated, Silus beckoned one of the riders forward from the ranks, spoke to him for a moment and then turned back to the volunteers. The cavalryman led his horse out of the squadron's ranks and stood waiting, the animal bending its neck to crop at the plain's lush grass.

'We've got forty-seven of you mules, including the officer, and that needs to be reduced to the thirty-one men who'll be riding instead of footslogging today, since that's all the horses we have spare after yesterday's fighting. So, here's a simple test. All you have to do is get on that horse over there.' He pointed to the sturdy mount now being held by its rider beside him. The horse was fully equipped, complete with a four-horned saddle and a leather chamfron to protect its snout, the eyes covered with perforated bronze eye guards. 'She's a docile enough beast, so I don't expect she'll kick too many of you, not unless you climb aboard her like you're trying to take your pork sword to her after a night in the beer shop. Perhaps you'd like to go first, Centurion, and show the rest of your men what we're looking for . . . ?'

Marcus gave Silus a long stare, holding his

gaze until the other man looked away, before turning to the mare, taking stock of her size and apparent demeanour as he walked over to the animal. He took the bridle from her rider and gently pulled the beast's head towards him, talking quietly into her ear, and stroking her muzzle gently. Once the animal was apparently comfortable with his presence, he took a slow sideways step towards the waiting saddle, continuing to stroke her neck, talking to the horse in soft tones. Grasping the saddle's projecting front horn, he vaulted into the saddle, making light of the weight of his armour, and turned to address the watching infantrymen.

'Soldiers, look closely and you'll see that I'm deliberately relaxing on to the saddle here, and allowing it to flex under my weight, rather than sitting up stiffly. I'm doing that because that allows these saddle horns to grip my thighs, and that will keep me astride this horse no matter what I might ask her to do. There's another reason for taking a relaxed saddle as well, if you can manage it, apart from the benefit of actually staying on the horse — if you try to sit up for any sort of time your legs will start to hurt more than you can imagine! Save all that standing up in the saddle stuff for the first time we see some fighting.'

The mare stood quietly, then allowed herself to be encouraged into a sprightly trot around a tight circle before the young centurion swung his leg back over its back and dropped neatly to the ground. Double-Pay Silus nodded his reluctant respect, his mouth twisted into a tight smile.

'Very good, Centurion, it's nice to see an officer that understands horses. You've got a lovely loose seat, and your mount and dismount were as good as any soldier in the Petriana wing could have managed. I'd like to see you handle a spear up there, mind you, but you'll do for today. Now, let's have another one of you mules up here and see what you're made . . . '

Marcus's voice rode over his instructions, harsh enough to raise Decurion Felix's eyebrow.

'A word, Double-Pay?'

Silus walked across to where Marcus was waiting for him, a wary look on his face.

'Centurion?'

'Come and look at this.'

Marcus took his arm and led him around to the horse's far side, pointing to the shoulder straps there to disguise his true purpose from the watching soldiery.

'These men standing around us, Double-Pay, are *Tungrians*.'

The cavalryman frowned, unclear as to this unknown officer's purpose but unnerved by the harsh tone of his voice.

'Sir?'

Marcus sighed, shaking his head slightly.

'As I thought. You haven't got a clue what you're dealing with. Allow me to educate you. You will remember, if you've been with the Petriana for any length of time, the battle of Lost Eagle?'

He raised an eyebrow, waiting for the other man's response, which was still bullish, despite a slight uncertainty in his voice, unclear of where this strange and apparently cavalry-trained officer was taking the discussion.

'It would be hard to forget, Centurion. We took hundreds of blue-nose heads that day, once the fuckers broke and ran. It was bloody wonderful . . . '

He flinched as Marcus interrupted him again, his eyes wide with barely restrained anger.

'And do you remember, Double-Pay, sitting on your big fat arse and watching some bunch of dozy mules hold off those blue-noses for an hour or so, before they broke and ran, and you big brave horsemen decided to actually take part in the battle?'

The other man's face took on a nervous look with the sudden hostility in Marcus's voice.

'That's a bit unfair, Centurion, we . . . '

'Not from where my men were standing!'

The cavalryman flinched at the anger in Marcus's voice. Decurion Felix, standing a dozen paces from them, heard his fellow officer's angry tones and smiled slightly, taking a sudden interest in the hilt of his spatha.

'We fought ten times our strength in barbarians to a standstill that afternoon, while the Petriana sat and did nothing to aid us. The Tungrian soldiers standing around you, Double-Pay, spilled blood and lost friends that afternoon, while you sat and waited for us to send them running for you to chase down. You all rode back from that hunt with heads by the half-dozen, but my men were too tired, too damned numb, to take their swords to the corpses of the men they'd killed. Every one of these men has been blooded, Double-Pay, and stared into the eyes of men that could have been their brothers as they died on our iron. They've seen more fighting in the last few months than is good for them, I'd say, or good for anyone else that tries to play the fool with them. If your intention here is to humiliate them because they can't vault into the saddle like a man that's been practising the trick for the last year, I'd advise you to consider what a man that's been humiliated, and who has no concern for the consequences of taking revenge for a slight, might consider doing to you once night has fallen across tonight's camp.'

Silus swallowed nervously, without even being aware of it.

'I see your point, Centurion. Perhaps I could . . . '

Marcus nodded, his disgust evident in the curl of his lip.

'Yes. Perhaps you could, Double-Pay.'

He gestured to the waiting infantrymen.

'After you.'

The cavalryman gave his decurion a swift glance, finding little in Cornelius Felix's face to encourage him. He coughed, groping for the right reaction, the words spilling out a fraction too quickly for any of the men gathered around him to be fooled.

'I think you're right, Centurion, that strap does appear to be worn. I'll have the saddler replace it once we rejoin the rest of the wing.'

Marcus nodded magnanimously.

'Quite so, Double-Pay. And now, you were

saying? Time for my fellow infantrymen to take their turn displaying the cavalry mount?'

Silus shook his head decisively.

'I don't think they can be expected to perform to that standard, Centurion. A hand up into the saddle, I think, and a quick trot round, that'll be enough to show me what they've got.'

Marcus nodded, shooting a quick glance at Cornelius Felix to find the decurion indicating his own approval, a hint of a smile on his face. He turned back to the volunteers, taking stock of the men from his own cohort who had stepped forward, looking for the chance to become cavalrymen. Lurking among them was a familiar figure, and while Silus took the next man out in front of the group to try his hand with the waiting horse, Marcus strode into the group, tapping the man on the shoulder and pulling him to one side.

'Scarface? I didn't know you could ride? In fact, if I didn't know better I'd say you were determined never to let me out of your sight, no matter what you have to put yourself through. Can you even get up on a horse without falling over the other side and breaking your neck?'

The soldier blushed, but stuck his chest out in response to the challenge.

'I was born on a farm, Centurion. I learned to ride young. And you're not going to go charging around the hills with this shower of donkey wallopers without one of us to keep an eye out for you.'

'Us?'

The soldier blushed a deeper shade of red, his

eyes narrowing with something close to, but not quite, righteous anger.

'You've been a bit of a wild one ever since you joined the cohort, Centurion. All summer you've been running from one fight to the next, and never a thought for your men, or for the pretty girl that's waiting for you at Noisy Valley. All the lads that matter in the Ninth Century think you've a death wish, and we've decided to keep you alive until winter at least. And I'm the only one that can ride . . . '

He stopped talking, having realised that Marcus was looking over his shoulder, a wry smile creasing his face.

'Perhaps you are, Scarface. And perhaps you're not.'

The soldier turned, to find Qadir standing behind him. Marcus raised an eyebrow.

'And are you another one of 'us', Qadir?'

The Hamian shook his head, giving Scarface a disgusted look.

'Well done, then, soldier. You're alone with the centurion for a moment and it seems that you've already spilled the beans to him. Go and climb on that horse, and leave us to talk.'

Red faced and abashed, the soldier slunk away to take his place in the queue to mount the long-suffering mare, while Marcus gave his deputy a puzzled frown.

'So how do you get to walk away from the Ninth so easily, given their lack of an officer?'

Qadir shrugged.

'I just told the tribune what I can do on a horse. He thought it would be a good idea if I were riding alongside you, so he gave Morban my stick to poke in the soldiers' backs for a while, and your trumpeter gets to polish Morban's standard twice a day.'

'And just what can you do on a horse?'

Qadir smiled, and Marcus caught a brief glimpse of a relaxed confidence he hadn't seen in the man's demeanour at any point in the weeks they had spent together since their first meeting in the port of Arab Town.

'I have some small skill in the saddle. I . . . '

Something behind Marcus caught the Hamian's eye, and his jaw dropped fractionally.

'Oh, Deasura, that's not a sight you'll see every day!'

Marcus turned and stifled a laugh in the face of an irascible German sitting uncomfortably on the now distinctly unhappy-looking cavalry horse. He walked around the mare, his face alive with the first smile since Rufius's death.

'Well, Arminius, I can't say you're the most natural horseman I've ever seen.'

Arminius sneered down at the men standing around him, then leaned out of the saddle and put a sausage-sized finger in Double-Pay Silus's face.

'Just so we're clear, I hate horses. Tribune Scaurus says I ride like a mule tender with bleeding piles, and that I have all the skill in the saddle of a sack full of shit. And despite that, before you open your mouth, I'm one of your thirty-one horsemen and that's official. You don't like it, I don't like it, but the tribune couldn't give a toss what either of us think. Wherever

Centurion Corvus goes, I go. So there it is.'

He climbed down from the horse and clenched both of his massive fists, scowling around him.

'And anyone that finds that funny had better be ready for an unscheduled sleep.'

Double-Pay Silus looked at him thoughtfully, then beckoned his pay-and-a-half across to join him.

'See that?'

He pointed at the German, and the other man nodded with pursed lips.

'What have we got that'll carry him thirty miles in a day without breaking down inside a week?'

⋆ ⋆ ⋆

South of the Wall, in a copse overlooking the Sailors' Town fort, Centurion Rapax and his colleague Excingus were exchanging uneasy glances. The fort was silent, without any movement, and Rapax had been watching its walls intently for long enough to be sure it was deserted. Excingus fished out his pocket tablet, once again checking their route against the directions he'd been given in Yew Grove two days before.

'North from Waterfall Town ten miles, across the river dam and then another nine miles north up the road to Vintner's Way, then carry on to Sailors' Town.' He paused, giving the silent fort another long, searching stare. 'Well, that's bloody Sailors'Town right enough, and it looks just as dead as the first two ghost towns we've ridden past this morning. I say we push on, and get to this Noisy Valley place soonest.'

Rapax spat on the copse's dry earth.

'That centurion you got the directions from was close to soiling himself, and there he was with half a cohort between his precious skin and the local thrill seekers. He had no patrols out looking for information, so he had no idea of what might have happened up this way in the last few days. I didn't like the last place, but we were close enough to friendly forces for the locals to be keeping a low profile. Here, on the other hand . . .'

Excingus nodded and stared across the three hundred paces that separated copse and fort.

'We're too far out to see what's in there. Perhaps we should get a little closer?'

His colleague shook his head decisively, sniffing the air.

'Smell that? It's faint, but we're downwind from the fort. That's the smell of rotting meat, old son. Once you've had a noseful of that reek you never forget it. That fort's full of nothing but corpses and flies, and the tribesmen are out there somewhere, lurking close to the road and waiting for some more soldiers to blunder into their trap. We can only guess what the men who were manning the place went through before they died, but I don't intend sharing their fate. We'll go round it, my friend, and give the barbarians plenty of chance to show themselves.'

The small party mounted their horses and walked them carefully and quietly round to the fort's east, putting the higher ground between it and them to mask their movements from any watchers in the fort as much as possible. Only when the fort was completely out of sight was Rapax willing to allow them to return to the road, and even then it was clear he was still reluctant. He gathered his men about him, looking hard into each man's eyes as he spoke as if weighing them for their ability to deal with the pressure they were all feeling.

'There are fifteen of us. If we bump into anything more than a couple of dozen of them we'll have no option but to run away from them as fast as these horses will carry us.' He cast a dark glace around his tent party. 'And any of you that decide that keeping your skin intact might best be achieved by outpacing the rest of us had better be ready to see the colour of your guts when I catch up with you. Right, then, march.'

less than a hundred paces from the two horsemen, a deer broke cover, sprinting away from them and eliciting an uncompromising response from Marcus's mount. The big horse pinned back his ears and went from their easy trot to a full gallop in half a dozen strides, almost throwing Marcus from his saddle with the speed of his reaction. Regaining his seat, the centurion decided to let the animal run, enjoying the unaccustomed sensation of his mount's raw speed. Looking back over his shoulder he saw that Qadir, despite the fact that he had been caught by surprise by the horse's sudden charge, was crouched over his own horse's back as the chestnut mare swiftly gathered pace. Supremely confident in his ability to stay in the saddle, the Hamian dropped his mount's reins and pulled his bow loose from the leather carrying case across his shoulder, reaching for an arrow as the chestnut started to catch Marcus's grey, eyes narrowed as he calculated the distance to the fleeing deer. Farther back, the double-pay and his deputy were also riding hard in pursuit, the rest of the newly formed squadron looking on with expressions of either amusement or amazement.

Marcus tightened his grip on his spear, putting his heels into the grey's ribs to encourage the horse to greater efforts, and touching the reins to guide him around a small copse of a dozen or so stunted trees. As he flashed past the thicket he glanced into the trees, his gaze momentarily catching a flash of red in the greens and browns of the undergrowth, and with a sudden hard tug at the grey's reins he turned the horse sharply, pulling his shield from its place on the horse's left flank and readying his spear to stab into the foliage. With a desperate shout a tribesman pushed his way out of the trees, bellowing his defiance and brandishing his sword at horse and rider, but the grey was seemingly as keen for the fight as he was for the chase, ignoring both the barbarian's noise and his blade as he pushed in towards the new threat, turning slightly to the right without any conscious effort on Marcus's behalf. The horse's move both presented his rider's shield and opened the angle for his spear as Marcus punched the weapon forward and down, sinking its heavy iron head deep into the tribesman's neck. The spear's razor-edged blade sliced open the warrior's throat, and he fell back from the challenge choking on his own blood.

Pulling the grey's head farther round to the right, keeping the shield between him and the trees, Marcus walked the animal along the treeline, searching for any sign that other tribesmen were lurking in the shadows. Without warning five men burst from the copse and ran from the horsemen, most of them clearly wounded from the previous day's fighting and incapable of much more than a limping shuffle. Marcus shook his head in disbelief, turning to follow them at little more than a trot and raising his weapon to strike again, slamming his spear's iron head squarely into the rearmost man's spine and shunting him forward half a dozen paces before heaving the weapon free and dumping him to the ground. An arrow whistled past his head with a foot or so to spare, dropping one of the faster runners in a confusion of limbs as the fallen tribesman arched his back and scrabbled for the arrow's shaft. A moment later Qadir loosed another missile, and a second warrior staggered forward and down on to his knees with an arrowhead lodged deep in the square of his back. The last two barbarians stopped and turned to face their pursuers with their swords drawn, one of them barely able to stand from a roughly bandaged leg wound, the other, a tall, powerful warrior, raising his sword and stepping forward to protect his comrade. Marcus cantered the grey past them outside the reach of their weapons, reaching round to stab his spear's bloodied blade into the wounded man's chest and dropping him to his knees in grunting agony. The last warrior raised his sword in futile defiance, and Qadir put one last arrow to his bow, drawing the missile back in readiness for the split-second flight that would bury its evil three-bladed iron head in the barbarian's chest. Marcus looked back at the man, and at the last possible moment realised that there was something familiar in the barbarian's stance as he prepared to fight and die.

'Qadir! Alive!'

The big Hamian stopped in mid-shot, not yet taking the tension off the arrow poised to fly from his bow, and Marcus trotted his horse back to within a few paces of the defiant warrior, aligning his spear's gore-slathered blade with the barbarian's chest. The tribesman stood his ground, his sword held in both hands ready to swing if the Roman came within reach, but his face spoke of desperate exhaustion rather than any eagerness to fight. Marcus peered hard at his face, nodding slightly as if some suspicion were confirmed by closer scrutiny.

'Surrender to me now and you'll get fair treatment! Lift that sword to me and I'll put you down with a wound like his . . . ' He pointed the spear at the fallen man panting for breath on the ground next to the barbarian. 'And if you wait here for much longer there'll be another half dozen or more of us, all looking for a head to take and only you on your feet. Decide now!'

The warrior closed his eyes and raised his head to the sky, then dropped the sword to the ground and slumped to his knees, just as Double-Pay Silus galloped his horse round the copse and pulled up alongside Marcus, levelling his spear at the defenceless warrior.

'Well done, Centurion! Do you need a hand sending this big bugger to meet his ancestors?'

Marcus shook his head, pointing at the corpses and dying men scattered around them, his voice hard with authority.

'If you want a head to decorate your saddle, take any one of those that takes your fancy, neither my comrade here nor I have any appetite for the practice. But this one, Double-Pay, is *mine*.'

He dismounted as the remainder of the squadron cantered up, stepping carefully up to the barbarian, picking up the man's sword and passing it to Qadir to remove any temptation for renewed resistance. His captive looked up from his kneeling position, glancing around at the hostile men crowding in to see their centurion's captive, speaking in rough Latin without any sign of fear.

'So what you do now? Torture, and then knife?'

Marcus shrugged, keeping his eyes on the other man and his hand on the ornate eagle pommel of his gladius.

'There's no need for me to torture you. All I want is for you to tell me your story since the last time we met, and if you do that with honesty then I will release you unharmed.'

'Centurion, I think we'd be best . . . '

Marcus spoke without turning away from the captured Briton, who was now regarding his captor with a puzzled look.

'No, Double-Pay, this is not negotiable. If this man tells us what has happened to him in the very few weeks since he and I last met, and if I believe that he's telling the truth, then he walks free. I suggest that you carry on with our patrol, and I will stay here long enough to hear him out. I'll keep a few men with me for safety, though, because I know from recent experience that he's a fighter. My men Qadir, Scarface and Arminius ought to be more than enough.'

There was a moment's silence from the man behind him, and Marcus found himself fighting a powerful urge to turn and pull the double-pay down from his horse, his blood still boiling from both the brief fight and the lingering frustrated rage left by the previous day's dreadful events. His right fist clenched so hard that he could feel the nails biting into the skin of his palm, and, looking up from his captive, he found Arminius, perched atop his new mount Colossus, shaking his head minutely, his eyes slitted in silent warning. Silus's response, when he spoke again, was bleak, and Marcus had no need to turn around to know that his new subordinate would be white with anger at being put down so hard.

'Very well, sir. We'll leave the wounded to you, though, that's the way the Petriana works. If you wound a man, then you finish that man. Squadron, follow me!'

Marcus waited until the squadron was halfway to the horizon before speaking again.

'So, Briton, before we talk, will you send your fallen brothers to their gods, or will you allow a Roman to do the job for you?'

The big man stirred himself, standing to face his captor and looming over the Roman. Arminius dismounted from the huge horse that Silus had allocated to him and took a pace from its side while keeping a grip on its reins, putting his muscular bulk close enough that the tribesman would be dissuaded from any attempt at violence, but the look he got from the Briton, almost a head taller than the German, was anything but intimidated.

'I have no weapon.'

Marcus shrugged, taking the long sword back from Qadir and holding its hilt out to the barbarian.

'Then use this. And don't forget that my colleague here could put three arrows in your back before you could run a hundred paces.'

The warrior took the weapon without comment, turning away to the man lying alongside him, now deathly pale and hovering on the edge of consciousness with his eyes staring glassily at the sky. He put the sword's point on to the dying warrior's chest, then turned back to Marcus with the weapon poised for the kill.

'This man was brother. I ask favour of coin.'

Marcus fished a sestertius from the pouch on his belt and handed it over without comment. The barbarian bent and slipped the coin into his comrade's mouth, patting the dying man's face and muttering a few quiet words, then stood again, quickly pushing the point into his chest to stop his heart. He turned away from the corpse with tears in his eyes, glancing around him at the dead and wounded men scattered around them. Marcus nodded, gesturing for him to continue.

'We'll wait here while you give them dignity.'

The tribesman nodded to Marcus, and turned away to the remainder of his fallen comrades. He worked quickly and efficiently, using the sword where he found that the sprawled bodies were not yet dead, and returned to the waiting soldiers once the task was complete, handing the sword back to Marcus. The centurion took the weapon from him, pushing its blade deep into the turf beside him and gesturing for the Briton to sit, folding himself down on to the grass at the same time.

'So, Briton, am I right in thinking that we know each other?'

The giant nodded, turning his arm over to reveal a 'C' branded into his flesh, with a line scored through the letter overlaying the original brand, the 6th Legion's bull emblem burned in below the marks.

'Yes, remember you.'

Marcus nodded, and of the other three men surrounding them, only Scarface showed any sign of understanding his centurion's meaning.

'This is the barbarian slave that fought with us to take the fort?'

Marcus put out his hand.

'Your name is Lugos, as I recall?'

The Briton looked at the offered hand for a moment before taking it in a firm grasp.

'Yes, I Lugos.'

Marcus turned to Qadir and Arminius, both of whom looked baffled and curious in equal measures.

'Lugos was captured after the battle of Lost Eagle, and put to work carrying the ram that battered down the gates of a Carvetii fort we were tasked to take a few weeks ago. Once we were through the gates the slaves were freed to run wild and distract the defenders, and a few of us, including Lugos here . . . '

Scarface bridled.

'And me!'

' . . . and this particularly insubordinate soldier, managed to fight our way through the fort's defences and finish the fight quickly and cleanly. After which he was clearly rewarded by the Sixth Legion with release from his captivity, and told to go home. But what happened after that?'

The Briton shrugged his shoulders.

'No escape war. Try go home, but Calgus men find. Make join warband. I find brother, we fight together when legion attack. Brother wounded, we run with many men. When dark come, we escape, hide in trees. Then you come . . . '

'And I killed him.'

Marcus closed his eyes, shaking his head at the situation's grim irony. Lugos stood in silence and stared wet eyed at the ground, his body sagging as the determination that had driven his efforts of the last few days seeped away and left only the numb reality of the corpse on the ground beside him. The young centurion took a deep breath, then turned back to face the stricken barbarian.

'I cannot apologise for killing your brother, Lugos. Nor can I regret the fact that I fulfilled my role in pursuing your group to destruction, no matter how painful that might be to you. All I can do is to wish that it might have been different, that fate had not brought us back together in such a cruel manner. And keep the bargain I struck with you.' Lugos lifted his gaze and looked at him again, his eyes still red. 'So, Briton, tell me of your last day. What have you seen since the legions brought the fire to Calgus's camp in the forest?'

The Briton spoke for several minutes, and when he fell silent again Marcus nodded his head slowly, looking at Arminius and finding his face equally troubled.

'You're sure about this? This man Harn was leading the warband east when you slipped away from them, not heading for the north?'

'Yes. Go to Alauna. Harn say plenty food

there, soldiers be gone.'

'And that didn't tempt you?'

Lugos shook his head with absolute certainty.

'Alauna holy place. Alauna mean 'shrine' my speak. Harn take warriors to Alauna, he insult great goddess. Bring death to he, and his sons.'

'Sons?'

'Yes. Sons. They march with Harn.'

Arminius shrugged.

'It's not unusual. I was only twelve summers when first my father and his brothers took me to war. It is in such company that a boy grows to manhood before his time.'

Lugus nodded his agreement.

'Good sons, strong and tall. Make fine warriors.'

'Yes.' Marcus stared bleakly to the east. 'If they live that long.'

* * *

'I don't know about you, but those hills scare the shit out of me.'

The legionary spat over the wall that ran above the Noisy Valley fortress's south gate, staring bleakly out at the hills that sloped down to the banks of the River Tinea as it swept past their walls, cold and dark in its course from the mountains to the sea, as hostile as any ground they had fought over to the north of the Wall in the last six months. His fellow soldier nodded dourly, turning his head to take the late afternoon's wind-driven drizzle on the side of his helmet rather than straight into his face.

'Not surprising, given what happened to those poor bastards in the Third Century. Fuck knows what the tribune was thinking of when he sent them south . . . '

It was a common theme in their desultory time-killing conversations, as the cohort's men patrolled their walls and worried about their immediate futures. A patrol in force had been sent out into the Brigantian countryside to the south of the river in the first days of this fresh rebellion, with orders from Tribune Paulus to march the ten miles to Sailors' Town. They had been intended to strengthen the small garrison that had been left to hold the remote fort when the rest of the cohort based there had marched north to join the fight with Calgus. It was a needless and stupid risk, the legionaries guarding the south gate had told each other as the cohort's 3rd Century had marched out grim faced to confront the rebellion on its own ground. Every legionary in the fortress agreed that the bloody auxiliaries should have been left to look out for themselves. Even the 3rd Century's centurion had seemed to share their opinion of his orders to make contact with the isolated garrison on the long road south to the legion's fortress at Elm Grove. As he had pulled on his helmet for the march, itself a rarity in that under normal circumstances it would have been carried across his chest until needed, he had confided to the duty centurion of the guard that he entertained small hopes of reaching the fort without trouble. Less than five hours later the 3rd Century, or rather what was left of it, had struggled back through the gates in bloody disarray.

'Those poor bastards looked like they didn't have another step in them. And that was the ones that hadn't stopped arrows or spears.'

The century's watch officer, a stocky soldier with fifteen years' service called Titus, the only surviving man of any rank, had sat shivering in the warmth of Tribune Paulus's office in his blood-spattered armour, eyes still pinned wide by shock, and had told a story that had chilled the blood of the senior officer sitting opposite in his crisp tunic.

'They came out of the trees on both sides of the road, two or three hundred of them. They went for the centurion like a pack of dogs, and they had the chosen man on his back a moment later. The front half of the century was chopped to mince, and the rear rank broke and ran. I tried to stop them, but it was useless, they ran like children. Last thing I saw was the fucking blue-noses waving the centurion's head around. *Bastards* . . .'

Tribune Paulus had been uncertain whether the watch officer had intended the epithet for the barbarians or his own men, although the look that the man gave him as he was dismissed made him wonder whether there might have been a third target for the other man's ire.

The legionary spat over the wall again, shaking his head and scowling out at the grey hills looming across the valley.

'We can only hope that the idiot's realised there's no way to get through to the south.

Whoever the Vardulli cohort left minding the shop at Sailors' Town is already on a stake or else in some very nasty shit indeed. And we can only hope that the bloody blue-noses decide that we're too tough a nut . . . ' He stopped, squinting out into the afternoon's gloom. 'Hang on, can you see what I can see?'

The other man followed his pointing hand.

'Horsemen, crossing the bridge!'

The riders were pushing their mounts hard, no more than a dozen of them where the soldiers guarding the fortress's walls would have sworn nothing less than a cavalry wing could have made it through the sea of hostile tribesmen blocking the road from the south. The legionary shouted down to the men guarding the gate below him.

'Call out the centurion. There's riders coming in!'

The century's full strength poured out into the street, spears and shields forming a hasty wall across the narrow gap between the buildings to either side while their centurion stalked forward with his sword drawn and bawled an order for the man-sized wicket gate to be opened. He peered through the gap into the drizzle, as the small party reined in their horses ten paces from the wall, sizing up the men astride their exhausted horses and seeing uniforms that were clearly Roman, but yet not familiar. Two of the riders were wounded, one grimacing at the pain of an arrow protruding from his thigh, the other man only still on his horse because another soldier was holding him up, a slow dribble of blood running from a deep wound on his right forearm to drip from his hand. All of them looked at the end of their endurance. Two of the riders wore the cross-crested helmets that were the mark of a centurion, but in a province gone wild with bloodlust, and with an unknown number of soldiers dead in the land south of the Wall, that meant little enough to a man entrusted with the security of a legion's supply base.

'Who the fuck are you? I see uniforms that I don't recognise, and two officers' helmets in a group of a dozen men, and that don't add up! Quickly now!'

The darker faced of the two centurions jumped down from his saddle and stalked forward, his face set in disdain. Stopping so close to the legion centurion that the brow pieces of their helmets were nearly touching, he fixed hard eyes on the other man, and when he spoke his harsh growl set the duty officer's nerves jangling.

'Who we are has nothing to do with you, Centurion. I am a Praetorian Guard officer, and my colleague here is from the Camp of the Foreigners in Rome. We've ridden fifteen hundred miles in less than a month, and fought our way through a barbarian ambush that took two of my men and wounded two more, so if that gate isn't open very fucking quickly I'll have you as a replacement for one of the men I've lost today!' He lowered his voice an octave and fixed the legion centurion with a gaze of such malevolence that it momentarily rooted the man to the spot. 'Your rank, Centurion, will be that of soldier, and I will take full advantage of that rank. Would you like to test out that promise?'

The centurion was turning away to order the gates open before the last words had left the praetorian's mouth, his face suddenly pale at their implication. His mind was still reeling ten minutes later as he escorted the pair to the tribune's office and happily took his leave of them.

'Gentlemen?'

The tribune was of the equestrian class, and if not quite as supremely self-confident as the legion's senatorial broad-stripe tribune, he had enough breeding and military experience to feel himself more than capable of managing any situation he might find put in front of him. He took his seat behind the desk, indicating that the two men should do the same. They sat, both men placing their swords across their knees, their wet armour dropping spots of water on the immaculately polished wooden floor. The burly praetorian took the lead, his voice rasping out in the office's quiet.

'Greetings, Tribune, I'm Quintus Sestius Rapax, centurion, Praetorian Guard, and this is my colleague Tiberius Varius Excingus, centurion, from the Camp of the Foreigners.'

The praetorian paused for a moment, watching the tribune's face intently. Sure enough, the man's eyebrows twitched upwards minutely, and while Rapax could find some respect for the man's almost complete control over his reaction to the identity of his travelling companion, he knew at that second that they had his measure.

'I'm Sextus Pedius Paulus, tribune, Sixth Imperial Legion and commanding officer here. What brings a praetorian and a corn officer to Noisy Valley? Surely you'd have been better waiting until this local rebellion burned out before risking the North Road? I hear you have lost men to an encounter with the rebels.'

Rapax shrugged, dismissing his losses as a regrettable necessity.

'We have travelled here from the imperial palace, Tribune, without pause for anything other than snatched meals and a few hours' sleep each night, changing horses several times a day at the courier stables to cover as much distance as possible. That will give you some understanding of the urgency of our mission, and the reason why we pressed on at the cost of two good men killed by those barbarian bastards. We carry authorisation to command the support and assistance of any man in the empire should we have the need to do so.' He paused to hand over a message scroll embossed with the imperial seal. 'And our mission, Tribune, is to . . . '

'One moment, Centurion.' The tribune held up a hand to silence the praetorian, whose eyes narrowed at the interruption, scanning the scroll as he unrolled it. He frowned, staring hard at the name written at the bottom of the document. 'This order is signed by the Praetorian Prefect. The Emperor's name is nowhere to be seen, other than where the writer states that 'the Emperor commands all true and loyal subjects to provide whatever service may be required by Centurions Rapax and Excingus, either together or individually'.' He waved the scroll at the praetorian with a puzzled frown. 'How is *this* an imperial decree?'

Excingus spoke for the first time, and Rapax sat back with a quiet smile as his colleague shook his head dismissively, his soft voice dismissing the objection without any hint of concern.

'You've been away from Rome for a good while, Tribune? I guessed as much. During your absence, Tribune, my colleague's noble prefect, Sextus Tigidius Perennis, has risen far in the estimation of our glorious Emperor. The prefect's colleague, co-prefect of the guard Publius Tarrutenius Paternus, has been executed for the crime of procuring the murder of the Emperor's *closest* friend, palace chamberlain Saoterus. Not only has Prefect Perennis been granted sole command of the Praetorian Guard as a result, but he has also been granted responsibility for far more than just safeguarding the imperial family. The prefect now conducts a substantial part of the throne's affairs in order to free the Emperor for more important matters. As the Emperor's right hand, therefore, the prefect has both the right and the *duty* to pursue the throne's enemies, no matter where they may seek to take shelter from his master's divine vengeance. It is the prefect's strong expectation that any man of integrity and loyalty to the throne will provide my colleague here with any assistance he might need, but he asked me to accompany centurion Rapax, as a means of ensuring that help under any circumstance. You will, I'm sure, be aware of the special trust reposed in the Camp of the Foreigners by every emperor since the divine Hadrian himself turned the corn officers to his service.'

Tribune Paulus sat back in his chair, taking fresh stock of the two men facing him. A praetorian centurion with the looks of a killer, and an imperial spy more than happy to lean on the unnerving reputation of his office to get whatever he wanted. And both of them, it seemed, operating under the authority of a man known to be gathering power at a fearsome rate. He thought quickly, calculating how far he might push any resistance before making a target of himself.

'I've heard of pairings such as yours before, gentlemen, and to be frank the example that's been set hasn't been a good one. What guarantee do I have that you'll exercise your powers with appropriate responsibility?'

Rapax stared back at him, with a look that sent a shiver up the tribune's back, his hoarse voice flatly uncompromising.

'There's nothing to fear from us, Tribune. Once we've tracked down this traitor we'll do our business quickly and quietly, and return to Rome to inform my prefect that justice has been done.'

'And seen to be done, Centurion?'

The praetorian shrugged.

'Anyone that's been sheltering the fugitive can expect to suffer imperial justice, that's inevitable, but we understand the value of restraint. After all, you're fighting a war here, and we wouldn't want to impede your efforts to put this barbarian scum back in their place.'

The tribune nodded.

'Quickly and quietly, then, and no excessive punishment of any officers who might have been deceived by this man Aquila?'

Excingus nodded firmly.

'I think we understand each other, Tribune. In return for your assistance we'll make sure that justice is served without a lot of unhelpful excitement.'

Tribune Paulus nodded, and shifted his weight forward in the chair, putting his hands on the desk in readiness to stand, but neither of the men facing him showed any sign of getting to their feet. Excingus frowned slightly, raising a hand to forestall Paulus.

'There is just one more thing, Tribune. Hearing your name just now, I was reminded of something I was told shortly before I left Rome.'

Paulus nodded politely and sat back, feeling sudden discomfort with this new and apparently spontaneous line of discussion.

'Yes, it was the day before we left the city. A former tribune of the Sixth Legion was found with his throat slit, apparently by his own hand. The bodies of his wife, child and closest relatives were found in the house with him, all dead from stab wounds. The assumption is that he must have lost his mind as a result of his experiences here in Britannia, and run amok with a dagger before using it to take his own life. A terrible shame, the child was less than two years old, and his wife was such a pretty little thing before he took his knife to her. I believe his name was . . . Quirinius?' He made a show of consulting his tablet. 'Ah yes, Tiberius Sulpicius Quirinius. He was a senator, since his father had killed himself only a few weeks before. Seems it ran in the family . . . '

Paulus stared at the two men with a growing sense of horror, both at the news they bore and its implications. Excingus continued, his expression suddenly almost predatory.

'Senator Quirinius left a journal, of sorts, in which he made several interesting statements regarding his experiences in Britannia. The most startling of these was his professed knowledge of exactly who killed tribune Titus Tigidius Perennis.'

He waited for Paulus to react, stringing the silence out until the tribune had no option but to fill it.

'But Perennis died in battle. He was . . . '

Excingus shook his head firmly.

'And that's what his father believed, until Senator Quirinius's journal came to light. It seems that far from dying at the hands of the barbarians, dying honourably with blood on his sword, the prefect's son was murdered by a Roman. The missing son of Senator Aquila seems to have made his way to Britannia in an attempt to avoid his fate, and Tribune Perennis in turn seems to have managed to find him. We believe that Aquila must have killed him in order to maintain the secrecy around his hiding place here on the frontier.'

Paulus pursed his lips and looked baffled.

'Who would have harboured a known fugitive? That would be a death sentence!'

Excingus nodded agreement.

'And not just for anyone foolish enough to protect the fugitive. Anyone else that became aware of his presence and failed to report it to the relevant authorities would carry the same burden of guilt. And the same punishment . . . '

He fixed Paulus with a hard stare, and his tone become accusatory as he continued.

'The thing is, Tribune, that Senator Quirinius's journal was quite adamant about two closely related facts. The first was that he had been told who it was that had killed your colleague Perennis. The second was that it was you who had shared that knowledge with him, apparently while you were under the influence of drink, one night after the battle in which your legion was stripped of its eagle and half its fighting strength. The battle in which the prefect's son died, in fact.'

Paulus sat back in his chair, his face pale with shock.

'I told him . . . '

'Yes?'

'I told him that a centurion serving with an auxiliary cohort attached to our legion was reputed to have killed the tribune before the battle.'

'And that centurion was the fugitive Aquila?'

Paulus shook his head, his face blank.

'I genuinely couldn't say, Centurion. He was just another auxiliary centurion to me.'

'From which cohort?'

'The First Tungrian, as I recall it.'

'And how did you know that this centurion was in fact the tribune's killer?'

Paulus looked up, a hard edge coming into his voice.

'If I tell you that, how am I to be sure you won't take your threats to another good man?'

Excingus smiled evenly.

'That depends on you, Tribune. There may be no need to involve anyone else in this, as long as my colleague here and I know where to go hunting for this fugitive. Of course, I'll interrogate my way through this entire province if I'm forced to do so, but it'll cost me time I badly need to avoid wasting, time in which the fugitive might be running for another hiding place. I should add that it would go badly for you too, in that case. And you have a large family in Hispania, I believe?'

The tribune's face hardened, and his knuckles whitened against the dark wood of his desk. Rapax slid a hand to the hilt of his dagger, his body tensing. After a moment Paulus slumped slightly in his chair, the fight seeming to go out of him as the consequences of any rash action sank in.

'Very well. I have no option but to take you at your word that you'll go after this Aquila, rather than carving a bloody path through a body of loyal soldiers.' He sighed, closing his eyes in resignation as he spoke. 'A man I've known since childhood is serving as an officer with another auxiliary cohort. He pointed the centurion out to me during the battle's aftermath. The Tungrians had held off ten times their strength for longer than we'd have ever thought possible, buying time for the other legions to reach the battlefield. Naturally we wanted to have a look at the damage they'd done to the warband, so we walked up the hill, over a carpet of bodies so thick that they were two and three deep at the point where the two lines had clashed. There were officers from half a dozen units standing around and marvelling at the scale of the slaughter, and that the Tungrians had survived such an onslaught. And the smell . . . ' He shook his head slightly at the memory of the reek of blood and faeces that had permeated his clothes for days afterwards. 'One of the Tungrian centurions walked past, covered in blood and wide eyed with the strain of what his cohort had endured, and I commented to my friend the decurion that he had two swords strapped to his belt. That's when he told me that he'd seen the same man earlier that day, standing over the body of Tribune Perennis.'

Excingus raised an eyebrow.

'And that's all he told you? None of the grisly details?'

Paulus laughed without mirth.

'Oh, I tried to get them out of him all right. I might not have liked Perennis very much, but he was still a Roman tribune and my colleague. My friend just smiled at me, and told me that the less I knew the safer it would be for me. It seems we'd both have been better off if I'd never heard any of it . . . '

Excingus nodded, a glint of triumph in his eyes.

'Yes. And better still for your colleague Quirinius, given that he couldn't keep his mouth shut. And now, Tribune, I'll trouble you for that one last piece of information. It'll be hard for you to give it to me, but it'll go harder on you and yours if you keep it from me. Who was this friend of yours, exactly?'

5

Out on the hills to the north of the Wall, the Venicones had restarted their long march to their homeland at first light. By mid-morning their pace across the barren hillsides was little better than a walk, despite the likelihood that the Roman cavalry would find them and recommence the deadly game that had played out the previous day. Many of Drust's men had not eaten anything since the previous morning. The day had dawned bright and clear, and was now warm enough to make the marching barbarians sweat heavily in the absence of any breeze to cool their labouring bodies.

'Come on, my lads, we'll all just have to keep marching if we're going to avoid being speared by those horse-shagging bastards! Another few miles will see us safe!'

The Venicone king's voice was hoarse with bellowing his commands, but there was still a hard edge to his shouted encouragement that compelled Calgus to open his legs and stride out, despite his own experience in the art of cajoling his own men to greater efforts. He had watched Drust fighting off the Roman cavalry the previous day, pulling a horseman from his mount's back with his war hammer's spike and cutting the stunned horseman's throat with a hunting knife the size of a short sword before he could recover from the fall, putting his head back in a savage howl of triumph as the soldier had spasmed out his death throes at his feet. More than once he had led the brief attacks that had punished those riders who had ridden too close to the warband, swinging his heavy pole-arm to fell their horses and leave the Romans easy meat for the men of his bodyguard clustered about him. Even the discovery that his body slave was missing, along with the gold torc that was the king's badge of authority, had failed to put the man off his stride, although for all of Drust's bravado, Calgus doubted that the loss was anything like as trivial as the Venicone was making out. Smiling wryly at his own acceptance of the need for pragmatism in defeat, when less than a week before he had been the leader of ten thousand warriors and on the verge of a victory to upset the balance of power across the entire province, Calgus put his head back and dragged down a lungful of air into his burning chest, forcing his feet to even greater speed despite the burning pains in his legs from the previous day's exertions.

'Are you enjoying this yet, Calgus?' He glanced wearily sideways to find that the Venicone king had fallen in alongside him, a grim smile on his face as he regarded his captive's gritted teeth. It's a long time since you walked so far or so fast, I'd imagine? I could always lend you a blade, of course, and let you make a run for it. We can't be all that far from your own land, so you might make it to safety.'

Calgus snorted, waving a hand at the treeless

hills across which the warband was making its laboured progress.

'You know as well as I do that their cavalry will be close at hand now, trotting happily along the trail we're leaving with their spears ready for use. One man alone in country this open wouldn't last any time at all.'

He coughed and spat phlegm on to the thin grass at his feet, and Drust laughed.

'This little march is doing you wonders, Calgus, we're working you harder than you've managed in years. And to think you could have been no more than a head on a pole by now if not for the Venicones.'

Calgus shook his head in disbelief.

'I imagine you're still planning to see me decorating some Roman's spear, unless by some good fortune they get to you first. So where are you taking me, my most unwelcome host?'

Drust leaned towards him conspiratorially, looking round to ensure that his people were all sufficiently engrossed in their own struggle to keep moving before speaking, his voice lowered to avoid it carrying.

'You know what, Calgus? I don't have the first idea. We're in the middle of nowhere, in land I've not trodden before in my life with a pack of Roman cavalrymen on our tail and nowhere to seek shelter from them. All I can do is keep my people moving, and hope that we'll reach some feature that we can defend against the Romans before they find some means of bringing us to bay on ground that suits them.'

The rebellion's former leader nodded, lowering his own voice in turn.

'Well, I know where we are, Drust, and I know where we need to go if you want a chance to hold these bastards at arm's length for long enough that they'll lose interest in . . . '

A tired shout of warning sounded from the rear of the column, and both men craned their necks to stare back down the wide track of flattened grass the warband was leaving in its wake. A body of horsemen had crested the rise over which the Venicones had laboured less than half an hour before, no more than a thousand paces behind them. Drust spat on to the ground, hefting his hammer, which, Calgus noted, still had a few hairs clinging to its flat face.

'It was too good to last. I'll leave you to contemplate your fate, and how you might want to buy yourself a little extra time rather than dying out here on their spears, while I make sure that our rearguard have their wits about them.'

* * *

Tribune Licinius had ridden hard, overtaking his leading squadrons minutes before their first sight of the enemy. Reining his sweating horse in alongside the leading squadron's decurion, he quickly sized up the sprawling mass of barbarians with a grim glance at his first spear.

'Still just as many of them as there were when we left them to it yesterday, I see. All we seem to have achieved is to have thinned them out a little, and even that small gain cost us over ten per cent of our strength. I suppose the best we can hope to achieve today is to harry them from their flanks, and keep them from any shelter so that they keep running all day. We need to herd them, like a flock of particularly vicious cattle, until they break from lack of food and shelter. Once they reach the River Tuidius we'll see how well they cope with an impassable obstacle to their front and hostile spears to the rear. Pass my orders to each squadron as they join the chase, no man is to go any closer to the barbarians than one hundred paces, other than to clean up the stragglers as they fall behind. We'll lose no more men unnecessarily today. I'm going for a look at them close up.'

He spurred his magnificent grey stallion forward, flanked to either side by the men of his bodyguard, and cantered up the length of the warband, keeping a sensible distance between himself and any bowmen lurking in their ranks. Spotting a small hillock a short distance from the barbarians' path he rode to its summit, using the elevation to look down into the Venicones. Licinius muttered quietly to himself as he watched the barbarians streaming past, straining his eyes to make out the finer details.

'That will be their king marching there, I can see his men clustered around him.' He squinted intently, a frown creasing his forehead as he caught sight of something that held his attention. 'And who's that marching alongside him in such a fine purple cloak, I wonder? I seem to recall my good friend Legatus

Equitius mentioning something similar in connection with another tribal leader of our recent acquaintance . . . '

⋆ ⋆ ⋆

Marcus and his small escort rode north-east in the wake of the rest of the squadron, following their tracks in the grass until they found their colleagues taking their lunch on the open plain, with lookouts posted to all sides. Marcus dismounted, summoning Double-Pay Silus with a quick gesture. The cavalryman walked briskly over to him and saluted crisply, his face expressionless, and Marcus took a deep breath before speaking.

'My apologies, Double-Pay, I've been in a foul mood ever since my closest friend in all the world was killed yesterday, and I've been taking it out on you. We don't have to like each other, but we do have to get along if this strange situation is going to work, so let's forget this morning and see how the afternoon shapes up, shall we?'

Silus nodded, his face relaxing a fraction.

'Agreed, Centurion.'

Marcus pulled off his helmet, scratching his head as he spoke, and the double-pay took a bite of the piece of hard bread in his hand, chewing vigorously as he listened.

'The barbarian we captured back there was a man I knew from another fight, in another place. He told us everything he'd seen in the last day, and part of what he told us was that there's a large tribal group heading east in front of us. They're making for a fort on the road to the north.'

Silus looked hard at the centurion, chewing on the bread for a moment before swallowing it.

'That'd be Alauna. I've been there a few times, it's a big place, built to house several cohorts, so that if the Votadini ever got stroppy with us we could use it as a base from which to put them back in their place. More of a trading centre now, though. It's got a decent-sized vicus too . . . ' The two men shared a knowing look. ' . . . which would make it the perfect place for them to find food, and take their frustrations out on any civilians who haven't already run for the hills. I'd imagine that a quick attack might find the blue-noses distracted enough to let us get at them before they even realise we're in the neighbourhood.'

Marcus nodded.

'Perhaps a careful scout forward would be the best idea? The rest of the squadron could go north to find Decurion Felix, and tell him what we've discovered, and perhaps we should send a messenger party to warn the tribune. Shall we go scouting, Double-Pay? I'd imagine that your deputy can manage well enough in your absence?'

Silus smiled happily at the prospect.

'Yes, sir. Perhaps you and I, Centurion, and a few picked men?'

* * *

Having overtaken the straggling Venicones, Tribune Licinius's men were a good deal more circumspect than they'd been the previous day. Even without their explicit orders to avoid a straight fight, there wasn't a man in the entire cohort who hadn't witnessed the fate of those men who had been unwise enough to ride close enough to the tribe's straggling mass and paid the price for doing so.

The cavalrymen had been horrified by the mutilated bodies of their fellow riders, and the horses that the tribesmen had swiftly and crudely butchered for their meat, and nobody was looking for the same fate either for himself or for the mount that was his closest companion. They rode alongside the warband at an easy pace, those men with bows loosing the occasional arrow in the hope of inflicting a wound that might cause the victim to fall out of the Venicones' punishing march north, while the rest of the cavalrymen ranged up and down the huge body of men searching for any signs of weakness to exploit. As the morning progressed, and the ground started to slope upwards again, a steady trickle of barbarians lost their painful struggle to keep up with the warband's main body, no longer able to cope with the pace being set for them, and were swiftly ridden down and speared. Their heads were unceremoniously hacked from their bodies and tied by their hair to the saddles of their killers as bloody trophies of the day's running battle, before the victorious riders spurred their mounts to rejoin the hunt, driving the warband pitilessly before them. As the morning wore on even the weak autumn sun's heat became torture for men denied any water since the previous dawn, and the number of tribesmen falling victim to their remorseless hunters grew steadily until most of the horsemen had at least a single head dangling by the hair to bump bloodily against their horses' flanks.

Marching alongside Drust, his throat so dry that his breath was coming out in harsh panting rasps, Calgus looked across at the grinning horsemen walking their horses less than a hundred paces away on either side of the Venicones.

'There's desperation in the air, Drust, I can smell it. And so can you, I'd guess. Any ideas?'

The Venicone king ignored him, keeping his gaze fixed on the ground rising before them as they tracked slowly up a broad dry valley.

'Your men need water, Drust. They're at the end of their tether for the lack of it. Another hour like this and you'll have another five hundred dead, and three times as many again before the sun sets. And in the morning you'll struggle even to get them back on their feet for lack of food.'

Drust turned a baleful eye on his captive, one hand caressing the hilt of his sword.

'Perhaps I should offer to trade the Romans your head for safe conduct.'

Calgus shrugged, watching a party of horsemen under a snapping dragon banner canter up the length of the warband.

'There's your chance, then. That'll be their tribune, mounted on that grey horse with the rather fetching armour. Why don't you call out and see if he'll bargain with you? I'd imagine you'll get a short reply, though. He's got you by the balls, and I'm pretty sure he's only wondering whether he can manage to have your head tied to his saddle horns without another night in the field.' He ignored Drust's tightly clamped jaw and continued. 'See how there are twice as many horsemen to your left as to your right? There's a reason for that, Drust, and that reason is that since those bastards know this ground like the back of their hands they want to keep you away from something.'

Drust raised an eyebrow, too weary to ask the question. Calgus grinned triumphantly, knowing that he held an advantage over the Venicone king.

'Water, Drust. Water and, although *they* don't know it, food too. Yes, I thought that might get your atten — '

His words were choked off as the Venicone leader took him by the throat, almost unable to draw breath past the pinching hold of Drust's fingers on his windpipe.

'Food, Drust . . . enough for . . . every man . . . still standing . . . '

The other man pulled him close, snarling into his face.

'*Where?!*'

Calgus shook his head, a feral grin showing his teeth despite the burning pain in his lungs.

'Fuck you . . . kill me . . . and you die too . . . '

Drust pushed him away, drawing his hunting knife and putting the point to Calgus's throat.

His voice was level again, the anger burned out by the truth of the other man's words.

'What food?'

Calgus shook his head, laughing despite the blade's cold point pricking at the stubble lining his throat, and the coughs racking his body.

'Put the sword away . . . If you were going to kill me . . . you would already have pinched my life out.' He hacked up a lump of phlegm, spitting it on to the turf at the other man's feet and sucking in a great draught of air before speaking again, his words acerbic in their new-found confidence. 'I'm not quite the fool you take me for, Drust. I knew that I might have to fall back to the north, and so I concealed enough meat in a location close to here for ten thousand warriors to fill their bellies three times over. Whole oxen, Drust, dozens of them. Butchered, salted, and wrapped in enough cloth to keep the worms out, and that was less than ten days ago . . . ' He paused, looking at the expression on Drust's face. 'And so the question, great king of the Venicones, is just what a belly full of meat for every man of your warband might be worth to you? And while you're thinking about that, just ponder what you'd give for a good strong stone wall between you and those horse-fucking bastards tonight.'

Drust stared at him without expression.

'You've already given me enough to tell me that I should drive my men to the west, and that I'm looking for a Roman fort that you've already conquered. What more do I need?'

Calgus smiled quietly, concentrating on

putting one leg in front of the other.

'I'm sure you're right. We're only ten miles from the place I've got in mind, so why don't you just blunder about the hills hoping to stumble across the exact spot, eh? I'll tell you what, why don't you just stop wasting time on me, and get on with leading your men to the right place. Feel free to come back for another chat if the need arises.'

He watched silently as the Venicone warlord turned away. Drust cursed quietly, looking about him at the cavalrymen walking their horses patiently on every side, their spearheads glinting in the sunshine. He shook his head, then turned back to his prisoner.

'Very well! What do you *want*, Calgus? Stop playing with me before I lose my patience!'

Calgus met his angry glare with a level stare.

'What do I want, in return for stone walls to allow your men to sleep without fear of sneak attacks, that and a belly full of meat? When your alternative is for those bastards to keep right on chopping your tribe up one man at a time, today, and tomorrow, and for as long as it takes them to run your last men into the ground? Let me think.' He put a hand to his chin, pretending to consider the question for a moment. 'I'll tell you what I want, Drust. I want to be a guest of the Venicones, an honoured ally, rather than a prisoner under threat of having my head handed to the Romans. That, and your sworn oath that my place with your people is safe for as long as I like. Either you guarantee my safety, and swear on something I can believe in, or I'll leave you to blunder round this country until you've all succumbed to your hunger and their spears. Those cavalrymen won't be going hungry tonight, they'll already have riders out hunting down game and collecting water, and their field supplies will be following close behind. They'll sleep a few miles away, where their camp fires won't be visible to you, and in the morning they'll find you again and keep on killing every man that falls out of the march. Best you choose now, Drust, while there's still time to make it to my refuge before darkness.'

* * *

After the midday meal Marcus's scouting party rode steadily away from the rest of the squadron, heading east in the direction that Lugos had indicated as the path taken by the tribal band from which he'd managed to escape. Looking to his left from the height of his horse's saddle, Marcus could see the distant figures of the rest of the squadron scouting away to the north, less the message riders he'd sent back to warn Decurion Felix of the warband's likely presence in Alauna.

The half-dozen men trotted their mounts along with each man set to watch an arc of terrain to ensure continual vigilance in all directions, and they rode in silence for the most part, still conscious of the clash of wills between their officers earlier in the day. After an hour or so Double-Pay Silus whistled softly, pointing at the ground before them with his spear.

'Tracks. Lots of boots.'

Marcus stopped his mount to look at the focus of his deputy's attention. The ground before them was thick with the imprints of the tribesmen's rough leather boots; every one pointed east.

'Any idea how long ago they passed?'

Silus shook his head with a faint smile.

'Could have been any time in the last few days, this ground's been damp enough to hold a mark for weeks now . . . '

Arminius dropped his bulk from Colossus, squatting to poke an exploratory finger into one of the bootprints.

'These prints are new, less than a day old. See the sharp edges? I'd say these are the men we're looking for. They were in a hurry too, the stride length tells me that they were running.'

Marcus looked about him before turning back to Silus.

'I think we should concentrate our attention on the front now. How far from the fort are we, do you think?'

'No more than five miles. We could work our way round to the north-east, there's a nice thick wood on a hill that'll hide us from anyone watching from the fort's walls. That's where I told Decurion Felix that we should regroup.'

Another hour's careful approach brought them within sight of the fortress town, its walls and gates apparently still intact. Leaving the rest of the party to wait in a thick copse of oaks, Marcus, Arminius and the double-pay slid quietly through the trees until they had a clear view of the settlement. Silus shook his head unhappily, staring at the fort's thick stone wall that loomed over the vicus's houses and shops, clustered around its sturdy main gate.

'If they realise we're out here, all they've got to do is stay in there with the gates shut, and we'll be reduced to starving them out.'

Marcus stared intently at the walls, searching for any sign of life.

'They might already have been and gone.'

Silus shook his head with the certainty of experience.

'Not likely. There'd be some movement in the vicus if they'd already pushed off, even if it was only a few survivors. As it is I'd imagine that they're busy drinking themselves stupid and screwing the arse off anyone who was stupid enough not to have run while the going was good. There'll have been more than a few of those poor bastards that reckoned it was a better gamble to stay with their homes and businesses.'

Marcus looked up at the sky.

'It'll be dark before we can get the infantry here, but we could at least make sure that Tribune Scaurus knows what's going on, and work out what to do tomorrow. You stay here, and make sure that Felix keeps his men out of sight when they turn up, and I'll head back down the road until I find the detachment. Come on, Arminius.'

* * *

'Gods below, what are they up to now?'

Tribune Licinius watched with disquiet as the Venicones veered from their steady march northwards, the warriors at the warband's head turning their path almost to the west in the space of a few seconds. The decurion alongside him shook his head in disgust.

'They're making for the bridge over the River Tefi, sir! Either they've been biding their time, or someone inside that bloody nest of rats has grown a brain.'

Licinius stared at the mass of warriors, his mind racing.

'Yesterday I wondered if I'd seen Calgus in their ranks. And today a body of men that has to date acted without any sign of understanding the ground they're stamping under their feet is suddenly making moves that look suspiciously as if they know where they're going. I wonder . . . ' Shaking his head decisively, he turned to his first spear. 'Well, we're not just going to sit here and watch them dig their way out of this hole, not after all the effort we've spent pushing them into it. Send three squadrons forward to gather firewood and prepare the bridge over the Tefi for burning if they get within a mile of it. I'd rather have to rebuild the bloody thing than watch them make their escape over it and then put it to the torch to stop us from following.'

The decurion saluted and turned away to issue his tribune's orders, and Licinius glanced over his shoulder, searching for the handful of men that were never far from his side, waiting their turn to carry his words across the empty landscape.

'Messenger!'

The warband seemed to be moving faster than had been the case during the long weary morning, as if some fresh purpose were invigorating the warriors, urging them to accelerate their pace across the rolling ground between them and the river. They surged forward, passing the burned-out wreck of Yew Tree Fort and splashing through the stream that skirted its walls in their determination to reach the river. The Petriana's riders paralleled their path, the leading decurions nervously calculating the distance between the leading tribesmen and the bridge for which they were driving until, with less than a mile left for the warband to run to the crossing, the lead squadron's trumpeter blew three notes long and hard, the signal for the bridge to be fired. A moment later the first smoke rose into the clear sky above the crossing, quickly darkening into a black plume as the fire took a grip on the structure's old timbers.

Licinius watched intently, muttering to himself as he waited for any sign that the Venicones understood the renewed depth of their predicament.

'So, what will you do now, eh? You can't go north, not with a river in the way, and south would be suicide, so it's either east or west. Come on, let's be . . . '

He fell silent as the warband, with a ragged cheer that was audible at a quarter of a mile distant, turned north and drove towards the river, seeming to slump into his saddle as he realised what had just happened, shaking his head as he turned to the senior decurion sitting alongside him.

'Balls! Well, that settles one thing, there's no doubt in my mind that Calgus has found some sort of home with the Venicones. First they make a lunge for the bridge and encourage us to burn the damned thing out, and now they're running for the river like fifteen-year-olds on a promise.'

The decurion nodded with a wry smile.

'Yesterday's disaster hasn't made the barbarian bastards any less sharp, then. Perhaps we should start running for another crossing place. I can't see them allowing us to use whatever handy little ford he's leading them to.'

The tribune sent ten squadrons, two-thirds of his remaining strength, away to the east to seek a point where they could ford the river and renew their pursuit of the Venicones, then led the remaining five in their close watch on the barbarians as they ran towards the point that had clearly been their objective since their initial change of direction earlier in the day. Eager to ford before the cavalry could get men across the river to resist their crossing, the tribesmen had their heads up and were running hard, the occasional man falling behind to be executed by the following cavalrymen, but the remainder covering the short distance to the river in a matter of minutes. Licinius watched with disgust as the tribesmen made their way across the ford, each man stopping to fill his water skin as the mass of barbarians made good their escape from the trap into which he had so carefully driven them. Something caught his eye, and he sat back, shaking his head in disgust.

'And just to add insult to injury . . . '

He pointed at the last few dozen men crossing the shallow river, walking backwards and throwing glittering objects into the stream as they retreated towards the far bank. It was too far for him to be sure what the Venicones were scattering, but even the threat of what he was watching was enough to change the game they were playing once more, further tilting the balance of power back to the barbarians.

'We have to assume that they're seeding the river's bed with tribuli, or something equally unpleasant, and there's no way I can risk losing dozens of horses to those sharp little teeth by trying to force a crossing. This ford will be unusable until it's been swept clean again, and that won't be getting done any time soon.'

His deputy nodded.

'East or west?'

Licinius shook his head.

'East. Ten miles to the nearest ford, and ten miles back again, plus whatever distance they can run in that time. They'll be tucked up nice and snug in whatever's left of the Three Mountains fort by the time we get back on top of them.'

* * *

'He looks like the sort of man we need.'

Rapax turned to examine the man that

Excingus was indicating, running critical eyes over the prisoner's face and body. The shackled legionary looked bored, standing in the weak afternoon sun and waiting to be told what to do next. His arms bulged with muscle, and a long knife scar ran down one cheek beneath close-cropped black hair. The praetorian strolled across to his place in the line of half a dozen men, tapping him on the shoulder with his vine stick.

'What did you do? And try not to make it sound like it's supposed to be funny.'

The disgraced soldier looked down his nose at the centurion, rolling his head as if to loosen stiffness before answering.

'I took a centurion's vine stick and put it up his ar — '

The praetorian struck with a speed that caught the prisoner completely unawares, ramming the stick into his solar plexus so hard that the breath exploded from his body, leaving him bent double and helpless.

'You didn't try hard enough.' He turned to the centurion of the guard. 'All right, what did he do?'

The centurion, recently come on duty and only too aware from the briefing from his predecessor of the heavily wielded authority of the praetorian's colleague, answered without any of the bombast that might otherwise have been the case.

'He stabbed another soldier to death in a bar fight. The dead man said something that upset him, apparently . . . '

'First offence?'

'Well, it *was* the first one where he got caught. He's been a right pain in the arse to the men of his century, forever pushing them around for their rations and just to show what a big man he is. He's also suspected of having given his watch officer a beating a couple of nights ago, but there wasn't any proof that it was actually him.'

'Name?'

The centurion of the guard shrugged without interest.

'No idea. I make sure they're fed and watered, and that they get a beating if they step out of line, but none of that means I have to pretend to be their mother.'

Rapax put his stick under the prisoner's chin, lifting his face to reveal a grimace of pain.

'Name?'

The soldier dragged in a breath before he answered.

'Maximus . . . ' He held Rapax's eye as the praetorian stared grimly at him. ' . . . Centurion.'

'I think I'll just call you Smartarse for the time being. Keep the manners and you may get out of here today. Why did you kill the other man?'

'He took the piss out of my century for getting cut to ribbons by the blue-noses when some idiot sent us south without any support, then pulled a blade when I gave him a spanking. So I took it off him and stuck it in his neck.'

Rapax nodded, calculating.

'And do you want to be freed, or would you rather rot here until your legatus comes back to hear your story? At which point he'll almost certainly order whatever there is left of your tent party to beat you to death for your crime. Something they'll be happy enough to do if they've seen battle while you've been tossing it off back here.'

The prisoner was clearly unconvinced.

'And in return, I have to do what? At least here I'm not risking a barbarian spear in my guts.'

'And in return, Legionary Smartarse, you have to join my party, and do whatever I tell you to do, whenever and wherever that may be. As it happens, we're going north, not south, north of the Wall to hunt for a fugitive from justice. I hear tell the rebellion north of the Wall is over, so you'll probably be safer out there than sat in here waiting for the Brigantes to break in and make you their new girlfriend. Choose now.'

He turned away, looking at the rest of the prisoners. Maximus stared at his back for a moment before speaking.

'All right.'

'All right what, Smartarse? Answer carefully, or I'll leave you here with the skin hanging off your back.'

'Sorry. Centurion. I'd like the chance to join your party.'

'Good choice. Let's have Smartarse here out of these irons, Centurion, he's got some soldiering to do.' He turned away, focusing on the next man in the line. 'Now, what else do we have here . . . ?'

The centurion of the guard nodded to his deputy, who busied himself releasing the prisoner from his shackles, then stepped forward and tapped each man's chest with his vine stick.

'Thief, thief, attempted murder . . . not very successfully from the look of him . . . rapist, and my special favourite, sleeping on guard.'

Rapax stopped at the rapist.

'Attempted murder doesn't look like he could pick a successful fight with my old mother, never mind collar a traitor. I don't like thieves, and the only thing I like less than a thief is the sort of weak-chinned fool that lets his mates down by falling asleep on duty. Eh, Sleepy? Your mates will make very short work of you when they're given the chance, and good luck to them.' He pointed at the rapist. 'I'll take *this* one, though.'

The centurion of the guard raised an eyebrow.

'I suppose you know what you're doing, but he's a nasty case. Put it to a woman old enough to be his grandmother by force and then killed her, and nobody would have been any the wiser as to who the sick bastard that did it was if his good-luck amulet hadn't been found by the body. Even now he keeps denying it. *Shut it!*'

Having opened his mouth to contest the centurion's story, the rapist closed it again, his face a picture of misery.

'See, all he does is piss and moan about how it wasn't him, despite the fact that he left the evidence and has no alibi worth a toss. You're sure you want him?'

Rapax smiled back at him imperturbably.

'Yes, I think I'll be able to find a use for him. We'll have to call him Granny Fucker.' He beckoned one of his men forward, indicating the two reprieved prisoners. 'Take Smartarse and Granny Fucker to the stores and get them kitted up. Make sure they look like soldiers, and not the ragged-arsed jailbirds they so clearly are. And if the stores officer gives you any trouble, just give him the usual 'you really don't want to meet my centurion and his mate the corn officer' speech. Meet me at the north gate in an hour. And now, Varius Excingus, we'd best go and see how our wounded are doing.'

In the fort's hospital they found a single doctor on duty, a woman who seemed utterly untroubled by their combination of muscle and bluntly wielded power.

'I can't release either of your wounded, Centurion, because neither of them is in any condition to be released. You can see them now, if you like, but they'll all need at least ten days' rest if their wounds are to heal cleanly. Now if you'll excuse me . . . '

The two men exchanged glances. Excingus raised an eyebrow at the doctor's departing back, nudging his comrade in the ribs.

'Just the way you like 'em, eh? High spirited and ripe for breaking in?'

The praetorian shook his head with a wry expression, and waved a dismissive hand.

'Not that one. There'd be a dozen nearly recovered soldiers in our faces if I so much as laid a finger on her. She'd be more trouble than she could ever be worth.'

His partner nodded sagely.

'I'm sure you're right. You'd better go and

have a few words with your men, then, hadn't you? Tell them we'll collect them on the way south once we've dealt with the Aquila boy. I'll go and do some research on the quality of the wine in the officers' mess.'

Rapax waved him away in mock disgust and strolled down the hospital building's narrow corridor, peering into each small ward in turn until he saw a face he recognised. The guardsman in question smiled wanly at his centurion, saluting despite the fact that he was sitting in bed with heavy bandages swathing his right thigh. The centurion looked around the four beds, finding two of them vacant and the last one inhabited by a heavyset bearded man who was fast asleep, a thin line of drool staining his pillow. Rapax squatted by his soldier's bed, keeping his voice low to avoid waking the sleeping man.

'How are you, then, my lad? Got the arrow out in one piece, did they?'

The guardsman nodded, holding up the iron arrowhead that had been buried deep in the muscle of his thigh earlier that day.

'Nice job she made of it, gave me some sort of honey mixture and I hardly felt a thing. Hurts a lot now, though . . . ' He bent closer to the centurion, beckoning with his hand to bring his officer's head closer to his mouth, whispering despite the lack of anyone else in the room to hear his words. 'There's some right chatty lads in here with us. *Tungrians*. Wounded at some big fight in the hills a few days ago, just starting to get their wits back about them and happy to talk the day away, if a man's willing to listen.' Rapax nodded silently. Having enough intelligence to know when to keep his mouth shut had been part of the reason he had recruited the wounded guardsman in the first place. 'Anyway, it seems that the lady doctor is a *very* close friend of one of their centurions and has been all summer, ever since he arrived from Rome. A centurion by the name of *Corvus*.'

Rapax raised an eyebrow in appreciation of the news, patting his man on the shoulder.

'Very good work. I'll make a point of coming back for you once we've found this 'Corvus' and put him where he belongs. For now you just concentrate on getting that wound healed. You're no use to me if you're not fit for battle.'

The praetorian nodded proudly, happy to have his officer's favour.

'I heard you were having a look at their prisoners. Found anyone worth recruiting?'

The centurion shrugged.

'I might have, it's too early to tell. There's one big lad that might have the makings, if I can be sure he'll do what he's told. He's quick enough with a blade from the sound of it . . . '

'And you'll have fun finding out?'

Rapax met his man's knowing look with a slight smile.

'Don't I always?'

* * *

Marcus and Arminius rode south at a brisk trot once they were out of sight of Alauna's walls, and able to use the road again. After an hour's riding they reached the spot where they had taken lunch, and Marcus reined his horse in, struck by a sudden impulse.

'Let's ride over to the spot where we captured Lugos.'

Arminius raised an eyebrow.

'You have a soft spot for the man, it seems.'

'I respect the man's courage . . . '

The barbarian shrugged his agreement, and the pair turned their horses off the road and cantered out to the copse where they had destroyed the desperate Selgovae remnant earlier that day. After fifteen minutes' riding into the late afternoon sun's glare Marcus spotted the lone warrior, and altered his horse's direction slightly.

'There he is. He doesn't seem to have moved since we left him, though . . . '

Lugos looked up as the riders cantered up to where he stood, then returned his gaze to the rough grave he had dug for his brother in the intervening period. Marcus and Arminius dismounted and stood facing him in silence, both men unwilling to break the grieving warrior's intent focus on his brother's last resting place.

'Was younger brother. Was five summers younger. No family left now . . . ' Marcus watched in grim silence as a single tear ran down the barbarian's cheek. 'Nothing left now. Death come soon.'

Arminius snorted, shaking his head.

'Very true. There are several thousand soldiers

not far away over there . . . ' He pointed at the setting sun. ' . . . any one of whom will be delighted to claim your head, but that's only if you get lucky. Worse than that, they might not kill you, they might just take a big lad like you for a slave. If you stay here you're likely to end up cutting down trees or digging for silver on starvation rations for the rest of your life.'

Marcus stepped round the grave's earth mound and stood face to face with the grieving warrior.

'He's right. If you stay here you will end up in a work gang, that or you'll be transported so far from your homeland that this place will be no more than a distant memory for the rest of your days. Come with us. We have other men like you serving with us, men who have been betrayed by Calgus. We can find a place for you, I'm sure of it.'

Lugos lifted his head and looked at the Roman with disbelief.

'Fight for Rome?'

Marcus shook his head.

'No, for yourself, and for others like you. We have one more job to do, before the winter sets in. We have to free the Dinpaladyr from Calgus's men.'

'Men like Harn?'

'Yes.'

The barbarian was silent for a long moment.

'And Alauna? Tell you, Harn insult goddess. You fight for Alauna?'

Arminius laughed again, a deep chuckle this time.

'Already he's bargaining with you. I like this man!'

Marcus smiled wryly at the warrior, raising an eyebrow.

'I expect my tribune is going to want to deal with Harn and his men before we march north. Although just how we're going to get inside those walls is beyond me.'

To his surprise, Lugos snorted derisively.

'You forget lesson from Carvetii fort. Get inside not the problem.'

* * *

Tribune Licinius stood on the slopes of the hill overlooking the former Roman fortress of Three Mountains, his horse happily cropping the lush grass while he gazed down at the abandoned fort below.

'The buildings have all been burned out all right, but the walls still look stout enough. I suppose Calgus was in too much of a hurry to get south to do anything other than torch the place and keep moving, which has played well enough for him now that he's forced to fall back on . . . '

He stopped in mid-sentence, pointing down at a huddle of men toiling at something outside the fort's walls.

'You've got better eyes than me. What in Hades do you think they're doing?'

The decurion at his side squinted down at the warriors on the flat ground five hundred feet below them.

'It looks like they're . . . digging? Yes, they're definitely trying to unearth something. There, that group are dragging something up from their pit. It looks like . . . like . . . '

'Like a sack full of salted meat, perhaps?' Licinius's voice was rich with irony. The decurion looked round at him, uncertain of his meaning. 'And there was me thinking that Calgus had met his match, that he'd lost his edge in the face of our overwhelming force. Just one day later I discover that not only does he have enough wits left about him to guide a Venicone warband clean out of the trap we've laid for them, but he also had the foresight not very long ago to have food stored here, just in case he was forced to retreat this way. King Drust had best be very careful that he hasn't got a snake by the tail.'

* * *

Rapax strolled up to the north gate to find his man waiting with the two released prisoners, both men fully equipped with arms and armour and sporting pensive looks.

'Well, well, Smartarse and Granny Fucker, don't you both look pretty.' He nodded to the guardsman. 'Very good. The stores didn't give you any problems, then?'

The guardsman grimaced, shaking his head dismissively.

'If you've met one storeman, you've met them all. A touch of the whip always has them running.'

Rapax smiled knowingly.

'Good, well done. Right, you two, let's go for a little walk, shall we?'

He led the three men through the gate, ignoring the surprised looks from the soldiers on guard at the sight of such a small party walking out on to what was, for the time being, tribal ground, and opened out his stride once the wicket gate was closed behind them.

'Come along, then, the pair of you, let's see how fit you are.'

Half an hour later, marching to the east after the long climb from Noisy Valley to meet the military road that ran along the line of the Wall, and with both men panting horribly under the unaccustomed load of their weapons and armour, he allowed their pace to fall back to a normal march, enjoying the burning sensation in his calves after so long without proper exercise.

'Feeling a bit tired, are we, gentlemen? Perhaps we ought to take a breather. Follow me!' He led them away from the road, and through the trees until he found a small clearing that would suit his purpose perfectly. 'Let's stop here for a little while, shall we? Relax. Take the load off your feet. There's no need for ceremony now, you've shown that you can drive along at the forced march with a full load, so just take it easy for a moment or two.'

He watched the two soldiers out of the corner of his eye as they slumped to the ground, both allowing their shields and helmets to lie on the grass, while the guardsman stayed on his feet and with a hand on his spear, knowing what was coming. The rapist lay back on the ground, dragging his breath in noisily with his eyes closed, while the murderer sat with his back against a fallen tree and his eyes searching the clearing, clearly equally exhausted but retaining enough awareness of his surroundings to have a curious eye on the centurion stood before him.

'So, soldiers, a rude reintroduction to the military pace, eh? Feeling nicely exercised, are we? Ready for your next test?'

The murderer's eyes narrowed, while his fellow convict lifted his head slightly to look up at the officer. Rapax smiled broadly, enjoying himself for the first time in several days.

'Your next test, gentlemen, is very simple. It is a test of your stamina, your skill at arms, but most of all it is a test of how well you listen and how well you respond to orders. The instructions for the test are very simple, but you're only going to hear them once so fucking *listen*!' The murderer tensed his body, ready to jump to his feet, while the rapist propped himself up on his elbows, looking puzzled at the sudden change in Rapax's demeanour.

'I've brought you both here for a reason, you maggots. For your next test there is only one instruction, and that is that very soon one of you is going to be the last man standing, while the other one is going to be a bleeding corpse. Go to it!'

He stepped back from them, watching the comprehension forming on the rapist's face even as the murderer pulled the sword from his belt and threw himself full length across the clearing to punch the blade through his rival's armour, and deep into his guts. He smiled quietly with the doomed man's first scream of outraged agony, watching as the victorious soldier ripped the blade free and thrust it into the rapist's throat to finish him off, a thick stream of blood bubbling in the dying man's windpipe. The victor stood up and turned to face him, his face fixed in the snarl that he had worn from the second that the meaning of Rapax's instructions had sunk into his brain. The centurion stepped forward into sword-reach without a hint of concern and took the bloody weapon out of his hands, patting him on his blood-spattered cheek.

'Good boy! Maximus, wasn't it? I think you're going to be rather good at this.'

* * *

Calgus smiled quietly to himself as the first load of meat was carried in through the shattered fort's empty gate arches. Drust was standing alongside him, with a look on his face that combined irritation and relief.

'Well, Drust, there's my end of the bargain satisfied. I took the cavalry off your back for long enough to get into the shelter of these walls without any further attacks, I led you to the one place for fifty miles where you can hold off an army, never mind a few hundred tired horsemen, and I've provided you with enough meat to put your men back on their feet ready to deal with anything those fools can throw at you tomorrow. I trust I can now depend on you to keep to your word, and that I'll be safe with your tribe for as long as I seek shelter with you?'

The Venicone leader nodded his assent, watching as his men lugged their heavy burdens into the fort and dropped them in front of the waiting warriors.

'You'll have a place with us for as long as you wish, provided you keep yourself to yourself. If I get any hint that you're making the slightest attempt to undermine me, however, I'll have you nailed up for the Romans to find when we leave this place. Do we have an understanding?'

Calgus nodded slowly.

'Yes, Drust, I think we understand each other perfectly. And when will we be leaving?'

The Venicone king looked about him, as if taking stock of the fort's stout stone walls.

'You buried enough meat to feed every man here for days, and the river will provide for our water needs, so I see no need to break camp until the day after tomorrow at the earliest. Those cavalry fools can stand on that hill and stare down at us all they like, they'll never dare to try forcing their way in here with so few men. Perhaps they'll get bored and leave us in peace . . . ' He paused, looking quizzically at Calgus's face. 'What?'

The other man shrugged.

'Nothing really, I was just wondering if there might be some value in sending out a few of your sharper men after dark to have a quiet look at their encampment. With a little bit of luck they might even take a captive.'

Drust nodded slowly, raising his eyebrows in

appreciation of the idea.

'A Roman prisoner. Information and sport for my men, something to take their minds off their surroundings. You might have something there.'

* * *

The sun was well below the western horizon by the time Marcus and his companions had found the detachment's overnight camp, and another hour passed while he made sure that his horse was fed and watered and sought out Martos.

'Prince Martos, there is a man I would have you meet. I found him wandering on the plain today, and took him into my custody rather than leave him to his fate, and in return he gave me news that I believe you'll want to hear.'

The Votadini nodded his agreement, and Marcus waved a hand at Arminius, who was lurking near by with Lugos, and the German escorted the reluctant Selgovae to Marcus's side. He nodded gravely to Martos.

'Greetings, Prince Martos. I trust that Two Knives here has told you the story of our hunt today, and how we ended up adopting this stray warrior to save him from sitting out on the plain until some undeserving soldier either took his head or sold him into slavery?'

Martos looked at Marcus, tipping his head to one side, then looked up at the silent Lugos, taking stock of the massive warrior's blood-stained clothing.

'I have the feeling that there is more to this story than you've told me so far . . . '

Marcus took hold of the Selgovae's right arm and turned it over to display his legion prisoner brand.

'We came across a party of men this morning on the plain, and rode them down, all bar Lugos here. I recognised him at the last moment as a man I fought with some weeks ago, while he was a captive of the Sixth Legion, and put my spear up. He tells me that he was forced into a warband by Calgus's men, and that he managed to escape in the confusion last night. The rest of the . . .'

He stopped, realising that Martos's face had taken on a hostile cast.

'This man is Selgovae?'

'Yes, but . . .'

The Votadini prince bridled with anger, putting a hand to his sword.

'You bring a warrior from the sworn enemies of my tribe to me, and expect him to be welcome at my fire? When his fellow warriors are busy plundering my tribe's home, and destroying my life!?'

Lugos took a step back, and for a moment Marcus tensed ready to unsheathe his own weapons, but Arminius put a heavy hand out and clamped it over the prince's sword hand.

'I suggest you listen to what the man has to say. Then judge how you should act.'

Martos stared into his eyes for a long moment before shrugging off his grip, and placing both hands on his hips.

'Very well. Speak, Selgovae, but do not expect to find me sympathetic to your tale. Your tribe has done more hurt to me and mine than a lifetime of retribution will put right.'

Lugos looked at Marcus and then shrugged, speaking in the language shared by the tribes.

'I understand. The Selgovae tribe has done many wrongs in one short summer. This man has every right to be angry for it is true, Calgus did murder his king.' He bowed to the bristling Votadini prince. 'Prince Martos, I went to war the first time of my own choosing, happy to fight the Romans and force them to leave our land, but I saw things in the first few days of our war that made me sad for my brothers. Death without reason, and things that would make our goddess turn her head away. Now a Selgovae warband has marched into Alauna, a holy place. They can only bring more disgrace on the Selgovae people, and I want nothing to do with this. More than that, I will do whatever I must to rid the shrine of their defilement.'

'Alauna?' Martos closed his eyes in despair, then opened them and turned to Marcus with fire in his eyes. 'Alauna is a sacred place, and long accustomed to the protection of your soldiers. A warband of any size will rip into the inhabitants and find no resistance worthy of the name. We must march on them tomorrow, and put an end to whatever suffering they are inflicting on my people!'

Marcus nodded.

'Agreed, but easier said than done. The fort at Alauna is intact, and it appears that they are strong enough to mount an effective defence. Tribune Scaurus will want the threat removed before he passes north, but he won't be able to ignore the fact that the time he can give to doing so is limited. Lugos here, however, has an idea as to how we might be able to resolve this problem in a swift and suitably bloody manner — if you're willing to play a part that might not come naturally to you and your men.'

* * *

The detachment's command conference was in full swing, and Tribune Scaurus's tent filled with officers by the time Marcus managed to disengage himself from the discussion between Martos, Arminius and Lugos. He stopped inside the doorway, saluted and turned to leave, intending to return at a quieter time to explain his proposal to his tribune, but Scaurus waved him into the gathering, calling for a chair.

'You've arrived at just the right time, Centurion Corvus! Perhaps you can tell us what's happening on the other side of the hill?'

Taking the offered seat, the weary centurion told the assembled officers the story of the day's events with a swift economy, watching the faces of the men around him as he outlined the likely fate of those of Alauna's inhabitants who had failed to flee. First Spear Canutius seemed unconcerned, unlike Frontinius and Neuto, who had both clearly served in the fort at some time or other to judge from the sick expressions both took on as the point of his story became clear. Unexpectedly, the first man to speak was Tribune Laenas.

'We should bypass this insignificant band and leave them to their own devices, Scaurus. Our duty is clearly to push on to the north and storm this 'Dinpaladyr' place. Any delay or detour might be construed as a failure to do that duty.'

Scaurus turned his head to look at his colleague, realising with amazed anger that the man was serious.

'Any man that accused me of any shyness with regard to my duty would stand need of both a sword and the skill to use it, *Tribune* Laenas. I've got ten years of service on the frontier with Germania, and my scars are all on the front of my body.'

The legion officer reddened and looked down at the floor after barely a second's withering stare from his temporary superior. His first spear smirked slightly, and Marcus found himself scowling at the centurion in disgust.

'My, ah, apologies, Scaur . . . Tribune Scaurus, I sought in no way to impugn either your record or your willingness to do your duty.'

Scaurus waved the apology away, looking slightly guilty at having browbeaten his colleague in the presence of their respective subordinates.

'Forget it, colleague, I know the spirit in which you spoke and I agree, we can't afford to spend any time camped out round five hundred barbarians when there's a tribal capital we're under orders to free. But I will not simply pass by and leave the inhabitants of Alauna to their fate. Nor can I leave five hundred Selgovae warriors loose in our rear, for that matter. You've seen the fort, Centurion Corvus, was there anything that sprang to mind with regard to getting in without a long siege?'

Marcus shook his head.

'No, sir, there's no quick way in without the legion's artillery to bang a hole in the walls. If the warband chooses to stand and fight, it could take us days to get men on the walls, and we already know that the Selgovae will fight like cornered rats. But somebody said something to me during the ride here that's making more sense every time I think the problem over. Perhaps getting in isn't the real problem?'

An hour or so later, with the last details of their plan for the following day agreed, Scaurus wearily dismissed the officers to their cohorts. As he'd half guessed would be the case, Laenas waited in his place while the others filed out, a penitent expression on his face. Raising a hand to forestall any apology, Scaurus shook his head.

'No, colleague, it's me that should be apologising. I was hasty and overbearing with you in front of our brother officers, and I should have reacted differently. I know you meant no harm by what you said . . . although you might reflect on a better way to have made the point?'

Laenas nodded glumly.

'I know I was wrong, Rutilius Scaurus, and truly it's me that must make amends. You had every right to be angry. I all but accused you of cowardice. Being the son of a powerful and outspoken man doesn't make for the best training in diplomacy.'

Scaurus shrugged, putting a hand on the younger man's shoulder.

‘Well said, and best we just both forget the whole thing. Our men will be looking to us to show a united command, given the risks we’re going to be taking over the next few days. Let’s try to give them what they need, eh?’

⋆ ⋆ ⋆

With the sun beneath the horizon, and the warband’s watch fires burning brightly at all corners of the fort’s walls, half a dozen men slipped quietly through the fort’s north gate, on the side facing away from the Roman camp. Their faces were darkened with mud, and their swords were strapped to their backs to leave both hands free without the risk of a scabbard catching on a rock or tree, and betraying them with unexpected noise. Moving slowly and silently, they eased around the fort’s walls until they reached the southwest corner, pausing for a moment to get their bearings under the night sky’s diamond-strewn vault before loping away towards the nearest of the three massive hills that stood guard over the Roman outpost.

Calgus ran with them, dragging the cold night air into his lungs with the delight of a man who had stood close to death only a day before. Drust had acceded to his suggestion that his local knowledge would be invaluable to the raiders with some reluctance, but had seen little choice once he realised the importance to Calgus’s tribe of the mountains towering over their refuge.

‘The hill closest to these walls was the Selgovae’s tribal capital, Drust, before the

Romans ever set foot on this land, and I know it as well as I know the lines on the back of my own hand. Allow me to guide the raiding party and I will take them around to the far side of the enemy camp, where the cavalrymen will walk without fear of attack behind the wall of their spears. I am your best hope of this night resulting in the capture of a suitable subject for our questions, rather than the loss of half a dozen of your men to no effect.'

The small party crossed the open space between the shattered fort and the hill's ancient and deserted settlement at a steady pace, every man alert to any sign of a Roman patrol, or for any hint that they might be the hunted rather than the hunters, but they reached the slopes of the northernmost of the three hills without either incident or alarm. Calgus took the lead, keeping their path close to the settlement's rotting wooden palisade in order to make the best use of its looming moon shadow, padding carefully through the darkness with one eye to the east where the Petriana wing's camp had been thrown up that afternoon. The Roman watch fires lit the camp's earth walls perfectly when seen from the hill's elevated perspective, and Calgus stopped the raiding party to point out in whispered tones the side from which he intended making their approach.

'You see, to their north they have men patrolling every fifty paces, all watching the men to either side? To attempt abduction there is to cut our own throats, they'll have a hundred men on top of us in no time. To the south, though . . . '

The Venicone warriors gathered around him followed his pointing arm. The camp's southern face was far less well guarded, with only the occasional patrolling soldier to be seen.

'We circle round to the place where the shadows lie deepest, and then we set up a lure and wait for a Roman to take the bait that we offer. I know these men, and the way they think, and I know how to bring one of them to us in complete silence for the sake of his own greed. Follow me.'

* * *

Centurion Cyrus stood in the knot of men facing Tribune Licinius as the Petriana's commander addressed them in the torchlit area in front of his command tent.

'It may be time to face the facts, gentlemen. The Venicones have wriggled out of the trap we set for them, with the aid of that devious bugger Calgus, and now they sit pretty behind walls that used to be our stronghold, with food and water enough to see them through tomorrow from the looks of it. They could hold Three Mountains against a force three times our strength without breaking sweat, and they may well be capable of outlasting us here. So, we can stay camped here and keep them bottled up in the fort, until the time comes for them to drive for the north again, or we can leave them to it and head south to join the rest of the army in putting down the Brigantes. I suspect that the latter choice might well be a good deal more satisfying than sitting here waiting for the buggers to do something.' He looked around the twenty or so decurions gathered about him, spreading his hands in invitation. 'Any views, gentlemen, before I make the decision?'

One of the more headstrong decurions spoke out quickly, hardly waiting for the sound of his tribune's voice to die away.

'They've killed more than enough of our men. I say we stay with the bastards to the end, until they fall to their knees with hunger and pray for a quick death!'

A few other members of the group nodded, although Licinius could see a larger number whose faces were creased in frowns. He raised a hand to the most influential of them, inviting him to speak.

'Titus?'

The decurion in question, a good ten years older than the first speaker, stepped forward a pace and looked about his brother officers with a hard stare.

'I say we leave these dunghill vermin to fester in their own shit. They are too many for us to take unaided, they mean nothing now that they seek only to run for the safety of their own land, and we can only throw more men after those we've already lost if we seek to pursue them further. To the south our own people may be in peril from the Brigantes, and my choice would be to ride to their aid, rather than to sit here watching these tattooed animals thumb their noses at us.'

He stepped back, his face flushed red with the unaccustomed attention, and a number of the older officers nodded and spoke quiet encouragement to him. Licinius opened his mouth to speak, but the words died as a third officer raised his hand to speak, waiting until his tribune had gestured for him to continue.

'Cyrus?'

The man stepped forward, pushing through the throng of his brother officers into the torchlight.

'Tribune, I say we have a third choice. Yes, we can ride to the south and war with the Brigantes, or stay here and ride herd on this rabble a while longer. Or we could, should we choose to do so, head to the north-east, and provide support to our brothers who have ridden with the Tungrians . . . ' Licinius's eyes widened slightly with surprise, unclear as to what motivation the officer speaking might possibly have. ' . . . After all, they've been sent north to liberate the Votadini tribal capital with barely sufficient strength for the task, and our speed and spears would doubtless be highly valued by their officers.'

The men around him were clearly equally as surprised as their tribune, and a moment of astonished silence hung over the group before Licinius spoke again, a faint smile gracing his face.

'So, gentlemen, we could stay here and hope to catch the Venicones in some error, or we could go south to a fight we know is even now raging across the northern frontier. And yes, we could even ride to aid the Tungrians in the liberation of the Dinpaladyr. Since there's no clear opinion in the room to which we can all cleave, I will consider the question overnight and tell you my opinion in the morning. Thank you and dismissed. Decurion Cyrus, a word, if you will?'

The tribune waited until the other officers had all left before speaking again, walking across to stand close to Cyrus, his voice kept low to ensure that his words remained between them.

'I would have found the words 'Support our brothers the Tungrians' a little hard to swallow coming from almost any of my officers, but to hear them coming from you was downright amazing. Have you been at the Falernian? Or is there some other piece of information you might like to share with me?'

The decurion kept his face imperturbable, shaking his head in response to the question. His answer was delivered in stiff, formal tones, his gaze locked on the tent's canvas wall.

'No, sir. I'm simply aware that there's a third of our strength out there to the north-east with the infantry, and since we're here anyway . . . '

Licinius held his questioning gaze for several seconds before turning away.

'And you'd be sure to tell me if there were *anything* you felt I needed to know?'

His subordinate nodded firmly.

'Of course, sir.'

The tribune walked around him slowly, his eyes fixed on the other man.

'Good. It's just that I still have the feeling that there's something I'm missing here, some reason why you'd want me to march the wing to join the Tungrians. And with your reputation for being a man of substance, a man with an eye to the main chance . . . '

He stopped in front of Cyrus, looking him up and down.

'One last chance, Decurion, and with no disrespect to your previous answers which I will happily overlook on this occasion should you choose to change your story. You really have nothing more to tell me?'

The decurion simply shook his head, never meeting his superior's gaze.

'Very well, off you go. Just bear in mind the way I'm likely to react if I discover that you've been keeping anything from me.'

* * *

Calgus led the Venicone warriors silently round to the Petriana camp's southern side, keeping to the darkest shadows and moving with a slow, cautious stealth calculated to avoid their being detected by any listening patrols the Romans might have out in the scrubland that surrounded their turf walls. When he judged that they had reached the optimum spot for their purposes, less than fifty paces from the patrolling sentry closest to them, he halted the group wordlessly and indicated that they were to spread out a few paces and take cover. Taking a silver pendant from his neck, he swiftly tied its leather cord to a tree branch, and silently stripped away any vegetation that would obstruct its line of sight to the men patrolling the camp's walls. He outlined his plan to the Venicones in a harsh whisper.

'When one of them comes to take this trinket, we will wait until he is in the act of removing it from the branch, then hit him from all sides. You,' he pointed to the warrior Maon, whose blow had flattened him during the Roman attack on his camp, 'you knock him senseless and put him over your shoulder, and then you all follow me away from here. We should be well away by the time they even notice that there's anyone missing, and by then it'll be far too late.'

Maon frowned.

'What if more than one of them comes for your bait?'

Calgus simply shrugged, tapping the hilt of his sword.

'Take whichever of them goes for the pendant, and put anyone else to your iron. We only need one.'

He reached up and spun the silver disc on its cord until the leather had a dozen or more turns to unwind, feeling the tension fighting his fingers.

'Ready?'

The men around him all nodded somberly, realising that they were about to lure a dangerous prey to them, and Calgus released the disc and allowed it to spin freely, the polished metal flickering as the moon's pale light reflected from its whirring surfaces. Sliding into the cover of a bush, he stared through its foliage at the

Roman he could see standing guard on the camp's western entry, willing him to look up and see the disc's silver twinkle in the darkness that surrounded them.

* * *

Cyrus strode from the tent with his face set stone hard, seething inwardly at the tribune's words and fearful of the potential consequences of his own failure to confess the prize that he still hoped would be his, despite the urge to tell his superior officer the full story. That fool Octavius had no idea of what he was capable of doing, or he would never have allowed him within a hundred miles of the deal, whether he was short of ready coin or not. Ignoring the sentry standing solitary guard on the camp's western gate, he pulled off his helmet and its felt liner in order to allow the night's cold air to take the itch from his sweat-sodden hair. No, he would find whatever idiot soldier was willing to sell the torc to the stores officer for a pittance and double the offer Octavius had made him, cutting the halfwit storeman out of the deal at a stroke. There would be no intermediaries between the frontier and Rome, just a two-year wait for his discharge and then a leisurely journey to the heart of the empire. He would have plenty of time to find the right man to broker the sale of the Venicone king's badge of authority to a wealthy collector on his behalf, and his presence and the story that he was the man who had hacked the barbarian king's head from his shoulders would help to ensure that the price paid would be a steep one. He could comfortably expect a hundred thousand from the sale, he estimated, enough money to . . . He snapped out of his reverie as the flicker of something shiny in the bushes to his right caught his eye and turned back to the sentry, ignoring the fact that the man looked half asleep.

'Stay here, keep your mouth shut and keep your fucking eyes peeled. There's something in the undergrowth and I'm going for a look.'

Pulling his helmet back on, he strode towards the spot where he'd seen the momentary flash of light, drawing his sword and scanning the ground around him suspiciously before returning his gaze to whatever it was that was hanging from the tree, now less than ten paces from where he paused to look around and sniff the air. He could see it now, a disc of metal hanging from a low branch.

'Must have snagged when the bastards came through, or been left as a marker and got forgotten. Their loss . . . '

The decurion sidled forward with his sword ready to strike and his other hand outstretched to take the object from its resting place, his attention fixed on the trinket. He didn't see the massive Venicone warrior who rose silently from the ground to his rear, an axe handle gripped in one huge fist, or even suspect the trap until the last second, with the rush of air as the stave's heavy shaft swept round in a vicious arc that ended with a thunderous impact with his helmet, smashing him to the ground despite the protection of its iron plate. Scrabbling disjointedly at the ground beneath him, shakily attempting to get back to his feet in defiance of his reeling senses, he felt another pulverising impact land on the helmet, and then knew nothing more.

6

The next morning was bright and cold, a harsh wind from the east making the Selgovae tribesmen occupying the Alauna fort huddle deeper into their thick woollen cloaks. They had gorged themselves on the fort's stores the previous evening, and taken their pleasure of the vicus's remaining inhabitants in an orgy of alcohol and rape, and many of the warriors were still the worse for wear by the middle of the next morning. A handful of corpses were scattered across the fort's cobbles like bloodied rags, left where they had been butchered by drunken tribesmen, and a faint echo of the stench of blood was carried by the biting wind. The faint cries of distress from those of the vicus's inhabitants that still lived bore witness that not all of the tribesmen had yet drunk themselves to the point of insensibility.

The tribal band's leader sat in the detritus of the former commander's residence, chewing on a piece of salted meat and basking in a quiet feeling of satisfaction. After their escape from the destruction of Calgus's forest camp his men had run long and hard to evade the inevitable pursuit, and to have found such ready shelter and food was little less than divine intervention. His warriors could recoup their strength over the next day or two, and the fort's intact walls and gate would protect them from any Roman units that happened across their hiding place. As he sat grinding the near-indigestible meat between his teeth, one of his men burst into the room, his sword drawn and a wild look in his bloodshot eyes.

'Harn, there are Romans advancing from the south! Looks like a legion!'

From the elevated vantage point offered by the fort's walls, Harn could see a long column of infantry approaching from the south, moving with a deliberate speed rather than hurrying to the attack as he would have expected. Straining his eyes, he could see that the leading soldiers were indeed legionaries, their detachment standard fluttering gaily in the wind, the stylised representation of a bull immediately identifying them as belonging to the hated 6th Legion.

He stared bleakly over the fort's stone rampart, looking across the empty landscape to the north and reckoning the odds. 'It would be *them*. At least there's no cavalry to be seen, and none of their stone throwers either. We could hold this place for weeks, given the amount of food they left behind, or we could make a run to the north without fear of being ridden down. It's a pity there's no way to know if they'll bottle us up in here, or just pass by and head north.'

As if in answer, the advancing cohorts' trumpets blew again, and the column split into three, one body of men deploying to the east and another to the west, while the foremost cohort spread across the southern arc. Within minutes the whole southern horizon was lined with troops apparently awaiting the order to advance to encircle the fort. Harn frowned out at them, looking again to the north.

'Looking to wrap us up, are they? If I could be sure there was no cavalry out there . . .'

A horseman rode forward from the advancing column with a dozen soldiers trotting alongside him, his armour and weapons shining in the morning light, and reined in his horse at the edge of any possibility of bowshot from the fort's walls. A warrior close to Harn put an arrow to his bow, ready to chance his skill at the distant target, but the Selgovae leader tapped him on the arm and shook his head.

'Let's hear what the bastard has to say before you start trying to put an iron head into his guts. Signal him to approach!'

The Roman officer dismounted, and approached the captured fort's walls with an escort of six men with shields held ready to protect him. At fifty paces from the wall he halted, bellowing out his challenge loud enough for every man gathered on the walls to hear it clearly.

'Selgovae warriors! I am Scaurus, the tribune commanding this detachment, and the man with your fates held firmly in my hand! You have been lucky enough to find a fort not yet burned out, and now you line its walls wondering whether to wait us out behind them or run for the north. I cannot make that decision for you, but I can provide you with a small clue as to the treatment you can expect when we break in and put an end to your pathetic remnant. I have with me a cohort from the imperial Sixth Legion, and these are men who want little more than a chance to take their swords to you. These soldiers are not the raw recruits that were shipped in from Germania, after the act of betrayal that destroyed six cohorts of their comrades. These are men who actually witnessed what you did to their comrades at the battle of Lost Eagle, and they are desperate to take prisoners rather than heads in this coming battle. Any of you that survive will find your last few hours more painful than anything you could ever have imagined. Anyone that lives through this day will be skinned, crucified and left for the birds to feed on their raw flesh!'

Harn leaned forward over the fort's wall, shouting back his defiance.

'Why are you telling us this, Roman?! Do you want us to run before you, and save you the grief of having to come and fight for these walls?!'

The tribune's reply was swift and purposeful, and sent a chill down the spine of any man listening with the learning to understand him.

'No, Harn! All I want is for my sworn oath to Mithras, for retribution on you and your tribe, to be honoured! And for that to come to pass, I need you to stay right where you are, and wait for us to break in and start killing you!'

Harn spoke out of the side of his mouth, not taking his eyes off the Roman.

'Shoot him.'

The archer raised his bow, pulling back the arrow until its iron head was level with the weapon's wooden frame, but before he could loose the missile at the Roman officer, and with a sudden scurry of movement, a group of twenty or so warriors threw open the fort's main gate directly below them. While they ran down the vicus's main street, heading for the road to the north, one of the running men, a big man at once strangely familiar and yet hard to place, turned as he ran and shouted back at the men lining the fort's walls.

'Run while you can! The goddess is angry with us, and she has called on these Romans to deliver her justice!'

Harn stared at them in amazement for a moment before turning to look down into the street below him at the cluster of warriors gathering around the gate. More than one of their staring faces was pale with fear, and, as he drew breath to put some iron in their backs with a swift series of barked orders, one of them bolted through the gate and down the road in the wake of the running men. An arrow from the waiting archer, loosed at Harn's terse command, left the man face down and writhing in the road's mud, but the damage was already irretrievably done. In the next few seconds half a dozen others followed, hurdling their fallen comrade without a second glance, and the trickle quickly turned into a flood as panic spread across the fort at the sight of more and more men running for their lives. Harn cursed loudly and bounded down the steps in pursuit of his fleeing warriors, his shouts of rage lost in the chaos of the warband's flight.

Scaurus watched and waited as the warriors streamed out of the fort, letting the rearmost men clear the vicus before signalling the legionnaires forward at the double march to occupy the fort, and secure it against any attempt by the Selgovae to return to the sanctuary of its walls. He watched for a moment longer, waiting until the running warriors were well clear of the fort, then turned to his trumpeter.

'It seems that the barbarian's ruse has succeeded. Give the signal.'

The trumpeter blew his horn, sending three long peals echoing across the empty landscape, and on the hill to the left of the fleeing barbarians a long line of horsemen crested the ridge to stare down pitilessly at their prey. Their upright spears glittered in the morning sun's cold light as Decurion Felix rode out in front of his command, his normally urbane voice raised in a stern tone of command.

'*Spears!*'

As one, the riders swung their spears down from the vertical to point down at the straggling line of barbarians fleeing to the north along the road's long dark stripe, five hundred paces down the hill's slope. Felix looked up and down the line of his men, while his mount Hades snorted and twitched beneath him, eager to run at the enemy warriors. Raising his voice to be sure he was heard along the line's length, the decurion issued his last instructions.

'No sword-work today, gentlemen, there are too many of them for us to stop and duel! Pick a target, and whether you hit or miss, ride through them and turn back for another go! Don't go spearing *our* barbarians, they're the ones at the front with the rags round their arms and their hands in the air! And listen for the horn signal; we need live prisoners as well as dead barbarians! *Advance!*'

He turned Hades through a prancing half-circle and led the detachment down the gentle slope, raising his good left hand in the command for the riders to keep pace with him while allowing Hades to lengthen his stride to a canter, controlling the stallion effortlessly with his knees as the hill's slope eased towards level ground. In the line of horsemen behind him Marcus clung tightly to the big grey's flanks with his thighs, pulling at the reins to lift the beast's head, physically holding him back from charging at the enemy prematurely. Looking to either side, he saw Arminius to his left, clinging to his mount with a look that combined exhilaration and terror, while to his right Qadir's face was alive with the joy of the moment as the chestnut mare increased her pace to match the animals to either side. The line of horsemen cantered steadily across the open space between hill and road, quickly closing the gap between them and the barbarians, who, rooted by the horsemen's thundering approach, had drawn their weapons and were readying themselves to meet the attack. When the horsemen were a hundred paces from the barbarians Felix lowered his hand to point at the enemy, his command delivered in an almost incoherent bellow.

'*Charge! Petrianaaa!*'

Ignoring the bit's hard grip on his mouth,

Marcus's mount responded to the command the way he had been trained, putting his ears back and gathering himself for a split second before he sprang forward to rip across the turf in a furious gallop that took the pair out in front of the surging line of horsemen. Horse and rider seemed to float across the ground, such was the animal's speed and purpose, and he barely had time to pick a target from among the mass of screaming warriors before they were upon the quavering barbarians. Putting his spear through the man's throat more by luck than judgement, Marcus dragged the blade free as the horse, disdaining any show of fear at the warriors' screams of pain and anger, burst through the enemy line in a scatter of bodies. He pulled the big grey back round for another pass through the enemy just in time to see disaster strike. As Arminius's mount Colossus crossed the road's slippery surface the animal lost balance, sending barbarians flying as he slid into them in a flurry of skittering hoofs before crashing unceremoniously to the ground with the German trapped under his struggling mass. The horse fought his way back on to his feet in an ungainly lunge, and a stray hoof clipped his helpless rider's head, stunning Arminius and sending him headlong across the road's hard surface. The warriors around him, momentarily scattered by the horse's flailing limbs, raised their weapons in anticipation of an easy kill, ignoring the chaos around them.

Marcus instinctively dropped his shield and pulled the grey up sharply, releasing his mount's reins and lifting his left leg to slide over the horse's side to the damp turf, dropping momentarily to one knee before springing back to his feet. Two hundred paces to the north Martos and his chosen warriors, having managed to outpace the fleeing Selgovae, had slowed to a walk while they watched the Roman cavalry tear into their sworn enemies. Lugos, standing among them and yet still in no way accepted as one of them, saw Arminius fall unconscious to the ground and reacted swiftly, drawing his long sword and sprinting back towards the embattled Selgovae with a roar of challenge. The leading Selgovae warriors turned to meet him but were already too late, one man falling with his stomach torn open while another reeled back with his nose spouting blood, smashed by the giant's massive fist.

Running towards his friend's prostrate and unmoving body, Marcus calculated fast as several barbarians moved in for an easy kill, their swords poised to stab into the unconscious German. Drawing back his spear as he ran, he slung the weapon at the man closest to Arminius and missed by inches, sending the weapon's wickedly sharp blade clean through the huddle of warriors without drawing blood, but scattering them in surprise and giving him the precious few seconds he needed to close the distance between them. Drawing his swords and screaming his rage at the warriors gathered around his friend, he confronted the half-dozen men poised for the kill. In the split second before the fight began, as the warriors took stock of the lone soldier confronting them, a rider clattered past the group, expertly spearing one of the barbarians in the back, dropping the man twitching across Arminius's body. With that, Marcus was among them with his swords blurred arcs of polished iron. Hamstringing the closest man with his spatha, he ducked under a wild swing to gut his attacker with the gladius's short blade, sending him tottering back with the stinking, slippery rope of his torn guts hanging from his body. Another warrior stepped in quickly, his powerful sword-thrust skating along the Roman's hastily raised gladius and slicing open Marcus's arm. Grimacing with the pain, the Roman arced his spatha through a full turn to hack the Briton's arm off at the elbow before he could pull back, then reeled away from the fight as another of the warriors caught his helmet a glancing blow with his sword, lucky in that the blade skidded across the iron plate rather than chopping through it and into his skull, but still seeing stars from the blow. As he staggered backwards, momentarily unable to defend Arminius from the men around him, Lugos burst into their midst, having run the length of the stricken warband at risk of being taken for a Selgovae and speared by the Petriana's riders, now roaming the battlefield at will.

Swinging his long sword two handed, he waded into the surprised warriors, scattering them in disarray as the heavy iron blade hacked deep into first one man's spine, toppling him limply to the road's cobbled surface, then chopped into another man's skull, sending him reeling out of the fight with his eyes rolling upwards to display only the whites. Shaking his head and blinking away the momentary confusion caused by the sword's impact with his helmet, Marcus hefted his weapons and stepped forward to confront the two men who had followed him out of the fight, a movement to his right catching his eye and making him back away again, shouting a swift command at the embattled Lugos.

'*Lugos! Down!*'

In a thunder of hoofs a half-dozen riders bore down upon the Selgovae and rode down the tribesmen, one of the horsemen smashing his chosen target reeling to the ground with a crunching impact between his shield's heavy brass boss and the hapless warrior's face, and Marcus found himself standing alone, surrounded by prostrate bodies. A horn was blowing insistently somewhere across the field, the signal for prisoners to be taken now that the fight was almost over, and Marcus stared about him, marvelling at the destruction wrought by the Petriana's men in the short time it had taken to avert the unconscious German's death. He walked slowly on shaking legs to where Lugos was sitting up after diving to the ground to avoid the cavalrymen's questing spears, straining to pull the big barbarian to his feet before wearily sitting down alongside the prone body of Arminius.

* * *

By mid-morning, Drust's torturer believed he had the key to the captured decurion's continued silence under his knives. He spoke quietly to his chieftain as he sharpened the tools of his trade one last time, dragging their razor-edged blades across the whetstone more for the effect that the rasping noise might have on the man strung up and waiting for the resumption of his attentions than to improve their already fearsome edge.

'He's a hard man, my lord, a warrior you would have been proud to fight alongside had he been born to the tribe. I have caused him great pain already, but he has given me no more than the occasional grunt as my reward. I can increase the level of pain he suffers, of course. I can sever the muscles that make his arms and legs work and leave him a cripple, saw off his manhood and show it to him before I blind him, if you like.' He looked back at the Roman, his eyes burning with defiance, before speaking again. 'But in all truth I doubt that this will break him, and he would die from the blood loss very quickly, and leave your men without the reward of hearing a Roman scream for mercy.'

Drust grimaced.

'Not what we'd hoped for. You have a better idea, I presume?'

The other man raised an eyebrow at the tethered Roman.

'I would say that he seems to be motivated by the need to avoid alerting his comrades to his agony at all costs. I would also guess that he is a proud man, and that to cry out would be to turn his back on his pride, to give in and show weakness at the end of his life. I do not believe that the knives hold the key to his tongue, but I think that he will speak readily enough if you can find a way to threaten him with the loss of his dignity. You must put him under the threat of the most degrading end that you have at your disposal.'

Drust stared at him for a long moment before nodding his reluctant understanding and turning to face the naked prisoner, looking him up and down to assess the damage already done to him by the torturer's knives before speaking.

'Fetch water. I need him wide awake.'

A warrior stepped forward and emptied his water skin over the Roman's head, and the cold liquid snapped his eyes open, wrenching him from the moment of respite provided by his loss of consciousness. Drust walked forward until he was close enough to the captive to prod his blood-smeared stomach.

'Well now, Roman, my expert in the art of persuasion tells me that he believes you cannot be broken by the use of his blades. He believes that you are too proud a man to allow yourself the slightest expression of pain or fear. And to tell you the truth, I am minded to believe him. Look at you — no, seriously, take a proper look at what he's done to you.'

The decurion stared back at him in silence with stone-hard eyes, their defiant conviction blazing back at the chieftain. Drust shook his head in mock sadness, turning away from his prisoner and looking out across the hundreds of men gathered to watch his humiliation.

'No, you'll keep your mouth shut no matter what I tell him to do to you, even as we wreck your body beyond repair, and at the end of that unhappy time all I'll have for my men's bravery in taking you from under the noses of your sentries will be a mutilated carcass of a warrior. Your fellow soldiers will revere you for the bravery of your death, and in time they'll erect an altar for you, somewhere where thousands of them will see it, to give them pride and fresh strength. Perhaps they'll name a new fort after you . . .'

He turned back to the captive with a half-smile.

'All of which is hardly what was in my mind when I ordered my men to bring me a Roman to make some sport with. What I had in mind was some screaming, something to put the fear of the gods into your comrades, and not a glorious end for you. So, I think it's time we tried something a little different. We think that you are a proud man, for whom any admission of weakness would be worse than death itself. So what, I find myself asking, would your reaction be to being degraded in the face of your comrades in a manner so gross that they will be revolted by what you have become?'

Cyrus's eyes narrowed slightly, and Drust smiled quietly back at him, seeing the Roman's face suddenly alive with the emotion he had been seeking to inspire in his captive.

'I thought that might get your attention. You see, there are men in every army who find the life away from women too much for them, and who turn to their comrades for the pleasures of the flesh. You, however, don't look like such a man. You probably make jokes about them, and use humorous names to make fun of the very idea, even though you know that this happens more frequently than you would ever admit to anyone from outside of your military world. And so what, I wonder, would your comrades think, what would they do, if we were to lash you up on the walls of this fortress and have a succession of my warriors bugger you in full view of your cohort. I have thousands of men, so I'm sure that a few of them will step forward when I offer the opportunity to fuck a Roman officer in the arse before we let my man with the knives finish what he's started. Perhaps a dozen of them would be enough to take that pride of yours and tear it into pieces so small that a man would have to get on his hands and knees to find them. And I'll guarantee you that nobody ever set up an altar to a man who got captured and ended up dying after taking a dozen barbarians in his backside.'

Cyrus glowered at him, his face twisted with repulsion and disgust.

'Nothing to say, Roman? Perhaps we could pull your teeth and allow two men to fuck you from both ends, just to complete the picture for your friends over there. 'Go to war with the Venicones', they'll tell each other for years to come, 'and if the barbarian bastards catch you they'll spit-roast you.' How about that?'

Cyrus spat a bloody wad into the dirt at his feet, staring down at the barbarian chief.

'Can I trust your word, Venicone?'

Drust raised an eyebrow at the growled response, taken aback by the unexpectedness of the Roman's retort.

'Trust my word? Why would that matter to a man facing imminent death?'

Cyrus grunted his answer from between gritted teeth, his voice pitched low to make the tribal chief lean closer.

'Because, King of the Venicones, I have information that I will trade for a quick and honourable death. I know where something is. Something that you have lost, and which can still be retrieved if you know where to look for it. If, that is, you have the balls to turn aside from your flight to the north.'

Drust's eyes widened, and he stepped in close to the captive, whispering into the Roman's ear.

'Tell me exactly what it is that you're talking about. If this is a trick I'm going to make you scream for mercy before you die.'

Cyrus grinned back at him through his pain, happy with the realisation that he had the Venicone chief hanging on his next words.

'You're missing something, Drust, something important. One of our soldiers found your golden torc in a tent, on the battlefield of your camp. The man you had entrusted to look after it was dead, with an artillery bolt through his spine, and so this soldier took your pretty piece of jewellery for himself. He tried to sell it to an associate of mine, who came to me for money to help him make the purchase, and so I know where that soldier is heading at this very moment, with your precious torc in his pack.' He spat another wad of bloody phlegm on to the ground at Drust's feet before speaking again. 'If you promise me, on your honour, to grant me a quick and honourable death, then I will tell you who that soldier was, and where he's marching. And I'll give you a clue to help you decide. His cohort has orders to march to the north, to a place close enough to this that you can be in battle with them inside two days. All you have to do is guarantee me an honourable death, and I'll tell you where.'

* * *

Arminius awoke from his temporary stupor to find Scarface sitting next to him under a clear blue sky, both of their horses contentedly cropping the grass where they were tethered a few feet away. He sat up with a gasp of pain, putting an exploratory hand to the lump on the back of his head, then looked about him, surveying the customary human detritus of any combat, hundreds of dead Selgovae lying where they had fallen, through pain-slitted eyes.

'What the fuck? I remember hanging on to that bloody horse for grim life, but then . . . '

Scarface snorted a laugh.

'But then your 'bloody horse' took a header, legs all over the bloody place, jumped back up and booted you in the nut. I might well have pissed myself laughing if I hadn't been so busy fighting off half a dozen of the hairy bastards, having left my spear stuck in the seventh.'

The German nodded, touching his head again as if to prove the story.

'I was lucky not to get carved up, then?'

'You were lucky that a certain young gentleman decided to hop off his own horse and fight the bloody Selgovae off you, that's what you are, mate.'

Arminius sank back on to the grass and closed his eyes.

'I might have guessed. How did he fare in the fight?'

'The centurion will be back soon enough; he went to get his arm bandaged, and make sure that Prince Martos is all right, given that he managed to avoid being skewered by this shower of donkey wallopers. He kept the long-haired fuckers off you long enough for these bowlegged bastards to get their shit in a pile and come to the rescue, him and that big Selgovae monster we spared yesterday. He collected a scratch and a couple of dents doing it, but I doubt it's knocked any more sense into him.'

Arminius got to his feet, his face taut with the pain in his head.

'I'll go and find him. And see who's doing all that screaming.'

He found Marcus sitting in a queue of men with light wounds waiting for a harassed bandage carrier to attend to them, and dropped to the turf next to him, ignoring the indignant looks of the men behind him.

'Scarface told me I'd find you up here. Any nice scars in the making?'

Marcus lifted the bandage covering his wound,

revealing a foot-long slice up his left forearm, the blood that had welled from the open flesh already mostly clotted.

'Nice. That'll be a good one to show off to the ladies once it's healed. Scarface said you got dented?'

He took the proffered helmet and examined the crease hammered into its surface.

'Impressive. And a good thing that whatever did this didn't get through it.' A noisy commotion from the small group of warriors who had been taken prisoner, held captive under the spears of the legion cohort, made him wince. 'Mithras, but I *wish* that shouting would stop! What are they doing to the man?'

Marcus lifted an eyebrow.

'We took nineteen prisoners, including their leader Harn and both of his sons. I'd imagine the noise has something to do with what the Votadini would like to do to them.'

The German caught the slight bitterness in his tone and nodded his understanding.

'Martos and his volunteers waited all night in the vicus for their chance to encourage the Selgovae to run for it. I suppose they had plenty of time to listen to the inhabitants of Alauna being raped and killed. Alauna being a Votadini settlement, you'll have remembered . . . '

He slapped the Roman on the shoulder encouragingly.

'I'll go and have a look, you stay here and get that scratch sewn up.'

He stood, rolling his head on his thick neck, and then leaned back down to speak quietly in the centurion's ear.

'And thank you for standing over me when I was helpless. I owe you a life.'

He strode away towards the source of the noise. In the middle of a circle of variously amused, amazed and horrified cavalrymen, Martos's warriors had erected a hasty tripod formed from the trunks of saplings felled from the copse behind which the cavalry detachment had taken shelter from view the previous evening. A group of his men had lashed a naked young Selgovae tribesman to the frame's apex by his bound wrists, his feet tied together to prevent him from struggling and his feet barely touching the ground, requiring him to stand on tiptoe. When they stepped away, having gagged him to stop his shouts of protest, one man remained in place before the helpless prisoner, a long-bladed knife held in one hand. Scaurus and Martos were watching the preparations with apparent interest, while alongside them an older man was being restrained by a pair of burly legionaries. Catching sight of his master, the German strode across the space around the prisoner and stood before Scaurus with a slight bow. The tribune greeted him with a wry smile, returning the bow with a nod of his head.

'You've recovered from your knock to the head, then, have you, Arminius?'

He nodded gingerly.

'Apart from a headache that may be with me until the day I die, yes, Tribune.'

Scaurus shrugged, raising an eyebrow.

‘Perhaps this is what will happen every time I order you on to horseback? You managed to end up on your backside the last time as well. Since the young centurion can clearly handle himself well enough to save both his own skin and yours, perhaps I should return you to your normal task of standing at my shoulder and glaring at anyone that comes near me?’

The German bowed his head slightly.

‘I will, of course, accept any duty to which you choose to put me, but I should point out that I now owe your centurion a life.’

‘In which case you’d best stay close to him a little longer, I suppose. I believe that your horse was unhurt in your accident, so perhaps you should reclaim it and prepare for our next move. And now, if you’ll excuse me . . . ?’

Arminius bowed again, watching as the tribune turned back to the barbarian being restrained by a pair of hefty soldiers beside him.

‘Have you seen enough of this to be sure I’m serious, Harn? I can’t say that I would enjoy having that young man tortured all that much, but then I’ve seen worse things done to my comrades over the years by men just like you, so please don’t imagine that it would trouble me in any way. And let’s not forget what we found when we searched the fort you’d just left in such a hurry.’ He looked at the fingernails of his left hand, nibbling at a rough edge before speaking again. ‘You know what treatment that boy will receive if I ask my ally Prince Martos here to let his man off the leash. In fact I’ll wager you know it better than most, given your master's tolerance for his men's brutality towards Romans, soldiers and civilians alike. Your man there will have his skin removed, one long strip at a time. Martos tells me that his man is an expert, and can keep his subject alive for up to a day while slowly but surely reducing him to a gibbering idiot with the pain of the whole thing. Or, of course, I can have your man there cut down and returned to his fellow prisoners. All that you have to do is swear to behave yourself, and provide me with just one little bit of help. Should you choose not to do so, I have quite a good supply of your men for these Votadini to play with. The same Votadini whose king your master Calgus murdered in cold blood, you will recall, and whose warriors were betrayed to us in order to remove the inconvenience they might have otherwise posed. I doubt they're going to get bored of hearing the screams of a dying Selgovae any time soon. So, what will it be?'

Harn stared at his feet for a long moment before raising his gaze to stare into the tribune's eyes.

'You'll spare that man his life?'

'Yes. I will personally take my sword and cut him down from where he's hanging.'

'And you'll keep these Votadini dogs from torturing any of my men?'

'If you keep your side of the deal, yes. It won't be hard, since they want what I want just as badly as I do. But I think you ought to listen to what it is that I want before you agree too quickly. Your man there will keep while we discuss how you're going to help us liberate Martos's people from yours. It's either that, or we'll all spend an entertaining day watching him peel your young lad there down to a strip of raw meat. And we have a plentiful supply of salt, should simple skinning get too repetitive.'

* * *

Rapax and Excingus swept into the hospital building in the middle of Felicia's rounds that morning, brushing aside her assistant's attempts to keep them from disturbing her. Excingus did the talking, while the praetorian stood impatiently in the background, tapping the floor with one foot in the manner of a man with a strong need to be elsewhere. The corn officer was insistent, despite the doctor's protests that she had more than enough to keep her busy in the hospital.

'I understand completely, madam, and I assure you that I wouldn't be asking you to leave your patients if this wasn't a matter of a man's life. Of course, we can all go and see Tribune Paulus if that's what's needed, but in the time that will take, this centurion's man will probably die . . . '

He stood waiting, while Felicia stared at her feet for a moment.

'He has a broken leg?'

Excingus nodded quickly.

'He slipped, jammed his foot into a gap between two rocks, then fell sideways. The sound it made was quite horrible. We didn't dare to move him, given that we were so close to the fort and your medical skills.'

She nodded decisively, turning to her orderly.

'Very well. Julius, could you fetch my instruments, please? And my cloak. Bring your own too, you might be required.'

Rapax stepped forward, shaking his head.

'No need, lady, we'll have all the men you need with us.'

Felicia raised an eyebrow at him.

'And your men are trained hospital orderlies, are they? I might well need some combination of a man's strength and a medically trained mind to free your man's leg. He's coming with me.'

The praetorian nodded his grudging assent, shooting a wry glance at his colleague.

'As you wish, lady.'

The party were mounted and on the road within minutes, the doctor and her orderly at the heart of a tight knot of riders who were waved through the fort's north gate, the purpose of their haste already made clear to the guards. They rode up the steep hill towards the wall's North Road gate in silence and were waved through the opened gateway with equal lack of ceremony. The party carried on up the road for another mile, until Rapax indicated a path that branched out into the open country.

'He's about half a mile down here.'

The party rode down the narrow track single file, with Excingus leading and Rapax at the rear, until they rounded a bend and saw the distinctive figure of a praetorian sprawled in the grass beside the path. Felicia jumped down from her horse with Julius at her shoulder, unaware that Rapax was close behind them and had drawn his dagger from its sheath. As the doctor moved in to take stock of the casualty's condition, he took a grip of Julius's hair and pulled his head back savagely, opening up the orderly's throat for a swift pass of the knife's blade. Felicia turned back from the unharmed soldier with a look of puzzled annoyance that changed in an instant to horror as her orderly's blood spurted across the grass, his body held upright only by Rapax's powerful grip on his hair as his eyes rolled slowly upwards. The praetorian pushed his tottering victim to the ground, leaning down to wipe his blade on the dying man's cloak before resheathing the dagger. Folding his arms, he stared back at the wide-eyed woman with a defiant glare, shaking his head slightly.

'You would insist on bringing him with you.'

Felicia's look of horror slowly transformed into understanding, her face hardening as she realised how badly she'd misread the two centurions' intentions.

'You want to use me to get to Marcus.'

Excingus nodded brightly over his brother officer's shoulder, a faint smile wreathing his lips.

'I told you she was clever enough to work it out on her own. Yes, my dear, we're going to hunt down your fugitive boyfriend, and you're going to provide us with the means of making sure he comes to justice quietly. Your Marcus

Valerius Aquila has been evading justice with his barbarian friends up here for long enough, and with your invaluable help we're going to put an end to his little game of hide-and-seek.'

Felicia shook her head defiantly, her chin jutting with anger.

'You'll get no help from me! Marcus is innocent of any charge your masters might throw at his family to justify theft and murder, and I won't be part of your evil!'

The corn officer strolled forward until he was close enough to the white-faced, trembling woman to see the sheen of tears forming in her eyes. When he spoke his voice was softer than before, almost apologetic.

'I'm sorry, my dear, but you most certainly will. When the time comes you'll beg for him to save you from the indignities you're being subjected to. You'll scream like a pig with a spear in its guts, and you'll provide us with all the distraction we'll need to do the job that should have been finished in Rome. Tie her wrists and put her back on the horse, we're riding to the north.'

* * *

'So now we march north and free the Dinpaladyr?'

Tribune Scaurus nodded tersely, watching as the young Selgovae warrior was cut down from the hastily erected wooden frame from which he had been suspended.

'Yes, Martos. Those are my orders, and now

that you've terrified this Selgovae remnant into obedience for me we'll strike as fast and hard as we can.'

The Votadini prince stared across at the captives, now huddled under the spears of the legion cohort and watching with evident resentment as the two centuries of Tungrians moved among their dead, carrying out the grisly task to which the tribune had set them.

'Obedience? From the Selgovae? I would rather trust a pack of wolves. These men will watch and wait for their chance to fight back and restore their lost honour. It would be better if we put them to the sword now.'

Scaurus shook his head firmly.

'No. *With* them I think we have a chance to get inside the gates of your tribal fortress. Without them we could be camped outside it for weeks, while the men Calgus sent to usurp you sit and laugh at us, praying to their gods for the snows to come early this year and abusing your people to their hearts' content. The prisoners will live just as long as they serve us, and your job, Martos, is to watch them like a hawk and make sure that they do. And besides, I have another trick up my sleeve with regard to ensuring Harn's total obedience.'

* * *

Tribune Licinius sat in the quiet of his tent, the daily rations report from the cohort's quartermaster unnoticed on the table in front of him, while his subconscious teased at the conundrum presented by the events of the previous night. Only minutes after their confrontation, Decurion Cyrus had marched out into the darkness beyond the temporary camp's walls and simply vanished into thin air. Logic told him that his officer must have been taken by barbarian scouts, and yet the man's behaviour just before his disappearance had been sufficiently strange to justify Licinius entertaining the possibility that he had chosen to disappear into the wilds for reasons that were as yet unclear. A shout from outside the tent snapped him out of his reverie, and another put him on his feet and out through the tent's door. A soldier dashed up to him, saluting hastily and gasping out his message.

'Tribune! The Venicones have got Decurion Cyrus!'

He hurried to the camp's eastern gate, pushing through the men gathered around the earth rampart to where a cluster of his officers stood watching the walls of the ruined Three Mountains fort in silence. A man's body had been lashed to a wooden frame on the stone wall's top surface, and a cluster of barbarians were gathered around him, staring out towards the Roman camp. As the tribune watched, his eyes slitted with anger, one of them cupped his hands to his mouth and bellowed something made unintelligible by the distance. Looking about him, Licinius saw that his bodyguard, ever mindful of his safety, had gathered around him. He made a quick decision, turning to the dozen or so officers staring at the scene playing out in front of them.

'I need to see what's happening here. Gentlemen, you and my bodyguard can accompany me to within bowshot of the walls. Any barbarian sufficiently brave to attempt an attack on such an ugly collection of specimens would have my utter respect, so I'm guessing we'll be safe enough. And besides, I have the feeling that Drust wants us to see whatever it is that he's arranged on that wall.'

He strode forward out on to the open ground between the cohort's temporary camp and the fort's blackened walls, his officers and body-guard fanning out around him and keeping their eyes open for any sign of either ruse or ambush, until their tribune halted at a distance he calculated to be at the very edge of bowshot. The men waiting on the stone wall's fighting surface parted, and Drust stepped forward, flanked by a pair of men with shields ready to deflect any attempt at missile attack. Putting his hands to his mouth, he bellowed a greeting to the Romans.

'Greetings, Romans! I offer you a truce if you'd like to come closer, and watch the entertainment I have arranged for my men.'

Licinius looked at the commander of his bodyguard, a leather-faced double-pay with the pale lines of old sword wounds decorating his muscular arms, and raised an eyebrow in question. The veteran soldier stared at the barbarians lining the fort's walls, and then grimaced and shook his head slowly.

'Not if it were my choice, Tribune, I can't guarantee to protect you if they have archers waiting behind the parapet. We should stay here.'

The tribune shook his head in turn, patting the other man's shoulder.

'That's one of my officers they're about to butcher up there. You'll just have to do your best, should this turn out to be a way to draw us in close enough for an attack.'

He motioned the men around him forward with the flick of his hand, his face set in dour lines as they drew close enough to the fort's walls to see the pitiful state to which their brother officer had been reduced. Barely recognisable as the proud and powerful decurion he had been less than twelve hours before, Cyrus had clearly been severely tormented since his capture. His body was a mass of cuts, its skin slicked with his blood, and his limbs were criss-crossed with the marks of a hot iron bar. Both of his eyes were closed behind swelling bruises from his initial beating, giving the impression that he was resting after his ordeal, gathering his strength for the last act in his gruelling drama. Licinius stopped barely twenty paces from the wall, nodding to the barbarian king.

'We're taking you at your word, King Drust. I would be failing in my duty to this man were I to refuse the opportunity to look into his eyes as he dies. And besides, the sight will help to strengthen my resolve to ensure that you end your days somewhere warmer and noisier, with a cord around your neck and your people either enslaved or scattered in their hiding places across the hills of your miserable land.'

The barbarian looked down from his place on

the wall and smiled broadly, nodding at the Roman's words.

'Your safety is assured, at least until our business here is complete. As to your pledge to gift me a trip to your imperial city for a chariot ride and an inglorious death, I'll respectfully decline. You're going to need more than a few hundred horsemen to scatter my warriors, and from what I've heard your army has other priorities at the moment.' He grinned wolfishly at Licinius, who in his turn kept his face blank of any emotion and gestured to the warlord to be about whatever it was he intended. Drust shrugged, lifting his hands in mock greeting. 'Welcome, Romans! It was good of you to come so far north with us while we make the journey back to our homelands! Tomorrow you may ride alongside us for a while longer, if you wish, north to the hills of my people, and the ground my men know as well as the hilts of their swords. And there, I promise you, we can make some real sport, a proper hunt rather than this slow procession, with every step taking you a little farther away from safety. Whether you'll still be the ones doing the hunting is a different question, of course . . . '

He paused, daring any of the men standing before the fort's walls to defy him, and Licinius felt compelled to roar back the answer that sprang to his lips without any conscious thought.

'It was our pleasure to make the journey alongside you, Drust! We especially enjoyed riding down those of you who failed to manage your gentle pace, and putting them out of their misery! That's something we expect to be doing a lot more of in the next few days!'

The Venicone warlord threw his head back in a laugh, his reply lightning fast.

'Aye, Licinius, tribune of the Petriana, as we enjoyed picking the shreds of horseflesh from our teeth once we'd finished our meal that first night. Although in truth we have so much meat now that your role of providing us with a convenient larder is really no longer necessary. And we may stay here a few days longer, if only to avoid our supplies going to waste.'

Licinius nodded, warming to the game the two men were playing, both of them ignoring Cyrus's battered body hanging motionless alongside the Venicone king.

'Yes, you were indeed fortunate to stumble over such a large cache of food. You should thank your gods that you took Calgus with you when you ran, I'd say, since such foresight has the mark of his cunning rather than any intelligence on your part. How is that slippery specimen of Selgovae duplicity? If he hasn't managed to depose you yet it'll not be for the want of trying!'

A long moment's silence hung in the bright morning air, neither man willing to speak again until at length the Venicone king spat on the wall's parapet and gestured to the prisoner lashed up alongside him, his arms and legs spread wide to render him helpless, and changed the subject to that which the Romans had been waiting for.

'As you will see, my men bumped into one of your officers in the darkness last night, and so they brought him back to our camp to see if we could make a little sport of him before the time to meet his gods arrives.' He paused, prodding the comatose body with one finger. 'He's provided us with little enough entertainment, but he's about to make up for that with the rather extravagant way that he's going to leave this life. You see, Romans, I've promised him an honourable death, to die on my men's iron rather than in some depraved and degrading manner . . . '

The hairs on the back of Licinius's neck stirred as if caressed by a cold breeze.

'And why would you make such a promise, Drust, when every other man you've taken alive in the last month has died long and hard, with their honour flensed clean away by your men's blades?'

Drust smiled down at him mockingly.

'Because, Tribune, he spoke nicely to me. Now be quiet, and watch your man take his exit, unless you want me to summon my archers to chase you away with their ironheads whistling past your ears.'

He held his hand out, holding Licinius's gaze with his own as one of his men put the shaft of a spear on to his palm, then turned with sudden speed and drove the weapon's blade deep into the helpless decurion's thigh, putting his weight on to the shaft to force the blade down through the limb's thick muscle and out of its underside until there was no need for him to hold the wooden shaft pointing back into the pale sky. Cyrus's eyes snapped open, and he strained at his bonds with knotted muscles, the cords in his throat standing out like bowstrings as the pain hit him in waves of red-hot agony, but no sounds left his mouth. A thin stream of blood ran from the wound, its paucity a testament to the amount of punishment that the decurion had already absorbed.

Licinius turned to find his first spear standing alongside him with a look that spoke volumes for his feelings about the man being tortured in front of them.

'Whatever else I might think of the man I've got to admit that he's got balls of brass.'

'Agreed. It's just a pity he seems to have had much the same between his ears last night.'

Taking another spear, Drust repeated the act, driving the weapon through Cyrus's other thigh and watching with satisfaction as the Roman once more contorted silently at the agonising pain being inflicted upon him. The men around Licinius drew in sharp breaths or turned their heads away, dumbstruck at the torture their comrade was enduring without making a sound. Taking a sword from another of his men, Drust leaned forward on the weapon's point, addressing the Romans arrayed before him in an almost conversational tone.

'I promised to make his death honourable. I didn't mention anything about it being quick.'

He pivoted and thrust the weapon's blade into the helpless decurion's guts, ripping it free in a stinking shower of blood and entrails. A deep groan of pain escaped the captive's lips, and his body twisted hideously in the ropes' unforgiving grip. Licinius spoke into the charged silence, raising his voice to a bark of command.

'*Decurion Cyrus!*'

The writhing body stiffened, and Cyrus's attention snapped down on to his commanding officer, his face distorted into a rictus of agony.

'Decurion Cyrus, you are dying with honour in the face of a brutal and remorseless enemy. You deserve the highest praise for your fortitude and stoicism. Now, before you die, tell me what it is that you've given to this barbarian!'

He glared fiercely at the dying man, willing him to answer. Cyrus opened his lips to display his teeth, clamped hard together against his suffering, drawing a quick breath to reply.

'Tribune! . . . I told him . . . about the Tung — '

Drust turned, ramming the sword into the Roman's throat and stopping him in mid-sentence with a horrible gurgle as what was left of his lifeblood ran down into his lungs and killed him in a few seconds of frenzied struggle for breath. The Venicone king turned back to stare down at the Roman officers gathered beneath him, his face flecked with Cyrus's blood and twisted in a snarl of frustration.

'Very clever, Tribune. I either allowed him to tell you something best left between the two of us or put him out of his misery to close his mouth.' He shrugged, a slow smile replacing the fury. 'No matter. I have his secret, and it remains exactly that. And you, Tribune, all of you dogs, have a count of one hundred to get yourself away from *my* walls. *On your way!*'

* * *

Ten miles north of the site of that morning's skirmish the detachment turned off the route of their march north and built the customary temporary camp. With the earth wall raised and the soldiers taking their evening meal, Scaurus had called his officers together for a cup of wine before darkness fell. Canutius had been delayed by a problem with one of his centuries, but both of the Tungrian senior centurions had attended with alacrity upon receiving the invitation, and found Tribune Laenas already in attendance. Sitting outside Tribune Scaurus's tent, cup in hand, First Spear Frontinius cast a jaundiced eye at the late afternoon sky and cocked an eyebrow at Neuto, shaking his head slowly.

'Rain before daylight, I'd say.'

His colleague nodded his head sagely.

'Yes. We should get them tucked up in their bedrolls early tonight; they're going to have a heavy day of it tomorrow.'

Scaurus raised an eyebrow but made no comment, allowing Tribune Laenas to fall into the veteran officers' time-worn trap.

'Do you mean to say that you gentlemen can tell what the weather will be doing just by looking at the sky?'

Frontinius nodded readily, his face a study in innocence.

'Yes, Tribune, when you've served on the northern frontier for as many years as myself and my colleague here, the weather no longer holds any mystery. And now, if you'll excuse us . . . ?'

He drank the last of his wine and stood to go, and Neuto, reading his expression, reached for his helmet and got to his feet.

'Yes, you'll have to excuse me too, Tribune, I've got a cohort to chivvy into their beds and a storeman to relieve of a new pair of boots.'

Laenas raised his hands to halt their departure, protesting at their apparent reluctance to further educate him.

'Gentlemen, gentlemen, not so *fast*! You can tell that it's going to rain from looking at *that*?' He pointed up at the sky, the clouds edged with gold as the sun dipped towards the western horizon. 'All I can see is the start of a sunset and a few clouds. What's the secret?'

The two first spears shared a glance, waiting for a long moment before Frontinius shrugged and turned back to face the legion officer.

'We'll tell you, Tribune, but you must promise to keep our secret between us. We don't want just anyone learning the secrets of frontier weather prediction.'

He stared at Laenas with a raised eyebrow, waiting until the Roman nodded his agreement, his face solemn.

'Your secret, gentlemen, is safe with me.'

The centurions stepped in close, beckoning the tribune from his chair and gathering round him in a conspiratorial huddle. Frontinius stared at him levelly, as if taking a gauge of the man.

'The secret of foretelling the weather in this harsh country is very simple, and yet known only to a few men. If we tell you this secret now, we are admitting you to a close-knit brotherhood of men who have this knowledge. Do you promise to keep it between us?'

Laenas nodded eagerly, his curiosity piqued beyond patience. Frontinius looked at his colleague, and Neuto nodded reluctantly.

'I suppose we can trust a tribune of Rome, a gentleman with a sense of honour. Very well, Tribune. The secret of predicting the weather here on the frontier . . . and you guarantee to keep this between us . . . ?'

'Senior Centurions Frontinius and Neuto, the phrase 'piss or get off the pot' is springing to mind. I'm sure you both have important duties to which you might be attending?'

The Tungrian officers nodded their understanding to a visibly irritated Scaurus, turning back to the tribune with pursed lips and raised eyebrows. Frontinius lowered his voice to a whisper, shaking his head almost inperceptibly

'The tribune gets annoyed because we haven't yet shared the secret with him.'

Scaurus spoke again without looking up from his scroll.

'I heard that. Get on with it.'

'Well then, Tribune, the secret of predicting the weather is this . . . '

Laenas held his breath with the tension, his eyebrows raised in expectation.

'Can you see that tree?'

Taken aback by the banality of the question, Laenas followed the first spear's pointing hand to stare at a distant lone tree on the horizon.

'Yes. Yes, I can see it.'

'And how far away would you say that the tree is?'

'Half a mile?'

'Excellent. If you can see that tree, or any other object at that distance, then it isn't raining.'

He stared at the Roman with a straight face, waiting for the other man to respond.

'Yes . . . I'd be forced to agree with you.'

'Excellent. So if you can see the tree, it's not raining. However . . . ' He raised a finger to underline the point. 'Colleague?'

Neuto inclined his head gravely, taking up the thread.

'If you can see the tree, and it isn't raining, it soon will be.'

The two centurions stood in solemn silence for a moment, watching the tribune intently. For his part, they told their own officers later that evening, he seemed to take it in good part.

'So if I can see the tree . . . if I've got this right . . . it will soon be raining.'

Frontinius nodded happily.

'You've got the measure of it. Use your new knowledge wisely, though, many men would cheerfully kill to have such insight. We . . . '

'*You* both have soldiers you could be beasting round the camp, if, that is, you wouldn't rather stay and regale my brother officer with further attempts at tent-party humour.'

The two men took their tribune's hint and strode away into their respective parts of the camp with a comradely nod to each other.

Scaurus cocked his head to one side ostentatiously, clearly waiting for something, and after a moment an outraged bellow of admonishment rang out as one of the pair spotted one of his men doing something outside the closely regulated activity prescribed for the soldier in question.

'Excellent! Normal service is resumed. Will you take another cup of wine with me, Tribune Laenas?'

The younger man paused for a second, as if expecting some further attempt at humour, then nodded his assent and sank back into his chair.

'Your officers, it seems, are little different to mine. The first cohort's centurions are always looking at me in that sideways manner they use to indicate my lack of suitability for my role in their closed little world.' The bitterness in his voice caught Scaurus's attention, and he dropped the scroll to give his subordinate his full attention. Laenas was staring out into the camp, his eyes unfocused as he gazed fixedly at the horizon. 'They're so secure in their certainty as to how everything works, and they give me so little help . . . '

Scaurus went into his tent and returned a moment later with a fresh flask of wine and two cups, pouring them both a generous measure.

'Here, this might help. It's the genuine Falernian, believe it or not, and it seems to have survived the journey in a more or less tolerable condition.' He took a sip, raising an eyebrow in mute appreciation. 'You were saying?'

Laenas shifted uneasily in his seat, taking a deep drink from his cup.

'I'm not a crybaby, you understand. My father made sure that I got enough training as a boy that I would give a fair account of myself were I ever to see any fighting, and yet these legion men have a way of reducing me to helpless frustration every time I try to impose my authority on them.' Scaurus watched him over the rim of his cup, taking stock of his officer's state of mind as he spoke. 'The battle to take the barbarian camp, there's a good example. I had orders to break in from the north with this very cohort, a critical role, Legatus Equitius called it, and I was very clear with my officers that we were going to play our part to the full. And yet when we got within spitting distance of the objective my first spear started prevaricating, finding reasons why we weren't ready to attack, and delaying our deployment until Licinius rode up and all but accused me of being afraid to advance into the enemy camp.'

Scaurus winced.

'Gaius Manilius Licinius does have a very special way of communicating his disappointment.'

Laenas nodded, warming to his subject.

'Quite so, but to make it worse, First Spear Canutius promptly started making it pretty clear to Manilius Licinius that *his* desire to get into action was being frustrated by *my* delaying tactics. Nothing I could challenge without looking even more of a fool, of course, but Licinius clearly went away with the impression that I'm not fit to command. And so I find myself here . . . '

' . . . under the command of a social inferior and probably doomed to this ignominy for the rest of your short career?'

Laenas winced at the words, for all that Scaurus's voice had been perfectly level.

'Yes, I'm sorry for my poor showing at our first meeting, I really wasn't thinking very clearly. Too busy feeling sorry for myself, I suppose.' He took another mouthful of the Falernian. 'Forgive me, colleague, I'm making a mess of this career on so many fronts I'm not sure what to do for the best, but I never meant to impugn either your office or your honour as a Roman gentleman.'

Scaurus smiled back at him.

'Cheer up, Tribune. Your first spear clearly has a problem that we can easily remedy, and you'll have plenty of chances to prove that there's fire in your belly in the next few days. As for first spears Frontinius and Neuto, their humour is of a different kind to that you might be used to suffering. You show them that you're fit to command and they'll soon enough come round to your side. Now, will you take another cup? That one seems to have emptied itself all too quickly. We'll drink to long life and glorious victory, and then I must spare some time for Prince Martos. I promised that I would read him the letters he captured during the raid on Calgus's tent, and it's about time I made good on the offer.'

7

Later that evening, with the evening meal taken and the three cohorts' soldiers busy about their usual campaign routine of cleaning their equipment and improving the edges of their blades, the detachment's tribunes and senior centurions came together in Scaurus's command tent to discuss the next day's march. Decurion Felix was ordered to attend as the commander of the Petriana's detached squadrons, and he brought both Double-Pay Silus and Marcus with him, despite the sour looks that the gesture earned him from First Spear Canutius. Scaurus opened the discussion, pointing to a sketchy map of the ground that lay before them to the north.

'Well then, gentlemen, I've ridden this route to the Dinpaladyr before, so I've made a start at drawing a map of the ground we'll have to cross to make our approach. Martos has given me all the help he can, but he's more of a warrior than a geographer, so I'm afraid that our knowledge of the route is still a little sketchy.'

'Tribune?' Double-Pay Silus stepped forward with an embarrassed salute, drawing inquisitive stares from the assembled officers.

'Double-Pay?'

'Begging your pardon, Tribune, but I've been riding these hills since I was a lad. The Petriana used to mount security patrols in the rear of the northern wall when it was still manned. We spent most of our effort in the west, keeping the Selgovae on their toes, but we rode this ground as well, when we could spare the time. Even after the pull-back to the old wall we still got around a fair bit, making sure the frontier tribes didn't mistake our retreat for weakness. I could add some detail to that map, if you'd like me to.'

Scaurus nodded, handing him a stick of charcoal. The cavalryman stood over the parchment for a moment, his eyes moving across its sparse detail, then put the charcoal to the map, drawing fresh lines with swift, confident movements.

'The River Tuidius runs here, and meets the sea here, and it can be forded by infantry here — but by cavalry here, and here.'

Scaurus's eyes narrowed, taking in the additional detail and its implications.

'So we can only cross the river in one place?'

Silus nodded.

'Yes, Tribune, unless we've got the time to build a bridge?'

The tribune shook his head with a grim smile.

'Neither the time nor the engineers, I'm afraid. So, if the men that Calgus sent to take control of the Votadini have their wits about them, they'll have scouts watching the ford and our element of surprise will be lost before we even cross the river.'

Silus shook his head.

'Not necessarily, Tribune. As I said, these two points can be crossed by horsemen. The animals will have to swim, but I've done it myself more than once.'

'How likely would it be for a body of horsemen to remain unobserved once they were on the far side?'

Silus nodded sagely.

'A good question, sir.' He drew on the map again, sketching in a range of hills that ran to the north-east between the river's course and the Votadini capital. 'The enemy scouts will most likely be waiting here . . . ' He pointed to a spot on the range just to the north of the infantry ford, ' . . . but we'd be crossing here, ten miles to the west and well out of their view. If we then went over the hills to the northern side we could make our approach without their ever suspecting we were there.'

'And if the Selgovae think to put watchers on *that* ford?'

Silus pulled a wry face.

'At the worst they could kill every man in that detachment before we ever got our feet out of the water, Tribune. A handful of decent archers could pick us off without any trouble at all.'

A silence hung in the air for a moment, broken at length by the thud of Scaurus's finger hitting the map at the spot indicated by the double-pay.

'Very well, Double-Pay, you've just earned yourself a temporary field promotion to decurion. And if you can take a party of men across the Tuidius and win us back the element of surprise, I'll ask Tribune Licinius to let you keep the title.'

Silus stiffened his back and saluted crisply.

'Thank you, sir. I'll get a party of volunteers together and make the preparations tonight. We can be across the river and on the far bank drying out our kit by early morning the day after tomorrow, and the road north will be clear by the middle of the day. It'll take you that long to get across the ford at the usual campaign pace.'

Scaurus nodded decisively.

'Then I suggest you get to it, Decurion. And now, colleagues, let's see what shape our three cohorts are in after the day's events . . . '

Outside the command tent both Felix and Marcus shook Silus's hand in congratulation, while the new decurion shook his head in bemusement.

'All that time wondering if I could ever get the promotion, and then an officer I hardly know drops it on me without any warning.'

Marcus smiled wryly, clapping a hand on his shoulder.

'Tribune Scaurus, as you are learning, isn't a man given to over-considering an idea if he can see its potential. Besides which, we haven't actually got across the river and dealt with the watchers yet, have we?'

Silus nodded briskly.

'True enough. And I need thirty men that can swim. What about your men, Centurion, there must be a few of them without the infantryman's usual hatred of water? After all, there's no soap involved . . . '

* * *

Arminius, by now more or less recovered from the blow to the head that Colossus had dealt him during the fight earlier in the day, sat by the fire burning in the 9th Century's lines and stared into its embers. Freed from guard duty by Scaurus's edict that the men who had volunteered to form Silus's cavalry squadron would need a full night's rest, he had accompanied Marcus, Qadir and Scarface back to their century once their mounts were settled for the night. Now, with most of the century already rolled up in their cloaks after the day's exertions, he found himself unable to sleep, and so had joined the century's standard-bearer in the fire's gentle glow. Morban was in an unusually reflective mood and the German, more used to finding the burly soldier a source of unceasing banter and rough humour, sat quietly and listened to his woes.

'I'm forty years old next month, and I joined the cohort at the age of sixteen. That won't mean much to you, I suppose — you barbarians are usually all dead before reaching such an age, I'd imagine . . . '

Arminius raised an eyebrow at the comment, but kept quiet as the standard-bearer ploughed on.

' . . . but for me it might as well be fifty. I joined at the age of sixteen, and so I reach my twenty-five years' service next year. Oh, they won't throw me out yet, of course, too many good men died in the last six months for there to be any danger of that, but a standard-bearer past his twenty-five, well, there's a blockage to another man's promotion and that won't do. Once the numbers are made up I'll be politely taken to one side and invited to enjoy the fruits of my service. Which will boil down to being given my pension and told, nicely, mind you, to piss off and give someone else a chance to wave *my* standard around.'

Arminius nodded, his face an unreadable collection of lines and shadows in the firelight.

'I can see the way of it. Other men will be ready to step into your shoes, and you will have to step out of them sooner or later.'

Morban shook his head sadly.

'And in truth, German, and strictly between us girls, I won't miss the job as much as I would have done ten years ago. Too cold in the morning, too hot by midday, never a drink to be had for weeks at a time and feet stiff with dead skin and sores. I'd swap it all for a nice little place in the Hill's vicus in an instant. My own alehouse and a guaranteed supply of thirsty customers, except . . . '

He paused for a moment, and the German saw his opportunity to lighten the discussion's tone.

'Except you'd drink it all yourself?'

A spark of the Morban that Arminius had come to expect resurfaced in his blinking indignation.

'No, you cheeky blue-nosed bastard, except for the *boy*!'

Arminius nodded again, having known full well the direction their discussion would take.

'I had high hopes that my colleague Antenoch

would take Lupus on when I retired, teach him his letters, and show him how to use a sword and shield. I hoped he'd make a better soldier out of the boy than ever I was. With the right learning there's no saying what the lad might achieve, but with Antenoch dead that's all gone.'

The German picked up a stick and poked the fire with it, summoning fresh heat from the dying embers.

'You think the boy might have the makings of a clerk? I think not, Standard-Bearer. I never met his father, but I hear he was a warrior, and that he died at your battle earlier in the year with great honour.'

Morban's face twisted into something between a memory of grief and one of regret.

'A life wasted, and my son torn from me. If he'd been a little less of a warrior and a little more of a soldier he'd still be with us.'

Arminius shook his head slowly, a gentle smile on his face.

'And yet he carried your blood, Standard-Bearer. He could no more have held himself back from the fight than cut off his own arm. A warrior has to fight, whether those of us left behind when they perish like it or not. And your grandson is no clerk in the making, not to my eye. He'll be the same man his father was inside a few years . . . with the right training.'

Morban snorted.

'Training from whom? Two Knives is too busy leading the century and trying to get himself killed, and there's no one else I can trust with his welfare when I have to leave the service.'

He fixed a level stare on the German, daring him to disagree, and Arminius smiled grimly back at him.

'Don't try to be clever, Morban, I know your game. You seek to shame me into helping you, and perhaps to absolve you from your responsibility for the boy. He's your grandson, and you cannot hand him off to another man so easily. However . . . ' He raised a hand to cut off the indignant standard-bearer's ire. ' . . . *however*, I do have a bargain to offer you, if you'll listen.'

Morban cocked his head to one side, and kept his mouth shut.

'I owe your centurion a life. He saved me from being butchered as I lay with my wits kicked out of me by that brainless mountain of horseflesh earlier today. He leapt from his horse and took on half a dozen of the enemy with nothing more than a pair of swords. He stood over me and saved me from the most shameful of deaths, and for that I owe him many times over. I do not take such a responsibility lightly, Standard-Bearer, and I will discharge it at any cost to myself that might be necessary. I have spoken with Scaurus, and for as long as my master is the commander of this cohort I shall serve this debt by watching over Centurion Corvus and keeping him from harm. However, like you, I was not created immortal, and in time I will age and my sword-arm will weaken. I will need a student to tutor in the skills of the warrior, with and without weapons, a young man who will grow to manhood and take over my duty of protecting the man sleeping in that tent. Your grandson will be my pupil, and with my training he will more than match his father in his skill at arms.'

Morban opened his mouth to speak, but closed it again as Arminius rode over him.

'Your part in this will be a simple one, but unavoidable. You will provide him with an income sufficient to ensure that his equipment is of a standard to match his skills, and to achieve that you will need to keep yourself from drinking and gambling away your pay as soon as it hits the table in front of you. If you feel unable to keep this part of the bargain, then you will have to resign yourself to his being every bit as brave as his father undoubtedly was, but insufficiently trained to survive his first rush of blood to the head. As, I am forced to add, also appears to have been the case with his father, Mithras grant him rest.'

Morban sat silently, staring into the German's face, his features unreadable. When he replied, his voice was taut with emotion.

'You'll take the boy on, train him to fight, and care for him until he can look after himself?'

Arminius nodded, the cast of his face as solemn as that of the man before him.

'For as long as Scaurus is tasked to lead these men, yes. If he is ordered to leave you, then the task will become one for someone else. Until that day your grandson will have the closest thing to a father I can manage.'

* * *

In the darkness of the hospital the wounded guardsman woke with a start, and spent a split second wondering what it was that had snapped him from his sleep so abruptly before a big hand closed around his windpipe, pinching out his shout for help before it was anything more than an idea. A dark figure leaned in close to him and whispered in his ear, the words as harsh as the tone in which they were spoken.

'You've got a big fucking mouth, Guardsman, and it's going to be the death of you.'

The praetorian shook his head slightly, incomprehension and panic already mastering him, and he attempted to rise from the bed despite the lancing pain in his wounded thigh. His unknown assailant's other hand reached into his tunic and took a firm grip of his testicles, exerting pressure strong enough to arch his back involuntarily. A long moment's silence followed, the guardsman unable to speak while the other man waited patiently for him to start to asphyxiate. As he began to feel light headed from the lack of air the big man spoke again, the menace in his voice unmistakable.

'I can burst these plums with a single squeeze, Guardsman. Keep still and I'll let you breathe. Any attempt to call for help and I'll watch you die blue faced and choking for breath.'

The grip on his throat eased slightly, enough to allow him to gulp down a breath of desperately needed air.

'You'd best keep still while I tell you about this problem I've got, and how I expect you to help me deal with it. You, Guardsman, had a quiet little chat with your centurion earlier today. You thought I was asleep, but I've got sharp enough ears when scum like you are spreading gossip about things best kept private. While I was lying there with my eyes shut and my ears open, I heard someone else tell your officer that our lady doctor was ripe for breaking in. Which upset me more than a little, given that she's to be married to my brother officer. Soon after that, I heard *you* tell him that she's close to a centurion by the name of Corvus. And now here we are, less than a day later, and she's missing, whereabouts unknown, but I'm told she was last seen riding out of the north gate with your centurion Rapax. From which I can only assume that he's kidnapped her, and intends to use her to get to Centurion Corvus?'

The praetorian nodded his head slowly. His eyes had adjusted to the shadow in which his assailant had placed himself, and he found himself staring at the hard features of the auxiliary soldier from the bed opposite.

'Where will he take her?'

If he'd been brave enough the guardsman would have laughed in the Tungrian's face, but he made do with a momentary smirk.

'I've no idea. They'll probably go north, find some ground where they can take Corvus off guard, and then lure him in with the woman. When he gets close enough Rapax will most likely have one of his men fuck her, get her to make some noise and bring the boy in angry and unprepared. Perhaps he'll even enjoy her himself. He's had a lot of practice in making the women scream recently . . . '

The Tungrian cut him off with a fierce look of disgust.

'So who's this Rapax's colleague?'

The praetorian couldn't hold back the smile any longer.

'Someone with more power than you could ever imagine. He's a corn officer, if you know what that means. He can . . . '

The Tungrian sneered back down at him, flexing his fingers around the guardsman's throat . . .

'I know what it means. And that's all I needed to know.'

He closed his fingers around the guardsman's windpipe, crushing his larynx flat and pushing him back on to the bed, waiting while the dying man squirmed for breath and clawed at the hand that was killing him.

'It's a quicker death than you deserve, and an easier exit than your centurion Rapax will enjoy when I catch up with him.'

* * *

Tribune Paulus was clearly unused to having his decisions challenged by the lower ranks, and appeared utterly nonplussed to find an auxiliary centurion in front of his desk and making demands of him that he could only regard as extraordinary. Having said his piece, the bearded officer standing at attention before him stared obdurately at the wall behind him and waited for Paulus to respond. The tribune spun out a long, calculated pause before speaking, wanting the silence to unnerve the other man enough to take the edge off his apparent arrogance.

'So, Centurion . . . ?'

'Dubnus, Tribune.'

'Centurion Dubnus of the First Tungrian *auxiliary* cohort. If I've understood you fully, you'd like me to detail a full century to join you in some wild journey north?'

'Yes, Tribune.'

In pursuit of Centurions Rapax and Excingus, who, you claim, have abducted the fort's doctor and carried her away in the apparently *mistaken* belief that her husband-to-be is a fugitive from imperial justice?'

'Yes, Tribune.'

'These two officers being, I am forced to note, a praetorian and a corn officer. Representatives of both the praetorian tribune and the Emperor himself?'

'Yes, Tribune.'

Paulus paused again, his eyebrows raised in an incredulous stare.

'Are you fucking mad, Centurion? I have five combat-effective centuries with which to hold this fort against who knows how many Brigantian rebels who might be gathering to attack us at this very moment. I'll remind you of what happened to the garrison of White Strength less than a month ago, and they had a good deal more men than we do. What is it that makes you imagine that I'm going to give you a century of my soldiers to chase after two men with the power to have any one of us — or all of us — tortured and executed at the merest whiff of treason?'

'They have the doctor, Tribune, and . . . '

'And if they've chosen to take her there's really not all that much I can do to stop them, given their *absolute* power to hunt down the state's enemies. Is there, Centurion?'

The centurion locked eyes with him, and held that gaze as he replied.

'No, sir. You can't. But I can. Give me the men and I'll make the pair of them vanish as if they'd never existed.'

The tribune bristled, fear and anger combined in his incredulous tone.

'You'll make the problem go away, will you? And what if you *don't*? What if this lethal pairing eludes you, and discovers what I've done? Why in Hades would I take such a risk?'

The centurion's face stayed expressionless, but his eyes burned into Paulus's with renewed intensity as he leaned forward, unconsciously accepting the senior officer's challenge.

'Because, Tribune, your legatus, Cohort Tribune Licinius *and* Cohort Tribune Scaurus have all put their faith and trust in Centurion Corvus. If these two so-called *officers* . . . ' he spat the word into the air between them ' . . . are allowed to do their dirty work, then all three of those men will likely die alongside him in some way or another. If you want to avoid that, you have only to give me the soldiers and turn me loose.'

Paulus sat back and pondered the centurion's point. A legion legatus and two highly thought-of tribunes would make powerful friends in the years to come. His mind turned, as it had many times since his interview with the praetorian and the corn officer, to his oldest friend in the world, north of the Wall with the Petriana and without any clue as to the doom bearing down on him.

'Let's imagine that I actually give you some legionaries. You'll take them north and hunt down these men how, exactly?'

The Briton smiled down at him from his standing position, his face almost feral with the intensity of his confidence.

'I am a hunter, Tribune. I learned to track and kill animals with my father and his people, the same people who are currently hunting down any Roman foolish enough to go into the countryside to the south of here without enough spears to make them think twice. And I know who it is these particular animals are looking for. I will hunt them, I will find them and I will kill them both.'

'And my part in this matter? Can I trust you to keep your mouth shut?'

The smile changed slightly, some hint of the Briton's contempt creeping into his expression.

'Oh yes, Tribune, I'll be very sure not to mention your name. You wouldn't want to be seen taking sides.'

* * *

Marcus snapped awake at the sound of a high-pitched scream which put him on his feet before any conscious thought was fully formed. Ripping the eagle-pommelled gladius from its scabbard, he stepped out into the cold morning air in his bare feet, ready to fight. A dozen of the 9th Century's soldiers turned on hearing the scrape of his tunic on the tent's rough canvas flap, their surprise at the weapon in his hand turning to amusement as they realised the misapprehension he was under. Looking beyond their grins, he saw the German Arminius standing with a wooden practice sword, the boy Lupus facing him with his own half-sized practice weapon held ready to strike.

'Don't squeal at me when you attack, boy, shout at me like you've got a pair of big hairy balls! And you're supposed to be carving my guts open, not trying to tickle me! Put your weight behind the blade when you thrust!'

Marcus strolled across to the pair, the watching soldiers parting to either side.

'You're teaching Lupus to fight?'

The German inclined his head in a slight bow, the closest he ever came to a salute.

'I have agreed with Morban that the boy needs to learn the arts of combat if he is to be a soldier. One hour a day, every day, I will spend on his education with the sword. Someone else can teach him to ride, though.'

The Roman's lips twitched slightly at Arminius's attempt at humour.

'It's a good idea. He'll be able to serve in two or three years, and he should have some preparation. But what, I wonder, will become of my equipment? There's little enough time spent on it as it is . . . '

Lupus turned and pointed to the tent in which he cared for Marcus's war gear, his high-pitched child's voice clear and confident.

'All cleaned and polished, Centurion, boots and belts shining, armour brushed, sword and helmet polished.'

Arminius patted him on the back.

'Wait here.'

He put out a hand, silently requesting Marcus to accompany him to the tent in question. Inside, the centurion stood in silence for a moment on seeing the condition of his equipment.

'Not bad. He'll have worked half the night to get it this clean.'

Arminius nodded.

'I sat with him and told him what to do, but it was all his own work. Once the idea of daily training was mentioned I could have told him to lick the soles of your boots clean.'

Marcus turned to the German with a serious expression.

'You know what you're letting yourself in for? The boy lacks a father, and Morban isn't much better than nothing, given his usual choice of pastimes.'

Arminius nodded with a wry smile of agreement.

'I know. I've promised your standard-bearer

that I'll play the role for as long as Scaurus leads your cohort, as long as he donates a regular portion of his pay to see the boy well clothed and equipped.'

Marcus snorted.

'And no doubt he promised that much and more in the wink of an eye. Just make sure you're standing next to him when he takes his turn at the pay chest, or he'll turn his coin into used beer, a pair of tired whores and somebody else's winnings before Lupus ever sees any of it. But for all of that, thank you.'

The German bowed again, a quiet smile on his face.

'The boy needs a father's guidance. And perhaps it will also be good for you *not* to be the one centurion on parade whose boots look like the floor of a legion latrine.'

* * *

Felicia woke from a troubled sleep to find herself looking into the eyes of the thin-faced corn officer, who had lain beside her staring intently until she awoke. He leapt to his feet with a chuckle, spreading his hands wide as if for applause.

'You see, I told you! Stare at a sleeping person for long enough and that person will wake up!' He turned back to his prisoner, holding out a hand with which to help her to her feet. 'Come along, my dear, we have a big day today, lots of riding to do and no time for lying about!'

The doctor got up from the ground without

touching his outstretched hand, looking about her to find the small camp a flurry of activity as the guardsmen packed their bedrolls and equipment on to their horses, few of them sparing her more than a glance as they worked. The praetorian officer walked across to her with a rough slice of bread wrapped around a piece of dried meat, his face creasing into a grin when she gestured her lack of desire for food. He reached out and took her hand, pushing the unappetizing food into her palm and wrapping the fingers around it.

'Eat it now, or eat it later, but you're going to want it some time today. We'll eat again at nightfall, but between then and now we've a long way to travel in search of your boyfriend. Throw it away if you like, but there'll be no more until then, not unless you've something tasty hidden somewhere about your clothing.'

One of the soldiers turned and grinned ferociously at the dismayed woman, his hands still busy with a reluctant buckle. The tunic beneath his padded arming jacket was a different colour from that of the men around him, and his armour constructed of segmented bands of iron where theirs was made of hundreds of overlapping bronze scales.

'I'll search her, Centurion. You just say the word and I'll be up that little missy's skirts so fast she won't . . . '

Rapax spun on the spot, putting his hands on his hips and shaking his head sadly.

'You can keep your hands and your thoughts well away from this one, Soldier Maximus, unless you want your end to come considerably sooner than I'd imagine you're planning.'

He stared levelly at the soldier until the other man lowered his gaze respectfully, than raised his voice to be sure he was heard by every man in the clearing.

'I won't tell you worm-beaters this more than once, so let's all be very clear about it. This woman stays untouched until I say her time has come. I want her screams of desperation when we get her boyfriend within earshot to be exactly that. *Screams*. Not the tired moans of a woman that's already been ridden half a dozen times by you whore mongers. Any man that doubts me in this only has to lay a finger on her and I'll relieve him of the hand it's attached to. You cross me on this one at your peril, gentlemen. Of course, once Marcus Valerius Aquila's cold on the turf next to her you can draw lots for her for all I care, but until then . . . you have been warned!'

Felicia shivered, pulling the blanket in which she had slept closer about her and crushing the bread and meat between the fingers of her right hand as she remembered the casual ease with which Rapax had murdered her orderly the previous day. She felt the sheath of Dubnus's knife hard against her thigh, and silently vowed to use it on herself before submitting to the ordeal so casually promised by Rapax.

* * *

After the cohorts had taken breakfast, the cavalry squadrons mounted up and headed north, fanning out across the route that the infantry cohorts would be following behind them, as they ground their way up the road that paralleled the east coast all the way to the Tuidius's estuary. Double-Pay Silus and Decurion Felix had briefly discussed the day's march for the former's squadron of volunteers, and agreed that it would be best if they headed straight up the road's relatively smooth ribbon, both for the sake of speed and to avoid the risk of the inexperienced riders among them coming to grief on the rough moorland that flanked the road's arrow-straight course on both sides.

Arminius rode alongside Marcus in the morning's pale sunlight, his green-eyed stare alternately flicking across the horizon and then down at the road's cobbled surface.

'It's a good joke on someone's part, to have me riding this monster along the very surface on which the slippery-footed bastard nearly managed to kill me yesterday.'

He touched the rough bandage tied around his head with a wry grin, but Marcus, sneaking a sideways glance, saw that his right hand had a good handful of the horse's mane along with the reins.

'Yesterday was pure accident. You'll be all right today, especially if you just relax your posture a little and let the horse do the hard work. The poor animal must think he's got a ceremonial statue on board.'

The German snorted disparagingly, but when he thought the Roman was no longer watching him he experimentally loosened the firm grip of his thighs on Colossus's flanks, allowing himself to sink into a more relaxed seat. Tempted to praise the improvement, caught out of the corner of his eye as he pretended to scan the horizon, Marcus took one sideways glance at the look on the German's face and kept his mouth firmly shut. Another mile up the road the German broke his reverie with a sudden question.

'The order was for men who know how to swim to form this new detachment, and so here we are. That means there's a river to cross. And after that . . . ?'

The Roman raised an eyebrow.

'It's a good thing for you that I was listening at the officers' meeting this morning, and not just admiring the unaccustomed shine of my boots. Martos thinks it'll take two days to get the infantry close enough for an attack on day three, as long as they keep bashing along at the thirty-mile-a-day pace. They've got the easy job, since all they have to do is slog it north until they get close enough to the Votadini fortress to fight. In the meantime we've got to make sure that their approach goes unnoticed and unreported back to the men that Calgus sent to take control of the Fortress of the Spears. So you won't have to worry too much about having these stones under your beast's feet for very much longer.'

Arminius rode on in silence for a moment, his face creased in thought.

'So we take their scouts, or just kill them. We make our way in close to the fortress under the cover of darkness, or bad weather, but even if we do manage to get all three cohorts in place outside their walls unannounced, how do we break in without any of the usual artillery the legions use to knock down enemy walls? Even if we surround the place, that only makes the bloody Selgovae more likely to run wild and fuck every living thing left breathing inside the fortress to death. Which would seem to defeat the purpose of our trying to rescue them.'

Marcus gave him a sidelong glance, a half-smile on his lips, and the German bridled at the thought of knowledge to which he was not privy.

'You already know, don't you?!'

Marcus grinned, leaning back in his saddle and yawning extravagantly.

'If you'd been in your usual place at the commander's conference, standing guard at the door with one ear inside the tent, rather than devoting your mornings to the martial education of undeserving children, you'd know too.'

Arminius leaned out of his saddle, poking the Roman in the shoulder and giving him a reproachful glare.

'To think that I stood over that child until I could see a shine on those boots of yours, only to be repaid with mocking laughter. You're a hard man, Centurion Corvus.'

Marcus looked about him ostentatiously, as if seeking to avoid being overheard, despite the fact that they had fallen thirty paces behind the riders ahead of them.

'I probably shouldn't share this with anyone not invited to the briefing, but since it's you . . . ' He beckoned the German to bring his head closer, muttering his next words in the other man's ear. ' . . . all you need to do is find out what it was that the Fifth and Ninth Centuries were doing yesterday, while Martos was persuading Harn to cooperate with us. When you know what it was they were collecting from the men we killed, you'll have a fair idea of the answer to your question. Now let's see how these beasts feel about having a bit of a trot, or we'll fall so far behind the squadron that the leading Tungrian century will overtake us. And I've no desire to find myself subjected to the kind of humour that would inspire. Have you *heard* the songs they sing about the cavalry?'

* * *

'Why the bloody hell aren't the bastards moving?'

Tribune Licinius turned to the speaker, his first spear, with a wry smile.

'They're not moving, First Spear, because they know very well that we can't stay here and watch them for ever. Not enough food, for one thing, given the impoverished nature of the game in these parts, and bigger fish to fry for another. My orders are explicit — to harry the Venicones until we've destroyed them or there's just no point to it any more, and then to ride south to join the campaign against the Brigantes. Drust ought to know that I don't have the luxury of sitting and watching him for very much longer, and if he's not bright enough to have worked it out I'm absolutely bloody sure that Calgus will have made sure he knows which way the wind's blowing. The longer we sit here watching a bunch of savages who're out of the fight as far as this particular rebellion goes, and as a consequence doing absolutely nothing of any value, the itchier my feet are going to get.'

His subordinate nodded his understanding.

'So we head south, then?'

Licinius stroked his beard for a moment.

'Yes. Sort of. Put the word out, as we discussed. It's time for a little bit of subterfuge.'

When the call went out for a volunteer to watch the barbarians from hiding, once the cavalry wing was away over the hill and apparently headed south, one soldier put his hand up without hesitation. He stepped forward to face the man who ruled his world with quiet confidence, sure that his long-practised skills would see him safe no matter how thorough the Venicones might be in their inevitable search for spies. Licinius paced around him before taking him to one side and speaking quietly in measured tones, as if sensing the inner calm that fuelled the man's self-belief.

'Soldier Caius, isn't it? Well, Caius, you know why I need a man to stay behind and watch this rabble while the rest of us are seen to ride south? I don't have the luxury of waiting for the Venicones to move, so instead I must use deception to bring them out of their hole. So tell me, Soldier Caius, how will you carry this trick off? The bastard that leads that rabble will promise to reward the man who finds you beyond his dreams, because he will know beyond a doubt that you will be lurking somewhere within sight of those walls, waiting for them to make their move. You know what they did to Centurion Cyrus?'

Caius nodded, just a touch of obstinacy showing in his face at the attempt the tribune was making to talk him out of the reward he'd been told was on offer, if he survived the barbarian search, and delivered news of their movements to the riders lurking far enough to the west to be undiscoverable.

'You heard that he took a long time dying, and left this life with his guts cooling in a wide pool of his own blood? And you're still determined to take this risk?'

Caius nodded again, with more pride than irritation this time.

'So tell me, just how do you plan to live through the hours after we leave then, and yet still keep your eyes on their camp?'

Caius looked him in the face before replying, his own face set in an expression of utter confidence in his own abilities.

'Tribune, before I was a soldier, I was a cattle thief. I was the man that watched the herds until the men paid by the farmers to keep us away from their animals were distracted. I would watch for days at a time, and never once did anyone catch sight of me. I'm going to dig myself a hide, and when it's done I ask that you should walk away for fifty paces before turning back to look for me. Walk closer, and every few paces look again, until you're back where you started. Then decide if you believe I can perform this task for you. I shall need my brother to help me with this. He serves in the same tent party.'

And with that he took up the sharp-bladed spade he'd carried with him from his tent and set to work, quickly digging out a two-foot-deep trench long enough to accept the length of his body lying flat, while his brother went to find branches of the right thickness and cut them down to the necessary length, dropping twenty of them at his feet and then standing back to watch him work his magic. Digging each one of the sticks into one side of the trench, two inches below the hole's lip, and then forcing each one's other end laterally into the facing wall's earth, he inserted them at finger-length intervals to form a slatted roof to the hide, then arranged the waiting turf strips across them in exactly the order they'd been removed. Working with slow and painstaking care, he made sure that the joins between each piece of turf were invisible, packing small sticks between the roof slats and the turfs where the resulting effect looked unrealistic, working until the hide's roof appeared no different to the ground around it. Nodding to his brother, he slid into the remaining gap with painstaking, delicate care, and then watched from below ground as the last turf was packed carefully into its place to complete the deception.

Standing to one side and watching, Licinius's face remained impassive, but his eyes narrowed as the soldier wriggled into his hiding place and the last turf was eased into the deceptive layer of cover arranged over the trench. With one final adjustment, a gentle touch to slightly flatten the turf, the remaining brother turned to face him and saluted, gesturing with a hand for the tribune to conduct the test that had been requested of him. Licinius nodded to him and turned away, walking a brisk fifty paces before turning back to scan the ground beneath which he knew the man was hiding. While he'd had no expectation of discerning any clue as to the hide's location at that distance, he was at first impressed and then bemused by the lack of any betrayal of its presence the closer he got to the spot where he assumed it to be. After a moment more he was standing more or less where he'd started, looking about him with resigned amusement.

'Go on, then, show me where he is.'

Caius's brother let out a piercing whistle, clearly intended to be heard in the hide, and to the tribune's astonishment the ground at his very feet erupted upwards, making him step back involuntarily as the hidden soldier burst from his hide with a broad grin.

'Jupiter's hairy balls! I nearly died of bloody shock!' Putting a hand to his chest and rolling his eyes, Licinius peered down into the freshly revealed hole. 'I would never have believed it. Can you do this at night, so that the blue-noses don't have the chance to see you digging yourself in?'

'Yes, Tribune, with enough moonlight to work by the result is no different.'

The tribune turned to his first spear, waiting impassively to one side.

'Very well, then, it seems that we have a scout. Detail a tent party, a steady one, mind you, to take this man and his brother out tonight, and dig him in somewhere with a good view of Three Mountains. Make sure it's well away from anything that the blue-noses might be poking with their spears once we've ridden off tomorrow. We don't want any of them falling through Soldier Caius's turf roof, do we? And detail a party of message riders to wait for him at a safe distance, ready to bring us the news once Drust has his savages on the move. I don't have a bloody clue where he'll lead them, but I'll bet you a flask of Falernian to a cup of warm piss that the one place he won't be taking them is straight back home.'

* * *

Dubnus surveyed the men the tribune had detailed to his command with a jaundiced eye, turning back to the centurion who had guided him to their barrack and called them on to parade to meet their new officer.

'What the fuck happened to this lot? They look like they couldn't fight their way out of a whorehouse, never mind take their iron to the blue-noses.'

The legion officer looked down his nose at the remains of what had clearly been a century at some point.

'That, friend, used to be our Third Century. Our genius of a tribune decided that it would be a good idea to send a century south to scout the road to Sailors' Town.' He shook his head, raising an eyebrow at his auxiliary colleague that encompassed the idiocy of senior officers across the empire. 'Eighty men sent marching south straight into a tribal revolt. I wouldn't have fancied my chances of getting to Sailors' Town with anything less than a full cohort. They got about ten miles south before the local nutters decided that enough was enough and jumped them in strength. Their centurion, a decent enough officer and a friend of mine, as it happens, seems to have realised that they'd bitten off far more than they could chew, but that they'd all be chopped to ribbons if they ran. So he rallied them, and led the front rank into the fight with their shields up and their swords drawn. It seems the rear rank weren't quite so keen . . . '

'And this is the rear rank?'

'Right in one. Bastards. The last thing they saw as they ran for it, or so their watch officer told Tribune Paulus, was their centurion's head being waved around. This lot are good for nothing more than scraping the latrines out, in *my* opinion, so if you're relying on them to put up a fight for you once you're north of the Wall . . . well, I'd be thinking very carefully before depending on *any* of them. And look out for the watch officer, he's a damage case. He got knocked about by one of his men once they were back in camp, and it's not done him any good.'

Dubnus nodded his thanks, watching the other man walk away until he turned the corner and disappeared from view. Turning back to face the ragged lines of soldiers, few of whom were managing to meet his level gaze, he folded his arms, biceps bulging against his mail armour, and looked up and down their ranks with a look of undisguised contempt.

'So you're what's left of the Third Century, are you? You're the men that abandoned your mates in battle and legged it home with your tails between your legs, or so the story goes. Anybody want to tell me otherwise?' He waited for a slow count of ten, running his eyes slowly over each man's face in turn and looking for any sign of dissent. 'No takers, it seems. So, you really are the lowest of the low, men that not only turned their backs on a fight but who left their officer, chosen man and forty good men to the blue-noses.'

He walked slowly, deliberately, across the open space to the first rank, his face twisted with disgust.

'If this were *my* cohort you'd already have drawn lots to choose which four men would get beaten to death by the rest of you, and then you'd have been sent out again in the company of *real* soldiers in search of another fight. The legions must be getting soft, allowing men like you to fester in your barracks rather than set a nasty bastard of a centurion on to you, with orders to clear out the rot.' He went face to face with the watch officer, his nose less than six inches from the other man's bruised features. 'Well, gentlemen, and fortunately for the army, I *am* that nasty bastard of a centurion. Life's about to get interesting for you men, and not in any sort of way you're going to enjoy.'

Turning away, he held his vine stick up for every man to see.

'Now some of you will already be thinking that I'm not a legion centurion, which means that I have no power over you. And you'd be right . . . ' He waited for a precisely judged moment before continuing again. ' . . . and yet so horribly wrong.' Turning back to face them, he slapped the stick into his calloused palm with a smack that made more than one man twitch involuntarily. 'You see, it's true, I'm not a legion officer, which gives me no formal power over you. And yet since I'm not part of your legion, I can do whatever I like to any or all of you tunic-lifting cowards and get away with it. Anything. I. Like. So, and here's where we see who's got any balls about them, do any of you useless ration thieves want to take me on, man to man? If any man can put me down I'll walk away and leave you to stew here in your filth. Come on, there must be one man out there that fancies taking me on. No? All right, then, any *two* of you. Any two men that think they could put me on my back. Come on!'

The century stood in silence, some of the soldiers shivering under his angry gaze, but not a man moved a muscle. Dubnus glared back at them, his mask of anger fading slowly to a sneer.

'No? The offer stands, gentlemen. If any two of you can put me on my back I'll leave you all in peace. Just one warning, though, in case one or two of the smarter among you wonder if it still counts if you try to hit me from behind. The answer is yes. It still counts. But if you decide to try it, make sure your first punch is a good one. Because if you don't put me out of the fight with that first punch, I'll break one or even both arms of every man involved, depending what sort of mood I'm in. And now, gentlemen, you've got a count of five hundred to fetch your marching gear and present yourselves in formation on the parade ground, ready to march north. Full armour, shields, spears, swords and your packs. Whoever looks after the century's cart had better be quick, because I want it loaded with your tents and ready to move inside another five hundred. Any man not on parade by the time I've strolled up to meet you will soon be getting used to the feel of my vine stick on his back. *Move!*'

⋆ ⋆ ⋆

After the lunchtime meal the volunteer squadron turned east, away from the road's course towards the east coast and down a long shallow valley that ran north-west for miles, down to a river plain lost in the misty haze. Double-Pay Silus looked down the valley's long slope and smiled happily, turning back to Marcus and pointing to the palm of his right hand.

'Well, Centurion, this is my ground now. I've ridden these hills a dozen times or more over the years, and I know it as well as I know this skin. The road runs almost to the coast, where the Tuidius meets the sea, but we're going to ease down this nice little valley and leave the stone path to the mules . . . ' He glanced quickly up at Marcus, but found his officer's face set in a wry smile. ' . . . if you take my meaning. They'll follow the road until it finishes close to the river late this afternoon, given that they're forced-marching, and camp out of sight of the ford tonight. Tomorrow morning they'll turn west to find the ford and they'll probably be crossing by mid-morning, ready to climb the hills on the far side of the valley. All of which will allow plenty of time for anyone set to watch for their approach to get a warning back to the Dinpaladyr, after which any idea of taking them by surprise goes out of the window.' He raised an eyebrow to Marcus, his face alive with the prospect of a hunt. 'And there's our opportunity. Anyone who's been set to watch for any sign of Romans is going to watch the road, since that's the way they know our infantry to make their approach. We, on the other hand, can sneak quietly down this nice little valley as far as the edge of the river's plain, cross it unseen when it's misty, early tomorrow morning, and then turn east and flush out any watchers in the hills on the far side before they even know we're there. And if we can deal with the watchers before they ever get sight of the infantry, then they can make their approach to the fortress of the spears with the advantage of surprise. And your improbable plan for getting inside without starting a massacre might just get a chance to work, eh, Centurion?'

* * *

By late afternoon the exhausted soldiers of Dubnus's temporary command were marching on little more than willpower, and the fear that whatever momentary relief might be gained from falling out of the line of march would be far outweighed by the punishment that their tormentor would bring down on them in the event that any man flagged. The auxiliary centurion had marched alongside them without any sign of discomfort since the half-century had marched through the Noisy Valley gates, despite the rumour that he had discharged himself from the fortress's hospital with a spear wound not yet completely healed.

'It's a right bastard, this road, don't you men think?' Dubnus's voice rang out along the small column as steady as if he were standing at ease, not marching along beside them at the standard pace. 'I've never liked it. The bloody thing goes up and down like a whore's skirts, so that one moment your calves are burning with the climb, and then the front of your legs feel like they're being caned with the pain of stopping them from running away with you in the dips. Whichever idiot engineer laid this one out straight needed his head examined.'

He looked up and down the detachment's length with a grim smile.

'On the other hand, it does provide you ladies with something a bit more testing than lazing around your barrack waiting for the tribune to decide what to do with a half-century of cowards.' A man in the file closest to him allowed a hint of a scowl to show on his face, and the auxiliary centurion bore down on him, putting his mouth six inches from the soldier's ear before speaking loudly enough for the entire detachment to hear him. 'Ah, so at least one of you doesn't like being called a coward. A pity that he's stuck with the rest of you, then, isn't it?'

The unit was breasting yet another crest, revealing the shape of a burned-out fort at the summit of the next hill. Dubnus turned and walked backwards, pointing his left arm at the shattered ruin coming into view.

'That, soldiers, is our home for the night. Fort Habitus, named after a legion centurion who served here soon after the Wall was first built.' He turned back to the line of march and strode alongside the detachment's front rank. 'Habitus was a proud old bastard by all accounts, old enough that he should have retired, but the locals weren't all that happy when the Wall went up and divided them from each other, and they expressed that unhappiness by killing Romans whenever and wherever they could, given the chance. Anyway, old Habitus was ordered to take his century out on patrol one day not very far from here, or so the story goes. He probably thought that patrolling in such limited strength was a good way to get attacked, but he was too much of a soldier to question orders and so off they went.'

He spat on to the road's surface.

'Poor bastards. They were ten miles or so from camp when the local blue-noses jumped them. Sounds familiar, eh? The barbarians were three hundred strong, or thereabouts, more than three of them for every man in the century. Old Habitus had seen it all by that stage of his career, of course, and he knew that if he allowed his men to run they'd all be dead inside a count of five hundred, and so he shouted at them to form a square, to stop the tribesmen from getting round their flanks, and to stand and fight.'

He glanced across their ranks, finding every man's face turned to his and their expressions taut with interest.

'And fight they did. Retreating when they could, with blue-noses surrounding them on all sides and the day wearing on into afternoon, and still they fought. A wounded man was a dead man, that far from help, and more than one dying soldier tried to take one or two of the savages with him by stepping out to fight man to man, but for the most part they held their ranks and slowly hacked their way back along the route they'd come earlier in the day. They left a trail of corpses behind them, their own and those of the tribesmen attacking them, but they held their nerve even when half of them had been killed and the remaining men were almost dead on their feet. The trumpeter kept calling for help, when he wasn't spearing blue-noses, and eventually, with evening drawing on, they heard the sound of an answering trumpet. There were Roman soldiers close by, and an end to their torment. The barbarians, well, they knew that their chance to take a centurion's head was slipping from their grasp, so they mounted one last wild attack, swarming around the detachment's shields in a desperate charge, but old

Habitus shouted for his men to hold on for just a little longer, and his soldiers stood firm in a circle of men that shrank with every casualty until another three centuries came over the hill and chased off the barbarians. There were thirty of them left standing, and not many of them without a wound of some kind, but they marched back into their camp with their heads up and their spears black with dried blood.'

He paused for a moment before continuing. The detachment was almost at the top of the hill, and the fort's burned and shattered timbers were looming on the skyline.

'Centurion Habitus was killed before his century was relieved. He stopped a spear in the back of his neck that dropped him like a sack of shit, poor old bastard. The men that survived said that they'd all have died in the first hour if it hadn't been for him bellowing at them to keep fighting, and that all the way through the fight he had a little smile on his face, as if he knew what was coming before the end. They named the fort after him to act as an example to the rest of the army . . . ' He raked a hard stare across their faces. ' . . . and to you, if you have the guts to follow it. Right, then, off the road here and into the fort. Get yourselves fed and then settle down for the night, one man from each tent party to stand guard with a two-hourly relief. And if I find any of you sleeping on guard there'll be no need to draw lots for who'll be beating you to death, because I'll already have done the job with my bare hands.'

Later in the evening, before darkness fell, he

called the watch officer to him with a request that raised the other man's eyebrows.

'Help me get out of this armour, will you, Titus? I can't bend enough to slide out of it.'

The watch officer shrugged and called another soldier over, the pair of them lifting the heavy mail armour from their new centurion's shoulders while he squatted to allow them to pull it clear. With the armour removed Dubnus pulled off the padded arming jacket and tunic that he wore beneath it, revealing his muscular upper body to the watching soldiers. A long strip of linen was wound around his stomach several times to form a thick bandage, and tied in place by its trailing ends, and as they watched he stripped it away, winding it up into a neat roll of cloth. As the linen fell away from his stomach it revealed a vivid red scar an inch wide, and Titus grimaced at the sight, his bruised face twisting in sympathy.

'Spear?'

Dubnus nodded curtly, wondering whether he was taking too big a risk in letting the soldiers see his weakness.

'Yes, two weeks ago at the battle of the Waterfall. The tattooed bastard put the bloody thing clean through my mail and skewered me from front to back. It's healing well enough, but it still hurts like the blade's still in there when I try to bend.'

He watched as the realisation that their new officer was not as invulnerable as he seemed sank into the soldiers' faces and laughed at them, putting his hands on his hips with a smile.

'Any two of you fancy having a try at me now?'

One by one they looked away, until only the watch officer held his gaze.

'You're not recovered from a spear wound and you've still got the apples to come north looking for a fight? Why?'

Dubnus smiled wryly, stretching wearily.

'I'll tell you once we're on the road tomorrow morning. If, that is, I'm still alive tomorrow morning.'

8

The volunteer squadron camped in the cover of the shallow valley that night, within a few minutes' ride of the River Tuidius. Silus had calculated that any watchers would most likely be hiding farther to the east, keeping watch on the ford that the cohort would use to cross the Tuidius rather than the apparently unfordable stretch of river to its west, but he was nevertheless loath to abandon the valley's cover. They spent an uneventful night, and awoke at dawn to find, just as Silus had predicted, that the river's plain was wreathed in a thick mist that restricted visibility to no better than a hundred paces. The newly promoted decurion gathered his men about him, his words made dull by the mist's muffling curtains of vapour.

'I was counting on a nice thick layer of river fog. It always happens at this time of year once the nights get cold, and it means that we can get across the river with no risk of anyone seeing us. So there's no time for breakfast now, we need to get swimming before it lifts. Get your kit packed but don't wear anything heavier than your tunics and your cloaks to keep you warm while we ride down to the river. Your armour and weapons will need to be strapped to your saddles, so make sure you roll your mail up nice and tight.'

The squadron followed his lead down to the river's edge, each man watching the horse in front of him intently as the mist gathered in thick curtains that curtailed visibility to a few feet in some places as they made their way across the river's flat plain. Silus gathered them around him again at the water's edge and pointed to his own equipment, already packed on to his horse's back.

'The Batavians are *supposed* to have swum across rivers like this and even wider alongside their horses in full armour, back in the days when the divine Julius conquered the south of this island, but I'm buggered if I can see how they managed it. There are those that think they might have used their shields for buoyancy, but there's no bloody way I'd risk slipping off my board and sinking like a stone in mid-river. We're doing it my way today, so go and have a look at my horse and see how I've got my armour laid across the saddle, and with my sword on top. Look at the way I've secured them with my rope, and used it to tie my spear and shield to the beast's side. Then take a length of rope and do the same yourselves, and I'll come round and see how good a job you've done. And make sure your spear isn't going to stab your horse in the eye if the poor sod turns his head to find out what the fuck you think you're doing, eh?'

He strolled around the horses, providing help to those men to whom the act of tying their equipment to their mount was proving difficult, eventually expressing his satisfaction with their preparations. Pulling off his tunic, he folded it neatly and slipped it under the rope holding his armour in place, then did the same with his blanket and boots. Standing naked in the cold morning air, he smiled wryly at the men around him.

'Well then, let's have you stripped down to your skins and ready to swim. And don't bother making the usual tired excuses about how cold it is.'

The soldiers stripped with the usual bathhouse ribaldry, albeit muted both by their circumstances and the admonishments of their decurion.

'Right, here we go. Stand by your animal's head and take a good firm grip of the reins. Walk the beast in and start swimming, and they will follow you. They might not enjoy it all that much, but every horse here knows how to swim. Just keep your arms and legs well clear of theirs, because there's only one of you that will win if you get tangled and it isn't going to be any of you girls. When you get to the far side keep your fucking voices down, and we'll have no squealing or shouting out how cold it is when you get in, you'll soon warm up with the effort of the swim. On the far bank get your sword drawn before you worry about getting dry and keep a tight grip on your horse once you've got your feet back on dry land, because some of them are going to be more than a bit pissed off at being made to do this. Now follow me . . . '

He strode forward into the river, walking into the chilly water without hesitation, and sliding his body into the horizontal position almost noiselessly, breaststroking out into the stream with his horse swimming alongside him happily enough. Marcus waded in behind him, and was surprised to find the animal's flanks shivering as he put his hoofs into the water. The big grey tugged against his reins without any real force, but strongly enough to indicate his discomfort. Pulling at the reins with a gentle insistence, Marcus led the animal into the deeper water, breathing in sharply as the cold water reached his groin, then pushed himself forward into the water and started swimming for the far bank, still lost in the mist. The horse surrendered to its rider's unspoken command and started swimming, surging up out of the water and then easing back into it alternately in a porpoising motion, his eyes rolling and his teeth bared at the unfamiliar sensation. Finding that the horse was starting to outpace him, Marcus waited for one of the animal's plunges back into the water and slipped a leg over his back, thanking providence that he had tied his spear and shield to the other flank. If the extra weight troubled the horse there was no sign, and freed of the need to keep pace with his rider, he forged through the water faster than before, passing Silus's mount in less than a minute. The river's northern bank loomed out of the fog more quickly than Marcus had expected, and getting a glimpse of dry land was enough to spur the animal to one last great effort. Horse and rider staggered ashore untidily, and Marcus slipped from his mount's back with his gladius drawn and ready to fight, despite the shivers racking his body with re-exposure to the cold air. Silus staggered ashore behind him, his sword already drawn and his body blue. His voice stuttered with the cold air's grip on his body, his lungs panting for breath.

'S-s-see? N-n-nothing t-to it . . . '

Another horseman wearily climbed the bank behind him, and the decurion pointed to the left.

'Ten paces that way, then dry off with your blanket and get your kit on. I want you ready to fight.'

Qadir waded out of the water next, the chestnut mare calm under his touch, and Silus raised a disgusted eyebrow.

'There's no justice. Not only the best horseman I've met in this whole bloody country, but his bloody manhood's still dragging in the water.'

The Hamian shook his head and hooked a thumb over his shoulder.

'If you want to be truly scared, take a look at that. Why do you think I was swimming so quickly?'

Both the officers looked past him, to see the impressive shape of Arminius as he waded out of the river. Silus shook his head slowly.

'Gods below . . . '

The German smiled complacently as he walked past them, and Silus pointed out into the fog still wreathing the riverbank.

'Get your sword out, bugger off into the mist and get that thing covered up.'

The squadron came ashore in ones and twos, until every man was accounted for and dry enough to put on their armour. The mist persisted, although it seemed to Marcus that it was thinning slightly as the sun climbed away from the eastern horizon, a slightly brighter spot in the grey. Silus cast a critical eye at the ascending spot of light, nodding decisively.

'This lot will have burned off in an hour or so, so mount up and follow me. I want to be safe on the far side of the hill before it clears, and out of sight of anyone looking out for us.

They rode carefully across the grassy expanse, at one point scattering a flock of sheep that was grazing in their path. Marcus looked around for any sign of their herder, tightening a hand on the hilt of his sword even as he wondered whether he could kill an innocent to maintain the secrecy of their task, but the running sheep were swallowed by the mist without any sign of their keeper.

'He's probably still asleep.'

He looked around to find Qadir at his shoulder, the chestnut trotting easily with the last of the river's moisture steaming off her body.

'It's his lucky day, then.'

The Hamian raised an eyebrow.

'And you could have put an innocent sheep herder to the sword?'

The Roman shook his head indecisively.

'I don't know . . . but I suspect our new decurion could.'

Qadir nodded knowingly.

'I think the word you're looking for is 'pragmatist'. And I suspect we're all going to have to stretch our principles if we're going to release the Votadini from their new rulers.'

* * *

Excingus woke Felicia with a gentle shake in the dawn's first light, wrinkling his nose and pointing at the stream by which the small detachment was camped.

'You smell, my dear, like a polecat. Come on, let's get you into the water and make you bearable for the rest of the day.'

She shook her head, painfully aware of the knife still tied to her thigh and certain to be discovered if she were forced to disrobe in front of the guardsmen.

'If you think I'm going to take my clothes off in front of these men . . . '

The legion soldier who Felicia had caught staring at her several times the previous day stood up from his place by the fire and ran his eyes up and down her body, the insolent smile playing across his lips in direct contradiction to his cold stare. Alongside him Rapax looked up from his breakfast and shook his head with a snort of amusement.

'Steady, Maximus, recall what I said to you and you might still be breathing by sunset. As for you, madam, go and have a wash before I come over there and throw you into the water. My colleague isn't going to give you any problems, he's not that way inclined. You've got more chance of persuading a sausage to stand up than you have of getting a twitch out of his wrinkle stick.'

She glared at the praetorian for a moment before standing, feeling the knife's hard length against her flesh and thinking quickly. Excingus led her up the riverbank, away from the small camp's bustle and into the trees that lined the stream's banks until they reached a small pool. He pointed impatiently at the water, clearly not willing to walk any farther.

'Get your clothes off and wash here.' Felicia submitted with a show of meekness, pulling off her stola, folding it up and putting it down on the grass, then removed her boots and turned to the waiting corn officer.

'Centurion, please could you give me a little privacy? I'm unhappy enough given my circumstances, without having you stare at me like a slave in the market.'

Excingus shrugged, spreading his hands wide.

'Didn't you hear my colleague? I, madam, regard the prospect of your naked body with all the anticipation I would normally reserve for looking at that tree.' He sighed, shaking his head slightly, then turned away, speaking to the foliage in front of him. 'Very well, you have your modesty, for now at least, although you must realise that it will be cruelly torn away from you when the time comes? Rapax will protect you until then, to keep you unsullied until the right moment, but he'll be quite merciless once your Aquila boy is within earshot. Speaking of your boyfriend, I'd be curious to know how the two of you ended up together. Weren't you the wife of a senior officer?'

Felicia worked quickly as she replied, keeping her voice level to avoid exciting his suspicions.

'If you want to know about my former husband, the story's quite simple. He was a brutal man, and no stranger to the idea of rape when he felt like it. He used to say it was just 'spicing things up'.' She unstrapped the knife from her thigh and dropped it into one of her boots before pulling off her tunic and stepping into the pool, gasping at the water's cold. 'He used to tell me he knew I enjoyed it once he had me helpless on my back, or pinned face down across a table with a handful of my hair to keep me there. He was a monster, pure and simple.' She climbed out of the water and dressed quickly, strapping the sheath back around her thigh beneath her tunic's thick wool. 'He didn't restrict his outrages to me, to judge from the little I heard about his behaviour towards the men who served under him. He was killed by one of them on the battlefield a few months ago, and I expect it was no more than he deserved.' Pulling on her stola as the centurion turned back to face her, she smiled wanly and nodded her thanks. The corn officer's eyes narrowed thoughtfully as he digested the fact that her husband was dead.

'Was he a wealthy man?'

Felicia shrugged dismissively, adjusting her clothes.

'He had a modest estate in Rome, I believe.'

'And you're not interested in how you might benefit?'

She shook her head, her hands spreading in a dismissive gesture.

'I have no entitlement, you know that well enough. And I don't want to touch anything of his ever again.'

'But the money . . . '

'I want nothing from him. I have all I want for this life.'

'And when we've killed young Aquila? What will you have then? Surely you'd be better off returning to Rome and taking your husband's property than staying here in poverty? I could help you, for a consideration.'

She turned hard eyes on him, understanding for the first time the depth of his cynicism.

'I'm sure you could. You could strong-arm my husband's family from their home, or worse, and then install me there as your creature, forever on your hook as the woman that consorted with a traitor, just a betrayal away from disgrace and even execution. But you're forgetting one thing, Centurion, in all your schemes of another man's money.'

Excingus smiled wryly back into her anger.

'And that would be what, exactly?'

She straightened her back, holding the stare with which she had him fixed.

'You haven't found Marcus yet, and you haven't faced him with swords in his hands. Be careful what you wish for, Centurion, because you might not like what happens when you get it.'

* * *

Dubnus stretched his stiff body, cursing the suspicion that had driven him to pad his bedroll with clothes until it looked to the casual eye like a sleeping man, preparation for a vigil that had stretched through the night with his sword drawn for the attack he felt would be inevitable now that the half-century had seen his wounds. With his endurance stretched to the point of exhaustion, and his body craving sleep more than at any time he could recall, he had stayed ready to kill the first man through the tent's flap if there were any sign that foul play was planned. Now, with the dawn's onset, his eyelids were red-rimmed slits in a face grey with fatigue. He'd heard the soldiers talking into the late evening until the authoritative tones of their watch officer had sent them to their blankets and silence had fallen, and suspected that their talk had mainly been a discussion of just how vulnerable their new centurion suddenly seemed. And yet no attack had materialised, making his night-long vigil seem an act of folly given the temptation to surrender to sleep. He closed his eyes and saw Marcus's face, willing himself to be strong for his friend and the woman to whom he would soon be married and remembering why he'd taken such a risk in coming north before his wound was fully healed.

The tent flap flicked open, light flooding the small space's interior, and the dozing centurion snapped awake, cursing his weakness even as he tried to work out how long he might have slept. Lifting the sword's point to strike, he stared bleary eyed at the doorway, waiting for the first of them to come through and die on his blade. A figure darkened the tent's interior as it blocked out the light, and Dubnus's poised sword-hand drew back six inches as the exhausted centurion prepared for the lunge that would put his gladius clean through the other man's guts and out of his back.

'*Centurion?*'

The sword stopped a hand-span from Titus's defenceless stomach, and Dubnus closed his eyes and blew out a compressed breath at the thought of how close he'd come to killing his subordinate. The other man stepped into the tent, brushing aside the weapon and staring wide eyed at him.

'I came to invite you to speak with the men. They've been talking . . . '

Dubnus smiled weakly.

'I heard them . . . '

The watch officer shook his head in amazement.

'And you assumed that since they'd seen your wound it would only be a matter of time before they decided to do away with you in the night. So you sat up all night waiting for them with a drawn sword? No disrespect, Centurion, but you need to get your head straight. My lads have spent half the night telling each other how big your balls are while you've been sat here sweating like a legionary's foreskin on payday. I suggest that you take a moment to get into the right frame of mind to listen to what they have to say without taking your iron to the first man that opens his mouth . . . sir. Come on, I'll help you get into your armour.'

An abashed Dubnus stepped out of his tent a few minutes later and walked slowly across to face the forty men standing waiting for him.

Titus snapped out the order, and the detachment stood to attention with a precision that raised his eyebrows. He turned to the watch officer and gestured with an open hand for him to say his piece.

'Centurion, the soldiers of this detachment have given consideration to the things that you've said to us since taking command. We couldn't fail to notice that you've matched us stride for stride with a hole in your side barely healed over. You've made us consider how we want to be regarded by our brother soldiers, since you've left us in no doubt as to how we're seen at the moment. We don't consider ourselves to be cowards, but we can see how our actions on the road to Sailors' Town make us look like exactly that. So the men have decided to take you at your word, and to put everything we can into proving that we can fight like men and regain our reputation.'

He shut his mouth and stood in silence, waiting for the centurion to react to his men's declaration of intent, but before Dubnus could make any response a soldier in the front rank stepped smartly forward, stamped to attention and then spoke out, his face reddening as he plunged into what was evidently a rare public display.

'We want to prove that we mean what the watch officer's said to you, Centurion. We can all see that you're a fighting man, out in the field again, and you with a wound not right yet, and it makes us feel ashamed of what we've come to. We want to take a detachment name, something that means something to all of us and reminds us of our promise to do better every time you give us an order.'

Dubnus nodded, resisting the temptation to smile at the man's blushing discomfort.

'And that name would be?'

'*Habitus*, Centurion. We'd like to use the old centurion's name to make us strong again, and to remind us what we're promising you.'

Dubnus smiled gently, but in respect of the sentiment rather than the manner of its delivery.

'Detachment Habitus? The old boy would probably be proud to have his name used for inspiration like that. You realise that you risk tarnishing his honour if you go looking for a fight and then fail to stand firm when you find it? Wherever he is now, you can't risk bringing shame to his name by doing this thing lightly.' He looked across the ranks with his eyes suddenly hard with conviction. 'I won't accept any man running from battle if you go through with the idea, in fact I'll be behind you waiting to cut down any man that runs in the face of the enemy.'

The soldier looked at Titus, and the watch officer stepped forward to speak again.

'We understand that, Centurion. You can kill any man that runs from a fight while we serve under Centurion Habitus's name, we're all agreed on that.'

Dubnus shrugged, turning away to his tent to hide the twitching of his mouth that was threatening to break into a smile.

'Very well, in that case we'd best be putting

some more miles under our feet. We're not going to find you a fight sitting on our arses here. Get these tents struck and your boots on the road, Detachment *Habitus*.'

* * *

Drust watched with satisfaction as the last of the cavalry cohort that had pursued his men north crested the ridge to the fort's west and vanished from view.

'A sensible decision by their tribune, I'd say. No point sitting here and watching us scratch our arses for the next few days, eh, Calgus? We'll wait here for a few hours just to be sure, then head north and find this detachment the captive told us all about.' Turning to discover the source of the Selgovae chief's silence, he found the other man's face sombre. 'What's the matter? I would have thought you'd be pleased to see the back of them. You can strike out for your homelands now, or stay with us if you will, but either way their threat is lifted.'

Calgus pursed his lips, shaking his head slightly.

'It's all a bit too easy, Drust, too easy by a long way. I know that tribune of old, and he's not the type to turn his back and walk away that quickly. There'll be men left behind them, you can be sure of that, watching and waiting to signal to the rest of them that we're on the move.'

Drust shook his head, laughing softly at the other man's caution.

'Nobody could ever accuse you of underestimating your enemy, Calgus — apart from allowing them to break into your camp and slaughter your army, that is. Once burned, forever cautious, eh? Well, just to make you happy I'll send a scouting party out to make sure they've really all left. Five hundred men ought to be able to clean the landscape of any watchers they've left behind.'

* * *

The volunteer squadron took a late breakfast once they had reached the southern face of the hills beyond the River Tuidius, each rider feeding his mount with oats from the sack tied to his saddle before sitting down to eat his own meal of dried meat and hard cheese, leaving the horses to crop the grass where they were hobbled. The hills to the north loomed above the group, their scree-littered upper slopes glittering with dew in the sun's pale morning light. Silus ate on his feet, staring hard to the east and chewing vigorously on a chunk of pork. Marcus stood and walked across to him.

'What next, Decurion? Up and over the hills?'

He waited patiently while the other man chewed hard for a moment and then swallowed with a grimace, washing the tough wad of meat down with a slug of water from his water skin, waving a hand at the hills to the north.

'Over that lot? Not likely, they're a death trap to cavalry, littered with small stones that will break a horse's leg, or make it fall and throw the rider, and the slopes are steeper than they look from here. No, I think we'll just take a gentle trot along the line of these foothills towards the coast in an extended line, and see what we can scare out of the landscape. Not that I expect to find anyone this far from the ford. We'll cross the hills in a few miles, when they're a bit less risky, and aim to meet the road, such as it is, about five miles north of the ford. If my guess is correct, that will put us well to the north of any scouts hiding to watch the crossing, and in the best possible position to intercept them when they make a run back to the fortress.' He turned to face the men sat eating on the hill's gentle slope. 'Get your nosebag down you and get back on your feet, we've a nice long ride ahead of us.'

* * *

The praetorians were still eating their breakfast at the roadside when a pair of message riders clattered down the road from the north, reining in their horses as Rapax stepped on to the hard surface and flagged them down, both men throwing crisp salutes to the centurion as they dismounted. The battle-scarred officer returned them with a swift gesture, waving a hand at the fire.

'I'm Rapax, centurion of the Fourth Cohort Praetorian Guard, and these are my men. We're marching north in pursuit of a fugitive from imperial justice and hoping for news of events that might lead us to him. Come and join us for a short time, and share what you know with us.

We'll do our best to repay you with whatever we have left over from our meal.'

The pair nodded their thanks to the soldiers as they shuffled round to make a space for them to squat in the fire's warmth, one of them glancing with a horseman's interest at the mounts tied to trees around the clearing. Rapax handed them a piece of bread apiece, warm from the fire's edge.

'You bear news from the north?'

The more senior of the two nodded, his mouth full of bread, speaking in staccato sentences as he ate.

'We defeated the rebels four days ago, Centurion, broke into their camp and massacred the Selgovae, but the Venicones got away, thousands of them, and we've been hunting them ever since. They took refuge in Three Mountains . . . ' The lack of comprehension on the centurion's face took him aback for a moment. 'Ah, it's a large fortress about fifteen miles to the north, abandoned and burned out when the barbarians came south. They captured one of our officers and tortured something out of him. We don't really know what, but we've pulled back to get them to leave the fort. Our tribune thinks they might be moving to attack one of the auxiliary cohorts for some reason.'

Excingus glanced across the fire at him, a look of mild curiosity on his face.

'An auxiliary cohort? I've got a cousin serving with one of the cohorts that defends the Wall. Begins with a 't', from memory . . . '

'Tungrians? That's the cohort they seem to have gone after.'

The corn officer wrinkled his forehead in apparent concentration.

'Tungrians . . . no, that's not it. Perhaps it was a 'v'. Anyway, you're riding south to take the news to the governor, I'd imagine?'

The double-pay man nodded sagely, while his silent companion put a hand to his belt in an apparent search for some item or other.

'Yes, we'll be at Noisy Valley before dark, and briefing message riders to take the word to wherever the governor is. Eight thousand barbarian warriors at Three Mountains and expected to head north soon, possibly heading to intercept the Tungrian detachment sent to free the Dinpaladyr.'

His colleague shook his head in exasperation, evidently unable to find whatever it was he was searching for, and stood with an apologetic shrug at the man next to him.

'It'll be in my saddlebag. Won't be a moment.'

Excingus's eyes narrowed.

'The Dinpaladyr?'

The seated horseman hurried to explain the term.

'Local tongue, sir. It translates as the Fortress of a Thousand Spears, or something close to it.' Excingus raised an eyebrow. 'It's the capital of the Votadini tribe, Centurion. The Tungrians and a few of our lads have been sent north to free it from the last of the Selgovae, though why the Venicones should want to stick their nose in is beyond . . . '

Rapax rammed his dagger up through the cavalryman's throat, springing up from his squatting position and reaching to his belt for another blade as the second rider ran the last few paces to his horse and leapt astride it, jabbing his booted heels into its sides. Pulling his arm back and holding the thin sliver of iron by the side of his head for a split second, he flicked the knife forward with a fluid jerk that sent it across the clearing in a split-second flash of polished metal to strike the fleeing horseman in the back of the neck. He teetered for a moment, stunned by the sudden, intense pain, but managed to keep his seat as his mount clattered away down the road, lost to view in seconds. Rapax shook his head, staring after the wounded man for a moment before turning back to his stunned soldiers.

'You can bring her out now!'

Excingus stood, the shock of the cavalryman's death starting to wear off but with his face furrowed with incomprehension.

'One moment I'm having a perfectly civilised conversation with a man who clearly has no idea of our little secret, and the next thing I know I'm watching you butcher the poor bastard and hurl the cutlery around as if you've got something to prove. Might I enquire quite what's got into you?'

Rapax pulled his dagger from the dead man's throat, wiping the blade on the sleeve of his tunic.

'Your man here was clueless all right, but his mate had worked out what was going on. All that playacting about looking for something that just happened to be in his saddlebag? That was just a pretext to let him get back to his horse without alarming us. I only realised it when he took one last look at the horses, and at one horse in particular. *Hers*.' He pointed to Felicia as she emerged from the trees with a guardsman at her back. I saw him do it as they walked to the fire and thought nothing of it, just a horseman taking a natural interest in our animals, but as he walked back to his horse he did it again. He gave her horse a good hard stare, and he wasn't walking like a man who was going to open his saddlebag and dig something out of it, he was winding himself up to jump on the horse and leave his mate here to face the music.'

Excingus's face creased as he considered the situation.

'If you're right then he must have recognised the doctor's horse, and put two and two together. In which case, we have a problem.'

The praetorian shook his head dismissively.

'Not really. I put that throwing knife clean through the back of his neck, so I'd guess he'll be dead from loss of blood before he's ridden five miles. There isn't another unit on the road all the way back to Noisy Valley, not with all the fun and games happening south of the Wall. No, I think our secret will be safe enough, once he bleeds out and dies by the side of the road. And now, given what we've just learned, perhaps we should consider how to find this 'fortress of spears' our dead friend here was so eager to tell us about.'

Excingus nodded.

'It's probably safe to assume that this road north will eventually lead us to the Three

Mountains fortress. Perhaps once we're there we'll find something to help us . . . '

* * *

Dubnus took the men of his detachment up the north road at the double march, a pace calculated to get thirty miles under a soldier's boots in a marching day while driving him to, but never beyond, the point of exhaustion. He'd explained the need for more speed to them as they strapped on their equipment, unburdening himself as to the purpose of their mission north of the Wall.

'A good friend of mine, an officer falsely accused of treason, is serving with my cohort somewhere out here. They're probably tracking down the last of the Selgovae, now that their warband's been scattered. His woman was the doctor in the Noisy Valley hospital, until a pair of Roman centurions took her prisoner and carried her away north of the Wall. They plan to use her as bait to draw him in, I'd imagine, put him to the sword and then finish her off at their leisure. And that, since I owe my friend my crest and vine stick, is not going to happen if I have anything to do with the matter.'

The watch officer had spoken quietly to him while the detachment were forming ranks for the day's march and putting their tents on to the ox cart that would follow along behind them, a look of disbelief on his bruised face.

'So you have no idea where these Romans may have taken your fellow officer's woman? They could be anywhere within a hundred miles of here.'

He'd nodded grimly, tightening his belt.

'Yes, but you're missing something. They're from Rome. They'll have no more idea of where to look for my friend Marcus than we do, and all they can do is follow the road north and look for information as to his whereabouts. And when they get that information, so will we. We'll march at the double today, it'll be good training for your lads and make sure that we lose as little ground to them as possible, given that they're riding and we're using boot leather. Now get your boys moving, we've a long way to go and no time to waste talking about it.'

The previous day's fifteen miles had hurt more than he'd have cared to admit, both from his lack of exercise over the previous weeks and the effects of prolonged double marching on the freshly healed wound, which tugged and dragged with every step, but Dubnus knew that to show any sign of weakness would only undermine the new resolve that his men had displayed that morning. Driving them on through his example, he pushed himself through first the discomfort and then, as the pace started to sink its claws into his stomach and lungs, the pain of the march, sweat running down his back beneath his armour to soak his tunic. Over an hour into the march, and reaching deep into his reserves of endurance, waiting for the agony searing his chest to abate as his long-delayed second wind took effect, he snapped his head up as a familiar sound reached his ears.

'Cover! Quickly, and keep your wits about you.'

The detachment scattered for the verge, pulling on their helmets and throwing their pack poles into the trees as they readied themselves to fight, their faces set in determination not to be found wanting a second time. Dubnus waited on the edge of the forest with his sword drawn, grimacing at the realisation that the detachment were alone in the heartlands of an enemy who, recently defeated or not, could still leave his men dead and dying with only a fraction of the strength still available to them. The sound of hoof beats strengthened over the space of a few moments, until to his relief a single horseman trotted over the road's brow. The rider's cavalry uniform gave him an instant of satisfaction, until he realised that the man was half out of his saddle and sagging precariously, on the brink of falling to the road's hard surface. He stepped into the road, gesturing his men forward to intercept the slowing horse and ease the semi-conscious cavalryman to the ground. Eyes slitted, and breathing stertorously, the rider was pulled carefully from his saddle, his head lolling back to reveal a blood-caked sliver of metal protruding from his throat. The soldier helping him ease the rider's weight to the ground goggled at the wound.

'Fuck me, he's been shivved!'

Dubnus turned the semi-conscious man on to his side, pain forgotten as he assessed the magnitude of the wound inflicted by a thin knife buried in his neck from back to front.

'It's a throwing knife. This man was running from something — or someone — when whoever it was put this into him with enough accuracy to very nearly kill him on the spot. A fraction to the right and he'd have dropped dead within a dozen paces. And as it is . . . '

He didn't finish the sentence, eyes narrowing as the rider's eyes opened and found his own, the man's hand clutching convulsively at his arm with surprising strength. He spoke, his voice no more than a whisper.

'Praetorian . . . killed us both.'

Dubnus bent close to his ear, speaking quietly but clearly to the dying man.

'A praetorian officer and a tent party of guardsmen?'

The rider nodded with painful slowness, the metal blade bisecting his neck making the effort horribly painful, and a fresh rivulet of blood spilled down the curve of his throat.

'Saw her horse . . . know it anywhere.'

'*Her* horse? The doctor's horse?'

The rider nodded again, a little more weakly this time, as more of his blood spilled on to the grass beneath him.

'Message for governor . . . Venicones going north . . . Licinius says to Din . . . Dinpal . . . '

'Dinpaladyr.'

The certainty in Dubnus's voice closed the dying man's eyes in what seemed a combination of relief and exhaustion, a long slow breath draining out of him with no more power behind it than was sufficient to maintain the processes of his life. With his eyes closed he spoke again, his voice now softer than before as he grasped at the last of his body's fast-ebbing strength.

'On my belt . . . purse . . . for my woman . . . '

Dubnus bent close to the dying rider's face, a note of urgency coming into his voice as he sensed the man's spirit slipping between his fingers.

'And I'll pay the ferryman for you. But which woman? And where?!'

The words were so quiet as to be nearly inaudible, the rider's last breath easing them into the still morning air as little more than the noise made by his lips as he uttered them.

'*Waterside . . . Clodia . . .* '

He lay still, and Dubnus bent close to listen for any more breath, at length getting back on to his feet and shaking his head decisively.

'He's gone. Dig that purse out, and let's see if he has a small coin for the ferryman. The rest goes into my pack, and we'll go and find his woman when this is all over and done with. And quickly now, that wound will have killed him before he'd ridden far from the scene of the attack, which means that we're closer to them than I could have hoped.'

He stared up the road's long grey ribbon, the earlier agony of the forced march forgotten as he calculated how far ahead of the detachment Felicia's abductors might be. His voice, when he turned to face his men, was harsh with purpose.

'Form ranks for the march! We're going to catch up with this man's murderer and show him and his men what happens when they kidnap the wrong person.'

The watch officer squinted at him from his place alongside the detachment's ranks.

'And if they've already found your man and killed him? What if this doctor's already dead?'

Dubnus spat noisily on the verge's damp grass.

'Well then, Watch Officer Titus, we'll spend a suitable amount of time making every one of them that lives regret his part in the matter.' He turned north, waving his hand forward in command. 'Any man that falls out of the line today gets left behind to live or die alone, so we'll have no thoughts of slacking. *March!*'

⋆ ⋆ ⋆

The morning sun was less than halfway to its zenith when the Selgovae watchers, waiting in the hills to the north of the Tuidius's last fording point before the river reached the sea, saw the first sign that the expected Roman advance had arrived. They had been waiting three days when the first of the Roman cohorts that they had been set to watch for marched down to the river's edge, and both men were dirty and tired.

'Time for us to run, right, Iudicael?'

The chief scout, a man chosen by the leader of the men occupying the Dinpaladyr for his steadiness under any circumstances, simply shook his head and kept watching as the leading cohort splashed into the river's shallow water, the soldiers driven forward by the inaudible shouts and curses of their officers as they hurried to form an initial defence of the ford's northern bank.

'These are Romans. They do everything according to their rules. They won't be moving any farther north than they have to until they've got every last man across the river.' He looked up at the sky. 'I'll wager you gold to horse shit they'll not be ready to move on until well after the middle of the day. No, there's no rush for us to run for the fortress. Besides, how often is it that you get the chance to watch the idiots playing their soldier games?'

His companion grunted a reluctant agreement, settling back into the grass to watch the Roman advance guard running to take up their defensive positions around the ford.

'Why do they take such precautions when there's no enemy to be seen for miles?'

Iudicael shook his head, a wry smile on his face.

'They have a way of doing everything that is agreed, and written down, and practised, and nothing will tempt them to break these rules, not even simple common sense. Not only will they form a defence on the northern bank for the rest of their men to cross behind, but they'll defend the southern bank against attack from the rear too. They are creatures of habit, and for that we can be grateful.'

* * *

The Venicone warriors chosen to scour the ground around the Three Mountains fortress were more than a little reluctant to carry out such a menial task, until Drust announced a handsome sum in gold for any man that delivered a Roman spy to him, and double that sum if the captive were still capable of talking. Suddenly enthused to their task, and persuaded by their king that the Romans must have set at least one man to watch them for any sign of movement, the tribesmen scattered in all directions across the hills surrounding the camp, probing with their swords and spears into any vegetation or feature that looked capable of concealing even the most improbably small of Romans, but without any satisfactory result. After several hours of increasingly dispirited searching the majority of them had given it up as a bad job, and trudged back into the ruined fort's walls with their dreams of fortune shattered. King Drust watched his men return from their fruitless hunt with a slight smile.

'And there you are, Calgus, it seems as if your caution, praiseworthy though it was, has overestimated our enemies on this occasion. It seems that the Romans have made a complete exit and surrendered the ground to us. That silver-haired tribune was probably under orders to get his men south and start carving up the Brigantes. I must confess that I cannot avoid the humour in their having risen to the fight just a week too late to have been any use to your dreams of conquest . . . '

His careless insult left the Selgovae leader untroubled, since in truth Calgus was not listening to the words directed at him. Staring out to the west, he was wondering exactly how the Roman spies that he was sure would have been left to keep watch on the Venicone warband had evaded discovery.

* * *

Scaurus and Laenas stood on the slope of a low hill and watched as the legionaries of the first cohort crossed the ford, the distant sound of shouting reaching the two men as the cohort's centurions roared out their orders and chivvied their men to carry them out with more speed. Martos stood to one side, just out of earshot, his face set hard while he watched the detachment's men crossing the Tuidius. Laenas rubbed his chin, staring down from their vantage point as his men fanned out to their defensive positions, quickly building a wall of shields and spears against any potential attacker.

'I'm somewhat surprised that there's no opposition, Rutilius Scaurus. Given that you think they'll have a good idea that we're coming, wouldn't you think that the barbarians would have been better advised to attack us here, while we're split on two sides of the river?'

Scaurus shook his head, waving a hand at the crossing.

'If they'd been waiting for us it would be far more in keeping for them to have been actually lined up on the riverbank waving their spears and daring us to cross. Besides that, I don't think there will be enough of them to mount a defence of the river, not against our numbers. Whoever's leading them probably has no more than four to five hundred tribesmen with him, and the Votadini won't be cooperating with them, not given the murder of their king. The men Calgus sent to take control were probably as nice as you like until they were inside the fortress, but after that I'd imagine that things have been rather ugly for Martos's people. Not to mention his family. Have you ever seen the Dinpaladyr?'

The other man shook his head, shooting a surprised glance at his colleague.

'I've not been north of the Wall in all the time I've served here. Have you?'

Scaurus smiled, taking a deep breath of the cool autumn air before replying.

'Oh yes, I've been all over this ground. I was tasked to scout the tribes to the north of the Brigantes' territory before this revolt ever started, to have a good look at them and report back as to how they would react if Calgus called for war against us. He wasn't exactly an unknown threat, despite the fact that the speed of his attack took the last governor somewhat by surprise.'

'You came this far north in the teeth of a civil war? With how many men?'

'Just one. My bodyguard Arminius was more than enough protection against the risk of an attempted robbery, and two men on horseback have a far better chance of fading into the landscape than a squadron.'

Laenas looked at him with a new respect.

'And your conclusions?'

Scaurus shrugged.

'Nothing that wasn't expected. The Selgovae were burning to go to war, the Carvetii would follow them on principle, and it was a coin-toss as to whether the Votadini would be willing to abandon their favoured trading status with the empire and align themselves with Calgus. Just how disastrous that decision turned out to be is borne out by their current predicament. During my scouting I made a point of getting a look around their main fortress, just in case we might find ourselves on the outside and in need of getting inside.'

'And . . . ?'

'It's impressive enough, built on a huge plug of rock that rises out of the ground like a sleeping dog's back, almost sheer on one side and still sloping steeply enough on the other that even the only possible route of attack would be an uphill battle all the way. The Votadini have ringed the hilltop with a palisade of mature tree trunks, thousands of them, so that from a distance it looks like a fence of spears. Their name for it translates as 'the fortress of a thousand spear shafts', and if it's defended by men who know what they're doing I'd say it's pretty much impregnable unless an attacker can bring artillery to bear on it. And even then . . . '

'Could it be burned out?'

'With a big enough catapult to get a missile over a wall that high, and with a good supply of oil to set light to the buildings behind it, yes. Neither of which we have in our possession, of course. Short of that, the only way into that fortress is going to be something that we've never lacked as a people, those Roman strengths that the empire was built upon. This is going to come down to a combination of old-fashioned guile and ruthlessness.'

* * *

The scouts waited until the sun was almost at its zenith before moving. On the river's grassy plain below them the last Roman troops were marching into the ford from the river's southern bank, and the soldiers on the northern bank were forming up for the remainder of the day's march, Iudicael nodded decisively.

'Let's be away now. They'll be moving soon enough. Keep flat until we're over the top of the hill and the risk of being spotted is gone, and then we ride for the fortress.'

His comrade nodded, and the two men squirmed away from their hiding place over the flat hill's summit, confident that their movement would go unnoticed given the organised chaos on the plain below. Once over the hilltop they stood, hurrying down the slope to where their horses were tethered by a small lake. Momentarily relaxing with the release of pressure once they were out of sight of the cohorts camped on the hill's far side, they were brought up short by the sudden realisation that their horses were missing from the trees to which they had been tethered. Before either of them could react to the loss, a man rose from the grass to their left and called a warning to them in their own language, his accent rough but understandable.

'I only need one of you alive, and there are men all around you. Surrender to us now or one of you will die quickly, the other slowly. Surrender to us now, and I guarantee you your lives.'

The older of the two froze, looking about him for the speaker, but the younger tribesman bolted without a second thought, running hard towards the lake. An arrow whistled through the warm air and dropped him into the hillside's long grass with his legs still kicking out his death throes, and Iudicael raised both hands, watching with resignation as the hillside's long grass around him came alive with armed men. The soldiers spread out quickly, their weapons facing outwards in defence, while three of them walked past his comrade's still-twitching body without breaking step. Their uniforms put paid to any last hope he'd had of the ambush being a mistake, and the small group's leader gave him a dismissive look.

'Tie his hands and put him on his horse. I want this man in front of the tribune as quickly as possible.' He turned back to Iudicael with a hard-faced stare. 'And you'd best make your mind up before we get there. With your mate dead you're the only source of information we've got as to what's happening inside the fortress of spears, and we're going to squeeze everything you know out of you in the next few hours. That can either happen in a nice, quiet and calm way, or it can take a lot of shouting and screaming, most of it being done by you, but the end result's going to be just the same. Me, I'd prefer it if we just had a nice chat and you told us what you know without any nastiness. I've heard enough of your lot screaming their lungs out in agony for one year, but only you can decide how it's going to be, and once we get into camp you're going to be asked a lot of difficult questions by some men who are in too much of a hurry to worry about hurting your feelings. So start thinking.'

The volunteer squadron rode down the shallow hill up which the legion detachment were leading the way and presented themselves to the command group riding at the cohort's rear. Silus jumped down from his horse with a smart salute to Scaurus and gestured to the surviving Selgovae scout with a flourish.

'As promised, Tribune, here's the last of the men sent to watch for our approach.'

Scaurus returned his salute, and turned his horse from the line of march before climbing down and walking across to look closely at the captive.

'Well done, Decurion, you've allowed us to steal a march on the men holding the Votadini captive. Tribune Licinius will have to confirm your promotion, but I can't see him arguing with my decision given this success. From this moment on you're a decurion. Well done.'

Silus saluted again, then tipped his head to the prisoner.

'Thank you, Tribune. What would you like me to do with this?'

Scaurus flicked an indifferent glance at Iudicael, who was sitting helplessly with his hands bound in front of him.

'I'm not sure there's much point in trying to get any information out of him. We know everything that we need to know about the Dinpaladyr, and anything he tells us about the Votadini holding it will likely be false. I think I'll just give him to Martos for entertainment when we camp tonight. He never tires of the opportunity to send another Selgovae to Hades with his balls in his mouth.'

Silus nodded and saluted once more, turning to take the horse's reins and lead it away.

'Spare me, Lord, and I will tell you everything I know! I swear to tell you the truth, I swear to my gods Cocidius and Maponus not to deceive you!'

Scaurus met the tribesman's imploring eyes with a cold stare, raising an eyebrow and snorting derision.

'You weren't listening, Selgovae. I already know *everything* I need to know about the Dinpaladyr. You're of more value to me as an offering to the Votadini prince your master betrayed and left to die than for whatever stories you think you can fool me with.'

The captive bent over his bound hands in supplication.

'I can tell you much that you cannot know, Lord. I can tell you who holds the fortress, how many warriors he commands, how much food they have . . . '

He fell silent as Scaurus stared hard into his eyes, then nodded to Silus.

'We'll have the prisoner down from his horse if you please, Decurion. And you, whatever your name is, the second I think you're lying to me I'll have you hamstrung and left to die here. I'm sure there are wolf packs roaming these hills that would appreciate the gift. You can start with the name of the man Calgus sent to take the fortress.'

* * *

The Venicones marched from the remains of the Three Mountains fort soon after noon with Drust and Calgus at their head. The Venicone king took a deep breath of the day's cool air, watching as his scouts loped forward up the road to the north.

'It's good to be able to move without the bloody Romans dogging our steps. We'll march to the north until we're over these hills, then turn east and head for the Dinpaladyr. Let's hope that your men are still in command of it.'

Calgus, marching alongside him in the chill morning air, laughed tersely.

'They'll still be there. I sent one of my more energetic men to take a firm grip of the Selgovae, and if I know him half as well as I think I do, he'll be riding them harder than they've experienced for many a year. I've visited the fortress on more than one occasion, and I can assure you that without a legion's catapults these Tungrians will still be camped out in front of those walls when we arrive, scratching their heads as to how they might get inside. Once your warriors have rolled over them and taken revenge for us both, I'll gather my men from inside the fortress and take them west to our own hills.'

The Venicone king raised an eyebrow.

'You'll return to your land? Why would you risk going back to the very place that the Romans will be busy putting back under their boots even as we speak? If they catch you they'll drag your guts out while you watch, and leave you for the crows. Your people will have a bitter winter ahead at the hands of the legions, and they may not be happy to protect you, given the size of your defeat. Why not come north with us, and spend the winter in the safety of the hills beyond the River Clut?'

Calgus walked in silence for a moment before replying.

'It might be safer for me to take up your offer, but we both know that the legions won't be off my people's land any time soon. Their cohorts will return to the forts that stud the road north from their wall, and their detachments will roam our hills as they wish. My people will be forbidden to gather without hard-faced centurions watching their every move, ready to set their dogs on us again at the first excuse. My people will suffer under their yoke once more, and if I desert them in such a time of need I will be unable to face any of the men that accompany me with any sense of honour.' He stretched, still stiff from his night's sleep. 'I must return to take up the fight for them, or the slaughter of so many good men in our uprising will be without meaning. And besides, we've been subject to their whims since before my grandfather was born, and we've always managed to make them pay a high price for the pleasure of treading our land, both in men and gold. There's an unfinished war waiting for me in the west, so while I thank you for the offer of protection, I cannot accept it and remain my own man.'

Drust shrugged, his eyes bright with the pleasure of marching without the Roman cavalry's constant threat.

'The offer stands. You may feel differently when this last fight is over.'

* * *

On the hillside high above Three Mountains, Soldier Caius waited until the tribesmen were well clear of the fort, poking away a lump of turf from the front of his hide to afford himself a better view of the sunlit ground below him. Satisfied that the warband was on the march, he bent his back and scattered the turf roof as he stood up in a shower of dirt. Brushing soil from his armour he turned away from the empty fort and started to run, heading down the hill's flank at an easy jog as he headed for the meeting point agreed the previous day. After an hour's run he trotted breathlessly up to the waiting cavalrymen, taking a moment to get his breath and gulp from a water skin before climbing wearily on to his horse and turning south.

Tribune Licinius received his report with a curt nod, turning to his first spear once Caius had finished his brief account.

'A note for the pay records, First Spear, Soldier Caius to be credited five hundred denarii for his retirement pension. As we agreed this morning, messengers are to be sent south with a report for the governor, and a full squadron is to be sent north immediately with orders to track the barbarians without being detected, and report back three times a day. We'll follow up at a respectable distance and wait to see what develops, but there is to be no attempt to engage the Venicones without my direct orders. The next time Drust sees our dragon banner I want it to be across a battlefield.'

* * *

Detachment Habitus staggered on to the ruined fort's parade ground on legs that seemed incapable of making another step. Half of Dubnus's command were leaning on their spears rather than carrying them, and even their centurion was grey with exhaustion after the day's exertion. Bellowing a command that restored some semblance of military order, he walked out in front of the soldiers with a tired but satisfied smile.

'Didn't think you could do that, did you? You've marched the best part of thirty miles today, and you're still all on your feet and ready to fight . . . ' He paused to share a moment of dark humour with those men whose heads were still up. 'Even if you do look like you've been beaten with hammers.'

He turned away and spread his arms wide to direct their attention to the burned-out shell of a fort that stood before them.

'This, Detachment Habitus, is Yew Tree Fort. Earlier on today we passed the forts at Roaring River and Red River.

The soldiers had spared the first of the wrecked forts no more than a passing glance, too deep in the effort of their forced march to care what they were passing, although more than a few of them had given Red River's burned-out shell a longing stare as they'd ground past it in the early afternoon, their hopes of camping there for the night dashed as their centurion's pace had continued unchanged.

'We are less than a day's march from Three Mountains, which is where I expect the men that murdered those cavalry messengers will be camping tonight. You might all be dead on your feet, but you've kept in touch with the men we're hunting, which is all that matters. Now get your tents up, light the watch fires and feed yourselves, then sort your feet out and get into your blankets. We march for Three Mountains at first light, and you're going to need your wits about you.'

Titus followed Dubnus as he walked away from the organised chaos of tent erection and made his way to the stream that would eventually swell to become the Red River.

'Centurion, do you really believe that we can catch a party of men on horseback? The men are shattered after today's march, and we'll be lucky to get as much as twenty miles out of them tomorrow.'

Dubnus turned away from the swift-flowing stream and nodded his agreement.

'You're right. I made a calculated gamble today, that something might slow down the men holding my friend's woman and give us the chance to take them unawares. I'd hoped that they might have delayed long enough at their camp last night for that to happen, but my gamble failed.'

The detachment had come upon the praetorians' campfire less than an hour after resuming their march, the embers still smoking gently and the other cavalryman's corpse face down in the bloody grass beside it. Felicia's captors had clearly mounted up and headed north without wasting the time required to give the murdered man any dignity in death, and neither had the detachment made anything but the briefest of stops to confirm that he was indeed dead. From grim necessity they had left his corpse where he had fallen, like that of the man who had ridden south from the scene of his comrade's murder before succumbing to the knife wound in his throat, untended other than for a coin hastily slipped into his mouth. Dubnus grimaced his distaste at the day's compromises.

'It didn't come any easier to me to leave those cavalrymen lying unburied than it did to you. We're soldiers, and we're taught from our first day never to leave a fallen comrade as carrion, but the needs of the living are greater than those of the dead in this case. And so tomorrow, Watch Officer Titus, and despite the fact that all of our legs will be as stiff as spears, we will climb from our sleep at dawn and head north again.'

'Won't these praetorians just ride on again

tomorrow, and vanish into the hills?'

Dubnus turned to face him.

'Which would leave us in the middle of enemy territory, forty men at the mercy of whoever comes by, and with no idea of what to do next?' Titus remained silent, but Dubnus could see from the set of his face that his estimation of the watch officer's concerns was accurate. He smiled gently. 'More than likely. And yet to gain the possibility of catching these bastards and freeing my friend's woman from her likely rape and murder, I would take that risk and many worse without a thought. That's what it means to be a Tungrian. Now, go and get your men moving, they're shuffling around as if they're already asleep, and the quicker we put them into their blankets the better they're going to feel when I root them out again at dawn. And when you're done, join me for a while before we turn in. I'd like to hear the story of how you got those bruises.'

He was sitting next to the century's cooking fire in his tunic by the time Titus had finished his rounds of the guards, and looked on as the watch officer pulled off his helmet and rubbed at his sweat-moistened hair. Standing with his back to the fire, luxuriating in its heat as the evening's air turned cool, Titus looked down at his new centurion with a face made taut by the anger he was clearly still feeling.

'You asked how I got these marks. The answer's simple enough. I got jumped in the dark, soon after our fight with the Brigantes on the road to Sailors' Town. My attacker hit me from behind, without any warning, and as a result he put me down with one punch. While I was down on my knees he then kicked me in the head good and hard a few times, just to be sure I wouldn't be able to get up and give him any sort of fight. Then, when he knew that I wouldn't be getting up again, and in the mistaken belief that I was already insensible, he bent over and said a few choice words to me. That was his mistake, because I might have been flat out with my head spinning, but I still had enough of my wits intact to recognise him. It was a soldier from my own century, a nasty piece of work called Maximus who I'd had call to discipline more than once. He took his chance to get some revenge that dark night, and less than an hour later walked into a bar fight that went wrong and put him in the fortress cells with a murder charge on his head. And that would have been fine with me, except that the men we're chasing up this road turned up and took him with them as a replacement for a man they lost on the road to Noisy Valley.'

Dubnus leaned back, stretching his body to test the still-healing spear wound.

'I see. So you have nearly as big an interest in catching these men as I do? That would explain your encouragement of their change of heart.'

Titus nodded, his face hard.

'Yes, Centurion, I do. And I'll drive these lads along just as hard as you will to get my chance at a rematch.'

* * *

The praetorians rode north from Three Mountains at daybreak the next morning, following the trail that the Venicones had stamped into the ground on either side of the rough trail that headed away from the ruined fortress to the north. Rapax sent a pair of riders north to scout ahead of them, with orders to ride back if they spotted any sign of movement, either Roman or barbarian. Soon after midday the outriders rode back towards their fellows at a swift canter, pointing back towards the north.

'Cavalry coming this way, ours from the look of it. Half a dozen of them . . . '

Rapax sent Felicia away into the forest with a guardsman, and told his men to dismount and act in the manner of soldiers taking a brief rest from the saddle. When the riders came down the road towards them it was immediately clear that these were not messengers, but soldiers hunting for the enemy with their spears ready for use. Two barbarian warriors were roped to their horses, half running and half staggering along in their wake. Their leader reined his mount in alongside the guardsmen, surveying their unfamiliar uniforms with a jaundiced eye.

'Greetings, whoever you are. We're a detachment from the Petriana Wing, with orders to sweep the enemy's trail for any stragglers, and capture them to use as an example to the Venicones before we fight them tomorrow. Have you seen any more of these scum in your day's march?'

Rapax stepped forward, his face set equally hard.

'Rapax, centurion, Praetorian Guard. No, we've seen none of these animals since we were ambushed on the road to Noisy Valley and lost two good men.'

They eyed each other for a moment before the cavalry officer spoke again, his voice a little less aggressive in the face of the praetorian's truculence.

'I'm under orders to sweep as far south as Three Mountains before turning back. We've only seen these two all the way from the road's fork to north and east, so you'll be safe to push on even if there aren't enough of you to put up a fight against any more than a dozen of them. Perhaps you should wait here, and we'll escort you north when we come back this way?'

The corn officer shook his head, stepping to Rapax's side with a slight smile.

'That won't be necessary, thank you, Decurion. My escort will be perfectly sufficient for the task, given that you seem to have scoured the way ahead clean for us.'

The decurion's eyes narrowed as he took in Excingus's white tunic and blue cloak.

'Yes, well, in that case we'll be away and . . . '

The corn officer raised his hand to forestall their departure.

'You mentioned a fork to the east? How far would that be?'

'About five miles, Centurion.'

'And from there to the 'fortress of the spears'?'

The decurion shook his head grimly.

'Another thirty or so, but I'd not recommend that you try to ride any farther east than the edge of the forest, once you reach it. You'll still be a good twenty miles from the hillfort, but there's a big angry warband sat between there and where you're trying to go. You'd be best setting up camp far enough into the trees that you can't be seen, and waiting to see what happens when we bring them to battle, tomorrow or more likely the day after. Either we'll clear them away or we'll lose, in which case you'll be better off heading back to the south.'

Excingus nodded his thanks and turned to Rapax, but turned back when the horseman spoke again.

'Centurion?'

The corn officer raised an eyebrow, waiting for the inevitable question.

'Might I ask what's so important that you're willing to risk the frontier zone with only a few soldiers to protect you? If it's none of my business you can tell me to keep my nose out, but I . . . '

Excingus raised a hand to forestall the decurion's apology.

'No problem at all, Decurion — indeed, you might even be able to help us. Just like you, we're hunting for an enemy of Rome. The only difference between us is that you're hunting barbarians, but our quarry is a Roman.'

* * *

'We need to move faster, Titus. Every hour we march at this pace sees them another five miles ahead of us.'

The watch officer met his centurion's scowl with a nod of understanding, but his face was set in a troubled frown, his voice pitched equally low to avoid it carrying to the men marching a dozen paces behind them.

'Agreed. But look at the state they're in. Even you look fit to drop, Centurion, and you're the hardest man here by some distance. After yesterday, some of these men are just managing to hang on at this pace. Push them to the double and we'll break them in short order. I say we just keep them moving, and aim to get to Three Mountains with the century still in ranks and marching.'

The centurion nodded reluctantly.

'I know. But I can feel them slipping away from me.'

He kept a brooding silence as the century struggled north, and his mood was little improved by the sight of Three Mountains as the fortress came into view in the mid-afternoon. The detachment staggered down the road's long slope towards the burned-out walls, their pace increasing as they realised that the ruined defences represented a chance to end their interminable march. The leading rank was still two hundred paces from the wrecked west gate when a flurry of activity caught Dubnus's eye.

'Horsemen! Form square!'

The legionaries were still struggling into formation around him when he realised that the approaching riders were friendly, and he pushed through the detachment's disordered ranks, standing in place and waiting to greet the cavalrymen's leader. The decurion reined his horse in alongside the big centurion and nodded his greeting.

'Greeting, Centurion. We've been watching you for a while now, and my double-pay and I have been pondering what might bring a half-century of legionaries north under the command of an auxiliary centurion? In fact we've got money riding on what it is you're doing out here, so be a good man and enlighten us, eh?'

The detachment's soldiers watched in exhausted silence as Dubnus chatted with the cavalry officer, who climbed down from his horse after a moment's conversation, clapping the big Tungrian on the shoulder, and then turned to another rider with his hand out. Squatting, he took out his dagger and drew a quick map in the dirt, then stood and clasped hands with Dubnus, remounted and led his men away to the north with a farewell salute. The Tungrian watched them go for a moment, then turned and beckoned Titus to join him.

'I told you something would turn up to tell us where to look for them. Those cavalrymen met up with the men we're hunting a while ago, and stopped to talk. They were heading north and then east, riding for the Dinpaladyr, apparently, and making no secret of their mission, although Felicia was presumably hidden in the forest while they talked. Their decurion said he was pretty sure that there was something not right with a small party of praetorians riding this far north, hunting for a traitor or not, never mind the fact that the other centurion in the party was so clearly a nasty piece of work. When I told him their purpose, and that they've taken the doctor as a hostage, he told me everything he could about them, including the fact that your soldier Maximus is still riding with them.'

Titus nodded, his eyes cold with the anticipation of revenge.

'So we keep marching?'

The Tungrian shook his head, casting a sideways glance at the exhausted legionaries.

'No, we need them rested for tomorrow's march. Besides, they haven't got any more than another few miles in them, not without losing half of them by the wayside. The decurion told me about a hunter's path that cuts the corner on their ride to the north and then east. Another thirty miles will see us within spitting distance of the spot where he told them to camp for the night *and* tomorrow. Seems that there's a Venicone warband camped between them and the Dinpaladyr, and he's advised them to wait it out rather than trying to get around the barbarians. They'll be stopped in one place, and with one last effort we'll be able to overtake them. And then we'll see how brave they are, *if* your boys can put away thirty miles tomorrow.'

Titus nodded slowly, turning to survey his men with hard eyes.

'They'll manage it. Every one of them. They owe me that much. I'll drive them on until they're hanging out of their own arseholes . . . '

* * *

The detached cohorts turned from the line of march in the late afternoon of the next day, guided by Decurion Felix's cavalry scouts to a location less than five miles from the Votadini fortress, as close as the experienced Tungrian senior centurions deemed was safe until the sun was beneath the horizon. The cohorts' centurions were instructed to allow their men to rest, and enjoy the unaccustomed luxury of not having to build the customary turf-walled marching camp for the night's stop. First Spear Frontinius gathered his officers and issued a terse set of orders that made very clear what the night held.

'We're not stopping here long, so tell your men to get their hard tack down their necks and be ready to move. The baggage train will be staying here when we move forward, so make sure they've all got their cloaks handy for later on when we're hanging about in the dark waiting for the fight to start.'

He stamped off to Tribune Scaurus's officers' meeting, arriving at the tent's entrance at the same time as Tribune Laenas and his first spear made their way in from the legion cohort's lines. To Frontinius's experienced eye, well used to looking for the signs as to whether a soldier was more disposed to fight or run when the time came, Laenas looked nervous, but steady enough, and his gaze was resolute when the Tungrian came to attention and snapped him a salute. His subordinate Canutius followed him into the tent without ever meeting Frontinius's eye, and the latter paused for a moment with a thoughtful look on his face before following him in, telling the guards to close the flap and withdraw a dozen paces.

'I'll be putting my head out to check on you at some point, and if there's any suspicion that you bastards are trying to eavesdrop you'll all be dancing to the tickle of the scourge before we go into action.'

Inside the tent he found the detachment's senior officers assembled and ready, every one of them looking serious as the reality of impending combat bore down on them. Scaurus waited for his signal that the entrance was secured before speaking, looking about his officers in the lamps' flickering light.

'Very well, gentlemen, let's get down to it now that we're all here. Decurion Felix?'

'All quiet, Tribune. We've had to take a few hunters prisoner rather than risk them alerting the defenders, but none of them resisted and most of them were keen to tell us everything they could about the men holding the fortress. They'll stay here with the baggage carts under guard when we move forward, and I anticipate no problems with any of them. Apart from that the ground between here and the objective is clear.'

Scaurus nodded.

'Approach routes?'

'Just the one, really, a nice wide hunter's path that'll get us to within two miles of the fortress undetected. After that it's wide open ground pretty much all the way to the gate.'

'So we're going to need our deception plan

after all. First Spear Frontinius, are your men ready?'

Frontinius nodded confidently, hands on his hips.

'Yes, Tribune, my Fifth and Ninth centuries will be going forward just before first light and attempting an entry to the fortress just as we've discussed before.'

'Thank you. I know I promised the next proper fight to the Twentieth Legion, but given that we seem to be wholly dependent on a fiction that my auxiliaries seem far better experienced to carry off, I'm going to have to put the First Tungrians in the first wave. I'm sorry, Tribune Laenas, I know how keen you were to take your turn at the sharp end. If it's any consolation, you'll have plenty of chance to spill blood for the Emperor if tomorrow morning's ruse is a failure, although much of it may be Roman if we're left outside the fortress's walls when it's done.'

Laenas bowed to his commander's decision with a slight smile of regret, but it wasn't the tribune that Frontinius was watching so much as his first spear. Canutius's face was a study in surprise and relief, his cheeks slightly blown out while his eyes lifted to the tent's ceiling.

Thanking his gods, from the look of it, Frontinius mused to himself, *and no kind of support to an uncertain young tribune*. The other man looked across the tent at him, and Frontinius nodded, keeping his face straight. *He knows. I keep my face expressionless and yet I'd swear he knows that I despise him. Probably because he despises himself just as deeply*.

* * *

When Martos heard that Votadini prisoners had been taken by the cavalry scouts he hurried through the sprawling cohorts in search of his people, Marcus walking alongside him at his request.

'There's no telling what will happen to them if someone doesn't point out that they're not your enemies, not since the . . . '

His eyes narrowed as he caught sight of half a dozen disconsolate-looking men squatting on the ground at spear-point, fully twice their number of legionaries standing guard over them. Marcus's face hardened, and he took Martos's arm before the Votadini prince could react, restraining the bristling warrior's urge to spring to his people's aid.

'Leave this to me.' He stepped forward, searching the guards' ranks for whoever was in authority. A squint-eyed watch officer was the only candidate in sight, and as Marcus approached he vigorously chewed and swallowed whatever it was he'd been eating, wiping his mouth with the back of his hand. Ignoring the man's somewhat half-hearted salute, he pointed at the prisoners and shook his head in a show of amazement.

'So tell me, why in the name of Jupiter first and greatest would these men be under guard? They're our allies, or hasn't anybody in the Twentieth Legion been paying attention for the last week?'

The watch officer dithered in the face of the

unknown officer's wrath, falling back on the time-honoured defence of his superior officer.

'My optio, sir, he said I was to make sure they don't go anywhere, and I thought . . . '

'Or you *didn't* think! These men are a valuable source of assistance and information, and you've got them looking at the business end of your spears as if they were being kept for sale to the slave traders . . . ' He caught the look on the man's face and seethed with fresh anger. 'Fuck *me*, so that's the game is it! Fetch your optio here, soldier. *Now!*'

The young centurion stood tapping one foot impatiently while the watch officer scurried off to unload himself of the responsibility for this unwelcome development, his face pale with barely suppressed rage, and by the time the optio walked up with a decidedly uncertain look on his face, he was very clearly fuming.

'Centurion, I . . . '

'*Slaves!?* You were going to slip these men into the slave take, were you, quietly ease them in alongside whoever we end up taking prisoner when the fortress falls? Make a nice little sum for the men involved, and nobody any worse off unless you count these poor bastards, sold into slavery alongside the men that have probably been working their way through the tribe's women for the last few weeks. You should all be ashamed of yourselves, and if there's a centurion involved you can fetch the bastard out here now and I'll tell him the same. Release these prisoners to me now, or whoever's responsible will be paying a high price for his stupidity. *Now!*'

The optio thought it over for a second or so before gesturing to his men to raise their spears. Marcus glared at him for a moment longer, then gestured to the waiting Votadini prince.

'They're yours, Martos. I think we'd better take them to join the rest of your men before anyone else takes a fancy to them.' As he turned away from the optio a final thought occurred to him, and he turned back with a raised finger. 'One last thing. I expect to have their personal possessions returned to me before we move again, or your tribune and mine will be discussing why these men can't return to the fortress tonight, and the danger of giving away our presence when they're missed. Weapons, clothing, boots, jewellery, the lot. Just one item short and you'll find yourself in the ranks rather than pushing them around. Try me!'

Safe inside the Tungrian ranks, the tribesmen lost some of the hunted look they had worn all the way through the camp, and when a selected handful of Martos's warriors joined the group they relaxed into the pleasure of greeting men they knew, and had feared were dead. Marcus nodded and walked away, leaving Martos to speak with his people in private in the time that remained before the cohort resumed its cautious advance towards the fortress. Squatting in the middle of the small group, he gently but firmly questioned them as to the events of the previous weeks, and the clearer their story became the darker his expression grew.

'And they allow you to leave the fortress to hunt?'

The man he was speaking to nodded dourly.

'They take our kills and allow us a portion to feed our families once, if we're lucky. I would have run for the north many days since if it weren't for my children. As for my woman . . . '

Martos put a hand on the hunter's shoulder, patting it gently.

'I know. And I'll make them pay in blood for this. But first I have to get in . . . '

He stopped speaking as a pair of legionaries dumped a pile of the men's gear in front of them and walked away quickly, looking about them at the Tungrians as they left, clearly less than comfortable in the presence of the auxiliaries. The hunters combed through the clothing and weapons, and were soon reunited with most of their possessions.

'Your friend the Roman is a decent man, it seems.'

Martos nodded in agreement with the hunter's quietly expressed opinion.

'I've not seen him that angry anywhere other than in the heat of battle. They're not all bastards. Now, I have a trade to propose to you. That cloak . . . '

When Marcus returned to rouse the century from their dozing an hour later, with orders from First Spear Frontinius for the 9th to lead the cohort to the closest point that they could get to the Dinpaladyr without being spotted by the inevitable watchers on the walls, he found the hunters waiting quietly to be told what to do, but no sign of Martos whatsoever.

'That's his cloak,' he told one of them, 'so he must have yours, right?'

The Votadini nodded with a quiet smile of pride.

'The master of the Dinpaladyr goes to war wearing my cloak to disguise him from the Selgovae.'

Marcus shook his head and turned to Arminius, who had accompanied him back from the command tent and was standing beside him with a knowing look on his face.

'He's lost it this time. One man against five hundred hostile warriors? What good can that do? We'll be lucky to even find his corpse.'

9

The sun's first tentative light was painting the Dinpaladyr's palisade wall in a delicate shade of pink by the time the Tungrian assault party had crossed the wide open farmland that surrounded it on all sides, and reached the base of the long slope that led to the Votadini capital's main gate. Marcus had studied the fortress as he marched, gauging the apparent impregnability of the city perched atop its massive hill as it loomed ever larger before the Tungrians, its very size at once daunting and challenging him.

'Gods below, it must be five hundred feet high.'

Julius, marching alongside him in a steady stream of curses at the distasteful nature of their disguise, nodded grimly.

'All of that and more. One almost vertical face and the rest of it steep enough on all sides that any attempt to fight a way in would be a bloody fiasco against any decent sort of opposition. We'll just have to hope that these stinking scalps deceive them long enough to get us inside. I still feel naked without my helmet, and a shield would probably come in handy some time about now.'

He turned to look back at the two centuries of Tungrians marching behind them, all similarly attired with their armour and weapons hidden beneath rough blankets taken from the Selgovae dead after the battle of Alauna, shields and helmets discarded in order to avoid their distinctive outlines betraying their bearers for what they were. As a macabre finishing touch, every man was wearing the scalp of a dead barbarian cut from the corpses after the battle, the long hair disguising the soldiers' cropped haircuts.

'Fuck me, but you lot look the part. Even your own mothers would never guess the truth. Now, before we get too close to the walls, stop marching and start slouching! You're not soldiers, you're a rabble of barbarian sheep molesters. You're tired and hungry, and all you want is to get inside and get a drink and a warm, so start looking pissed off and dragging your feet. And keep your hands away from your weapons, we're all friends here. Nobody makes a move until I give the signal, and then you lose the blankets and air your iron. Nothing fancy, just get inside the fortress, start killing the bastards and keep killing them until the rest of the cohort gets to us. You can keep the hair on as long as you like if you think it makes you look better, just as long as you can stand the smell.'

The men of the 5th and 9th Centuries smiled grimly. They had been selected as the most experienced men available in the sort of no-quarter fighting that would ensue from the second that they dropped their disguises and went at the tribesmen holding the fortress. Marcus gave Julius a rueful grin, his eyes alive with the prospect of combat, and his nose wrinkled at the stink of the scalp he was wearing.

'I'd hoped never to have to do this again after the last time.'

Scarface, marching just behind him in a bloodstained blanket and peering through the purloined hair that threatened to obstruct his vision, muttered morosely.

'Still owes me a scalp from the *last* time. Ten denarii I was offered for that, and now every bastard's got one.'

Ignoring the veteran soldier, Marcus looked up at the fortress again as the soldiers reached the foot of the hill's slope and started the climb up to the gate that was the only feature in an otherwise unbroken wall of mature tree trunks circling the rock. In the uncertain light of dusk, the hill looked like a massive ship that had struck a rock and had listed heavily to one side, one face almost vertical while the other sloped to meet the plain at an angle that was sufficiently shallow for the inhabitants to be able to build level platforms for their dwellings, making the interior beyond the wall a sea of straw roofs that stepped up to the hill's summit, where a single large hall stood out above the buildings around it. He tightened his grip on the arm of the man walking alongside him, applying a subtle but insistent pressure to keep him moving towards the fortress.

'Just remember to make this convincing. You know what will happen if we're still stuck outside these walls in an hour's time.'

Harn turned his head, a snarl of frustration distorting his face.

'I recall your tribune's words clearly.'

'Then you'll be very sure to play your part once we reach the gates. We don't want to carry out the threat, but I want you to be very sure that we will.'

Scaurus had spoken to Harn in the moments before the raiding party had left the safety of the forest, his face set hard against what Marcus could only guess was his own discomfort with the role he was forced to play by the situation. The Votadini fortress's dark bulk had loomed on the horizon in the first light, already massive despite the two miles that separated it from the forest.

'Very shortly now I'm going to send an assault party forward to the gates of that fortress, Harn, soldiers disguised as your people. The men Calgus sent here to rule the Votadini are going to line the walls trying to work out exactly who they are. Our only hope of getting in through those gates is you, and just how convincing you can be when they call down to you, and you face the obvious choice of either your own death or the betrayal of your own people. So let me help you with that choice. Fetch them out!'

A party of soldiers stepped into the ring of men surrounding the Votadini captives and pulled out a pair of young warriors. Harn's face went white with shock, as he realised that his last secret was secret no longer. Scaurus nodded grimly.

'Yes. Your sons. Did you really think we wouldn't find out that you brought your boys with you when you went to war with us?' He walked around the young men, one of them barely old enough to carry a sword, then returned to put his face close to Harn's with a sneer of contempt. 'One of them's no more than a child, you fool. What were you thinking? Did you imagine that this was going to be an easy victory, and that we would just melt away when you charged out of the hills? All you've done is provide me with a lever to use against you, and sadly the situation leaves me with no choice but to do exactly that. You brought me two boys, Harn, and there are two very different ways for them to die, *if* my men are not inside that fortress by daybreak tomorrow. There's the Roman way, and then there's *your* way.'

Turning away, he'd looked at the young men for a moment and then shaken his head sadly.

'Which would be a shame. They look like fine young men, and likely to grow to powerful manhood if you give them the opportunity. If you accompany my men out to the gates of the Dinpaladyr, and if you succeed in ensuring that those gates are opened to them and stay open long enough for the rest of us to arrive and secure the victory, then I'll be able to spare them. And you too, if you live through the fight. But if not, if we're forced to camp out on that plain and I have to work out another way to get into the fortress, then I'll have both of your boys executed in full sight of the walls as an encouragement to your people to abandon their resistance. Not that it'll do any good, of course, but I'll have fulfilled my promise to you that the price of your failure will be their slow and painful deaths.'

Harn had stared at him aghast, his mouth hanging open in horror.

'No . . . '

'Yes. One of them will be lashed with a scourge, just enough to open his back up like raw liver but not enough to kill him, and then he'll be crucified with his legs left unbroken. They both look healthy enough, so I'd imagine it'll take a day or two for him to give up the fight and choke to death, when his legs finally lose their strength. And the other . . . well, it'll be obvious enough to you that Martos and his men still harbour a certain sense of resentment at having been betrayed by the Selgovae. By *your* people. I don't think that he'll be overly troubled at a request to make an example of your other son, and provide the defenders with something to think about. In fact I'd imagine that he'll be happy enough to carry out my request, but I'll leave the fine details for him to decide just as long as I'm guaranteed plenty of agonised screaming to set the defenders' teeth on edge.'

Harn had shaken his head in denial, his eyes moist.

'You can't. You won't . . . '

Scaurus had looked into his eyes with a cold certainty that Marcus had never seen before, speaking quietly and without bombast.

'Yes, I will. I'm a tribune of Rome with orders to fulfil and only one way to carry them out. I may not like it, but I'm not about to let my superior officers down by getting squeamish with a pair of barbarian children, not given the number of innocents your people abused and murdered in Alauna alone. Think about that, while you make the walk across to the fortress, because the time to choose is upon you . . . '

The disguised soldiers were drawing close to the fortress, and the first signs that they had been spotted became apparent as men began appearing on the walls of the palisade to either side of the massive, iron-studded gates. Alongside Marcus, Julius raked a hard stare across the defences.

'Twenty-five. Perhaps thirty. Less of them than I'd expected . . . '

A harsh shout from the rampart interrupted him, a voice used to speaking with authority and to being obeyed.

'That's close enough! I am Haervui, warrior of the Selgovae tribe and the master of this fortress! One of you can come forward to explain yourselves, the rest of you stay where you are!'

Julius pushed Harn forward with a hand in his back, muttering into his ear.

'Off you go, and don't forget what the tribune told you.' He watched as the tribesman walked forward into the brightly lit space before the gate, his voice hard as his eyes swept the walls looming over them. 'Staying here works for me, it keeps them from getting too close a look at us. And whoever that is drawing his sword behind me, I can hear the bloody thing rasping on your scabbard's throat so put it away before I come back there and sheathe it where the sun doesn't shine. These are supposed to be our mates, so relax and concentrate on looking pissed off and shagged out. That shouldn't be too hard for you lot . . . '

Marcus watched in silence as Harn walked slowly forward, guessing what might be going through his mind. The voice from the wall above them spoke again, the tone a little less hostile as the barbarian got close enough to the fortress wall to be recognised by his fellow Selgovae.

'*Harn?* Harn, is that you down there?'

The tribal leader stared up at the walls, his voice level despite his inner turmoil.

'Aye, Haervui, it is.' He gestured back with his arm at the waiting Tungrians. 'And this is all that's left of my men. The Romans overran our camp and put most of us to the sword. Calgus is . . . '

Haervui spoke over him, clearly unwilling to have such news broadcast to the warriors listening along the palisade.

'Wait there, I'll come down.'

Julius nudged Marcus on the arm.

'*Fuck!* Get ready, we're only going to get one chance at this.'

Marcus tensed, understanding his brother officer's concern. Viewed from the palisade the Tungrians resembled a footsore and hungry remnant of Harn's warband, but it would be a different matter entirely were the Selgovae leader to get close to them, and a single shout of warning would see the fortress gates closed, and their hopes of storming the Dinpaladyr by surprise ruined in an instant. A man-sized door set in the right-hand gate opened to allow the speaker to step outside the fortress, and Haervui strode across to Harn, his glance flicking across the men standing behind him.

'We've got scouts out on the main road to the south, I'm surprised they didn't report your approach.'

Harn shrugged, giving no sign of betraying the Romans waiting anxiously behind him.

'We stuck to the hills, brother. I didn't trust the roads, there'll be Romans hunting for us now that the warband is scattered.'

The other man nodded, staring past Harn at the Tungrians with appraising eyes.

'So we're all that's left, my men and yours. We'd better get you inside, then!' He barked a command at the gate, and the muffled sound of wooden bars being removed from their housings told the waiting soldiers that the way into the fortress would be opened to them within seconds. 'Come on, then, get moving and get inside! I don't want the gate open any longer than necessary, there are Romans . . . '

He stopped in mid-sentence, his attention caught by something unexpected, and Marcus realised that he was staring at their boots. He allowed the blanket to fall from his shoulders as he started running, drawing both swords from their scabbards and sprinting at the two barbarians, knowing that there was no way he could cross the gap before the barbarian leader could shout the command to close the gates. With a whistle of ragged-edged iron slicing the air, Arminius's axe spun lazily over his shoulder, missing Harn by no more than a foot, and slamming into the barbarian leader's head with a wet thud as he turned to bellow the alarm to the gatekeepers. The Selgovae leader dropped to the turf in an untidy heap of twitching limbs, and Marcus grasped his chance, angling his run to charge straight at the fortress's gateway. As the two centuries ran forward the gates began to open with a groan of timbers, spurring Marcus and Arminius to greater speed as a fragile moment of opportunity opened before them. The men on the wall, realising what was happening, started to shout the alarm to the gatekeepers, while a couple of hastily aimed arrows hissed past the Roman to bury their iron heads in the ground behind him.

Marcus was the first man to the massive wooden gate by several paces, at the precise moment when the gatemen responded to the alarmed shouts from the warriors on the walls above them and released the winches at which they were toiling to pull the gates apart. In the split second before the gates started to close he squeezed through the thin gap between them, and found himself in a courtyard occupied by half a dozen men caught in various states of surprise as they dithered in the face of the panicked shouts from the wall above. One of them threw himself at the Roman with a knife in his hand and ran straight on to the spatha's point as Marcus thrust it into his chest. Arminius had reached the gate, but was unable either to squeeze through after Marcus, or even to stop the massive wooden doors' ponderous but irresistible closure. Marcus realised that the gateposts were angled slightly inwards, so as to make the gates fall back into the gateway and close upon themselves if the winches that opened them were released, and that he was, for the moment, beyond any assistance from their other side. He could hear the tribune's bodyguard shouting at the Tungrians to help him as the gates fell shut with a heavy thump, leaving his friend alone inside the fortress.

'Push, you bastards, before they get the door bars back in place!'

Marcus turned back to face the enemy, realising that half a dozen men were running at the gates with heavy wedges and hammers, seeking to secure the doors against the increasing press of soldiers straining at them from the other side. Kicking the dying man off his spatha's blade, he twisted away to evade another attacker, who charged in swinging at him wildly with a heavy stave, ducking in under the staff's reverse swing and stabbing the gladius down into the barbarian's neck and deep into his chest. He wrenched the short blade free in a shower of blood, leaving the fatally wounded man to stagger away with his eyes rolling up to show their whites. Pausing for a split second to judge the distance to the nearest of the gatekeepers, as the man bent to thrust his wedge between gate and ground, he leapt forward and stabbed the eagle-pommelled gladius through his neck, pinning the hapless man to the gate with the short blade clean through his throat and buried in the gate's timbers, his blood spraying across the gateway's roughly paved courtyard. The gatekeepers hesitated for a second, and then broke in the face of their comrade's last frenzied struggles against the cold iron draining the life from his body, running screaming from the gate into the gloom beyond the courtyard.

Marcus made to kick away the wedge that the dying man had managed to force into the space where the gates met, securing them both closed against the Tungrian soldiers throwing their weight against them, ignoring a poorly aimed stone that crashed to the crude flagstones a foot to his right, but something made him glance to his left. A long blade swept past his face, close enough that he felt its passage through the air. Dancing back with the spatha held blade up and to his right in a cocked stance, ready to either attack or defend, he watched with a sinking heart as the warrior who had so very nearly put a sword into his face advanced slowly towards him, another man behind him taking up the dying gatekeeper's hammer to batter the wedge more firmly into place. Within seconds the gate would be irretrievably and firmly shut against the Tungrians, and his fate would be sealed — either a quick death or the same protracted end that would be meted out to Harn's sons in the morning. His mind racing, he barely registered the arrow that flicked past his head close enough to graze his left ear, inflicting a stinging cut on the lobe. Distantly he was aware of the horn blowing on the other side of the gate, the signal for the remainder of the detachment to cross the plain and join the fight.

Taking two shuffling steps forward, he snapped the spatha downwards in a slanting cut to attack the barbarian's left-hand side, sending the other man skipping backwards with his sword flung wide to his left to deflect the attack. Fighting the sword's momentum with wrists muscular from years of incessant practice, Marcus altered the sword's course, sweeping the blade straight down and evading the block, then whipping it back up to his left shoulder before striking again with blinding speed at the swordsman's extended sword-hand, hacking it off at the elbow and dropping the severed limb to the ground with the long sword still gripped in its nerveless hand. Shouldering the horrified warrior aside, he swung the blade back to his right shoulder and put every ounce of his power into a vicious horizontal cut that buried the long steel blade deep into the second man's body, dropping him in agony to the courtyard's flagstones with the blade lodged against his spine and blood fountaining from the horrific wound opened in his side, his hammer falling to the flagstones with a dull clink.

Feeling the spatha's refusal to come free from the dying barbarian's body, Marcus released the weapon and spun away to take a firm grip of the gladius's hilt, only to find it still stuck fast in the gate's fine-grained oak. A memory flickered into his racing mind, of an afternoon in the hills above Rome on the day after his fourteenth birthday, when he had walked out to meet his tutors in the arts of combat to find no sign of the practice weapons that usually awaited him. The burly former gladiator who had until that day been his teacher with sword and shield had stood waiting for him with a long wooden staff held in one hand, a gentle smile on his face, while the taller, leaner man who was teaching him to fight with his fists and feet sat to one side with a neutral expression. Both men had walked alongside him in his unaccustomed toga the previous day, part of a full turnout of the villa's household staff to escort the young man to the forum, and witness the ceremonies and sacrifices that celebrated his accession to adulthood, and both had been granted a place at the feast held to mark the occasion the previous evening. Festus bowed slightly, the smile staying fixed on his face despite the show of deference.

'Fourteen years old, then. Not Master Marcus any more, but Marcus Valerius Aquila, a man. You'll wear that tunic from now on, and your purple stripes will tell everyone that you're the son of a senator. A man of influence, a man of breeding . . . and a target.' He lifted the staff, tapping one of the tunic's two crimson stripes where it ran up and over his right shoulder, the dusty iron tip leaving a dirty mark on the garment's white cloth. 'This will make you a mark for every thief and bandit that comes across you, and you'll need to learn to defend yourself or risk having your dignity removed along with your purse.'

He'd shrugged, not seeing the point that his tutor was trying to make and impatient to start the afternoon's lessons.

'So teach me. Where are my weapons?'

The gladiator had shaken his head wryly, tossing the iron-shod staff and a helmet to his pupil before turning to pick up his own practice weapons.

'Not today, Marcus. We have orders from your father that today your training is to change in recognition of your manhood. Until now we've concentrated on teaching you how to use a sword, on the techniques of fighting, and practising those disciplines until they have become automatic to you. From today we're going to teach you how to *fight*.' He'd settled behind the shield, staring over its rim at his bemused pupil. 'This is where the classroom ends and the real schooling begins. And here's your first lesson. I'm a robber, with my sword and shield, and all you have to defend yourself with is that stick. When I say the word 'fight' you'd better be ready to put me on my back with my ears ringing, because that's what I'm going to do to you if you can't work out how to use the staff quickly enough.'

A dozen heartbeats later Marcus had found himself face down in the practice ground's sand, his ribs aching and his nose bleeding, turning over to find the gladiator standing over him with the same sad smile and a hand outstretched to help him back to his feet.

'That wasn't easy for either of us. You don't train a boy from the age of seven without gaining some fondness for the little bugger, but you're not a boy any more, not since you put the ceremonial dagger to that goat's throat yesterday. Now that I've made the point let's go over that again, and see what you can learn from it. For a start, you're holding the staff with your hands too wide apart . . . '

Shaking his head to clear his mind, he stooped and plucked the staff discarded by the dying barbarian from the flagstones, turning to face a trio of men charging at him from the right. Ducking low under the leading warrior's swinging sword, he hooked the staff behind the man's ankles and pulled it towards him sharply, wrenching his feet out from under him and sending his attacker crashing heavily to the stone floor with a grunt of expelled breath. The Roman spun away, planting the staff's flat end squarely between another's warrior's eyes with enough force to stun him for a moment, finishing him off by slapping its other end across his throat with enough power to rupture his larynx. With two men on their backs, the first still struggling to get back to his feet after his heavy fall, Marcus focused on the last man left standing. The barbarian hacked down with his sword, cutting the raised staff into two halves and raising the weapon again in preparation for a killing stroke on the unarmed Roman's head. Marcus saw his opening and took it, stepping in and ramming one of the cloven staff's two sharp-edged halves up into the underside of the lunging warrior's jaw, burying the jagged wooden edge deep in his head before turning to smash the other half across the back of the remaining barbarian's head as he struggled to his knees.

Stooping to scoop up the hammer dropped by the man dying with the spatha buried in his side, he spun to face another warrior as the man screamed incoherently and ran at him with a battleaxe, swinging the heavy hammer up to clash with the axe blade as it swept towards him. The weapons met in a shower of sparks and the combatants spun apart, Marcus crouching low and sliding the hammer's handle through his hand to extend its swing, smashing its heavy iron head into the axeman's knee. With a loud crack of breaking bones the barbarian's leg folded beneath him, sending him headlong with a shriek of agony as the Roman spun another full circle, smashing the hammer's head into the wedge holding the gates closed and sending it flying across the courtyard.

With the weight of dozens of Tungrians pressing hard at them, the gates opened wide in seconds, admitting a tidal wave of angry soldiers who fanned out into the courtyard looking for someone to fight, leaving the half-dozen men killed or stunned by stones thrown down on to them from the palisade lying inert behind them. Julius shouted orders at the men around him, sending them hurrying to break into the buildings surrounding the courtyard in a search for anything with the potential to act as part of a barricade, intended to keep the inevitable barbarian counter-attack away from the gate long enough for the rest of the detachment to arrive, and turn the struggle into a one-sided contest.

Qadir stepped through the gates with an arrow nocked to his bow, barking a command to his Hamians as he chose his first mark, and sent an iron head up under the ribs of one of the men on the palisade. While Marcus stalked over to retrieve his swords from their resting places, the archers made short work of the men on the wall, leaving half a dozen dead and dying men slumped against the timber and the remainder lifeless across the courtyard's flagstones. More barbarians lurked in the shadows to either side, unwilling to advance for fear of the Hamians' arrows. Hearing his name shouted, Marcus turned away from the gate to find Julius pointing his sword at the two narrow roads leading away up the fortress's steep slope from the gate, bellowing an order at his brother officer.

'There'll be more of the bastards coming down from farther up the hill soon enough, and we haven't got our shields. Get your caltrops out and your men ready to defend the gate.'

Marcus nodded tersely, looking about him for his watch officer.

'Cyclops, where are the men with the caltrops?'

The one-eyed veteran pointed out two men waiting to one side with large sacks held well away from them, the steel points protruding through the rough material glinting in the torchlight. Marcus pointed at the scanty barricade that presented a flimsy barrier to any barbarian attack that might be mustering farther up the fortress's steep slope.

'Get them laid out on the far side of the barricade, and quickly!'

Cyclops walked to the barricade behind his men, watching as the first of them lifted his sack to pour the contents over the flimsy barrier, and then froze, his head cocked.

'What is it?'

The soldier turned back to him with a puzzled look.

'Sounds like . . . men screaming?'

Marcus stood alongside him and listened, hearing faint echoes of sound from the streets farther up the massive hill. A man's voice was raised in a shout of rage, and then, a second later, in a howl of pain and despair. Other voices were raised, some higher in pitch, angry shouts and screams of agony. Realisation hit him with a jolt of amazement, and he turned to Julius with an urgent wave to get his friend's attention.

'Something's happening higher up the hill, something violent, and there's no sign of any counter-attack! I'm going up there with a few men to find out what it is, you hold the line here and wait for the rest of the cohort!'

Not waiting for Julius's reply, he vaulted the barricade, selecting Arminius, Qadir and a pair of archers to accompany him, and shaking his head in resigned amusement as Scarface gave him a dirty look and followed them across the piled-up furniture with his face set against any idea of his being sent back. The small party advanced cautiously up the steep and narrow street, their weapons held ready to fight if the expected threat materialised from the fortress's shadows. In the buildings above them another scream rang out, the lingering, despairing sound of a man with cold iron in his guts and no hope of either rescue or release from his pain, and before the sound had time to fade a sudden glow sprang to life in one of the side streets to their right, accompanied by a noise that would stay with Marcus for years to come, haunting his dreams with its otherworldly echo of damnation.

A burning figure staggered out into the road, a man blazing from head to foot with the bright yellow flame of a freshly lit lamp and howling at a pitch and volume that made the Tungrians stop and stare in horror. A woman's figure followed the apparition from out of the buildings with a blazing torch, her face demonic in the rippling firelight as she pointed the torch, screaming incoherent abuse as the burning figure fell to his knees, holding his hands out in front of him as if unable to believe what was happening to him. In the light of his death throes half a dozen other fallen bodies became apparent, previously hidden in the street's shadows.

'Mercy?'

Marcus turned to find Qadir with an arrow nocked to his bow and drawn back, ready to loose into the blazing man's body and release him from the torment that was racking him in convulsive shudders. Arminius put a hand over the arrow's head and turned it aside, shaking his head in a manner that seemed almost contemplative as he watched the tribesman burn.

'These men have in all likelihood made their captives' lives a misery over the last few weeks. Who are we to deny them their retribution?'

The blazing figure fell slowly face first to the street's cobbles, flames continuing to lick at his flesh even as their initial exuberance died away, and the woman lowered her torch, retreating back into the shadows as she caught sight of the Romans advancing up the hill towards her. The Tungrians walked on carefully, peeping warily down each side street before crossing to continue their climb, until they stood over the blackened corpse with their scarves held across their faces against the stink of scorched flesh. Looking about him, Marcus realised that they were being watched from the houses on both sides, the glinting of human eyes in the cracks between window frame and shutter betraying the presence of the fortress's inhabitants. Raising both hands from the hilts of his swords he turned a slow full circle to display his open hands.

'We mean you no harm. We have come to release you from the Selgovae warriors who have been tormenting you . . . '

'Looks like they've done that for themselves to me.'

Ignoring the wide-eyed Scarface, he opened his mouth to continue, closing it again as a man stepped around the corner of the nearest building with an axe in one hand, the other knotted in the long hair of a struggling prisoner. The writhing barbarian was clutching at his groin, trying to stem the flow of blood from a horrific wound that seemed recently inflicted, to judge from the flow that was pulsing between his fingers. His captor's entire body was blasted with blood, both fresh red arterial spray and older stains, dried black with exposure to the air, and one of his eyes was an empty socket with a deep cut in the cheek below it. Despite the man's evident exhaustion, his stance as he contemptuously threw the mutilated man to the ground was unmistakable in its confidence and sheer muscular vitality.

'*Martos?*'

As Marcus walked disbelievingly towards him the Votadini prince put the axe's head down on the road in front of him and leaned wearily on its handle. The Roman stopped in front of his friend and stared in amazement at the thickly caked blood that painted him from head to foot.

'How . . . ?'

Martos looked up, his remaining good eye wide with the strain of whatever it was he'd done since leaving the detachment's camp. When he spoke his voice was dull, as if his usual vitality had been drained from his body.

'I climbed the south wall, Marcus. I climbed it a hundred times as a boy, so I thought why not do it one more time, eh? It nearly killed me, but I did it. Loose stones, fucking birds, but I made it . . . ' Holding up his right hand, he showed his friend the remains of his fingernails. 'A small price to have paid, given what I found when I reached the top.'

His face slowly split into a wide grin, a triumphant smile that seemed to contain an edge of maniacal glee.

'I knew you'd be making a move on the gate around dawn, so I hid myself until an hour ago and waited. And listened. Remember, I was born and brought up in this tiny little world, and I know every hiding place there is. I still fit a few of them too. So I waited, and listened, and I heard what these scum were saying about my wife and children, where they were keeping them and what they were doing to them. And when I judged the time had come, I left my hiding place and I went for the bastards. At first I just cut their throats, but when I found what was left of my family I realised that just killing them was too quick. So I started doing *that* . . . ' He pointed to the emasculated Selgovae, still writhing on the ground in front of him with both hands clutching his ruined crotch. 'It seemed fitting.'

'How many have you killed?'

The barbarian shrugged wearily.

'Twenty? I didn't ever stop to count.' Marcus looked about him at the ruined bodies of the fallen Selgovae warriors, and Martos read his glance. 'I stopped to free the warriors who were still here when the Selgovae took control. They were penned up in the great hall, kept under control by the threat of death and torture for their families. When I released them, and told them that the Selgovae were openly boasting about the number of women they'd violated, it seemed to give them an extra interest in ridding the Dinpaladyr of them. Any of them that are still alive won't be breathing for very long. The women have been released, and they've got oil and flame to take their revenge with.'

Marcus frowned, looking about him.

'We expected there to be hundreds more of them. Wasn't Calgus supposed to have sent five hundred men to occupy this fortress?'

His friend smiled tiredly, waving a hand at the scattered corpses.

'We seem to have been lucky, or perhaps the men that aren't here were the ones with the luck. Their leader sent more than half of his force east the day before yesterday, with orders to bring back supplies of food to stock the fortress in readiness for a siege. They're expected to return tomorrow. I'm sure that my people can find a fitting way to greet their return, given the way they've been treated over the last few weeks.'

* * *

By the time the cohorts had reached the fortress, what little was left of the Selgovae resistance had melted into a handful of terrified fugitives from the vengeful Votadini warriors and their incensed womenfolk. Leaving the bulk of his command outside the palisade wall, Scaurus walked though the massive gates with Tribune Laenas alongside him. A bodyguard of the 10th Century's hulking axemen surrounded the two officers as they looked about them, noting the neat rows of barbarian corpses piled against the walls on either side. Marcus had escorted Martos down to the gate to get medical attention for his gaping eye socket, and the tribune winced as he caught sight of a bandage carrier cleaning out the cavity with a vinegar-soaked rag.

'Centurions Corvus and Julius, my congratulations on your victory, although I'd say the prince here seems to have been the spark that ignited his people's reassertion of their will.'

Martos angled his head round to look at the tribune, ignoring the soldier's efforts to remove what little tissue was left clinging to his eye socket and speaking through teeth clenched at the vinegar's bite. The removal of most of the blood from his face had revealed features bruised with exhaustion, but his remaining eye still burned with suppressed rage.

'Once this man's finished making my eyehole feel as if I'd got a red-hot dagger stuck through it I'll walk you up the hill and introduce you to my tribe's elders. They're going to want to know what you intend, given that you've got enough soldiers camped outside their gates to level this fortress to the bare rock in a few days. And I might have a few words for them too . . . '

Scaurus nodded reflectively.

'The thought had crossed my mind. You can be assured that the governor took a very dim view of your people's decision to join the revolt, and that was before you massacred one of our cohorts and left their corpses burning on stakes for us to discover. Come along, that wound isn't going to get any prettier, not even if my man here were to pack it with myrrh rather than slop sour wine into it. Here, put this on, you're making my men feel queasy.'

He untied the scarf from around his neck, passing the square of clean white linen to the barbarian and leaning close to whisper in his ear.

'As it happens, I do have a small jar of the stuff in my war chest, cost me a bloody fortune. I can spare you a dab or two once this is done, it's supposed to take away some of the pain, and prevent wounds going bad as well.' He watched as Martos tied the scarf across his empty eye socket, nodding once the job was done. 'That's better, although it's going to hurt *a lot* for the next few days, I'd say. Come along, then, let's go and see what your elders have got to say for themselves . . . '

The party started climbing the hill's steep slope, but Scaurus stopped after fifty paces to look at the bodies of the dead Selgovae. Almost every corpse had the same vicious wound inflicted in the groin area, some of them with the severed genitalia pushed into their dead faces' mouths. The tribune shook his head soberly, turning back to face Martos.

'Whatever it was these men did, I'd say they're paying in the afterlife. These mutilations were inflicted while they were alive, I presume?'

Martos nodded impassively.

'They were on the men that *I* killed.'

Scaurus turned to Julius.

'Centurion, I'd be grateful if you could arrange for these bodies to be collected and prepared for burning somewhere out of sight of the gate. Have each one searched for anything that might provide us with any intelligence, and make sure that nobody gets soft and provides them with coin for the ferryman. I know I can trust you with this delicate duty . . . '

Julius saluted him with a slightly sideways look and walked back down the hill, shouting for soldiers to carry out the grisly duty of collecting up the corpses, while Scaurus turned to Marcus with a slight smile.

'Forgive me for giving your friend a job that any one of my officers could have carried out, but he's not famed for his diplomacy. What's needed now is some calm reflection on the Votadini tribe's uncomfortable situation, not hard-faced Romans sticking their chins out and looking down their noses at whatever passes for tribal authority round here. If anyone's going to throw his weight around, I rather believe it ought to be someone with a longer-lasting authority over these people than I can exert.'

He raised an eyebrow at Martos, who had watched the scene play out before him in silence, then turned and walked briskly up the hill with no more attention to the litter of dead and dying warriors than he would have spared on beggars in the streets of Rome. At the hill's summit Martos led the party into a towering hall a full fifty feet high, through massive wooden doors intricately carved with figures of warriors in battle. Inside the hall, illumination was provided by a line of guttering torches down each wall, and in the flickering light Marcus saw a group of men at the far end of the space. Scaurus strode down the hall's length to stand before them. Tribune Laenas at his shoulder and a pair of Titus's axemen flanking them. One of the elders stepped forward to meet him, bowing his head slightly in greeting and waiting in silence for the Roman to speak.

'Greetings. You are Iudocus, chief adviser to the king of the Votadini, if I am not mistaken?'

Scaurus spoke slowly and carefully, allowing time for another of the elders to whisper a translation into the old man's ear. After an initial startled glance at the use of his name by the Roman, and a moment's muttered discussion between the elders, Iudocus turned to face Scaurus with an expression of carefully composed neutrality. He spoke, and the translator spoke his words in Latin after a moment's pause.

'Greetings, Roman. While your presence is welcome to us, you can see that we have removed the Selgovae usurpers from among us and dealt with them as is appropriate with the warriors of a hostile tribe. We will provide you with the little hospitality we can, given the rather damaging events of the last few weeks, but I see no reason for you to trouble yourselves further on our behalf. This fortress is . . . '

Scaurus raised a hand, turning to Martos and beckoning him forward. He spoke to the prince in Latin, loudly enough to be heard by the watching elders.

'Prince Martos, Iudocus here has obviously failed to recognise either me or the perilous situation that your tribe finds itself in. Perhaps you could help him to regain a secure footing in this discussion, before he does his people some irreparable damage. The translation thing's a bit overdone too . . . '

Martos nodded and stepped out in front of his tribe's remaining leadership, and it was immediately apparent that something was making them nervous. Marcus's eyes narrowed as he watched them fight to keep their expressions neutral, and wondered whether it was their prince's blood-blasted aspect that was troubling them, or something less obvious. Clearing his throat, Martos addressed his words directly to Iudocus, speaking in Latin rather than his own language.

'The tribune has requested that I speak directly to you. You all know me, I am Martos, prince of this tribe and its rightful king with the murder of King Brennus. I went to war against the Romans alongside our king with your agreement. I fought alongside Calgus and the Selgovae as he directed, and I was betrayed to the Romans at the same time that he died at the hands of the Selgovae.' The elders looked at each other with disquiet, and Iudocus turned to the translator, only to find Martos's broken-nailed finger in his face, his lips twisted in anger. 'You may not like me, Iudocus, you sour-faced, long-toothed pedlar of half-truths and outright deceits, but you will listen to me, or else I'll do to you what I did to the Selgovae I found in the dark beyond this hall, once I'd finished climbing the south wall! You're not too old to have *your* cock carved off and stuffed into your mouth just like them, you old bastard! And since it was your idea that we went to war with Calgus you can be sure I won't hesitate to push you out there to share their fate at the hands of the women, if you give me any more cause. And you can forget the pretence that you don't speak the tribune's language, he's been here before.'

He folded his arms and stepped aside with a dark stare that left the elders under no illusions as to the depth of his anger, while Iudocus looked at Scaurus with narrowed eyes, the ghost of a smile touching his lips. When he spoke his voice was clear and strong, with only a hint of the tremors of old age in his almost unaccented Latin.

'You were here in the winter, I remember you now. A quiet visitor, content to watch and listen. Looking for signs that we would go to war with your people?'

Scaurus smiled with equal insincerity, cold eyes boring into the older man's.

'Not really, Elder. I knew the Votadini would join Calgus in his doomed rebellion as soon as I laid eyes on you and heard you speaking with your king. It was clear to me from the start that the 'lord of the northern tribes' had you in his pocket, and that you in turn had sufficient influence with your king to seal his fate. No, Iudocus, I was here to make an assessment of your people, and how likely it was that they could field an effective force after fifty years of peaceful trading with Rome. I didn't rate those chances very highly, but then I didn't have much of a chance to take the measure of Prince Martos here until we met on the battlefield.'

'Where he was taken prisoner rather than face his end in battle, I believe?'

Martos bunched his fists, but stayed silent with his face set granite hard.

'Where he lost, in point of fact, as the result of being betrayed by Calgus, which was a part of his plans of which I'm sure you're perfectly aware. Martos and his warriors were abandoned in the path of two angry legions, with the expectation that they would be slaughtered to the last man, I should imagine. Luckily for your people, he survived. Luckily for most of them, that is. Not so lucky for you, though, Iudocus. The prince here joined with us in the hope of gaining revenge for his king's death, and I'd say he's within an arm-span of dealing out a good-sized piece of that retribution at this very moment. Martos?'

The warrior stalked forward again, turning his face so that his remaining eye's cold stare played on the elders. He pulled an ornately engraved hunting knife from his belt, turning the blade to send reflected flecks of light from the torches across the hall's lofty roof beams.

'This, elders of my tribe, is an honourable weapon which I have sworn only to unsheathe when the blood of my betrayers is within reach. I have already used it to take the life of one of the men responsible for my king's death, a man called Aed. He was a man very much like you, old and clever, an adviser to his king and responsible for much of the needless destruction done by Calgus since this war began. I found a way into the Selgovae camp, after our betrayal and the slaughter of most of my warriors, and I put him at the point of this blade. When we were discovered I took his life with it. I sliced open his belly and allowed his guts out, but I took something else besides his life. Aed had a box full of his masters' documents which, when the Romans read them to me, made sense of much that had puzzled me before.'

He turned away, speaking into the hall's dark shadows.

'One letter in particular made me realise what

fools we all were to believe that Calgus was at war simply to expel the Romans from our lands.' He turned back to face Iudocus, his face white with anger. 'It was from you, Iudocus, telling Aed that Brennus was an old man and past his prime, with no 'reliable' successor. Telling him that you could ensure the support of the elders, and therefore the people of this tribe, for a change of leadership should this prove necessary.' He walked deliberately towards the elders, who to a man were slowly but surely inching away from their white-faced leader. 'You condemned your king to death, Iudocus, and thousands of our warriors with him. Did you hope to take control of the tribe yourself, and find some innocent to be king while you pulled his strings from behind the throne? Some child, father recently dead in battle and whose mother was expected to pose no problem? Except my wife wasn't taken in, was she? She saw through you in an instant, the way I should have done before we ever marched away to war and sealed both their fates. So you had her, and my daughter, tossed to the Selgovae dogs for their sport, and my son thrown to his death from the south rampart.'

Iudocus put his hands out as if to defend himself, his face pale with terror.

'It was the Selgovae, they . . . '

A sheathed knife landed on the stone floor before him with a quiet clang, a small weapon more suited to a child's hand than a man's.

'Before I started the climb up the south wall yesterday I found his body on the rocks near its foot, broken by the fall and picked clean by carrion birds. I knew it was him, this was still on the belt he was wearing. I gave it to him for his last birthday . . . ' He walked slowly to where the child-sized weapon lay, scooping it up and ripping off the rain-stained scabbard. 'You had my son thrown from the palisade and you gave his mother and sister to the Selgovae as playthings. She's dead, the women tell me, by her own hand rather than face any more of their torment. She killed my daughter first, a mercy killing you could say.'

He tossed the child's blade at Iudocus's feet and turned away to stare into the hall's shadows, wiping a tear from his cheek before turning back to face the elders.

'You're all guilty of this. You all nodded at this goat-fucker's suggestions, and you all turned a blind eye when he murdered my son and condemned my woman and child to a slow death at the hands of dozens of Selgovae warriors. By rights I should kill you all, here in this den of your evil . . . '

Scaurus stepped to his side, his face creased with anger and his hand raised to point a finger at Iudocus's white face.

'And we won't raise a hand to stop the prince if that's his choice. In fact I'd put good money down that Centurion Corvus here would take his swords to you alongside Martos, given the chance. He understands more than you can imagine about this sort of crime.'

Martos nodded his thanks to the tribune before turning back to the terrified elders.

'I should kill you all . . . but to do that would leave the tribe without leadership. I can't take the throne, I was as much to blame for the king's death in my pride as you were in your deception and plotting. And with my son dead I have no heir to follow me, nor the appetite to take another woman for the purpose of breeding a successor. So, I shall be the kingmaker rather than the king, and my word will be law unless you all want to suffer a death as undignified as that of those you betrayed, and for your daughters and granddaughters to be whores for the legions. My sister's son will be king, and you will guide him in the years that remain until he is old enough to rule alone.'

One of the elders opened his mouth to speak, but Martos raised a hand to forestall him.

'The new king's first act will be to sign a new friendship treaty with Rome, and this will include routine and frequent inspection visits to ensure that you fools are keeping your end of this distasteful bargain. This tribe will be an ally of Rome once more, and you will all work to ensure that friendship, or you will find this tribune, or one very much like him, calling you all to account.'

The elders exchanged glances, hardly daring to speak for fear of upsetting the delicate balance in Martos's words. Iudocus stepped forward and nodded solemnly, spreading his arms as if to welcome the prince's words.

'Most regal, my lord, you have shown as us all . . . '

He stopped abruptly, looking down in

confusion at the torrent of blood and bile pouring from his ruined belly. Martos had lunged forward with his hunting knife, concealed behind his back throughout his judgement on the elders, and ripped him open from hip to hip. He stepped back with a satisfied smile, watching as the stricken Iudocus fell to his knees and stared at him imploringly, a wavering moan of distress escaping from his lips as his blood puddled on the hall's stone floor. The prince stared down at him contemptuously.

'I said I was a realist, Iudocus. I didn't say I was stupid. Besides, these sheep needed a reminder to take away with them of just how ruthless I'll be if they ever stray from this agreement.' He raised his voice. 'I was careful not to open him up too widely, or to spill too much of his blood. This ruthless old bastard dies here, unaided and without any succour, and any man that touches him will die alongside him in equal agony. And when you're dead, Iudocus, there'll be no coin for the ferryman. I'm going to behead you and throw *your* headless body from the south rampart, where it can lie on the rocks to make a meal for the crows. Your head comes with me, as my guarantee that you'll forever be caught between this world and the next. And as for you all . . . ' He pointed the knife at the horrified men standing around the elder's spasming body. 'This is the last and best warning that you'll get. Cross me in any of what I've just commanded, and I will make sure you die just as slowly, and with just as little honour. Try me.'

10

Back at the fortress's main gate, Marcus found a scene of orderly chaos as the Tungrians carried the last of the Selgovae dead through the wide archway and down the steep approach towards a rapidly growing pyre of wood that the other two cohorts were gathering from the nearby forest. Julius was standing in the gate's shadow barking orders at the tired soldiers, and when he saw his fellow officer approaching down the fortress's slope he waved a hand out over the plain below them, indicating the toiling soldiers crossing to and from the forest with bundles of firewood.

'Once again the Twentieth Legion seems to have found its true role. You should have seen their first spear's face when I told him and that tribune of theirs that the fight was already over. He looked like it was his birthday, and . . . '

A shout from the wall above him interrupted his musing.

'Horsemen! To the west!'

Both centurions hurried up the ladder that led to the palisade's rampart, turning to stare in the direction indicated by the sentry. At the limit of their vision, perhaps five miles to the west, Marcus could just make out a flicker of movement. A small band of riders with a long white banner trailing above them was riding for the fortress, the standard's forked tail flickering in the wind of their passing. Julius shook his head with a disgusted look.

'It's the bloody Petriana. I'd know that dragon standard anywhere. I stood and watched the bloody thing fluttering in the breeze while they sat and watched us fighting and dying at Lost Eagle. And wherever that thing twists its tail you'll usually find that wily old bastard Licinius. *You!*' He shouted down to Scarface, who was standing at the bottom of the ladder. 'Stop following your centurion around like some love-struck goat herder, go and find Tribune Scaurus and tell him that Tribune Licinius will be at the gate by the time he gets down here. *Go!*'

Scaurus joined his two officers in time to watch the last mile of the horsemen's approach to the fortress. He stared out at the approaching cavalry squadron without any visible sign of surprise.

'I've sent Martos to get some sleep, he was almost beside himself with fatigue. So, what have we here, just when I thought life was finally about to turn dull for the rest of the year? My colleague and his men aren't riding like men who've decided to come by and see how we've done for the want of anything better to do.'

The Petriana's tribune dismounted a dozen paces short of the gate and stalked up to the palisade wall with a grim smile, squinting up at Scaurus and his officers and then glancing back at the men building the pyre on the plain below the fortress. He called up to them, shielding his eyes with a raised hand.

'Well now, colleague, I see you've accomplished your orders with the usual efficiency.

Perhaps you ought to come down here and join me, though. I've something to tell you that will give you some pause for thought.'

Scaurus climbed down from the wall after instructing Julius to keep the men inside the Dinpaladyr at their tasks.

'You'd better come with me, Centurion Corvus, I suspect I'm going to need someone to take notes of whatever it is my brother tribune has to tell me. I may well be too busy banging my head on the palisade in frustration.'

The two tribunes clasped hands, and Licinius waved a hand at the fortress with an appreciative nod.

'Well done, Rutilius Scaurus. How long did this take? It looks as if your men are only just digging out your marching camp.'

Scaurus nodded happily, jerking a thumb at Marcus.

'We got lucky, or rather Centurion Corvus here got lucky on our behalf. That and a little intervention from Prince Martos.'

He talked his colleague through the story of Marcus's fight for the gate, and their subsequent discovery of the havoc wrought by Martos and the released Votadini warriors, and the young Roman found himself on the receiving end of a long stare from the veteran cavalryman.

'Outstanding work, young man. Perhaps you should have chosen a more heroic name to hide behind, since it seems that you positively refuse to blend into the landscape and be forgotten. Which reminds me, there are imperial agents loose in the border area hunting for you. It's hardly a surprise, but it seems that the praetorian tribune discovered that you've taken refuge with this cohort through a piece of battlefield gossip that eventually reached the wrong ears. Apparently that knowledge has already cost more than one innocent life in Rome, and the report I've received tells me that Perennis believes the combination of a praetorian and a corn officer will be strong enough to ensure that you're brought to justice. Although I have to admit to being somewhat baffled as to what's to stop a ruthless senior officer from simply putting them both in the ground and nobody any the wiser.'

Scaurus frowned.

'While I thank you for that warning, I can't see you having ridden this far north to deliver that unwelcome news in person.'

Licinius nodded his head, grim faced.

'You're right. My other intelligence for you is of a rather more pressing nature, and concerns a Venicone king that seems to have a hard-on for your cohort.'

* * *

Scaurus gathered his senior officers in the Dinpaladyr's great hall, its stone floor still wet where the blood that had poured from the dying elder, as he had bled out under Martos's unforgiving stare, had been scrubbed away. Tribune Licinius took a cup of wine with Scaurus, Laenas and their senior centurions, lifting it in salute as the small group drank to their success in capturing the fortress.

'But that's not all we're here to do, is it, Tribune?'

First Spear Frontinius had greeted the arrival of the Petriana's commander with an instinctive reserve, and now he asked the question that was on every lip in a respectful but questioning tone. Scaurus nodded in recognition of his senior centurion's question, tipping his wine back and placing the cup on the table beside him.

'No, First Spear, indeed it isn't. Tribune Licinius?'

The cavalry officer stepped forward, looking around the small group to take their measure before speaking.

'Gentlemen, for what it's worth, I don't think that Drust has any intention of attempting to take this fortress. He has neither the time to spare in his march north, nor the equipment for any sort of siege. But if it isn't territory that's on his mind, something else must be dragging him so far out of his way home. Something that matters to him more than anything else. Think back, gentlemen, to that morning that we broke into Calgus's camp in the forest, the day that we broke this rebellion into splinters and scattered it to the wind. It was your men that were detailed to search the Venicone section of the camp, if I have it right?'

Frontinius and Neuto nodded with a grim glance at each other, both seeing where the cavalry commander's reasoning was taking him.

'And nothing of any great importance came to light? Or at least, nothing that was surrendered by your men . . . ? I thought so. My guess, gentlemen, is that one of your men found something of the utmost importance to King Drust, and that he promptly stuffed it into his armour and kept quiet as to the discovery. Something small enough to conceal, perhaps a piece of tribal jewellery, a crown, or perhaps a torc, something worth enough money to make an entire tent party join the finder in his crime. I also think he tried to sell it to someone known for such dealing, even though I won't be able to prove it until I get back south of the Wall and catch up with a certain stores officer. I'm pretty sure that *he* in turn recruited one of my centurions to help him with the coin needed to buy this trinket. A centurion who was then captured and tortured to death by Drust's men, during which agony I'd be surprised if he didn't buy a quick death with news of Drust's lost treasure. All of which means, if I'm right, that your command is about to receive the undivided attention of eight thousand angry barbarians, all bent on recovering whatever it is that their king mislaid.'

Tribune Laenas frowned for a moment before asking the obvious question.

'So why can't we just march everyone into this fortress, shut the gates and wait for these barbarians to get tired of camping outside and resume their journey north?'

Scaurus shook his head.

'That was my first reaction too, but the rainwater cisterns are almost empty and we don't have time to refill them. The Selgovae haven't allowed anyone out to fetch water for weeks, and the rain hasn't been anything like enough to do the job for them. Add to that the fact that they've just about stripped the place bare of food, and there's no way I can order almost three thousand men to take refuge here. If we camp inside this fortress we'll end up having to feed the population as well as ourselves, and our water will be exhausted within a day or two. Unless Drust were to take one look and then turn around and head for home we'd be bottled up in a trap of our own making. No, gentlemen, I'm afraid that we're going to have to fight Drust and his warband. Either that, or we run for our lives and abandon the Votadini to their fate. Not much of a choice, is it?'

* * *

The tribal elders reacted to the news of the approaching warband with the smug equanimity of men well accustomed to the idea of their fortress's invulnerability. It was only when the Romans had explained to them the parlous state of their supplies that they realised their predicament.

'And if you think the Selgovae were bad then you'll find the Venicones a revelation. They need food, and since you don't have anything to offer them I'd predict that they'll leave this hill a smoking ruin populated only by your corpses. Perhaps they'll spare your children for a life of slavery, but the rest of you will die in ways that will make you beg for your ends.'

Licinius stepped to Scaurus's side, his face set equally hard.

'You may live beyond the edge of the empire, but you've become accustomed to life in the shadow of what those of us on the southern side like to consider the civilised way of life. You trade your cattle and grain with us in return for luxuries, and many of you speak our language. The Venicones, on the other hand, despise us, and in consequence they also despise *you*. You'd be well advised to do everything in your power to ensure that they never come within sight of your walls, or you may find your entire tribe erased from existence.' He stared hard at the dismayed elders. 'If you don't believe me, just sit back and wait for a while If, on the other hand, you'd rather take a hand in ensuring your survival, you'll have every able-bodied person that can wield an axe or a spade gather at the gates as quickly as possible. I've an idea that just might get us all through this, but it won't work without enough labour. To put it simply, your people can either dig or die.'

The Romans turned away to leave the tribal council to their deliberations, and Scaurus raised an eyebrow at his colleague.

'Got somewhere in mind, have you?'

The older man smiled grimly and nodded.

'We passed it during the ride here. We can make it ready in an afternoon, and Drust's men are too far out to reach it before dusk. All it needs is a few hundred feet of earthworks, a few hundred carefully felled trees, and then some ankle-breakers and lilies, and it'll be perfect. And now, if you're amenable, I suggest that we go and find whatever it is that's drawing Drust towards us like a runaway bull. Got any ideas?'

Scaurus nodded tersely.

'Just the one.'

* * *

The Tungrian cohorts mustered as ordered, watched by the 20th's bemused legionaries. Scaurus stepped out in front of his command, his eyes sweeping across the ranks of his men. He nodded to First Spears Frontinius and Neuto, and at their command the cohorts' centurions barked the order that brought their men to attention. An uneasy silence settled across the ranks, disturbed only by the gathering number of men and women mustering at the fortress's gate with spades and axes. The tribune raised his voice to be heard across the mass of men standing before him, raking them with flint-hard eyes.

'Soldiers, you doubtless think I've paraded you in order to congratulate you for taking the fortress! And I have. Well done to you all! You will no doubt be fondly imagining that your fighting for the year is finally over, and looking forward to the march south and some long-overdue time in barracks. Perhaps you are wondering if you will be returning to your own forts. All of which is quite understandable . . . except for the fact that *your* fighting isn't over yet. One tent party here, a few men among fifteen hundred, have presented us all with a problem. They are hiding a secret from the rest of us. These men are in possession of something that doesn't belong to them. It used to belong to the king of the Venicones, and it now belongs to the Emperor by rights. One of you discovered it while we were searching the enemy camp, most likely, and tucked it away to sell later. We suspect that the man in question probably tried to complete the transaction that same day, once darkness had fallen, but for some reason the deal fell through, and he was left holding his prize.'

He allowed that possibility to sink in for a few seconds before continuing, watching the cohort closely. In the 7th Century's ranks Soldier Manius stiffened, the awful possibility that his centurion might recall their encounter in the torchlit darkness that night sending a physical shiver up his spine.

'The problem that the rest of us have got is that the Venicone king seems to have worked out that we have it, and he wants it back so badly that he's coming in our direction with his entire warband. Eight thousand warriors. In just a few hours, soldiers, whether we like it or not, we'll be fighting for our lives against the Venicones again. And in case any of you have forgotten that it was us who stopped them at the Red River ford, and left them stuck on the eastern bank with a bloody nose, let me assure you that they will know exactly who we are. They will be looking for blood in vengeance for their losses that day, and they will know that if they can find us outside of this fortress then they have their chance to slaughter us to the last man. And this time we have no river to hide behind . . . '

He turned away for a moment, allowing time

for his blunt words to sink in. Manius's eyes were locked on to Centurion Otho's back, and he forced himself to look away, and feign bored indifference, as the officer turned to search his century's ranks with a stony face.

'And so, soldiers, you will understand that I'm feeling somewhat let down by these few men that have put us all at mortal risk. In point of fact I'm angry enough to have them all beaten to death by their century, once I find out who they are. And trust me in this, I *will* discover them within the next hour. If I have to I'll have you all remove your armour for searching by your officers, and if the men holding this precious object make me waste that much time, time we should be using to dig defences, I'll make their deaths appropriately brutal. But, in the interests of getting this thing over with quickly, I'm offering a limited amnesty to these men, *if* they surrender themselves to *justice* promptly.'

Otho was moving now, walking swiftly along his century's front rank and making the turn at the point they met with the 8th, coming back along the rear of the soldiers' line. Manius could sense his approach, for all the fact that his gaze stayed locked on the tribune right up until the moment that the centurion pulled him backwards out of the line, ripping off his helmet with an impatience that tipped the soldier's head back hard and left his chin pointing into thin air, just as the first punch landed. Scaurus fell silent at the sudden commotion, watching impassively as the enraged centurion battered the defenceless soldier, tearing off his weapons and armour in between blows. At some point in the one-sided struggle the object of his search must have revealed itself, for he seized the other man by the ear and dragged him out of the century's ranks with his knees buckling from the savage beating, a shining piece of gold held aloft for the tribune to see. From behind him he heard First Spear Frontinius's snort of barely restrained laughter.

'It's a good thing we don't need the idiot to tell us the story, I expect he'll be eating nothing but gruel for the next few weeks.'

* * *

Late afternoon was turning to early evening when the two tribunes rode into sight of the Venicone camp. Halting outside of what they judged was the most optimistic of bowshots, they waited while the word was carried back to the warband's leader that there were three enemy horsemen waiting outside the camp in the sun's fading warmth. Having estimated that Drust was bright enough to recognise an opportunity to talk, the Romans were nevertheless relieved when a party of three warriors strode out of the smoke drifting from the barbarian campfires. Drust walked out towards the waiting horsemen until he was close enough to shout a challenge, his hammer carried over one shoulder and a wry smile on his face.

'Have you come to discuss the terms of your surrender, Roman?!'

Licinius leant forward, muttering quietly to his colleague.

'Leave this to me. He already knows who I am, but you're a different matter. Let's allow him a little uncertainty, eh?' He raised his voice to a parade-ground bellow. 'Far from it, barbarian! My colleague and I have come to have a good look at your ragged warband. My colleague here is keen to get some measure of how many of them we'll have to kill tomorrow before the rest of you turn tail and run for home!' He lowered his voice a fraction, speaking to the Venicone king rather than simply shouting at him. 'Perhaps you'd like to come a little closer, and avoid the need for all this shouting? I owe you one safe passage, if you recall?'

Drust nodded and led his companions closer, until the Romans could see the grey hairs in his red beard. Licinius dismounted with an easy grace that belied his years and beckoned for the other two to follow his example.

'If he wants to try cracking my head with that hammer I'd rather be on my feet than stuck up there on a dithering horse.' He waited until the two parties were lined up facing each other before speaking again. 'You amaze me, Drust. To have marched your men all this way for the sake of a simple gold trinket? Surely you could have had another one crafted for far less trouble than the likely price of attempting to recover *this*?'

He pulled the torc from inside his cloak, holding it up to the evening sun's golden light in a hoop of liquid gold. Drust started in surprise, and the warrior standing to his right put one hand to the hilt of his sword. Licinius smiled, his quiet chuckle of amusement creasing the

Venicone king's face into a frown.

'I'd restrain your man there, if I were you. Do you imagine I would be waving the bloody thing around this close to you without some assurance of my safety?' He gestured to Marcus, standing alongside him with both hands on the hilts of his weapons. 'Your tribes have both suffered at the hands of this young officer before. You, Drust, failed to cross the Red River because of the large numbers of your men that his soldiers left face down in the water as the price of their attempts to cross, and as for you, Calgus . . . ' He smirked at the Selgovae leader's surprised expression before continuing. 'Yes, I know you. That purple cloak, that and your pig-ugly face, were both described to me in detail by the last Roman officer to speak with you at such close range. You had a little chat with him before the battle that we've taken to calling Lost Eagle, if you recall? And if he were here, I'm sure Legatus Equitius would want me to thank you for your quite spectacular stupidity in sending your men up that hill to die on his men's spears in such an unimaginative fashion. He was given the command of a legion as a result of his victory over you, you know? You lost a battle you already had in your grasp that day, for all that you captured an eagle. But I digress, it's a common fault of the elderly.'

He smiled without humour at Calgus, but if he'd expected the Selgovae leader to be discomforted by the revelation he was disappointed. After a moment of stone-faced thought,

Calgus's face lit up with malicious glee.

'So you're the one! I read the legatus's private papers that we captured during the battle, and I was intrigued to discover that he had a son whose identity was hidden from the world. I still have his head hidden away, you know, preserved in a jar of . . . '

Marcus tensed, but Licinius waved a hand dismissively.

'*Enough!* I came to speak with Drust, not bandy gossip with yesterday's man. Your tribe is scattered to the four winds and your time on earth is limited, so hold your tongue and leave those men at the table who still have stakes to play with to talk. You can take the matter up with the centurion in the morning, when he has you at the point of his sword.' Licinius fixed Drust with a level stare, ignoring Calgus's scowl. 'King Drust, it's still not too late for us both to avoid yet more bloodshed. I'll happily return this bauble to you if you'll turn your warband's path to the north and return to your lands in peace.'

Drust shook his head slowly, holding Licinius's stare and pursing his lips.

'I think not, Roman. It would be a shame to have come all this way and left without a decent tithe of heads for being put to the trouble.'

The cavalryman shrugged expressively.

'As you wish. You know how the battle will go tomorrow as well as I do. You'll charge our line, and find yourselves on the wrong side of a turf wall that will expose your men to our spears as they try to get over it. It will all come down to a bloody slogging match, and that could last hours and leave thousands of men dead. And, I should warn you, we have more than enough strength to hold you off for as long as you choose to batter your heads against our defences.'

Drust shrugged.

'I'll take that 'trinket' from your dead body, and your head besides. It will remind me of the victory. And when we're done with you we'll march on to the Dinpaladyr and see how pleased Calgus's men are that we've lifted your siege.'

Tribune Licinius smirked, and tossed the torc on to the grass at his horse's feet.

'In that case you'd better have this. It will help my men to pick you out as you run before us, and since the reward I've put on you both is doubled if you're taken alive I'd guess they'll be grateful for that. And with that, colleagues, I think we've wasted enough time on these gentlemen.'

He turned away from the barbarians with one last calculating glance at Drust, whose attention was fixed on the torc lying before him in the grass's tangle, and then turned back to face them again.

'Although it would probably only be fair of me to temper your expectations as to the Votadini fortress. Should you by some strange chance manage to overcome our defence tomorrow, you might find the Dinpaladyr a little less receptive to your triumphant entry than you clearly expect would be the case . . . '

Calgus narrowed his eyes, and his head shook in disbelief.

'Never try to deceive a master of deception, Tribune. My man Haervui will have had that fortress buttoned up tighter than a duck's backside the second he saw you coming over the horizon. There are no secret approaches to the Dinpaladyr, and he'll have had scouts . . . '

His voice trailed off as he saw the smile on Licinius's face broaden to a grin.

'Scouts, yes, we found them and took them prisoner. That there's no secret approach to the fortress, well, again, yes, I can agree with that. But darkness, Calgus, covers up all kinds of sins, as I'm sure you'd be the first man to agree. So when two hundred beaten barbarian scum turned up at the fortress gates at dawn, led by a very persuasive Selgovae chieftain well known to all inside, who then proceeded to talk the defenders into opening the gates . . . well, we've all heard of stronger defences than the Dinpaladyr that have fallen to *deception*, haven't we?'

Calgus bristled.

'No man of my tribe would submit to being part of such treachery!'

Licinius shrugged, turning back to his horse and spoke his final words back over his shoulder.

'You know your men better than I do, Calgus, so I'm sure you're right. Your kinsman Harn would never play a part in such a scheme, not even with his sons at the point of a Roman spear. So the Dinpaladyr must still be in your hands, mustn't it . . . ?'

The Romans rode away, leaving their barbarian counterparts staring quizzically at their receding backs. Tribune Scaurus leaned out of his saddle to mutter in his colleague's ear, his tone bemused.

'So you've told them that we have the fortress. You've told them that we're going to be fighting them in 'the usual way' in the morning, and you've given that red-faced barbarian sheep-fucker his pretty gold neckpiece back. Did I miss something?'

Licinius winked across Scaurus at an openly curious Marcus before replying, a sardonic smile wreathing his face.

'Firstly, respected colleague, I want them . . . no, I want *Calgus* to fester in his own juices this night, at the thought that his brother warrior might have betrayed his cause. Secondly, yes, he now knows exactly how we'll be meeting their attack tomorrow, in precisely the same way we always do, in a nice straight line with spears, swords and shields. And that's just the way I like it. And lastly, with regard to that 'red-faced barbarian sheep-fucker's' pretty gold neckpiece, please believe me when I tell you that I meant every word. I want my headhunters to be looking for that tidy little fortune when they chase those horse-eating bastards back into the hills they came from. I'd rather have him in one piece for shipment to Rome, but I'll settle for his head. And whoever brings me his head will only get their reward if the torc's still attached. As far as I'm concerned it's only on loan.'

* * *

Later that evening, as the Tungrians prepared for sleep in rather different circumstances to usual, Licinius walked into the 9th Century's lines with a thoughtful look on his face. Directed to where Marcus lay stretched out on his rough woollen cloak, he left his bodyguard waiting at a discreet distance and stood over the young officer with his helmet in both hands. Opening his eyes, the younger man saluted and started getting to his feet, but Licinius waved him back with a gloomy smile that was barely visible in the twilight.

'I thought I might find you here. It seems I owe you an apology, young man, and I've been too busy to come and see you until now. Bit of a first for me, y'know, to be apologising for *not* saying something. Usually it's because I can't keep my bloody mouth shut. May I sit?'

The younger man gestured to the ground alongside him, and Licinius lowered himself on to it with a grateful sigh.

'So, that rascal Calgus has let the cat out of the bag and I have no choice but to acknowledge the truth, if not the helpfulness of the bastard's words. Yes, Legatus Sollemnis was your birth father. He got your mother pregnant while he was serving in Hispania. Your adoptive father was serving alongside him and was already married, and so he and your mother agreed to take you as their own rather than see their friend's child farmed out to some peasant family, or worse. And he was, after all, a senator. His house was not a bad place for an infant to find himself.'

He paused, rubbing his face wearily.

'Sollemnis told me all this when I discovered that the senator had arranged for you to be spirited to Britannia, rather than share his fate in Rome. He enlisted me in the plot to keep you alive, and he also swore me and everyone else that knew the secret to keep it that way until the rebellion was over, and he had the chance to tell you the story in his own time, rather than in some snatched conversation with no chance to explain his actions. And then, of course, he was betrayed to the Selgovae by Praetorian Prefect Perennis's arsehole of a son, and murdered on the battlefield at Lost Eagle. And yes, I could have told you the truth after his death, but I decided that you'd had enough mourning for one year. My mistake . . . '

He looked up to find Marcus staring at him with a level gaze, with no hint of the emotions he was feeling on his face.

'Enough mourning for one year? That's true enough, Tribune, more than true enough. My father — because he'll always be *my father* — and all my family, and then the best friend I have left in the world, and now the man I discover to have been my birth father. All of them dead in less than six months. I would mourn for the legatus, if I had another tear in my body, but I can't. Don't apologise to me for keeping this from me, because believe me, I would much rather never have known. And if Calgus thinks he's left a wound on me with his words, he'll do well to make very sure that he avoids me on the battlefield tomorrow, if he wants to live to enjoy the memory of my face this afternoon. Given the misery that man's heaped on me in the last few months, taking his head would be a good way to pay him back. Eventually.'

* * *

The Venicone scouts slid noiselessly through the night's silence, slipping along the forest's edge until they came within sight of the Roman camp. Going to ground in the trees, they watched their enemies in the full moon's light for long enough to be sure they understood the precautions the soldiers were taking before making their next step. A dozen watch fires lit the camp's interior, and patrolling soldiers paced along the length of the earth wall, staring out into the night's shadows. At length one man removed his boots and detached himself from the scouting party, slipping into the forest and moving silently through the trees at a stealthy pace, feeling forward with his bare feet for any potential source of noise as he took each step. His progress was painstakingly slow, but without any disturbance of the surrounding foliage or any noise to betray his presence. An hour's quiet stalk brought him within sight of the camp's rear wall, and he sank into the shadow of a tree to listen intently to the forest for one hundred patient breaths before moving again. Eventually, satisfied that he was alone in the night, and that the apparent lack of any patrol on this face of the Roman defences was as it seemed, he slithered over the waist-high barrier and into the heart of his enemy's stronghold.

A tent loomed before him, and he snuggled into its shadow to wait for any sign that he might have been detected, but none came. The camp was quiet, eerily so, and with a faint frown he put his ear to the tent's leather wall and listened carefully for a moment. No sound could be heard from within, no snores, no conversation, and his frown of uncertainty deepened. Taking a small blade from his belt, he sliced into the thick leather with a smooth, slow stroke, then put an eye to the hole thus created. The tent was empty. Eyes narrowed with suspicion, he crawled forward and around the corner, his hands outstretched to feel for anything that might betray his presence, and as he reached the tent's doorway they encountered a hole in the ground covered with slender branches cut from the forest behind him. Parting the leaves, he reached cautiously down into the pit, his fingertips searching for and exploring the trap's contents with delicate care.

Grim faced, he looked out across the camp, shaking his head at the utter and complete lack of movement. Watch fires burned untended amid a sea of empty tents, their faint hissing and popping of burning sap the only disturbance in an otherwise silent scene. Nodding to himself, he turned back to the wall, a slight smile creasing his face. Drust would reward them well for the knowledge that the enemy camp was an empty shell, a trap set for the unwary to blunder into, and provide a hidden enemy with the perfect opportunity to strike at them from the rear. Going back over the camp's wall, he allowed himself to relax slightly, confident that there was nobody to see him roll across the earth barrier and cross the gap into the silent trees. As his feet touched the ground he jolted back against the wall, a sudden searing pain in his chest rooting him where he stood, sudden torture tearing at his lungs as he fought for each agonised panting breath. Looking down, he saw the shaft of an arrow protruding from his rough shirt, and even as his shocked wits fought to make sense of its presence another arced out of the trees and slammed into his body, ripping a hole in his heart that killed him in seconds. His glazed eyes stared vacantly out across the forest as the hidden archers broke from their cover and moved with hunters' caution to stand over him.

'Not bad. But not good enough.'

Qadir nodded at his fellow Hamian's whispered verdict on the dead man's abilities, leaning close to speak quietly into his ear.

'Good enough to have got past anyone but us, I'd say. You'd better go and tell the tribune about this while I keep watch for any others. And be careful, there'll be more of them between us and the cohort.'

His fellow archer jerked his head in silent amusement and vanished into the forest without a sound. Qadir turned and slid back through the trees, settling back into a hiding place within bowshot of the dead scout's cooling corpse to wait for the dawn, silently mouthing a prayer for his victim's spirit as he nocked another arrow to his bow and froze into perfect immobility.

* * *

Drust roused his warriors before dawn the next morning and gathered their family leaders around him in the grey light of the sun's waking beneath the horizon. The previous night had been the time to fire his men up with tales of the riches they would win once the Romans were swept away, walking from one campfire to the next to show them his confident, wolfish grin. He stood in the middle of his warband, in the heart of a gathering of the fifty or so men who provided their leadership, thousands of warriors beyond them straining to hear his words.

'One cohort and a few miserable horse boys aren't going to hold us up for long, but I want to do this the true Venicone way, in a storm of iron and blood. *Their* blood. I've run from them for long enough to crave battle, to swing my hammer into their shield wall and see men shrink away in terror.' He stared about him, his heart swelling with a savage pride in the host of warriors gathered about him, and raised the hammer over his head in one hand as he turned in a full circle to stare his chieftains in their eyes. 'Not one of those Roman bastards is to survive to tell the tale of how we tore them limb from limb. Let it be as if they simply marched into the autumn fog and never came out again, as if the very hills wearied of their presence and rose up, crushing them flat without leaving any trace. Let there be no word of their deaths for their families, not even the bitter comfort of knowing that their men are dead, and not enslaved for the rest of their short lives. No more running, my brothers! Let the Romans know what it feels like to run . . . at least for as long as it takes for us to catch every last one of them and put them to the sword!'

When the cheers had died away he gathered his chieftains about him, speaking softly to avoid being heard beyond their tight ranks.

'Once we move, we move quickly. Tell your men that any one of them that falls out of the march will be left to face his shame alone. We'll meet the scouts I sent out last night on the road, and they will guide us into the enemy camp. We must mob the Romans, my brothers, like wolves bringing down a stag. When we find them there can be no hesitation, we must run straight into the fight and overcome their defence with simple weight of numbers. If we respect their shield wall they will hold us at spear's length all morning, bleeding us from behind its shelter in their usual cowardly way. Run to the fight like wolves, my brothers, sink your teeth into their throats and bring them down in the way that we fight best. Spill blood for me, my brothers!'

The warband ran to the east in the dawn's growing light in silence, their passage marked only by the jingle and clatter of their weapons, with the king and his twenty-man bodyguard running at their head. Three miles out from their camp, the scouts sent out by Drust the previous night rose from the vegetation at the side of the track that headed east to the Dinpaladyr, and Drust raised his hand to stop the warband's forward progress. His men panted their steaming breath into the cold morning air while he walked to meet his men.

'Only three of you?'

'One of my men went closer to the enemy camp, my lord, but he did not return. We heard nothing, but they must have found him and either killed or captured him.'

Drust nodded unhappily, telling himself that the man's loss would inform the Romans of nothing more than they already knew, but nevertheless cursing the lost opportunity to learn more about his enemy's disposition.

'Go on, then, tell me what you know.'

'We found the Roman camp by the light of their watch fires, my lord, and stayed within sight of them until dawn, to better see what awaits us. They have camped in a gap in the forest, my lord, with the ground to either side made impassable by trees they have felled with the tops facing outwards, but the ground before their earth walls is clear and flat.'

Drust scowled, his face contorted with the ache in his chest from the effort of the run.

'So they may be alerted, but no more so than would have been the case anyway. You can lead us to them?'

The scout nodded, pointing down the track with a dirty-nailed finger.

'Simple enough, my lord. If we run another thousand paces we will come upon the break in the forest on your right, five hundred paces deep and the same wide. The enemy camp occupies the last third of the open space, with flat ground all the way from the track to their earth wall.'

Drust nodded, thinking fast.

'How high is their wall?'

The other man tapped his leg where the thigh joined with his groin.

'This high, my lord. A running man could be over it in one jump, if it were not defended.'

'You read my mind. And when you left it to meet up here, was it defended?'

'No, my lord. There was noise inside the camp, but no sign of any shields at the wall.'

'Good. Now walk with me and give me a warning when we are within one hundred paces of the gap in the forest. We will make a quiet march from here, and only run again at the very last moment.'

The warband paced forward in silence, the lead scout walking alongside Drust as they crept down the track towards the Roman camp. With no more than fifty paces left before the point where he judged they should start the attack, the scout stiffened and grasped his master's arm, pointing at a handful of men who had marched out of the mist to their front, each of them carrying a pair of leather buckets. The group's leader bore the marks of a man who had recently taken a beating, and he carried himself gingerly, as if every movement were painful. Romans and barbarians alike goggled at each other in a moment of indecision before the soldiers reacted, tossing aside their buckets and turning to flee, screaming out warnings as they ran.

Too late, Drust told himself gleefully, much too late. He sprang forward, bellowing the only command required to unleash his men.

'*Attack!*'

The men of his bodyguard ran with him, the faster of his warriors passing him within a dozen paces as they sprinted in pursuit of the fleeing Romans. Rounding the edge of the forest gap within which the enemy camp had been constructed, the Venicones stormed down the slight slope towards their objective, every man howling a battle cry as they swept towards the camp's unmanned defences. Looking beyond the fleeing soldiers, Drust saw a sea of tents across the breadth of the Roman encampment, with smoke rising from dozens of cooking fires, while the few isolated sentries patrolling outside the earth walls took one look and bolted for the illusory safety of the camp's interior. The warband's onrushing tide reached the slowest of the soldiers fleeing before them, and the man went down with a spear in the back of his neck, his gurgling scream driving his comrades forward in their headlong flight from the howling warriors behind them.

The desperate soldiers reached their walls, running through the doglegged gap left open to allow unobstructed entry and exit, one of them falling on the mud-slicked grass and crashing to the ground. He was overrun in a second, dying in a flurry of blades as the leading Venicone warriors hurdled the earth wall to either side of the entry with ease and charged on into the Roman camp. Drust slowed a little as he reached the camp's walls, his eyes narrowing in calculation. There was no ankle-breaker, the square-bottomed trench that the Romans usually dug alongside their earth walls to fell the unwary attacker with broken foot or ankle bones. Driven forward by the sheer mass of his men, he climbed on to the wall to stare across the leather tents that filled the camp, resisting the press of his warriors to keep his balance as they poured over the wall to either side and charged forward into the heart of the enemy position.

'Cunning *bastards* . . . '

There, behind the camp's far wall, there they were. A wall of round shields faced the Venicones across the empty camp. The cooking fires, the few patrolling sentries and even the apparently surprised water carriers, all a ruse to make him believe the Romans were unprepared for his onslaught, and a part of his mind wondered what trick might yet wait for them even as he pointed at the defenders and screamed the only possible command under the circumstances.

'*Kill them all!*'

* * *

'They've bitten off the bait and swallowed it whole.'

The three tribunes lay flat among the trees, looking down the long slope that ran down to the empty camp so painstakingly prepared the previous day. While the two Tungrian cohorts' pioneer centuries had laboured with their axes to build an impassable abattis of fallen trees to either side of the earth walls, making an assault through the camp towards its rear wall the only way to reach its defenders, the soldiers and tribesmen had painstakingly prepared the ground inside the walls for an influx of unsuspecting Venicone warriors.

Licinius nodded in response to his colleague's comment.

'Just a little longer. Let them get properly mired before we show our hand.'

The barbarians stormed over the camp's outer wall and charged through the cohort's tents towards the real defence at its rear, a wall fully four feet tall and defended by a thicket of sharpened stakes set to rip the throat out of an unwary attacker.

'There you go. What a delightful sound . . . '

Higher notes were piercing the berserk roar of the Venicone onslaught, screams of agony rising as the warriors charging across the empty camp found the other defences readied to greet them. Scaurus's grimace when the older man had first outlined his plan for the battle had brought a smile to Licinius's face, and blank incomprehension to Laenas's.

'Lilies? That's a bit classical, colleague.'

Licinius had smiled grimly, holding the fire-blackened stake up for his brother officers to examine more closely.

'You like the idea, then?'

Scaurus had nodded, taking the sharp sliver of wood and testing the point on the ball of his thumb before handing it to Laenas.

'Very much so. If it was good enough for the

Divine Julius in his conquest of the Gauls, it's more than good enough for us to use on these animals.'

Judging that the volume of agonised screaming had risen to the level they were waiting for, he raised an eyebrow at Licinius, who nodded his agreement, raising his voice for the centurions waiting behind them to hear.

'Very well, gentlemen, let's go and show these tattooed bastards what it means to push Rome too hard.'

All three men climbed to their feet, and behind them the wood that overlooked the decoy camp came alive with the shouting of centurions and the rattle of equipment, as three cohorts stirred from their long wait and came to battle.

⋆ ⋆ ⋆

Still standing on the false camp's front wall, Drust watched in dismay as his warriors blundered into the trap waiting for them, As they charged through the sea of tents, intent on bringing the defenders to battle, dozens of men lurched and fell within a few seconds, their screams merging with the war cries of their uninjured comrades in a cacophony of rage, pain and terror. The warriors following them turned to the left and right, seeking a way round the sudden chaos of fallen bodies twisting in the agony of their wounds, and blundered into more of the hidden traps, each hastily dug pit containing several stakes arranged to point in different directions like the petals of a flower.

'Lilies. Nobody could ever accuse the bastards of failing to learn from their mistakes.'

Drust turned to find Calgus standing alongside him atop the low turf wall. The Selgovae leader shook his head slowly, watching as Drust's warriors gingerly felt their way across the field of traps laid out in front of the rear wall's entire length. Even advancing with caution, their progress suddenly reduced to a slow walk, the occasional man still found his foot vanishing into the apparently solid ground and impaled on the fire-hardened wooden stakes concealed in their well-camouflaged pits. Both men watched as the first warriors reached the defended rear wall, snaking around the long stakes protruding from the earth wall's defence to attack the men waiting for them behind their shields. Calgus shook his head slowly.

'I've seen this before this year. They'll hide behind that wall and slaughter your men with their spears as they try to climb it. You've been fooled, Drust, they'll hold us off all morning . . . '

'So we'll kill them all by the afternoon. They're still stuck there behind that wall, and all I have to do is send a force around to their rear and we'll have them bottled up like rats in a barrel.' Drust turned to look at Calgus, who was staring at the defenders with an uncertain look in his eye. 'What?'

The Selgovae king's frown deepened.

'There's something wrong here. The Tungrians have oval shields . . . ' Drust turned to look again with fresh focus.

'You're right, they're round. Like . . . those fucking horsemen!'

He spun and looked back up the slope, his jaw dropping at the sight of armed and armoured men pouring from the trees to their rear. Turning back, he pointed at the member of his bodyguard who carried the signal horn used to gain the warband's attention in battle.

'*Blow!*'

As the horn's echoes rang across the field, and the Venicones paused in their struggles to reach the camp's defended rear wall, Drust raised his hammer high over his head, then pivoted to point the weapon's heavy iron head up the slope at the trap closing around the warband.

'Warriors, there is our enemy! *Attack!*'

⋆ ⋆ ⋆

The detachment's first centuries broke from the trees at a dead run, their centurions bellowing encouragement as hundreds of men hurled themselves from their hiding places and sprinted for the line that Licinius had indicated to Scaurus and Laenas the previous afternoon. The three men had walked across the long shallow slope as the late afternoon's shadows slowly lengthened, discussing the course that they expected the next morning's fight to take.

'Assuming that Drust displays his usual bull-headed behaviour, and attacks quickly rather than standing back to consider what might be wrong with this scene . . . ' Licinius paused and waved a hand at the soldiers labouring to construct the marching camp that he hoped would lure the Venicones into their trap. ' . . . then there will come a moment when he knows he's been fooled. And at that moment he will turn his men round and they'll come charging back up here like the hounds of Hades, and if they get here . . . ' He pointed at the ground they were standing on. ' . . . before we can get a decent line established to stop them then they'll overrun us in no time.'

Scaurus had looked back at the trees behind them, then turned to stare down the slope, gauging the distance with a practised eye. He shook his head unhappily.

'Hiding three cohorts in that wood is all very well, but the men will be packed in like spectators at the circus games. It'll take longer to get them out and into line than we'll have. We might be better just meeting them on open ground . . . '

Laenas put a hand on his arm.

'What if . . . '

The two tribunes turned to look at him, Scaurus raising an inquisitorial eyebrow and Licinius frowning slightly. His voice when he spoke was impatient with the younger man's interruption and Scaurus saw his subordinate flinch almost imperceptibly at the tone.

'*Yes?*'

'Well, I was thinking . . . '

Licinius put his hands on his hips and narrowed his eyes with frustration.

'Tribune Laenas, we are . . . '

'Colleague?'

The older man looked at Scaurus in slight surprise, taken aback at the studiedly neutral tone of his brother officer's voice.

'Rutilius Scaurus?'

'If our colleague has an idea, then I'd like to hear it.'

He'd raised an eyebrow at the younger man, opening his hands in encouragement, and Laenas had stolen a nervous glance at Licinius before speaking again, his voice riven with uncertainty.

'I was just thinking that if our problem is the time we'll have to get our soldiers out of the trees and into line, then we'll have to find a way to slow the Venicones down as they come back up this way. A way they won't notice on their way down the slope.'

Both men had stared at him curiously, their interest piqued. As he kept talking, his voice strengthening as the idea took shape, Licinius's sceptical expression had transformed into a slow smile by the time he turned to call to the nearest officer.

'*Decurion!*'

Silus had hurried across to the trio, saluting briskly.

'Tribune?'

'I need you to take a party of twenty men back to the Dinpaladyr. There's something the Votadini will have plenty of that we need, and as much of it as you can find.'

The Venicones massed at the decoy fort's wall turned at their king's command and surged back up the slope, yelling out their fury and frustration. A clear trumpet note rang out across the battlefield, and, as if by some arcane magic, the horde of charging tribesmen were suddenly reduced to a chaos of struggling bodies, hundreds of them sprawling over previously unseen obstacles while the men behind them were felled in their turn by the chaotic sprawl of bodies. In seconds the onrushing warband's attack was reduced to a crawl, those men still on their feet having to pick their way around those still recovering their balance. Hacking furiously at the ropes which had tripped them, raised from the thumb's-width trenches in which they had been run across the hillside the previous day, each one snapped up and tied fast by men hidden in the woods to either side, the Venicones were quickly able to remove the unexpected impediment, but as Drust looked over his men's heads at the scurrying Roman troops he shook his head and spat on the ground with disgust.

The cohorts had formed a rough line by the time their enemies had resumed their progress up the slope, Tungrians and legionaries intermingled by the speed of their rush from the trees and kept that way by a decision made by the three tribunes the previous afternoon. Licinius had watched the 6th Legion's men going about their preparations for the following day's battle and turned to the other two senior officers with a questioning look for Laenas.

'Tribune, have your men actually seen any fighting this year? I believe your cohort was shipped in from Germania after the disaster at Lost Eagle, and you were too late into the battle to destroy the rebellion to see any proper fighting.'

Laenas had slowly nodded his reluctant agreement.

'In that case they are an unknown quantity, whereas our Tungrian cohorts have fought in two battles this year already. We know that they will cope when the barbarians' first attack breaks on their shields, but we cannot know how your men will react. I suggest that we deliberately mix some of your legionaries in with the Tungrians, and let them work out their ranking when they get to the line of defence. That way the experienced men will help the new boys cope with what they're about to experience. The rest of you can form our reserve. After all, no good commander ever put everything in the shop window, did he?'

Marcus's 9th Century were among the first men to the point where Licinius had decreed the defensive line would be held, in the company of the first men of the legion cohort out of the trees. Scarface pushed himself into his accustomed place in the front rank, hefting his spear and looking to either side at the legionaries beside him, grinning at their expressions as they watched the barbarians regain their momentum to charge up the slope at them.

'Nice shields, ladies. Best get ready to use them, the tattoo boys will be here in a moment. *Get your spears ready to throw!*'

'Thank you, *soldier*, I'll be the one that decides what we're to do if that's all right with you?'

Marcus, standing to the line's rear with his gladius drawn, kept his rebuke level enough and his eyes fixed on the oncoming Venicones. Julius's 5th Century had taken their place in the line next to his men, as equally mingled with the legion cohort's men as were his own, and the big centurion was stalking along the line of his men and barking his last instructions over the din of the approaching barbarians.

'There's no river to stop them this time, only your shields and your desire not to end up with your head on the point of a blue-nose spear.' Marcus winced with the involuntary memory of his first glimpse of Rufius's head held aloft at the battle of Forest Camp as his brother officer raised his voice to bark an order at his men. 'Both ranks, spears ready!'

All along the straggling Roman line the soldiers that had reached their places gripped their spears more tightly, readying themselves for the next command as the Tungrian and legion centurions waited for the right moment. Julius, gauging that the Venicones were as close as he wanted them without starting the fight, bellowed an order that rang across the battlefield.

'Front rank, spears . . . *throw!*'

Legionaries and auxiliaries alike ran forward the few short paces needed to give them the momentum to throw their weapons, hurling their spears and javelins into the onrushing Venicones and dropping to one knee in order to provide the rear rank with a clear throw.

'Second rank, *throw!*'

The rear-rankers threw their spears in flatter

arcs, their targets fewer than a dozen paces distant, the auxiliaries' broad-bladed spears and the legionaries' arrow-headed javelins dropping hundreds of the enemy warriors to the slope's turf in screaming, writhing agony. The soldiers quickly reformed their line and braced for the barbarian charge's impact as the stricken warriors were shrugged aside or trampled underfoot by the warband's charging mass. Scarface grimaced at the sight of a dying warrior, a spear spitted clean through him, being propelled forward on faltering legs by the mass of men behind him, and set himself a little lower behind his shield as he waited for the warband's impact. Muttering as much to himself as to the men around him, he raised his gladius until the sword's point was held level with his shield's brass boss, ready to strike.

'Steady, boys, steady. We get this wrong and we're all fucked . . . '

The Venicone charge broke on the defenders' shields with an impact that rocked the Roman line back half a dozen paces, the warband's wild-eyed warriors hammering at the wall of shields that confronted them with a rabid intensity, a wild desperation born of their realisation that they were trapped inside their enemy's line. The Romans gave ground grudgingly, forced back one pace at a time by the barbarian onslaught and fighting back from behind their shields with well-timed sword thrusts. Aiming for the barbarians' vulnerable thighs, guts and throats, their stabbing thrusts ripped open the warriors' unprotected skin in hot sprays of blood, killing or disabling several of the enemy for every legionary or soldier who fell to a barbarian weapon.

The soldier Scarface, his tunic already wet with blood running down his neck from a shallow spear wound to his chin from the initial barbarian attack, pushed his shield forward as the spearman stepped forward and struck at him again, watching as the weapon's long blade punched through the board's layered wood and stuck firm. Wrenching the shield back to pull the weapon from its wielder's hands and drag the barbarian forward an involuntary pace, he stepped forward to meet the momentarily unbalanced warrior with a snarl of triumph. Stabbing his gladius deep into the other man's thigh, he twisted the blade savagely to open the blood vessel running beneath the ruined flesh, wrenching it free and punching the stricken spearman back into the mass of men behind him with his shield's heavy boss.

Behind the battling soldiers, centurions spaced down the length of the line watched hawk eyed for casualties, bawling at the men of the rear rank to pull any casualty who failed to stagger clear of the fight out of the line by his arms and throw him clear, quickly pushing a replacement in. Where the majority fought back in silence, save for their grunts of exertion, a few of the Romans, those close to being unhinged by the horror unfolding around them and those for whom these few precious minutes of combat were the potent elixir of their lives, screamed in desperation and wide-eyed defiance at the barbarian warriors railing at their shields as they fought.

Drust climbed the slope behind his men with a speed born of his sense of urgency, Calgus close behind him as he pushed through the warband to reach the Roman line with his bodyguard gathered close about him. Looking between the heads of his warriors he saw the Roman line holding firm, the determined soldiers fighting hard to hold off his men's attack, and the evidence before him told its own story. Many more warriors than soldiers lay dead and wounded in the trampled mud between the two lines, and the sour stink of their blood and the contents of their guts was already strong enough to make his gorge rise. Stepping back a few paces, he looked grimly around the men of his bodyguard, nodding slowly at them as the knowledge of what would be required to escape from the Roman trap became clear on their faces. He spoke over the battle's din, looking each man in the eye in turn as he told them what he needed.

'Warriors of my household, you above all other men of the tribe are as brothers to me, after all these years together. And now, my brothers, I must ask a difficult thing of you. Unless we break this Roman line, and quickly, our own dead will form a wall over which we must climb to make our escape, making such a thing nigh on impossible. We few must do what another five hundred champions might struggle to achieve, hamstrung by their very numbers. We must throw ourselves into the Romans without regard for our lives, and kill enough men in one place to allow our warriors to exploit the gap we carve in their line, and break it asunder. When their line breaks I will lead the warband through the gap and fall on them from the rear. Victory will be ours, but to break their line will need a mighty sacrifice, my brothers. I will lead you in this, but you must be willing to attack the Romans with desperate speed and raging fury if we are to make this happen. Can you do that for me, my brothers, knowing that many of you will be drinking with your ancestors tonight?'

He looked around his men again, seeing the resolution harden in their faces as they met his gaze, some nodding their assent while others simply stared back with the expressions of men who knew full well that their time had come. Brushing away tears of pride, he opened his arms and beckoned them into a huddle of bodies, smelling the tang of their sweat as he spoke the words he knew would unleash their full fury on their enemy.

'Brothers you have been to me, but no longer will I call you so. From now you are not brothers to me, but sons! Those of you that fall will be venerated as my children, those of you that live respected as members of my family. We shall be remembered far beyond our lifetimes, my sons, for what we are about to do, for we go to bite out our enemy's throat, and tear his body to pieces. *With me, my sons!*'

The huddle broke as the king stepped forward to face the Romans, swinging his hammer in an overhead stroke to bring it sweeping down on the head of a legionary, the heavy iron head smashing the Roman to the ground with his helmet staved in, and while the men to either side goggled at their comrade's inert body he swung the hammer low, breaking the ankles of one man and upending another with a vicious hook and pull that used the last of the weapon's momentum. As the line's rear-rankers stepped in to take their places, peering from behind their shields at the fallen soldiers, his bodyguard surged forward with snarls of defiance, taking their iron to the men to either side of the breach in order to stop any attempt to reinforce the endangered section of the line. Their reckless attacks broke on the obdurate Roman defence in sprays of their own blood, but their sacrifice, as Drust had predicted, gave him a precious moment of time in which the soldiers to either side of the terrified rear-rankers were preoccupied with their own defence, and could give no thought to reinforcing the point of his attack. Turning back to face his warriors, Drust raised his hammer high and bellowed the only command his men would require.

'*Forward, my brothers! Forward to victory!*'

Turning back to the Romans, he sprang forward and swung the hammer up and then straight down, punching the pointed end of the weapon's head down into a soldier's helmet, breaking through the iron shell and felling its wearer instantly, blood flowing from the fallen man's ears as he pitched full length atop the turf. The warband surged forward with a roar of triumph, pouncing on the weakened section of the Roman line in a welter of blood and iron, killing half a dozen soldiers and smashing its way through what was left of the defence in an unstoppable stream of men. First Spear Neuto ran from his place behind his cohort's line towards the break in the defence, shouting a request to his colleague Frontinius as he drew his sword and plunged into the fight.

'Quickly, send me your rear-rankers!'

Julius and Marcus, the nearest of the 1st Tungrian Cohort's officers to the break in their sister unit's line, had already reacted exactly as Neuto had requested, ordering their rear-rank men to leave the fight and follow them towards the slowly but inexorably expanding hole in the Roman defences. They ran head on into the Venicones who had fought their way past the soldiers struggling to contain the breakthrough, dozens of wild-eyed warriors spilling out into the open space behind the line, whose next act, unless they were contained, would be to fall on the rear of the men still struggling to hold back the barbarian wave.

Marcus drew his spatha and pointed it at the warriors, urging his men forward alongside those led by Julius, their few dozen soldiers advancing into the teeth of the barbarian attack, and momentarily shoring up the right-hand side of the line's breach. Facing fresh opposition where they had thought to find nobody to oppose them, some of the barbarians turned to fight while others pushed up the slope towards the legion cohort waiting under the forest's edge, seeking to outflank the newcomers. Reinforced by the increasing numbers of men running to re-establish the line's integrity, even as more warriors pushed and fought their way through the slowly widening gap, forcing the defenders back pace by anguished pace, the 2nd Cohort stood their ground and fought back, despite their precarious position. Stubborn determination, and the knowledge that to break under the pressure being applied to them could result only in their deaths, fuelled their desperate resistance, but the two centurions shared a knowing glance, both realising that the defence was hanging by a thread that must snap at any moment with the Venicones' simple but irresistible weight of numbers. Marcus looked in puzzlement up the slope to the reinforcements standing in front of the forest before turning to shout a question to Julius above the cacophony of battle.

'*What are they waiting for!?*'

11

Tribune Laenas stood in front of the detachment's reserve, five centuries of his legionaries waiting one hundred paces to the rear of the Roman line, and watched with growing unease as Drust's hammer rose and fell above the defenders' heads. He had been every bit as unhappy as Scaurus had predicted would be the case when he was detailed to stand ready with the reserve centuries, one hundred paces behind the main line of defence.

'Tribune Scaurus, I must . . . '

Scaurus's response had been terse, his patience stretched thin by the young aristocrat's pressing desire to put his cohort in the coming battle's front line.

'Follow your orders, Tribune? That would be wise!'

The young Roman had recoiled at the harsh tone in his superior's voice, seeing something unexpected in Scaurus's face as the older man had turned to face him in the previous evening's gloom.

'I only . . . '

Scaurus had shaken his head uncompromisingly, putting a finger firmly on his subordinate's breastplate.

'No! I understand, Laenas, but you're just going to have to do as I tell you. This is going to be a world away from anything you or your men have ever experienced before. I need battle-hardened soldiers in the line when the Venicones realise that they're the rats in this particular trap, because they're going to fight like wild animals to escape. My auxiliaries have faced down barbarians exactly like these more than once this summer, which means that they know they can beat Drust's men given the right circumstances. If some of your legionaries can get into the line alongside them then so much the better for all concerned, but my men need officers that they can trust standing behind them. Your first spear is going to be of questionable value in a fight from what little I've seen of him, and you've never experienced this scale of bloodletting at close quarters, for all your unquestionable willingness to fight . . .'

He'd smiled tightly at the younger man, shaking his head slightly, and when he spoke again his tone had been gentler.

'I'd be content to stand as our reserve, if I were you, Tribune Laenas, and let your first experience of this vicious way of fighting be an easier introduction than my Tungrians had at Lost Eagle. And while you're standing there, you should pray to all of your gods that there's no need for your men to unsheathe their swords. Because if there is, then the barbarians will have broken through, and you and your five centuries will be all that stands between my command and bloody disaster. And in such circumstances, colleague, your chance for death or glory will be upon you quicker than you can appreciate.'

With a sudden, sick lurch of his guts, Laenas

realised that the line was breaking before his eyes. As he watched, the tiny breach in the detachment's defences began to widen as the inexorable force being exerted by the mass of barbarians pressing upon it forced apart the soldiers fighting to hold them back, and despite the reinforcements running from the line's rear on both sides of the breach. Realising that he had only seconds in which to react, the young tribune ripped his sword from its scabbard and turned to Canutius.

'Come on, then, First Spear, it seems that we're needed after all . . . '

His subordinate was staring across the narrow space between the reserve centuries and the milling barbarians, his eyes pinned wide and his face red with fear. Laenas stared at him for a moment, both horrified at the man's apparent loss of control in the face of battle and uncertain of how he should react. As the moment of decision hung in the balance, a shout rang across the battlefield, Scaurus's voice cutting through the fight's rising din.

'*Tribune Laenas! Your time for glory is here!*'

He nodded decisively and turned away from Canutius with a slight smile, suddenly calm in the realisation that there was only one possible course of action. Raising the weapon above his head, he summoned the strength to steady his wavering voice.

'*First Cohort! Ready spears!*'

The legionaries pulled their javelins from the damp earth into which they had been pushed butt spike first moments before, and hefted their shields from their resting places in a dry rustle of wood and iron. Laenas turned back to the barbarians forcing their way through the rupture in the Romans' line, their numbers already doubled in those scant seconds, and fixed his gaze on the red-haired giant who had smashed his way through the detachment's line with such brutal ease. For the first time in months, it seemed, he felt his heart lift with the moment's simplicity, felt liberated from the need to worry about the slow bleeding away of his reputation at the hands of his subordinate. Fighting back a sudden wild urge to laugh aloud in the first spear's terrified face, he pointed his sword down the slope at the Venicones.

'*First Cohort! Follow me!*'

Stepping off down the slope without looking behind him to see whether his men were following, he locked eyes with the Venicone king, watching the man with an almost detached interest as the warlord lifted his massive war hammer and strode forward to meet the reinforcements, his bellowed challenge lost in the fight's tumult. The two men stalked closer to each other with their eyes locked together, neither willing to look away in the last seconds before they met. Above the roar of the fight Laenas thought he heard his name being called again, but ignored the distraction as the barbarian warrior broke into a run, covering the last few paces between them in seconds with his hammer swinging high.

The weapon slashed down in a humming diagonal attack, its spike intended to crack the tribune's breastplate and smash his ribs, but he sidestepped and ducked beneath the blow, slashing at his opponent with his sword's blade and drawing a bloody line across the man's thigh. Drust staggered and snarled, reversing the hammer and thrusting the heavy iron counterweight at the base of its handle into the Roman's face, sending him reeling backwards. While Laenas was off balance, blood spurting from his shattered nose, a tribesman leapt forward and rammed his sword deep into the tribune's armpit before dying on the shaft of a thrown javelin as the 1st Cohort's centuries hurled their weapons in a devastating low-slung volley that withered the ranks of the attacking Venicones.

With a roar of anger the legionaries drew their swords and charged at the stunned barbarians, stabbing viciously at their enemy in their fury at seeing their officer fall. Drust and what remained of his bodyguard fought in a tight knot, briefly holding the legionaries at bay in a circle around them until Maon, standing back to back with his master, was spitted by a javelin thrust, staggering forward on to his enemy's blades with blood frothing on his lips, falling under a hail of hacking blows. Another legionary stepped in and drove his spear through the Venicone king's back, heaving and twisting on the weapon's wooden shaft to force its barbed iron head deeper into the stricken barbarian's body. Drust's spine arched with the cold iron's first agonising thrust into his kidneys, and he stared down in disbelief as the spear's head ripped through his stomach wall.

Dropping to his knees in agony, he allowed the hammer's handle to slip from his grasp as he reached down to grasp the javelin's iron head with both hands, his teeth bared in a silent scream of pain. Scaurus ran the few paces from his place at the rear of the Tungrian line, a dozen of the 10th Century's axemen around him hacking a path into the remaining barbarians before them. He pointed his sword at the breach in the line, hurling an order at the legionaries over the fight's hubbub.

'*Sixth Legion, advance! Close this gap!*'

At the shouted command the cohort's front rank marched onwards down the slope, their implacable attack scattering the remaining barbarians to either side in panicked attempts to escape before the line was re-established. Behind the marching centuries another soldier raised his gladius and chopped down at the fallen king's exposed neck, the blow sufficiently strong only to half-sever Drust's head from his body but enough to put him face down and unmoving in the grass. The sword rose and fell again, and its bearer lifted Drust's severed head by its mane of red hair with a bellow of triumph while the owner of the javelin buried in his corpse's back tore its barbed-iron head free from the headless body. The king's gold torc fell from his severed neck into the hillside's long grass, and the spearman bent to retrieve it, goggling at the fortune in gold in his hands.

'I'll take that! And the torc!'

The legionaries turned to find First Spear Canutius striding towards them, his panic of barely a moment before wiped away by his men's success.

'Those both belong to the Emperor. I'll make sure they reach the governor, rather than have you thieving bastards . . . '

The legionary who had decapitated the Venicone king looked about him quickly, getting a quick nod from his mate, who had raised his spear as if to examine its bloody blade with a critical eye. He allowed the dead king's head to dangle at his side and replied to the officer's challenge with a curled lip, fixing Canutius with a disparaging glance.

'Not this time, *Centurion*. You're too shy when the fight's on for my liking.'

Canutius raised his vine stick, his face hard with fury, only to stagger as the legionary behind him lunged forward, ramming the javelin's vicious point through his armour and deep into his body. The man holding Drust's head bent close as the officer stiffened, jerking spasmodically as the spear's barbed-iron head tore into his heart.

'That's what you've been terrified of all this time, pushing us forward to keep your skin intact. Not so bad now, is it?'

He nodded to the spearman, who deftly withdrew his weapon's pointed head through the hole it had punched in Canutius's armour, and lowered the dying officer to the ground alongside the spot where Laenas lay, his open eyes staring blankly at the clouds above them.

'That's vengeance for you, I'd say, young Tribune. You fought well enough for a lad when you finally got the chance . . . '

He reached out to close Laenas's eyes and then, spotting a minute movement of the fallen officer's chest, bent closer to examine the fallen tribune with a critical eye.

'Young gentleman's not dead, not yet anyway. *Bandage carrier!*'

* * *

While the battle raged on fifty paces down the hill's slope, Scaurus and Licinius hurried to the rear of the attacking legionaries surrounded by their escort of Tungrian axemen, heading for the spot where they had seen Tribune Laenas go down under Drust's attack and finding a huddled knot of men gathered around the bodies of several men. Licinius scattered them with a barked command, pushing one man out of his path.

'Stand aside!'

The legionaries cleared a path through to the stricken Laenas, and Scaurus, noting the body of Canutius alongside that of the young tribune, hung back behind his colleague with his eyes roaming across the scene. The bandage carrier shook his head unhappily, looking up at Licinius with a look of certainty.

'Nothing I can do for him, Tribune, the wound's too deep inside. He should be dead already, by rights.'

Scaurus found what he'd been looking for, a pair of legionaries sidling towards the edge of the group with neutral expressions on their faces.

'*You two!* Stop where you are! The rest of you, get back in line and fight. This battle has a while to run yet!'

The two soldiers snapped to attention, eyeing the hard-faced tribune as he stalked towards them. Licinius put a toe under Canutius's shoulder, turning the dead man's body over.

'He was speared in the back, from the look of it.'

Scaurus reached out and took the spear from the taller man, examining its point with a critical eye.

'There's blood on this weapon, legionary.'

The soldier shook his head dourly.

'Barbarian blood, sir. I did for their king.'

The tribune shook his head in turn, then handed the weapon back and turned away, bending to kneel alongside the dying tribune.

'Well now, Popillius Laenas, you'll be in the company of your ancestors soon enough. Hold your head up high when they greet you, for you've won this fight for us. See?' He lifted the Venicone king's head for the dying man to see. 'This was their king. Without him to lead them they'll give it up soon enough, and you're the man that took the fight to him and sealed his fate. I'll make sure your family know you died with a soldier's honour . . . ' He bent closer to the prostrate tribune, speaking quietly into his ear. 'But now I need you to tell me one more thing, brother. You see, your first spear lies dead alongside you, murdered by one of your own men in all likelihood. It's common enough when an officer is hated by his soldiers, of course, but we can't allow it to stand unpunished. So tell me, Tribune, did you see it happen?'

Laenas moved his head with painful slowness to stare at the two soldiers standing behind the kneeling tribune, a faint smile ghosting across his face, and his lips moved in speech so quiet that Scaurus had to put his ear to the dying man's mouth to hear them.

'*Saw . . . nothing . . .* '

Scaurus stared into his eyes for a moment, watching as the life left them. He patted the dead man's shoulder and then rose, turning back to the waiting legionaries with a flat stare.

'Today, legionaries, is your lucky day, or so it seems. Rejoin your century.'

Glancing at each other with scarcely concealed relief, the two men turned back to the fight, freezing into immobility at the sound of the harsh metallic scrape of Scaurus's sword leaving its scabbard.

'Of course, I could still have the pair of you lashed to death, or simply execute you both myself, here and now. So I suggest you surrender that pretty gold neckpiece before I decide which of the two would be preferable.'

The spearman turned back white faced, pulling the massive gold collar from inside his armour and putting it into the tribune's hand. Dismissing the men with a flick of his hand, Scaurus turned back to his colleague, who stared back at him with raised eyebrows.

'If Laenas was willing to condone their murder of Canutius then who am I to deny him that last pleasure, given the number of times the man was the cause of his humiliation?'

Licinius nodded, taking the torc from his colleague's outstretched hand and looking over his shoulder at the battle still raging on the slope below them.

'Agreed. Now let's go and finish what Drust was so keen to start. We have a chance to bring peace to the north for a generation to come. I'll see every last one of these bastards dead or a slave before night falls.'

* * *

With the gap in their line closed, and reinforced by the five legion centuries that had pinched off the Venicones' desperate attack and killed their king, the Romans began the process of inexorably grinding the resistance out of the tribesmen trapped between their shields and the forest. Advancing down the slope behind their shields, spears and swords stabbing out to kill and maim those barbarians still willing to face them, they herded the beaten tribesmen into an ever smaller space, until their only alternatives were surrender or death. Increasing numbers of men threw down their weapons and knelt under the detachment's spears, cursed and spat on by those of their comrades still willing to fight on in defiance of the odds facing them as more and more men fell under the Romans' unrelenting assault or gave up the struggle.

'It's a hard choice. In their place I chose to fight, but . . . '

Marcus raised an eyebrow at the tone in

Arminius's voice, both men watching as another sullen tribesman was dragged through the Tungrians' line at spear point, his hands swiftly bound before he was pushed into a group of his beaten comrades under the swords of a pair of lightly wounded soldiers.

'But what? You'd have missed this life of adventure if he'd just beaten your brains out. Can you really say that you'd . . . ' He raised his sword and pointed at one of the wounded guards. '*You!* Keep your distance from the prisoners and stop waving your iron at them, unless you want me to come over there and do the same to you!' The soldier saluted gingerly with his wounded arm and stepped back from the tribesmen, lowering the sword whose blade he'd been passing inches from their downcast faces. 'Where was I? Yes, can you really say that you'd exchange a quick death and an unmarked grave for . . . '

He looked up as a squadron of riders rode up to his place in the line, their leader reining his horse to a halt alongside him with another mount led alongside him.

'Centurion! Would you like to be a cavalryman one last time? There are Venicones who escaped when your line was broken to be hunted down, and Tribune Licinius has ordered me to take the best men available in their pursuit. Leave this hairy gentleman to watch the fun, and join us in the hunt!'

The Roman looked up at the rider, shielding his eyes from the sun's glare.

'Is that Bonehead you've brought for me to

ride, eh, Decurion Felix? Perhaps this is really just one more chance to get my neck broken?'

The decurion grinned back, gesturing to the horse with his free hand.

'Nobody else can ride him, not now you've encouraged the unruly bugger to have his own way whenever he fancies it. Come on now, the blue-noses will be gone without trace at this rate, and your tribune gave me a message for you. He said to tell you that Calgus ran . . . '

'*Qadir!*'

The chosen man turned from his place at the line's rear, where he was supervising the capture of the continual flow of barbarian prisoners.

'I've a score to settle! The century is yours until I get back!'

Felix watched as Marcus plucked a spear from the nearest rear-ranker and jumped into the saddle alongside him.

'Yes, he said that would have the spring back in your step.'

The two men rode hard up the slope, with the remainder of Felix's squadron following close behind in an extended line. They quickly overtook the hindmost of the barbarians who had fought their way free as the legion centuries had closed the door on their route to freedom, a tall skinny warrior limping painfully away from the battlefield as fast as his damaged body would carry him. The decurion lowered his spear and rode the straggler down, expertly thrusting the weapon's long blade through his neck and tearing it free in a shower of blood, not bothering to look back as his victim sank to his knees and then pitched headlong to the turf.

'There's more of them! Form skirmish line!'

The horsemen rode down several groups of barbarians, initially wounded men, unable to flee fast enough to have any chance of escape, but soon they began catching the unharmed warriors who had taken their chance to run for their lives. Those that prostrated themselves were spared, and a rider detailed to guard the survivors of each group, while those that continued running or turned to fight were killed without compunction by the fast-riding cavalrymen.

'*There!*'

Felix pointed his blood-slathered spear at a small group of warriors running hard for the shelter of a forest still a mile distant, and Marcus's face hardened at the sight he'd been waiting for.

'It's Calgus! Cut them off, but nobody touches the man in the purple cloak!'

Brought to bay too far from the trees for there to be any chance of escape, the barbarians threw down their weapons and pushed the Selgovae king forward towards the horsemen. Calgus shrugged off their hands, stepping forward to meet the point of Marcus's spear with his head held high, advancing until the point of the weapon's iron blade rested firmly on his chest.

'Very well, son of *two* dead fathers, take my life. If you have no interest in what your real father wrote about you in all those letters he never sent, put that spear through me and take your revenge.'

Stabbing the weapon into the turf, Marcus

dismounted and stepped up to the barbarian leader with one hand on the hilt of his gladius and his face dark with anger. Calgus smirked back at him.

'As I told you yesterday, the legatus was quite a writer, it seems. I captured a writing chest full of his correspondence, and among it was a sheaf of scrolls that he wrote to you, over the years. It was quite touching really, full of his hopes for you, and talking about the few times he managed to see you by visiting your father when you were younger. He . . . '

'No.'

The barbarian blinked in surprise and then opened his mouth to speak again, but found himself looking down the length of Marcus's gladius.

'No. For all I know you're spinning me a tale from your own desperation. You want me to escort you back to my tribune, who will send you back to Rome for the triumph that you assume must follow this victory. There, you presume, you might live another year, or more, and there have always been those barbarian leaders who are spared when they get the chance to work their wiles on the Emperor. What's to say that you can't pull the same trick?'

Calgus grinned wryly.

'You'll never know, then, will you? You'll have to . . . '

He staggered back as Marcus punched him hard in the face, a straight jab that sent him reeling dazed to the ground. Before the barbarian leader could respond, Marcus stepped forward with the eagle-pommelled gladius raised, spearing the blade's point down into the barbarian leader's left calf with careful precision before pulling it loose through his Achilles tendon. Calgus raised his head and screamed in agony, jerking again as Marcus repeated the process with the other leg. He pulled a knife from Calgus's belt, ripping the purple cloak away from the prostrate chieftain and cutting two long strips from it before stepping back and tossing them to the wounded man, his eyes pitiless as the barbarian leader twisted in pain.

'That's your death sentence, Calgus. Use these to bind your wounds and you're not likely to die from them, but you'll never walk unaided again. You can stay out here and take as long to die as you like. Of course, the wolves will find you soon enough, once there's nobody else here to frighten them away, and if they don't I'm sure the Votadini will be happy enough to provide you with a protracted death if they get to you first. You could kill yourself, of course, if you have enough will power to open your wrists with your teeth, but I suspect you'll hang on to the very last moment, hoping against hope for some improbable rescue. Not much of a choice, I suppose, but it's a good deal more than you gave my birth father.'

He turned away and remounted the big grey without a backward glance, meeting Felix's raised eyebrows with a steady, expressionless gaze.

'That will be the last of them, I'd say. Anyone that reached the forest deserves to live. Shall we take the survivors back to join their fellow slaves?'

* * *

The small detachment rode back down the slope an hour later, the heads of the tribesmen they had overtaken dangling from their saddle horns and their prisoners staggering exhaustedly before them. Marcus trotted his mount over to the tribunes with Felix following him, and dismounted wearily, saluting the two senior officers before holding out what was left of Calgus's cloak to Scaurus. The tribune took the garment and passed it in turn to Licinius. The senior officer nodded solemnly, tossing the prize to one of his bodyguard.

'You took revenge for your father, then?'

'I crippled him, and left him for the animals.'

Licinius grimaced, casting a wry smile to Scaurus.

'Remind me never to get on the wrong side of this young man. Still, with both Calgus and Drust dead we'll have no more problems from the tribes any time soon, at least not until the current crop of barbarian children reaches maturity and decides to come looking for revenge, by which time it'll be somebody else's problem to handle. Who knows, perhaps we'll even be able to reman the northern wall with this many of the tattooed bastards either dead or on their way to new homes.'

Marcus looked out across the battlefield from the vantage point of his mount, surveying the aftermath of the Venicones' disastrous attack. A mound of enemy dead was being stacked unceremoniously where the fighting had been the heaviest, at the point where the line had momentarily broken. Other soldiers were carefully collecting the detachment's dead and stacking their corpses in neat lines, each body stripped of its armour and weapons in preparation for the funeral pyre for which the two Tungrian pioneer centuries were cutting wood at the forest's edge. In another corner of the clearing a large group of tribesmen were huddling under the legion cohort's spears, while soldiers pulled them one at a time from the mass of their comrades to be searched before they were roped into lines of downcast men ready for the long march south into slavery.

'How many of them did we kill, sir?'

The Petriana's commander followed his gaze.

'About five thousand of them at a guess. It was a bit of a bloodbath, if the truth be told. The killing was almost impossible to stop once we had them pinned against the forest, especially given the casualties our men took holding their first charge.' He caught Marcus's frown and smiled grimly. 'We've lost over four hundred men, mainly in the struggle to close the line after Drust had battered his way through it. Apart from Tribune Laenas and that worthless fool Canutius, we've lost First Spear Neuto and three other centurions holding them back while the Sixth Legion decided whether to join in or not. If Canutius hadn't been speared by his own men I'd probably have done the job myself. I suppose a couple of thousand slaves will make a decent contribution to the burial fund, and see the widows and children right, even if the sheer number of them drives their price down. And now that you've restored some measure of the Sixth Legion's honour by dealing with the maniac that started the whole bloody mess off, I'd suggest that you . . . '

He paused as a trumpet sounded. Marcus turned and looked over the heads of the labouring soldiers from his vantage point on the horse's back.

'There's a rider coming in from the west. An officer from the look of it.'

Licinius frowned with bemusement for a few seconds, then nodded slowly.

'Of course. They'll have followed the Venicones' tracks. I should have expected this. You'd better come with me, gentlemen, because if I'm guessing correctly this concerns all of us.'

Marcus and Felix dismounted, leading their horses behind them, and followed Tribunes Licinius and Scaurus across the slope, none of them noticing that Martos had detached himself from the body of his warriors and was following them at a discreet distance. The small party waited at the battlefield's edge until the lone rider reached them. Equipped as a centurion, he was tall and thin, with a sardonic twist to his mouth.

'Greetings, Centurion . . . ?'

The newcomer looked down at them curiously, making no attempt either to dismount or salute.

'Greetings, gentlemen. You, sir, must be Tribune Licinius, if my estimate is correct. And as to these other three gentlemen, I'd guess that *you're* Gaius Rutilius Scaurus, recently promoted from prefect to tribune. Your colleague Tribune Paulus at Noisy Valley gave me an excellent description of you, and I would have recognised the youngest of you without any such help, since he bears a distinct resemblance to the physical description I've been given for Marcus Valerius Aquila, son of an executed senator and therefore a fugitive from imperial justice.' He stared at Felix for a moment before shaking his head with a wry smile. 'And you, Decurion, are perhaps the most unexpected of all. You *are* Amulius Cornelius Felix, I presume? Tribune Paulus told me how you got that scar on your chin sparring with him as a boy. Your presence is a *very* welcome bonus, since your friend Paulus also told me, only after the application of quite significant personal duress, I should add, that you hold the key to a question that Praetorian Prefect Perennis is most keen to have answered.'

The corn officer looked down at the three men in silence for a moment before speaking again, his expression one of utter confidence. I don't suppose for one moment that you're actually wondering who I am, since I'm sure that bad news always travels faster than good, but just for the formality of the thing, my name is Tiberius Varius Excingus. I've come a very long way to meet the four of you, all the way from the Camp of the Strangers in Rome, in fact, but it seems that I've arrived at a most propitious time, doesn't it? A battle won, barbarians routed, everything as it should be with the exceptions standing before me, eh, gentlemen? One murdering traitor, the two most senior officers guilty of harbouring him for these last six months, and the one man who will eventually provide me with the proof of your collusion to protect the fugitive and enable me to identify just who it is that's been writing such unpleasant letters to the prefect on the subject of his son's death. And all in one place, which makes matters so much simpler.'

He sat back on the horse with a smile, waiting for one of the men facing him to speak. Scaurus put a hand on the hilt of his sword, stepping forward and glaring up at the corn officer.

'You do realise that you're surrounded by soldiers who were fighting for their lives less than an hour ago? Men with their comrades' blood still drying on their armour, and who have killed so many times today that one more death would make as little difference to them as swatting a fly? And you're a long way from the Camp of the Strangers, Centurion. Doesn't that make you feel a little vulnerable?'

Excingus snorted, shaking his head in amusement.

'I was told that you would be the pugnacious one, Rutilius Scaurus. And to answer your question, I feel as safe here talking to you as if I were walking through the forum in Rome. For one thing, I'm sure that neither you nor your colleague Tribune Licinius will want to jeopardise the lives of those you hold dear in Rome by any intemperate action. You might have been away from home for too long to know just how far the praetorian prefect has risen in the estimation of the throne, but suffice it to say that he's been permitted to grant certain members of the Guard quite extraordinary powers. More than that, he's provided them with sufficient latitude with regard to their personal conduct that they're more than adequately motivated to carry out whatever orders he passes down to them. Let me stress that, gentlemen, *whatever* he orders. No matter how bloody, or distasteful. Given that I knew exactly who you were, do you doubt that I have already provided my associates with sufficient information to point these men of dubious honour at the very people you hold most dear?'

A long silence hung in the air between the four men before Excingus spoke again.

'In addition, should any further explanation of the threat my presence here poses both to you personally and to your loved ones at home be required, I should also point out that my approach to the scene of your triumph here is being witnessed with great care by the two horsemen that you'll see waiting for me some distance away. Should any violence be done to my person here, they will ensure that the truth of it is known to both the governor and the Emperor . . . '

'In which case Ulpius Marcellus would have no choice other than to have us put to death immediately.'

'Exactly, Tribune Licinius, both succinct and

correct. Which would leave *your* family here in the province somewhat at the mercy of anyone minded to make them pay for your treason, wouldn't you say?'

Licinius stared up at the corn officer with murder in his eyes, and then shook his head in slow, angry resignation, his eyes burning with hate as he spread his hands in a gesture of surrender.

'Very well, *Centurion*. You have us all by the balls. What do you want?'

Excingus nodded gravely.

'Very pragmatic, sir, and just as I expected. What I want is very simple, Tribune, and without either choice or alternative. Put simply, both Decurion Felix and Centurion *Aquila*, to use his former name, will divest themselves of both weapons and armour, and then ride with me and my escort to a place not very far from here, where Aquila will be executed for his treason by my praetorian colleague. This will be carried out quickly and cleanly, for we take no special pleasure in this duty, and when sentence has been carried out then Felicia Clodia Drusilla will be released and indeed escorted to join you here . . . '

Scaurus raised a hand to restrain Marcus as he tensed to leap at the corn officer.

'No! Unless you want her dead, or worse, you *must* restrain yourself! Explain yourself, Centurion!'

Excingus leaned forward on his saddle horn and smiled down at the hostile faces gathered around him.

'There's not really all that much to explain, Tribune Scaurus. Having gathered that the centurion here has something of a reputation as a fighting man, we thought it best to have an additional means of subduing him for our short ride to justice. If I fail to return within a specified time period then the lady will find herself on the receiving end of some rather degrading behaviour on the part of my praetorian escort. It's just a precaution, of course, I'm sure there'll be no need for any unpleasantness. Now, given that time is passing, shall we proceed, or would you rather keep the centurion here and allow all the consequences of non-cooperation that we've discussed to come to pass?'

Marcus shook his head, fumbling with the buckle of his belt.

'There's no choice. I'll go with this reptile and face the 'justice' that's been stalking me ever since the throne decided my father's estate would make a nice contribution to the treasury.'

He met Excingus's eyes with a contemptuous stare, but the corn officer's shrug was eloquent in its indifference.

'I don't judge the men on whom I'm ordered to exercise the imperial will, Valerius Aquila, I'm simply an instrument of my master. If Prefect Perennis says that you have to die, that's simply the way that it is. Shall we? You too, Decurion Felix, although obviously you'll be staying with us for a while longer. I have so *many* questions to ask you.'

Marcus tossed his belt and swords aside, and

tried to lift the heavy mail shirt over his head but was frustrated both by the armour's weight and his own sudden exhaustion in the face of his impending death.

'Let me help you, Centurion.'

Martos stepped forward with a look at Scaurus, and took a firm grip of the heavy mail coat's shoulders, lifting the armour over the Roman's head. As he did so, Scaurus stepped forward with renewed anger, putting a hand on his sword's hilt and sliding the weapon halfway from the scabbard before Licinius caught his arm and stopped the movement. Excingus, momentarily startled, resumed his confident pose as he watched the two tribunes' momentary battle of wills, grinning smugly as the older man tightened his grip on Scaurus's arm and clamped his other hand on to his incensed colleague's sword hand. Shaking his head firmly, Licinius pushed the blade home into its scabbard, ignoring the rage in his colleague's eyes and speaking to him calmly, in a tone akin to that used by a father to a recalcitrant son.

'I don't know about you, Rutilius Scaurus, but I'd like to keep my family out of this mess. If you draw that sword he'll have his praetorian animals rip apart the lives of everyone we care about. Think about it.'

Scaurus stood stock still for a moment, his body shaking with repressed anger, and then turned away, putting a hand to his eyes. Excingus smiled wryly at the sight, shaking his head.

'You really do need to learn to take this sort of

thing with a touch more equanimity, Tribune. If this is the worst thing that ever happens to you then you'll have had a fortunate life by comparison with most of us.'

Marcus stepped past his tribune with a reassuring pat on the other man's arm, staring up at the mounted man with a look of disgust.

'Very well, *Centurion*, if you're ready?'

Excingus gestured wearily to the horse alongside his own.

'Climb aboard, Valerius Aquila, and let's get this over and done with. You, Decurion, can ride your own beast. A fine-looking animal, you really are a very privileged young man.'

The three men turned and rode away from the knot of officers and soldiers watching them, while Scaurus, Licinius and Martos stood and watched them disappear over the ridge. Licinius raised an eyebrow at his colleague, his tone reflective.

'That went about as well as we could have expected. The rest is up to the pair of them.'

⋆ ⋆ ⋆

Martos walked away from the tribunes briskly as soon as the corn officer turned his horse away, knowing that Arminius wouldn't be far from his master at such a moment. He found the German waiting a dozen paces distant, his arms folded with disapproval.

'We should have fought. Allowing them to take our friend away without any resistance shames us all.'

The Votadini prince shook his head.

'They have his woman. And that bastard was very clear that he will tear through the tribunes' families if he even suspects them of attempting to rescue the boy.'

They shared a dour glance before Arminius spoke.

'All of these things will happen whether we resist or not. Those animals are strangers to any idea of honour.'

'So you think we should follow them?'

The German nodded.

'They'll be looking behind them for horsemen, but they won't see a pair of dirty barbarians trailing them along the forest edge if we stay far enough back.'

Martos snorted with laughter.

'If we stay far enough back? With them on horses and us on foot? Staying far enough back isn't going to be much of a problem. Come on, then . . . '

He turned for the treeline, only to find Lugos standing behind them, towering over both men. Martos raked him with a hostile stare.

'What do you want, Selgovae?'

The warrior flexed his shoulders, great ropes of muscle moving beneath his scarred skin, and hefted the war hammer that he had liberated from the growing pile of captured barbarian weapons. Similar to Drust's heavily decorated weapon, the hammer hanging nonchalantly from his hand was, if anything, heavier, its iron beak sharpened to a point and the handle's counterweight formed from a disc of iron which had been patiently worked to produce a ragged edged and a viciously hooked half-moon blade.

'Roman spared my life, now I pay back debt. And you not call me Selgovae. I have no tribe.'

The prince grimaced at Arminius, tightening his sword belt a notch in readiness for their run to the east.

'It's up to you. Does he run with us?'

The German nodded, tossing aside his round wooden shield.

'Yes. Since you and I are also both dispossessed of our tribes, it seems we have no option but to accept a fellow exile. Now *run!*'

* * *

Marcus managed to hold to his initial resolve, to treat the corn officer with a frosty silence as they rode to meet the praetorians waiting on them, for no more than a minute. Felix kept silent as his friend's indignant anger boiled over, stroking Hades' neck gently as if savouring the feeling one last time.

'So this all means nothing to you? You're happy to carry out your master's instructions without giving any thought to the innocent lives you're destroying?'

Excingus's response to the question was a look of near-incredulity.

'And what would you have me do, Valerius Aquila? Tell the second-most powerful man in the Empire that I'm sorry, but the man you've sent me to kill isn't really guilty of anything, other than being born into the wrong family at the wrong time. Should I tell him that his son, far from being the innocent victim of a fugitive from justice, was in reality a traitor who betrayed his legion and caused the loss of their eagle, one of the worst possible military reverses possible? Because believe me, I've heard all those stories before over the space of the last couple of months. And doubtless most of them are true . . . '

Marcus snorted his derision.

'Most of them?'

Excingus laughed, shaking his head.

'Very well. All of them, if that helps you to feel better, and more besides, no doubt. The fact remains, young man, that I am an imperial enforcer, and, having reached the dizzy rank of centurion in the Camp of the Foreigners, therefore without any real choice in this matter. Gentlemen, I am an urbane version of the men that collect their tribute from the businesses of the Subura district, but no less of a hired sword for all that, and I am as subject to the praetorian prefect's will as if he were riding alongside us. Were I sufficiently weak minded to yield to the 'justice' in your words, and release you to run again, what do you think would happen to me, eh? I would be dead before the sun kissed the western horizon, of course, and dead, I should add, at the hand of the very man with whom Prefect Perennis has paired me for the task of finding you, and erasing you from this pathetic existence that you've chosen as being preferable to a quick death. I have neither illusions nor any choice in this matter, Valerius Aquila, and neither do you, but to play your part, and die with as much dignity as can be managed under the circumstances.'

A long silence held for a few moments before Marcus spoke again.

'And the decurion here? What has he done to merit whatever torture you plan to subject him to?'

Excingus raised an eybrow at the cavalry officer.

'Do you want to tell him? No? Very well. Cornelius Felix is here because on the day of the battle in which the Sixth Legion lost their eagle he watched you take part in the violent death of the man who had betrayed the legion to the barbarians. Since that man was Prefect Perennis's son, our pursuit of you has been invested with more than a little of his personal interest. But that wasn't the end of it. The decurion here told a friend of his, a legion tribune called Paulus, what you'd done as you walked past them one night in camp, and that friend got drunk and told his colleague Quirinius, the legion's senior tribune. Quirinius was then sent back to Rome, fell on hard times and imagined that he could bargain with Prefect Perennis. He sought to trade the identity of his son's killer for some favour or other. Fool . . . ' He shook his head sadly. 'He had a beautiful wife, and a sweet child, and I had no choice but to turn my colleague the praetorian and his thugs loose on them as part of the routine cleaning up after such murders. Anyway, he told Perennis who it was that had told him about your hiding place here on the edge of the world. The prefect, being rather unhappy about a series of letters he's received from Britannia, threatening him that the truth about his son might easily become public knowledge, gave us a second mission, more important to him than the quest to find you and put you down, believe it or not. He ordered us to find the letter writer and to silence him for good, and that trail leads from Quirinius to Paulus and from Paulus to Felix here. After that I'll wager there's only one more link, the letter writer himself. I'm pretty sure that the final link in the chain is your tribune, in fact I'd put good money on it, but I'll need to be quite sure before unleashing the hounds on him and his family, which means that your questioning is likely to be somewhat *enthusiastic* . . .'

He tipped his head to the two riders set to watch his approach to the Tungrians, who had left the shade of the trees, and were cantering their horses towards the three horsemen.

'And so that, Centurion, is why your friend Felix is accompanying us back to our camp. And now, I suggest, you might want to keep your complaints about the injustice that you're about to suffer to yourself for a while. I like to pride myself on having a good deal more understanding of the contradictions inherent in the role that my kind and I play than my companions, but I think you'll find these particular gentlemen a little less informed than me. That, and a lot more willing to take out their frustrations on an unarmed prisoner. So, unless you really want your woman to suffer at their hands as a means of teaching you to keep your mouth shut . . . ?'

He raised an eyebrow, waiting until Marcus had wearily conceded the point with a dispirited nod before looking away, speaking out into the empty landscape as if talking to himself.

'Good lad. I knew you'd see the sense of it.'

12

'They're here, Centurion, Excingus has them both!'

Rapax nodded at the man he'd set to watch for his colleague's return, getting up from the fallen tree on which he'd been sitting.

'Good. Once this Felix tells us who witnessed the death of Perennis's son we'll be able to finish the job and get out of this shithole of a province and back to some sunshine. Come along, my lovely, let's you and I get ourselves out of sight before your boyfriend gets here. You two, come with me. The rest of you can provide the centurion with a suitably warm welcome once I've got his woman squawking.'

He pulled Felicia into the trees, retreating far enough into their cover that he could see out into the clearing without being visible. The remaining soldiers spread out in a half-circle to receive the riders, who rode into their midst and stopped at the corn officer's command, the two praetorians who had escorted them in peeling away to either side. Rapax dragged Felicia deeper into the forest's cover, his hand clamped over her mouth to prevent her from calling out to Marcus.

'All in good time, he'll hear you screaming for me to stop soon enough, but let's not spoil the surprise, eh?' He turned to the guardsmen following him. 'You two, stop gawking and stand guard. I don't want anyone creeping up on me while I'm otherwise occupied. Now then, Doctor, let's get down to . . . '

In the moment of his distraction Felicia, knowing that she could wait no longer, reached under her skirts and pulled the razor-sharp blade free from its scabbard. As Rapax turned back to her, and before the watching soldiers could shout a warning, she struck with all the speed and strength she had, plunging the knife up into the soft skin beneath his jaw until only the bone handle protruded. The praetorian staggered backwards, his eyes flickering as the weapon, stabbed up through his tongue and palate, ran with blood that streamed down the bone handle and on to his boots. He reeled back another step with his eyes rolling up to show only their whites and then straightened, gripping the knife and tearing it free from his jaw with a terrible groan.

Slack jawed at the sight of their officer's wound, the guardsmen failed to notice that their prisoner had turned and run deeper into the trees, wrenching their attention back to the fleeing woman only when the stricken centurion pointed after her.

'*Ged 'er!*'

Turning away from their officer as he swayed and staggered, blood running down the front of his armour in rivulets, the praetorians did as they were bidden, Rapax's plight quickly forgotten as they chased the running woman into the forest with the smiles of men who intended to fully enjoy the fruits of their hunt when they ran her to ground.

* * *

Marcus looked about him at the praetorians gathered in a half-circle around the three horsemen, shaking his head wearily.

'Eight of you? To kill one tired soldier?'

Excingus shrugged, gesturing for his prisoner to dismount.

'My colleague Rapax is a thorough man, and your reputation with a sword goes before you. Now do get down and meet your fate with a little composure. The decurion and I will provide an audience for your commendable stoicism.'

Marcus frowned and spread his empty hands before him.

'If I had a sword I could understand your colleague's caution. But then if I had a sword you'd already be face down with your guts hanging out, and this scum would be in the fight of their lives, rather than putting an unarmed man to death.'

One of the praetorians stepped forward, resheathing his gladius with a slow metallic scrape.

'Well then, sonny, why don't you come down here and show us how tough you are without a weapon in your hand. But keep your ears pricked for the sound of your woman squealing her lovely little lungs out, our centurion should be putting it to her any time now. Beating you to death with our bare hands will give you more time to appreciate the thought that we'll all be taking a turn at her once he's done.'

Marcus climbed slowly down from his horse

and turned to face the men gathered in a loose half-circle around him, his face white with anger both at the guardsman's words and the look of satisfaction on his face. Taking up a loose stance with his hands hanging by his side, he looked the praetorian up and down, shaking his head slowly and sighing loudly.

'Very well, then, come and put me out of my misery!'

He watched through eyes slitted in concentration as the guardsman turned to his mates with a confident smile.

'Hold off, boys, I'll take first turn at him. It isn't every day that I get the chance to knock an officer about.'

He stalked towards his would-be victim, clenching his impressive fists in readiness to fight.

'You see, *Centurion*, the advantage I've got over you is that I fought my way up from the gutter to where I am today. I've beaten hundreds of men into the dirt in my time and you're going to be just the same as all of them once you're on your back seeing stars. I'm going to . . . '

He leaped forward in mid-sentence, clearly intending for his words to have distracted Marcus sufficiently for the sudden attack to take him by surprise, throwing a fast punch at the Roman's face with the intention of putting his opponent on the defensive. Swaying back to evade the blow by the width of a finger, Marcus hooked the guardsman's forward leg with a swinging boot and dumped him on to his back, the breath audibly knocked from the praetorian's body as he hit the ground. Reaching into the neck of his tunic, following the thin leather cord that ran down across his chest, he grasped the handle of the hunting knife that Martos had slipped over his head during the act of removing his armour and ripped it from its hiding place. Then, dropping to one knee, he thrust the knife's blade up under the praetorian's jaw and ripped his jugular open in a spray of blood, pulling the dying man's sword from his scabbard and jumping back to his feet. The remaining guardsmen gaped for a moment before one of them drew his sword, prompting the others to reach for their own weapons. His knife-hand red with blood, Marcus turned to face them, speaking to the wide-eyed corn officer without turning to face him.

'If I were you, reptile, I'd run while you still can . . .'

Excingus backed his horse away from the knot of men, shaking his head in amazement as his erstwhile prisoner stepped forward to meet the armed soldiers, raising the bloody knife for them all to see and nodding at the dead guardsman's corpse.

'You can all either run now, and save yourselves, or you can add your blood to his.'

One of the soldiers shook his head, raising his sword to fight.

'You can't fight all of us, not if we come at you together.'

Marcus smiled, shaking his head at the man who'd spoken and pointing the sword at him.

'Well volunteered, you can be first in that case.'

Felix stepped Hades sideways, the coal-black horse responding easily to the familiar pressure of a knee in his ribs, then nudged the animal's flanks with his boots, telling him wordlessly to advance a few steps while he made a show of pulling back on the beast's reins as he goaded him forward with his feet. As the closest of the guardsmen turned to face the big horse, raising his sword to threaten mount and rider, Hades responded exactly as he'd been trained, rearing up and kicking out with a powerful forefoot which sent the soldier flying backwards in a spray of his own blood, his face smashed by the sharp edge of the animal's hoof. Stepping down from the saddle, Felix slapped Hades' rump, sending the horse cantering away from the vengeful swords of the two guardsmen who had turned to face him, and stooped to retrieve the dying soldier's gladius.

'I'd suggest you men get on with it and finish these two off, before they kill any more of you.'

The remaining soldiers advanced in response to Excingus's goading, spreading out into a semicircle around the two men. One of the older guardsmen looked Marcus in the eyes, speaking to his comrades as he balanced on the balls of his feet, ready to attack.

'When I give the word, we rush them. Nothing fancy, just mob the pair of them and get your iron into them. On my command . . . ready . . . '

As the praetorians readied themselves to storm their victims, each of the soldiers looking to his comrades for the signal to attack, a one-eyed barbarian warrior, covered in sweat and panting as if from a long run, broke from the trees behind the two prisoners. His sword was held ready to fight, and he weighed up the situation as the praetorians gathered around the two officers stared at him in surprise, panting out a question to Marcus.

'*You've not . . . killed them all . . . yet, then?*'

The Roman shook his head, a slow smile spreading across his face, and another warrior burst out of the forest to stand alongside the first, his chest heaving with the effort of their pursuit. He glanced around the men encircling Marcus and Felix, a wheezy chuckle fighting its way past his efforts to drag air into his lungs.

'*You made . . . me run . . . all this way . . . to fight . . . these children . . . Martos? He could have . . . managed this many . . . on his own.*'

The last man to emerge from the trees topped the first two by a head, but he was barely breathing heavily despite the effort of the run. A massive war hammer was held loosely across his torso, its heavy iron head still smeared with blood and hair. Hefting the huge weapon on to one shoulder, he clenched his other fist and stepped forward into the ring of praetorians, his face a mask of snarling hatred as he gazed about him and spat out a challenge in his own language.

'At last! Romans I can fight!'

While the praetorians were still staring at the newcomers with growing uncertainty, Lugos swung the brutal weapon in a wide single-handed arc, his massive strength making light of its dead weight and smashing the hammer's wicked beak against a hapless soldier's chest, dropping the man writhing to the grass with his ribcage smashed. Lifting the pole arm high over his head, he roared in triumph and smashed it down through the crippled man's helmet to break his skull with a sickening crunch of iron and bone. The other two warriors exchanged a look and stepped forward alongside him, raising their swords to fight, but as they did so the praetorians broke and ran for their lives despite their weight of numbers. Lugos went after them with a bellow of rage, running down the closest man in half a dozen strides and snagging his shoulder with the hammer's hooked counter-weight blade, dropping the praetorian to the ground in a flurry of arms and legs and leaving the downed man to his fellow warriors as he chased after another panic-stricken soldier. Excingus took one look at the fleeing guardsmen and turned his horse away, spurring it away from the clearing and on to the road south.

Marcus sprang forward, running down the slowest of the soldiers and tripping him, kicking away his sword and dropping his own gladius before pouncing on him to grip his throat in one hand, raising the bloody hunting knife to tear out his windpipe. His voice was a feral growl, snarled through bared teeth, and the helpless guardsman went rigid with the threat of impending death.

'The woman! Where did your officer take the woman!?'

The soldier pointed into the forest with a trembling hand.

'Th . . . that way!'

The Roman jumped to his feet, dropping the bloodied knife and picking up both swords.

'Stay down and they might let you live . . . '

He ran for the trees with a speed born of desperation, hurdling a fallen trunk and tearing through the undergrowth to find himself in a small clearing. Propped up against a massive oak on the open space's far side was a man in the armour of a praetorian centurion, his chest covered in the blood that was still running from the small but deep wound under his jaw. Marcus stepped forward, raising both swords ready to fight in case the wounded officer were part of some trap, but there was no movement in the tiny glade other than the slow dripping of the other man's blood. Struggling to focus, the wounded praetorian shook his head and laughed painfully, the movement causing the flow of blood to accelerate for a moment. His voice was almost inaudible, and Marcus had to lean close to hear the words, made almost impossible to understand by the praetorian's horrific wound.

'*Young Aquila, is it? The things you see when you don't have a sword in your hand . . .* '

Marcus stepped forward and put the blade of one of his swords to the centurion's throat, watching as the blood streaming from under his jaw ran across the polished metal.

'Where's my woman?'

Rapax studied him from beneath drooping eyelids for a moment before speaking, his eyes fighting to stay open from shock and blood loss.

'*No idea. Bitch stuck me with a knife and then made a run for it. Sent my men after her* . . . ' The wheezy laugh came again, and with it a hardening of the dying praetorian's face. '*One little girl alone in the forest with two big soldiers? I doubt she's enjoying that very much* . . . '

Marcus locked eyes with Rapax for a moment, then ran the gladius up into the wound in his throat, pushing the blade upwards until it stopped against the back of the praetorian's skull. Ripping the blade free, he ignored Rapax's slumping corpse and turned away, stepping silently into the trees.

* * *

Felicia ran blindly through the trees, hearing the sounds of pursuit behind her as the two praetorians burst through the undergrowth in her wake, remorselessly closing the gap she had opened on them with her initial burst of speed from the clearing. She ducked into the shelter of a towering oak at the edge of a small glade, pulling her stola tight to her legs in the few seconds she had before the soldiers charged past a few feet to either side of the tree. The sounds of their pursuit died away, and she stared into the forest for a long moment, torn between staying out of sight and putting more distance between herself and her pursuers. The sound of their voices reached her faintly, and she realised that they must have stopped chasing her and started thinking through where she could have given them the slip. Their words were becoming clearer, and to her horror she realised that not only were they coming back towards her, but that they clearly had a good idea of where she was. A voice called out into the forest's quiet, and she had no difficulty seeing the face behind it in her mind's eye, the legionary whose stare had so disturbed her over the previous days. Maximus.

'You can't run from us, woman, we're going to find you soon enough and make you sorry for what you did to the centurion.'

A new voice broke in.

'Oh yes, we're going to spend hours making you sorry, we're going to . . . '

Maximus kept speaking, ignoring his colleague's attempts to intimidate her into leaving her hiding place.

'I'm good with women, you see. I've got a way with them.' He paced around the small clearing, and Felicia could feel his eyes raking the vegetation, looking for her place of concealment. 'Want to hear something funny? The same night I was jailed for killing a man in the Noisy Valley alehouse, another soldier from my tent party was brought in for the rape and murder of an old woman. 'Disgusting', they called him, and 'animal'. They knew he'd done it, because his amulet was found by the body. They reckoned she must have torn it off his wrist while he was raping her. The other soldiers would have done for him there and then, but he was locked up separately and the only people that got to have a go at him were the duty centurions, when they were in the mood. I used to watch him in his cell, his face a picture of desperation, pleading that he hadn't done it, but nobody was having any of it, not for a moment. The only person that believed he was innocent was me, because I knew he hadn't been near her. Have you guessed how I knew that, little missy? I'll bet you have . . . '

He stopped talking for a moment, allowing the suspense to build until it was all Felicia could do not to scream the answer to his question at him.

'That's right! I knew he was innocent because it was me that killed her! What a night that was! I jumped my watch officer and gave him a good kicking, then I followed the old girl back to her hovel and saw to her as well. I'd slipped into another tent party's barrack and lifted his good-luck charm from his kit before I went out, you see, so I snapped the cord and left it by her body, and that was all it took to see him in prison. It almost made up for getting pissed and killing that idiot from the Fourth Century when he tried to take his knife to me. And when I find you, little missy, I'm going to do all the things to you that I did to her . . . '

He darted into the vegetation on the other side of the clearing with a rustle of leaves, thinking that he had her hiding place located. In the moment of his distraction Felicia was on her feet and running almost before the decision to do so was fully formed. She would stay low, run to one side of the returning praetorians as quickly and quietly as she could, and hope to get far enough away that she could hide again. Shouts in the forest behind her told her that she had failed in her hopes of escaping unnoticed, and she abandoned any pretence of stealth and ran as fast as she could, knowing that she could never expect to outrun the soldiers. So intent on escaping from the pursuing praetorians that she failed to see the soldier waiting in her path until she was only a few paces from him, the startled woman tripped over a tree root and fell to the ground at his feet. Smiling at the look on her face, he thrust his spear's butt spike into the earth and held out a hand towards her as she shrank away from him, holding the knife out in hopeless defiance.

'Hello, my lovely! We've been looking for you!' He shouted back over his shoulder. '*I've found her!*'

The first of the pursuing praetorians came into sight, and drew his sword on seeing the legionary, walking slowly forward with a cruel gleam in his eye.

'Whoever you are, you can fuck off. This one's ours . . . '

He frowned in recognition as he stalked forwards, then snorted with laughter as he realised that he knew the other man.

'Fuck me, things must be getting desperate if they've put the Third Century back into the field. Run away from any good fights recently, have you, old son? Now fuck off double quick, there's a good boy, and I'll spare you the indignity of being put on your back. Leave that to little missy here . . . '

He grinned broadly at the legionary, who, to his surprise, shook his head grimly and pulled his spear loose from the forest's hard-packed earth, raising the blade to point at his face.

'Not this time, Maximus. You've missed a few important things since you ran away with your new boyfriends. *Habitus!*'

While the guardsman was still taking in his former comrade's unexpected show of bravado another legionary came crashing through the undergrowth, his spear held ready to throw.

'Fuck me, there's another one. Is that you, Decimus? Don't say you've grown a set of balls as well . . . '

Both legionaries pointed their spears at his chest, stepping forward either side of Felicia and facing off against the baffled Maximus.

'You can run for it now, mate, or you can stay and find out what Roman iron feels like when it's deep in your guts.'

Watch officer Titus broke through the wall of greenery and stopped, recognising his former tormentor in an instant, his face hardening.

'Well now, the big wheel turns in its own good time. Look what the gods have rewarded me with. I'll have this bastard's balls off and poke them up his backside before he's stopped breathing! *Century, to me! Habitus!*'

Maximus took one look at his one-time superior's face and turned, running for the shelter of the forest. Titus shook his head in disgust.

'He always was too quick on his feet.' He offered the bemused Felicia his hand, helping her to her feet. 'And you, madam, have a friend looking for you.'

A scream of agony sounded from the trees into which the two praetorians had made their retreat, the sound cut off after only a second as whoever had struck the first blow finished the job. The soldiers stepped forward with their spears raised, only to shuffle backwards as a ragged figure in tunic, leggings and infantry boots stepped out before them, his clothes and swords dark with the blood of whichever of the praetorians he had killed moments before.

'*Marcus!*'

Felicia ran across the clearing and fell upon the bloodied figure in sudden tears. After a long moment, during which the number of soldiers gathered around them had swollen to nearly twenty, he prised her loose and looked into her tearfilled eyes with concern.

'Are you . . . ?'

She nodded tearfully, wiping at her wet face with a sleeve, ignoring the knife she still held in the other hand.

'All right? Yes, my love . . . we both are.'

A frown creased Marcus's face.

'You *both* are . . . ?'

'Cocidius help me! For the son of an intelligent man you're really quite stupid when it comes to anything but butchering everyone that gets in your way.' The frown became a gape of amazement as the young centurion realised that Dubnus was lurking behind the gawping soldiers. His friend strode out to meet him, putting an arm round his shoulder and speaking quietly into his ear. 'If you don't know what a pregnant woman smells like then it's time you took a good deep breath and found out. And it's also time for you to make an honest woman of her, I'd say.' He stamped on the blade of his spear twice, first bending it and then breaking it clean off the shaft before handing it to the amazed Marcus. 'Here you go, that'll do for the ceremonial hairstyle you lot are supposed to favour in your women on the big day. It's not been stuck in a gladiator for luck yet, but I did one of the bastards that carried her away with it just now, if that counts.'

* * *

'Tribunes Licinius and Scaurus! Welcome back to civilisation, gentlemen, if we can characterise the never-ending din of Noisy Valley so generously!' Governor Marcellus advanced around his desk, his normally sombre face wreathed in a beaming smile, and clasped hands with his officers. Behind him Legatus Equitius, commander of the imperial Sixth Legion and former prefect of the 1st Tungrian Cohort shot them a wry smile, raising amused eyebrows at his superior's unaccustomed bonhomie. 'I've asked Legatus Equitius to join me in greeting you both, given his previous connection with your Tungrians.' Equitius inclined his head as the governor continued his greeting. 'My congratulations to you both. You have brought great honour upon your cohorts, and extinguished a threat to Rome's frontiers for years to come.'

Licinius saluted, handing King Drust's heavy gold torc to the older man.

'Governor, this belonged to the king of the Venicones. We took many more items of jewellery from their dead, but I thought you might want to take personal charge of this particular item.'

Marcellus raised the torc and admired its workmanship for a moment.

'Indeed, Tribune, an item of such value will make a fitting accompaniment for the news of this victory when it reaches the Emperor. And now, gentlemen, you must take a cup of wine with us, and explain how you achieved this unexpected triumph.' When the story of the previous few days' events was told he sat back in his chair with a contented smile, nodding his head slowly in satisfaction. 'Excellent work, gentlemen, simply excellent. Any threat the Venicones might have presented to the frontier is broken, and the Votadini are free to rebuild their kingdom without any external interference from either north or west. All of which means that we can focus our attentions to the south of the Wall, and on putting these Brigantes scum back in their place. They still control most of the country between here and the legion forts to the south, and I fear that the campaign to root them out will be a bitter struggle. They're not coming to battle as the northern tribes did, but seem happy to fight us with a dirty little war of raids and ambushes. Which means that your cavalrymen, Manilius Licinius, will have their hands full scouring the country for them. You are to ride for Waterside Fort today, and join with the Second

Legion and the western wall cohorts in hunting down and eradicating these savages wherever you find them.'

Licinius nodded his understanding, and Marcellus turned to Scaurus with a gentle smile.

'And as for you, Rutilius Scaurus, I must presume upon your cohort's willingness to endure hardship once again. I had originally intended sending you west with your colleague's horsemen to strengthen the Second Legion's forces, but I have received a request for assistance from my colleague in Gallia Belgica in the last few days, assistance I feel well suited to your particular blend of skills and experience, not to mention your cohort's original recruiting base.' He turned to the desk behind him and picked up a scroll, handing it to the young tribune and raising his voice to issue his formal orders. 'Rutilius Scaurus, you are hereby ordered to march your men to the port of Arab Town at the eastern end of the Wall, and there to take ship for the mainland. Once landed, you will make your way with all possible speed to the fortress town of Tungrorum. Once there, you are to establish a secure camp and then to carry out whatever operations you see fit to disperse and destroy the various bands of bandits, both large and small, who are plaguing the region.' He shot Scaurus a glance. 'Of course, you will be wondering exactly why your men should be needed, when there are three perfectly good legions only a few days' march away in their fortresses along the River Rhenus, any one of which might comfortably cope with any local problem. As it happens, not only have the German legions been somewhat depleted by the need to reinforce our losses of earlier this year, but they have also been stretched too thin by a series of barbarian incursions in the last few months. Things are not so bad that the barbarians could attack across the river in strength, but bad enough for the area around Tungrorum to have fallen prey to the worst kind of scum, deserters and brigands who are making life intolerable from the accounts I've received.

'They've tried to deal with the problem, of course — indeed, three detachments of increasing strength from their auxiliary cohorts have been sent into the area. They were either defeated by force of arms or, as seems to have been the case with the last force that was sent to the area, a full cohort of infantrymen mind you, they've chosen to desert to the enemy.' He took another sip of wine before continuing. 'There are three reasons why I've chosen to send you and your men to deal with this situation, Tribune. First, the legatus here tells me that your men are the best we have for hunting down and destroying these brigands.' Scaurus shot a glance at his cohort's former commander, who could only shrug apologetically. 'Second, your command is two cohorts strong, which ought to be sufficient to deal with the deserters who, I suspect, will be your main problem. And third, your men are more likely to want to protect their original settlement than the local auxiliaries, who are after all drawn from lands thousands of miles distant.'

He fixed the tribune with a level stare, tapping the order scroll in his hand to underline the significance of its contents.

'In dealing with these matters you are to cooperate as fully as possible with the local authorities, but you are also to consider your command as independent from civilian control and make any necessary decisions required to remove the threat to civil order represented by these criminal scum.' He smiled thinly at Scaurus. 'Everybody, Rutilius Scaurus, is going to want you to achieve everything at once, which is why I've deliberately written these orders to allow you to set your operational priorities as you see fit. In the meantime, it will take at least ten days to gather enough ships to carry your command across the German Sea, so I suggest that you march your men back to their home fort and allow them time to say their goodbyes. And that, Tribunes, concludes my orders. May the gods smile upon you both.'

The governor nodded and turned back to his desk, and the two men saluted and began to leave, only to stop at the office's door as he spoke again, frowning at a tablet he'd picked up from the desk's highly polished wooden surface.

'Ah, but there was one more thing. Trivial, perhaps, given the events of the last few weeks, but potentially serious for all that.' Both men turned back to face him, sharing a quick glance. 'It seems that a pair of imperial investigators rode through here a few days ago. Tribune Paulus reported the fact to Legatus Equitius when we arrived here. Apparently they were seeking some fugitive from justice who has managed to upset the praetorian prefect in some way or other . . . '

Scaurus kept his face neutral, thanking the foresight that had made Licinius send a rider south in advance of the legion, taking the news to Paulus that Rapax and Excingus's mission had failed with the death of one man and the complete disappearance of the other.

'Anyway, gentlemen, it seems that these two officers and their escort have been lost without trace. As an essential formality I must ask you both if you made any contact with them after they left this fortress?'

Both men answered the question with blank stares, and when Licinius spoke his voice was hard with suppressed anger.

'None of my men have reported any such encounter, Governor, although I lost two message riders around that time, left to rot where they fell by unknown assailants. When we found them one was lying unburied beside a roadside campfire, and the other was face down in a ditch five miles to the south. He had a throwing knife stuck through his neck, a knife that my armourers tell me was Roman in design. The presence of imperial spies might go some way to explaining their deaths . . . '

Marcellus frowned in his turn.

'I see. Well, there's probably little to be gained from any official comment on the matter, and since these men seem to have been operating independently of my office I intend to leave the matter where it lies. In any case they're certainly dead. Only a fool would have ridden this far north into the heart of a tribal uprising with such a flimsy escort, never mind crossing the Wall with the northern tribes still in ferment.' He shook his head and dropped the tablet on to the desk. 'Dismissed, gentlemen, let's get on with this war and leave the mystery of their disappearance to a quieter time.'

Stepping out of the principia into the supply fort's usual bustle, the two tribunes exchanged a glance, and Scaurus breathed a slow sigh of relief before speaking.

'It seems that young Paulus decided that he was better off having a legatus and two tribunes beholden to him than to spill the beans to the governor.'

His colleague nodded slowly.

'Yes. But I'd still be happier knowing exactly what happened to that odious creature Excingus, and that last praetorian for that matter.'

Scaurus nodded thoughtfully as he stared down the fortress's main street to the opened gates, watching as the guard century supervised the arrival of the first supply convoy to reach Noisy Valley from the legion fortress far to the south since the start of the Brigantian rebellion. His men had buried the praetorian dead after hunting them down through the forest, but no sign had been found of either the corn officer or the soldier who had hunted Felicia through the trees after her escape.

'Dead, or enslaved, I'd guess. They had a long stretch of road to cover just to reach the Wall, and the tribes won't be in a forgiving mood. And now, if you'll excuse me, I have a cohort to get on the road west. If they miss any more of the time they have left at the Hill than necessary they won't be all that forgiving either, given where I'm about to take them.' He turned away to head for the infantry barracks, then stopped and turned back.

'Colleague, given that I'm detached to go hunting bandits, I'd be grateful for the continued loan of your horses until we return. A squadron of cavalry could make all the difference when we're chasing around the forests after shadows.'

Licinius gave him a jaundiced look.

'You've got sticky fingers, young man. Every soldier that comes into contact with your cohort seems to end up as part of it. Hamian archers, borrowed cavalrymen. I'll even wager you that the half-century of legionnaires Dubnus borrowed from the Sixth will end up in your establishment. And yes, you can extend the loan if you think it'll do you any good, and you can keep that decurion you promoted to command them. But there is a price you'll have to pay for the privilege.' Scaurus raised an eyebrow, waiting in silence for the older man to make himself clear. 'Given that young Aquila seems to have put the cart before the horse by getting our lady doctor with child, I'm assuming that they'll be quietly marrying each other some time in the next few days. And don't try to fend me off with all that nonsense about it being illegal for soldiers to tie their hands together, because we both know it happens. So, if you want to hang on to my horses a while longer, you'd better make sure that I'm there when it happens. She'll need someone there that's known her for more then a couple of days to stand in for her father.'

* * *

'You're sure that you want to go through with this, m'dear? We both know that it's illegal for a soldier to marry. Are you sure you want your centurion to take that sort of risk, just to . . . '

Felicia's stare silenced Licinius's playful words, her voice pitched low to avoid the words carrying to the priest waiting at the other end of the main hall of the Hill's principia. The holy man had been escorted in from Noisy Valley by two centuries of Tungrians, and had eyed the hostile hills and forests along the route with unashamed fear, making his low opinion of such risk-taking very clear to all who would listen.

'Just to give his child a father, Tribune? Yes, I'd say it's worth the risk, given the sentence of death hanging over all of us.'

The cavalryman smiled gently.

'Forgive me, madam, it's just the rough humour of an old soldier who should know better. I only meant to say that while I can see that you've become attached to the man, marrying him is a bolder step altogether. I was a good friend of your father, and while I have every respect for your husband-to-be, I would be remiss in my duty were I not to make sure that you understand the risk you're taking by joining your life to his.'

Felicia smiled back at Licinius, taking his hand in hers.

'Gaius, you're such a sweet man beneath all that ridiculous military bluster. You mustn't worry about me, though. I'd rather spend a year with Marcus than a lifetime regretting that I didn't take this chance. And besides . . . ' She lifted a hand to indicate the knot of centurions gathered at the far end of the hall. ' . . . have you ever seen a more forbidding collection of physical specimens to have between a lady and anyone that would do her harm? They wouldn't even let me out of the gate to pick flowers for my headband without a tent party of soldiers to keep me from harm. Legatus Equitius has agreed to Tribune Scaurus's request for me to provide medical services to his command, now that his replacement doctors have managed to reach the legion, and I can't see very much happening to me once I'm part of this cohort, can you?'

Licinius raised a knowing eyebrow, muttering under his breath and drawing a sharp glance from the doctor.

'Sticky fingers again . . . no, nothing madam, just my little joke with my colleague. I'm sure you'll be as safe with these housetrained barbarians as if you were sitting comfortably in your father's villa in Rome. And in any case . . . ' The principia's double door opened, and Marcus stepped into the room with a smile for Felicia, the extent of his wedding finery a clean tunic and leggings, and a belt decorated with highly polished brass openwork. He saluted First Spear Frontinius and nodded to his colleagues before crossing the room to stand before her with a broad smile.

'You look lovely.'

Felicia smiled back at him tolerantly, lowering her veil.

'So do you. And you're not supposed to see my face until after we're married!'

Tribune Licinius laughed uproariously, drawing another aggrieved glare from the priest.

'In point of fact, young lady, you're also *supposed* to have a matron of honour to supervise the proceedings, instead of which you've got a first spear who couldn't crack a smile if his life depended on it. Nor do we have anyone to read the auspices, much less a sacrificial animal from whose liver they might be read. And for that matter . . .'

'We have each other, Tribune, and that's all I need today.'

The cavalryman acknowledged the finality of her tone with a slight bow.

'Indeed you do, madam, and long may it remain that way. Perhaps this mission to Germania will provide you with some respite from the fear of discovery. And since none of us are getting any younger, perhaps we should proceed?' He held out an arm to her. 'Come along, m'dear, I think we ought to go and stand in front of that particularly disgruntled-looking priest. We've got our ten witnesses, so let's get your hands wrapped together and the sacred wheat cake eaten, shall we?'

Later, with the ceremony complete, the happy couple exited the principia beneath an arch of first the officers' swords and then those of the 9th Century, and ran the gauntlet of dozens more soldiers happily throwing nuts into the air to cascade down on them in the time-honoured fashion. As they sat down to a celebration meal in the praetorium, with plentiful wine on the table, the conversation inevitably turned to Dubnus's charge north to rescue Felicia. Julius, for several years the younger man's centurion during his time as a chosen man, waved a chicken leg at his former subordinate, his cheeks flushed and his voice a little louder than usual.

'Only you, Dubnus! Only you could have shamed a gang of disgraced road menders into following you into the teeth of a rebellion with barely enough strength to put a tent up! Not only that, but with a scar on your guts only three weeks old! A scar you earned, as I recall, by jumping into a losing fight with those tattooed head jobs!' He raised his cup to the younger man. 'Colleague, I salute the size of your stones, but one of these days you'll end up face down unless you learn to think before you jump!'

Where a younger Dubnus would have bridled at the implication of rashness, the centurion simply nodded slowly, raising his own cup and taking a sip of his wine. Felicia, who had allowed much of the discussion to wash over her as she enjoyed the sensation of having Marcus beside her, watched her rescuer intently.

'You may be right. Perhaps I do need to think a little more before I act. But I can tell you this:

I will never stand idle while any friend of mine is in danger. I would have gone north alone if necessary, healed or not, to find and rescue this lady, and to Hades with the consequences.'

He locked stares with his sparring partner, a faint smile of challenge on his face. The older man nodded solemnly, raising his cup again, looking about the table to be sure he had his colleagues' full attention

'Gentlemen, a toast! I'll drink to the man that made sure our brother had a bride to marry today. To my friend and brother Dubnus, the man with the biggest balls in all the cohort!'

When the officers were seated again Felicia, recognising that the time had come for the officers to celebrate the event in their own exuberant manner, stood up and begged the party's forgiveness for her inevitable fatigue, a request greeted by a chorus of understanding and concern. Marcus took her arm and led her from the room with a grateful nod to Tribune Scaurus for his hospitality, leaving the centurions grinning knowingly at each other. Otho raised his cup, a broad grin splitting his battered face.

'Well, it is their wedding night! And young Marcus needs to get as much sack time in as possible before the lady's too far gone for riding!'

Dubnus leaned over and clipped him playfully around the head, ducking away from the return blow and raising his own cup in challenge.

'A song! Come on, Knuckles, you punch-drunk old bastard, start us off!'

Otho glared at him in mock annoyance, then

threw his head back and bellowed the first lines of an old favourite at the ceiling.

'When I'm on patrol the farmers hide their chickens and their eggs, And watch their daughters just in case I sneak between their legs, But they forget that I will take my pleasure where I can . . .'

The other centurions joined in for the verse's last line, their voices raised to a roar that put a wry smile on Scaurus's face.

'So I shag the sheep and the billy goat too, 'cause I'm a Tungrian!'

As the other centurions joined in Julius went to fill up Dubnus's cup, only to find the younger man's hand covering it. He raised an eyebrow, bending close to shout in the younger man's ear.

'What's wrong with you? Losing your taste for the wine already?'

Dubnus shook his head, pointing at the cup.

'Just half a cup, and I'll water it. I've got to march east tomorrow with half a dozen disgraced road menders who insist on coming along for the walk.'

Julius raised his eyebrows in question, but Dubnus shook his head disparagingly.

'It's no big thing, just an errand I promised to run for a man I met on the North Road.'

Otho threw his head back again, bellowing out the next verse while his brother officers raised their cups to him and drained them. Outside, in the fort's torchlit road, with the boisterous singing audible over the wind's moan as it pulled at the fort's exposed roofs, Felicia stopped walking down the steep slope to Marcus's quarters at the end of the 9th Century's barrack, and turned to her new husband with a gentle smile.

'Go back in, Marcus. Go and join them, just for a while. I'm too tired to do anything but fall asleep the moment I get into bed, so you might as well enjoy the company of your friends. They've taken you into their family, so you should go and be part of it when you have the chance.'

The young centurion walked back into the praetorium's dining room to a chorus of ribald abuse centred on the obvious fact that he had clearly been unable to satisfy his woman, smiling resignedly as he took the brimming cup offered to him by Julius.

'Well, if you've come back to join the party, Two Knives, you'd better sing the next verse!'

Egged on by the raucous centurions, he stepped forward and took a gulp of wine, then roared out the lines he'd sung so often with his century on the march.

> *'I'm back from bloody battle, I've got money on my belt, And I'm full enough of spunk to make an armoured codpiece melt . . .'*

Outside, standing close to the room's window, Felicia heard his voice raised in song and smiled to herself, putting a hand to her gently bulging belly and moving off down the road's slope to their quarters.

'A lifetime or a year, my love, we'll make every moment precious.'

* * *

The wind from the sea was bitingly cold by the time Clodia had finished her work at the Waterside Fort's official guest house, her legs aching from a day spent on her feet, cleaning and cooking for the house's guests. She stepped out into the torchlit street, shaking her head in disgust as a pair of soldiers paused in their staggering progress from the vicus alehouse back to their barracks to leer drunkenly at her, but her discouragement only seemed to encourage the pair to push harder at her misery. One of them stayed rooted to the spot, too drunk to participate in the fun, but the other man, a heavyset watch officer who had long expressed an interest in her, persisted with a staggering walk that put him firmly in her path, swaying and pointing a finger at her with a knowing leer.

'Come on, Clodia, you know he's dead and gone. Give us a kiss and I'll show you what you've been missing all these months. And I've got a bigger . . . '

Without warning, a big bearded infantry centurion loomed out of the vicus shadows and stepped in front of her, putting one massive hand on the cavalryman's chest with the other clenched behind his back, visible to the harassed woman but not to her assailant.

'The lady doesn't want your pissed-up attentions, soldier. Take it away to your bed and come back for another try when you're sober.'

The drunk staggered backwards, then bridled and went on the offensive, jabbing a finger at the newcomer.

'Fuck you, you mule bastard! You and your mates . . . I'll do the lot of you . . . ' Clodia looked around, and found that half a dozen hard-faced infantrymen were backing up their centurion. The senior man nodded respectfully to her, speaking quietly in a moment of silence while the drunken cavalryman swayed and smiled to himself with pride at his defiance.

'Don't mind us, ma'am, the centurion will put this idiot to sleep soon enough and then we can all go back to what we were doing.'

Another pair of Petriana men exited the beer shop to find out what the shouting was all about, stopping in the doorway when they saw the auxiliary soldiers waiting for them.

'I'll fucking do the lot of you, you sheep-shagging bastards . . . '

The drunkard swung a fist at the officer, who leaned back far enough to allow it clear passage, then stepped forward and pushed at the other man's chest, sending him back half a dozen steps.

'If you try that again I'll be forced to put you on your back . . . '

The cavalryman charged forward, spreading both arms in a clear attempt to grapple with his assailant, but the centurion, rather than stepping back to avoid the attack, took a pace forward. His first punch was a jab, stopping the drunk in his tracks with a sickening pop of broken cartilage, his second and last blow a leisurely right hook that dropped his assailant senseless to the street's mud. He looked around at the meagre audience, spreading his hands in question, while the unconscious cavalryman's drinking partner goggled at him in drunken bemusement, and the other two men scowled their anger from a safe distance.

'And *that's* why you're on your back. Now, does anybody else think they want a go? I've not had a proper fight in months, so I could do with the practice. Nobody? You two, you look like you fancy trying your luck . . . ' The men watching from the beer shop's entrance blanched and walked quickly away, drawing amused looks from the soldiers behind their officer, who shook his head with something approaching genuine regret as he called after them. 'Good choice. Now bugger off and mind your own business.' He turned back to the woman, bowed and offered him her hand. 'Madam, my apologies for that unfortunate scene.' He took a deep breath, steeling himself for the task at hand, and the woman stared up at him with mute distress. 'I cannot pretend that I'm here with good news, but I do bring something that will soften the blow I'm sure you're expecting. My name is Dubnus, and I was the last person to speak with your man before he departed this life. Perhaps you could take us to somewhere we can speak privately.'

In the privacy of her tiny room, with the other men of his century waiting outside, he told her how she had been at the heart of the dying man's last thoughts.

'He died in battle, fighting to the last, but we were the only men to see it happen. He was carrying a message for the Petriana's tribune, and he fought to the death to defend it. Your man was twice the soldier those drunken fools will ever be, and his last wish was that we should bring this to you.'

Nodding her tearful thanks, the woman looked wanly at the purse. It was somewhat heavier than had originally been the case, the product of the 3rd Century's vigorous fund-raising throughout their cohort upon their return to Noisy Valley. Their new-found reputation, built on the back of a wild charge north to rescue the fortress's doctor with an apparently insane auxiliary centurion at their head, had paid dividends, and reduced the number of their fellows willing to accuse them of cowardice to a foolhardy few who had swiftly found the 3rd Century in their faces and ready to fight for their reputation. Clodia opened the purse and peeked inside, her face brightening slightly at the amount of gold it contained.

'It can't replace your man, but it can make life easier for you for a while. It can give you time . . . to . . . well . . . '

Sensing the centurion's embarrassment, she took his hands in hers, silencing his stuttering flow of words.

'Thank you, Centurion. You're all very kind. I've known he's dead for weeks now, when the wing came home without him, but it helps to know the truth. Will you be here for very long, you and your men? I'd like to show my gratitude in some way, if only with enough money to buy you all a drink?'

Dubnus stood, looking down at the woman with a gentle shake of his head.

'Thank you, ma'am, but we must march east in the morning. These men will have a new centurion waiting for them, and my own cohort is ordered to cross the sea before the winter comes. We're to strengthen the defences in Germania, or so it seems, and I daren't risk my friends taking ship without me.'

He bowed and withdrew from the tiny room, gathering his men by eye and leading them back to the transit barracks. He'd been in his centurion's quarters for no more time than was required to light the room's single lamp and shed his armour when his watch officer stepped through the door, a leather flask in one hand and another lamp in the other.

'If you'll forgive me, Centurion, I thought a drink might be appropriate . . . '

Dubnus waved a hand at the room's only chair, lowering his massive body carefully on to the bed and accepting a cup of wine with a nod of gratitude. The two men drank, then shared a moment of silence before Titus raised his cup in salute.

'To you, Centurion, pig-headed, single-minded, and the making of the Third Century. You may have been a bastard, but you were just what we needed.'

Dubnus raised his cup, drinking again before he spoke.

'Cocidius knows I hate to admit it, but I'll miss your miserable shower of fight-shy soap-dodgers too.' He leaned back on the bed with a broad smile, waiting for the watch officer to reply. Titus nodded wryly, offering his own cup up.

'And we'll miss you. Being part of a legion cohort is going to be dull as ditchwater without your inventive turn of phrase and compulsive need to fight anything and everything that moves.'

Dubnus snorted derisively.

'You poor fools must have led quiet and boring lives. I've a colleague by the name of Otho who'll put a soldier to sleep the hard way if the man as much as looks at him sideways. It was one of his boys that carried good old King Drust's torc all the way to the fortress of the spears, and when dear old Knuckles found out, he beat the poor bastard half to death in less time than it takes to tell the story.'

A long silence fell, both men looking into their cups at their remaining wine.

'Take us with you.'

Dubnus started from his reverie, his eyebrows shooting up at Titus's sudden plea and his voice acerbic with barely restrained humour.

'Oh yes, I'll just have it away with forty-three legionaries to Germania, nobody will miss you for a few weeks . . . ' He met the watch officer's eyes and saw the certainty in them, his voice softening with something between surprise and respect. 'Bugger me, Titus, you're serious, aren't you?' The other man said nothing, his face hot with embarrassment. 'You're actually serious. You want to walk away from a place with your legion, seventy denarii more per man a year than our lads earn, an extra five years to serve, *and* getting the shitty end of the stick every bloody time there's a choice between getting the legion's hands dirty or sending in the second-class soldiers. Are you fucking mad?'

The watch officer shifted uncomfortably.

'We understand all that . . . but the last few weeks have made us feel part of something different. We all feel like real soldiers for the first time in a long while.'

He stopped talking, aware that the centurion was staring at him with something close to amazement. Dubnus shook his head slowly, staring hard at the other man in astonishment.

'I've genuinely seen it all now. You want to turn your nose up at the best job a man can have in the army and pitch your luck in with a bunch of rough-arsed country boys? And it's not as if your officers are just going to say 'Very well, Tribune Scaurus, off you go with half a century of our men'. Even your legatus, decent bloke though he is, will be hard pushed to justify that to your new first spear, not to mention that complete prick of a camp prefect. No, you'll just have to . . . ' He stopped speaking, tipping his head to one side. 'Did you hear that?'

The sounds of raised voices reached them, and

Dubnus grinned happily, draining his cup and heaving his body off the bed, making for the door with Titus just behind him. In the gap between the two transit barracks a dozen or more angry men were gathered, some of them armed with staves and practice swords, and their leader stepped forward when he saw Dubnus in the barrack's doorway, raising a wooden sword to point at the Tungrian.

'You! You broke one of my men's jaw, and you're going to fucking pay double for that!'

Dubnus stretched his massive frame, rolling his head and flexing both arms' biceps to their full girth before stepping out into the confined space.

'And you might well make me pay for teaching your idiot some manners, but if you're stupid enough to come at me with weapons I'll have half of you in the hospital for a month or more before you put me down. If you're ready to pay that price, let's get on with it.'

Titus stepped out beside him, muttering out of the side of his mouth.

'If we fight these bastards off, you, me and the boys, you'll take us with you?'

Dubnus held up a hand to the cavalrymen, his voice harsh with authority.

'One moment, gentlemen, my watch officer wants to ask me a question.'

The infuriated cavalrymen seethed, but none of them was yet brave enough to be the first man to rush the intimidating centurion, and so they contented themselves with indignant looks while he turned to the watch officer with a raised eyebrow, his voice softened so as not to cross the gap to them.

'You're telling me that you want to *fight* for your place with the cohort?'

Titus nodded slowly.

'There's fifteen of them, and seven of us. If we send them away with a spanking, and the cohort's honour intact, you agree to get us on to your boat for Germania?'

Dubnus nodded slowly.

'Very well, you cheeky bastard, you're on. I have no idea how, but if we send these donkey wallopers home to Mummy with their arses kicked, I'll find a way for you to be Tungrians. And may Cocidius forgive me.'

Titus smiled happily back at him, putting two fingers to his mouth and blowing a piercing note. After a moment's pause the barrack door behind them burst open, and the five other men who had accompanied Dubnus to Waterside Fort crowded through it, led by the grizzled soldier who had made the impassioned plea on their behalf at Fort Habitus. Their watch officer flicked his wrist, allowing a heavy leather-lined cosh to fall from his sleeve, pointed at the cavalrymen and bellowed a single word, lifting the weapon and stepping forward to find his first victim.

'*Habitus!*'